Cryers Hill

Kitty Aldridge

W F HOWES LTD

This large print edition published in 2007 by
W F Howes Ltd
Unit 4, Rearsby Business Park, Gaddesby Lane,
Rearsby, Leicester LE7 4YH

1 3 5 7 9 10 8 6 4 2

First published in the United Kingdom in 2007
by Jonathan Cape

A CIP catalogue record for this book is available
from the British Library

ISBN 978 1 40740 554 4

Typeset by Palimpsest Book Production Limited,
Falkirk, Stirlingshire
Printed and bound in Great Britain
by MPG Books Ltd, Bodmin, Cornwall

Cryers Hill

To Isabella, Joe, Ben and Katya

The heart of our trouble is with our foolish alphabet.

Mark Twain

CHAPTER 1

The dogs are beginning to bark. Every day it is this; same hour each dawn, precise as any farmyard rooster. Each has a distinct voice. Sean leans out of his bedroom window. Above him a dirty sky sparks gold in the far corner, where the green hill waits. Below him he can see the diggers, their yellow cooled to amber in the half-light. Forklifts and cement mixers, resting with yesterday's last brick or crumble of mortar gone cold in their teeth.

The fastened-up houses are dark; the sleepers inside still strewn in their sheets. The air is turning pink; Sean breathes it in and feels his scalp creep and his legs chill. Everywhere you look are the orange-brick houses and the promise of more and more and more. Here are the houses-in-progress, the houses-in-waiting, the partial houses with their innards hanging out. Here are all the things you're not meant to see: the metal prongs and foam and breeze block, arterial pipes, asbestos fillings, and waterfalls of wiring. The serrated, sharp, jagged and gelled are all on display here: ducts, tubes, cavity walls, sheathing, joists, waste pipes. The bits, pieces, livers and lungs, dissected, cross-sectioned, unfinished. The families may watch, as they move in, their neighbours' houses in the next cul-de-sac growing from a set of spikes in the ground.

Sean looks at the sky. Somewhere beyond the smeary grey, God is watching, deciding. Sean scans the estate. You must keep your eye on the ball; it is a known fact. Even when there appears to be no ball at all. There is always a ball. This much he knows.

Sean Matthews stands at the bottom of George's Hill, more or less the very centre of the housing estate, with his hands on his hips. School is finished for the summer and last night, 20 July 1969, two men landed on the moon. This morning somebody mentioned that the earth was spinning at hundreds of miles per hour. Sean narrows his eyes against the grit and dust from the diggers, mixers and trucks, and tries to take all this in. His shaggy head is yellow and as round as the sun that hangs directly above him. His legs are sturdy; they carry him each day, in reasonably straight lines, after the girl he believes he cannot live without. He is her attending page, his chin low under his gold helmet of hair. Sean, flat-nosed, slope-eyed Sean, with his scooping walk and his hiccuping laugh. A boy whose waking thoughts drift high above the clouds, even while he traipses on his stout legs, limping, dragging, perhaps the wail of a radio song drifting over his shoulder.

Sunlight falls across the estate-in-progress, sending the dust rising like steam at a sulphur springs. Sean glances down at his feet encased in their Clarks sandals and he wonders, what if they can't get back to earth, Neil and Buzz? Whatif?

Nothing will grow well here. No one knows why. There are stones in the soil; it is full of rocks and lumps of chalk that crumble into powdery pieces, flecking the earth with white, and dry, dry, dry. But it doesn't stop people gardening. On the contrary, they appear encouraged. In the coppery evenings made soft with brick dust you can see them leaning on rakes and hoes, pale and fleshy in their flip-flops, strolling about their few square feet, oblivious to the neighbour, identically occupied, the other side of the chicken wire. The air is filled with the ting-ting of rakes combing over broken stones and the sweetly ripe pong of fertiliser as it folds into the sorry soil in big hopeful spadefuls. Everybody sprays and digs and hoes and starts again, sleeves rolled up and mouths set firm like the Pilgrim Fathers. Some things grow, weeds do well, especially nettle and dock and dandelion, and the piles of bricks grow too and the dust and the fat rubbery babies whose banshee yells can be heard over the roar of machinery. Above the earth two men are prancing about on the moon. They cannot be seen with the naked eye. *The naked eye*, Sean thinks. Whatif they never come back?

★　　★　　★

'Want to see something magic?'

Sean is confident. He has combed his hair to the side and leans with his hands in his pockets. Ann narrows her eyes, stops chewing.

'No. I'm having my tea p'sof. What?'

'You'll have to come.'

'No. Where?'

Sean raises his eyebrows, hinting, he hopes, at unfathomable mystery. 'Not far. See something. Want to?'

Ann is annoyed by this acquisition by him of some mysterious fact she knows nothing about. She is mildly revolted also by his display of showy confidence. She waits until her silence unnerves him and he blinks first.

'Wait then.' And she slams the door in his face.

They go the short way, as fast as they can, past the school where they are learning to read a modern alphabet – not the traditional true one, a new one, a kind of liar alphabet. It is an official experiment, like space travel. Along the dirt paths they go and then across the fields. You have to watch what the farmer puts in here. There are bulls sometimes; a man from Hazlemere was very nearly speared through the spleen. Now whenever he goes to the pub everyone shouts, 'Olé!'

Sean tells Ann. She stares at him, but does not comment. Ann does not blink if she can help it. Anyway, she has other things on her mind. There are no dangerous beasts in the field today. Only grass, dock and dandelion, and a tall blue sky, flaring in the corner where the sun lies idle.

Sean tries to chase but Ann will not run, so he is forced to trot circles around her and burp, which she ignores. She walks elegantly, with wading-bird aloofness. Sean tries fart noises.

At the farm they turn left and head for the woods. The dairy herd are in for milking; some of them waiting by the fence turn to watch them pass. Something about their fixed, white-lashed stare, unblinking, and only the briefest pause in their chewing, reminds Sean of Ann. Then their big heads swing away again as one.

Cockshoot Wood is dark and still. Sean and Ann skirt around it, scooping through grass that clicks and sizzles with insects. From the wood comes the voice of a pigeon, oo-look, oo-look, he coos. A woodpecker laughs.

To the left is the first of several dewponds, fringed with brown and purple grasses and busy in summer with frogs and snails and numerous insects busily rowing themselves to and fro on copper-wire legs. The tiny muntjac deer tiptoe from the wood to drink here at the start and end of the day; foxes come too and tumbling balls of hedgehogs.

The pull of the wood is strong enough to prevent you looking where you are going; the shadows are tempting. Sean and Ann look back at it over their shoulders as they run, as though they are expecting something to rush out, or fearful they may themselves be drawn helplessly in. The noises, exotic and inexplicable, come one at a time, magnified by the pauses. Fluty notes, then nothing. A sudden *ptchoo*, as though something unseen were unable to contain a sneeze.

Sean and Ann run. Sean wants to be fastest, to beat her. He pumps his elbows and rushes till there is a wind in his teeth. He cannot help admiring his running. He notices that Ann appears not to rush at all, but merely glides sideways while the grass flows under her feet. This is the kind of girl she is. Nature itself is careful around her. You will never stare down Ann Hooper; she can outstare anyone, she is undisputed champion. She does not blink unless it is absolutely necessary, nor giggle, nor cry, nor chatterbox with girls.

Sean has realised over time that Ann's loveliness comes from the things in her face that are not quite right. Her eyes are wide apart, the same shade of brown as her hair, and would be pretty if not for the look they carried, which is stupefied and mildly criminal. She has a broad meaty nose that is softened by a downpour of freckles, and a small sullen mouth filled with sharp teeth. In the point of her foxy chin is a dent, hollowed as if it were done hastily with the end of a spoon. Ann doesn't laugh often, but when she does it is like your life being spared.

Sean can't help it: the world stops where she stands. She is older than him by a year and a bit. He likes to place himself before her, a soldier to his Queen, and stare up at her face, while she gazes, unblinking, over his head. She has awoken in him a courage he hadn't known he possessed. She has made him want to run and fight; she has made him think of blood and rockets and battles and nudity. He wants to tap her on the shoulder and say, 'Come on. You're with me.' But he doesn't. Instead, Sean presents himself daily at Ann's house, arriving either around the back, by the garages, where he waits for her to fly up over the fence on her swing, 'Wotcha', or, at the front, where he sits on the mounds of dirt and builders' sand gawping up at her bedroom window. He can easily be viewed from the house, kicking something off his shoe, rolling bricks around with a stick, staring into space. Sometimes Ann opens her mouth to shout something down at him, then changes her mind. Sean sits like a weary traveller, elbows on his knees, mop of yellow hair blinding him to the obvious. He does not know enough to be vain about his hair, though it hangs glossily in his eyes like the kind of yellow hair you find on the heads of righteous characters in fairy tales.

He decided the first time he saw her. 'Hello. Your name's Ann.' His first words to her, telling her like that, asserting what he knew. It had been his only moment of power, those first few seconds between them. After that she was in charge.

'P'sof, spastik.'

He clung on, obstinately, for a while.

'Make me, then.'

7

But she was already lost to him.

'Pissof, oppit.'

'Says who?'

'P'sof, don't talk to spastix, do I?'

'P'sof yself, then.'

Then she walked away and he followed. And this was the beginning, they had got the formalities out the way. Her leading, him following, flaxen page in royal footsteps. Sean Matthews fell in love with an older girl before he was nine. Nobody thought it would last.

Sean cycled as fast as he could past the newest nearly-houses; past the diggers and mixers and waiting towers of bricks that touched the sky. Clouds of red dust obscured the road and billowed up in drifts like battle smoke. He rode blindly on, directionless, while a Dixieland of jackhammers and electric saws shrieked and thumped behind him.

He went around the front and rang the bell. He wasn't going to wait all afternoon for her at the back fence, life was too short, his life at any rate, lately. The house seemed dark and cool inside. He thought he heard a sound like singing, or perhaps a person speaking in a swirly way, a kind of complaining. He put his finger to the bell to ring again and the door opened, as though someone had been there all the time.

If he had checked his reflection in a car wing mirror beforehand, Sean would have seen a small ghoul, recently dug from the ground, with hot red eyes, dusted from head to toe with brick and cement dust. Ann stared gravely at him for a long time. 'I'm dying,' he said. Very good – he was pleased with that.

She didn't move at first. Her eyes travelled up and down him, and then a thing from the gods for which he would for ever rejoice: she blinked.

They run the usual way, along the dirt paths, across the fields and alongside Cockshoot Wood. Everything is strangely still today. There is no bird-song or vixen bark. There is no clue as to why. They go past the dewponds and then away from the ancient castle that is no longer there, to the woodland pond.

When they arrive they are breathless and hot and have to collapse noisily for a while in the long reeds. Sean looks up and sees Ann's face blotting out the sun. And though he has imagined it a thousand times, it surprises him. It is where it ought to be, above him, falling to earth. He hopes it might kiss him, please God try. She does open her mouth, but she talks.

'You could drown yourself it doesn't hurt.'

He waits while the words fall down on his face. He waits for them to make sense, to realise she didn't say that at all, but something else like, *Can't you see I love you, darling, I've always loved you*, the way they talk in the black-and-white films on Sundays. After a moment he realises she said what she said. He wasn't sure if he should reply or not.

'Drowning is quick and you don't feel none of it.' She smiles softly. He wants the smile to go on and on. He wants to stop his life right here. He wants to pull the bus cord – ding – like you do when you want to get off. He will lie back under her smile for a hundred years. Maybe drowning wouldn't be so bad.

'Nah,' he says. 'No ta.'

She moves away. 'Spaz.' And the sun lands in his face. He feels her body falling next to his. The air feels cooler in spite of the glare. He has her smile though, he has held it in his mind, trapped it under glass so he can look at it any time.

CHAPTER 2

There is a naked man at large. Three sightings so far. Four if you include this morning, when he appeared to Ann and Sean. They walked to school the long way, by Widmer Farm to pinch the ripe plums that fell when you shook the trees along the fence, then ran to the allotments, and sat on the gate opposite the lower fields to eat them. They had each eaten two when a tall man without a stitch on, nothing except for shoes, came bursting out of the covert by the ancient oaks and started to sprint across the grass in front of them.

There was nothing to be done about it, so Ann and Sean carried on chewing, and watched. He ran well, long arching strides, arms pumping. Ann noted that his hair, though balding, was rather wavy and grew out of his shoulders too. They watched until the man reached the perimeter of the field, where he paused under a giant sycamore. He did not appear to be out of breath. On the contrary, he began a series of slow, inexplicable movements, before fastening himself against the tree, where he remained for several seconds. Ann and Sean looked at one another, their mouths purple-raw from plum juice, and Sean became aware that he might quite like to press the plum stone in his hand against Ann's teeth until she struggled and then he would have to use his body to pin her down, p'raps kneel on her. But instead he said, 'That's not right.'

Ann didn't reply. She chose silence for a response, in the hope it might convey superior knowledge. Sean remembered the bus-stop snoggers, interlocked at impossible angles, all joined up at the mouth, two by two, like they were waiting for Noah's Ark to pull up, instead of the 11 and 14 to High Wycombe. A naked man. A streaker. Streakers were modern; they were all the rage; they were on the news, chased by crowds of police officers. What was a streaker doing in Cryers Hill? Where were the policemen who were supposed to be chasing him? Sean wished Lothian were with them. Lothian Dickey, a boy with a hero's name. Only the coils of sable hair hinted at his Celtiberian inheritance, a clue to the bronze and iron heart. 'Black as a tinker's pot,' was how the mothers agreed to describe the raven black of those curls. Lothian would have known what to do about a streaker. Lothian was from Dumfries. When he spoke, a strange beautiful sound came out, like words blown through some sort of gas; a Scottish riddle with a daring rise and fall that pulled the words taller and shorter at the same time. 'Aye,' he would say, as though referring only ever to himself, as if no one else mattered. But mostly Lothian said very little at all.

Lothian's dad worked at Harwell, with the graphite reactors. He had blown-up hair and wild eyes, like he'd swallowed the uranium. Once upon a time he had made his son a bow and a set of arrows with cardboard flights and Lothian had become quite the little archer on the streets of Glencaple. Subsequently the cello-throb of his bowstring could be heard each evening as he stalked the Cryers Hill estate, releasing his arrows over the diggers and brick piles, firing them through the nearly-windows like one of King Malcolm's own archers at Carham. The Dickey family stayed a few months, before moving to Southampton. Sean had kept Lothian's address in his pocket until the pencil words faded completely away.

'Bang bang pop pop, you're dead, I'm not.' This is what Kevin Atkinson says. Kevin has worn the same limp blue shorts and red pullover for months, even now that it's summer. Nobody takes him seriously. He runs sideways, with his mouth open. Bang bang pop pop.

'Waaaah!' replies Charlie Burns.

Adam Duke wheels around with his hands on his hips, eyes bulging. 'We need gunpowder!' He kicks the ground and walks showily up and down.

The girls are standing in a straggly group. There are no straight lines; hair, ankles, arms, heads, all

13

angled, crooked, curled. In their faces a mixture of indifference and incomprehension. What are girls for? Sean used to think. Apart from pushing prams around. What are they actually for? He concluded there was no obvious point to them. He knows better now. Now that he is eight and a half. The boys run in straight lines between one pointless task and another, bawling out live reports. 'I am running! Aaagghh! I are here! A big hole! Charlie! It's got water! Quick! Get off! Run! Waaahhh!'

The girls, in contrast, sidle, idle, circle. They communicate in whispers, murmurs and coded giggles. They sway in groups, like exotic fish, swirls of hair and skirt, watching the boys with a practised air of disapproval, already softening into a sort of resigned affection. The boys regard the girl groups with fear and disgust. Girls produce an invisible magic that turns each boy into the other's vilest enemy, enchanting them so that they fall on one another with fists, feet and threats, while the girls giggle approvingly.

Jason Smith has a secret he is telling everyone. He says he can understand bird talk. He says what they say is mostly rubbish not worth listening to. He says it with his hands behind his head and his foot tapping as if it's an actual truth. Sean reckons if this is lying then it's very good. Jason doesn't know any breeds of bird. He only knows that the fat brown ones make jangling calls all summer and like to sit on high perches. However, he insists birds are very intelligent, in spite of all their chatter. Calling someone birdbrain is not an insult, it's a compliment. Jason says this twice. He is pleased with the way it sounds: official. Sean realises he has never thought about the word birdbrain before, that it is a compliment in disguise. He hopes he is one.

Sticks and stones can break my bones, but names can never hurt me. Astride their bikes the Dewell gang lean against fences at increasingly unlikely angles. They fold their arms and sway in the saddle, cocky and sure as a circus troupe. Rod is their leader. In truth, Sean prefers the idea of sticks and stones; it is the names he can't tolerate. The way they are broadcast for a start. If only they could be written down on slips of paper, folded, for only him to see, edged through his letter box, or handed to him quietly. Why does everyone else have to know? This way they become official, like a replacement name. The worst part is their killing accuracy. Spaz, dwarf, germ. It is uncanny. Pygmy, squirt, runt, leg, Nelly, midge, spaz. Spaz had stuck. He is Spaz now more than he is Sean. He is rarely Sean; only in the classroom, at Christmas, and during the police interviews that were taking place every day in the school dining hall.

'Want to see a streaker?' Sean asks Rod, hoping this might buy him some time. Whole summers in the saddle meant the Dewell gang ride as well as any highwaymen; backwards, sideways, in the air and after dark; as though boy and bike were a whole animal, fused together. They fly up and down the hill day and night, unearthly as centaurs. They ride inside the almost-houses on their rubber-tyre horses, up and down the splintery staircases, through the wind-blown bedrooms, down the precariously balanced plank ramps that lean out of naked window holes. They fill the houses with screams and disagreement before any family has even had the chance. You can't know where they'll appear next. Their faces pop out of window holes and doorways, rear up over fences and burst from behind brick mountains. They flit between puffs of diesel smoke like fiends. Their presence signals that things are poised to go awry. They appear not to be interested in his streaker.

'Sorry, but can I get past please?' Sean says it as pleasantly as he can. He waits while his brain plays the pictures of them flinging young adders across the stream by Widmer Farm.

'Sorry but can I get *past please!*' they chorus, a satanic choir at the creosote gates. There is nothing Sean is actually sorry for, except maybe being in this moment, in this place, at this time, with boys whose legs are wheels, and whose hearts have cemented over, along with the farmland. Afterwards, as he hunches down and walks briskly away, he realises that, in spite of everything, he believes one day he will foil them. This is what happens in stories, even liar-alphabet ones. The baddies always get what is coming to them.

The camp is empty. Just Steven Bone, sitting with his back to them, cross-legged in a recently purloined steel sink. He flashes around, stubby fringe in his eyes. 'Can I help you?' he cries archly. He is ignored. The camp is in the wilderness. The wilderness is the remaining shred of green on the estate. A surviving tangle of vegetation and trees. Dazzling green where the sun flares and darkening in the shadows. At the height of summer it is jungle-lush with things that climb and twine. You can listen to the creaks and whispers of the vegetation, you can feel the sensation of its animal eye, the hush while it remembers its secrets. From here you can still hear the rumble of diggers and thump of piledrivers. The diesel throws a brown haze over the sun, making the sky hot and oily, making the clouds slide and curdle. One of these days the forgotten bit of wilderness will also be dug out and thrown away to make room for more houses and dirt gardens where nothing new will grow. For now it belongs to the estate kids, their own patch, to do with as they please. They have built a house. What else? An improvised copycat among all the orange-brick examples. Three estate dogs lie in the shade, belonging to who knows who. Estate dogs roam free.

There is a noise like the cry of metal birds. Everyone stops to listen, all the kids and dogs with heads tilted high. It's louder now, a terrible scraping, a scream. Keith Dodd's stubby legs appear first, through the leaves, beneath the branches, short, determined strides. Then his fish-bone body, shirtless, and his sharp face, bright with anticipation. He stops and the screaming is silenced. He waits, watching everyone watching him, savouring his Trojan moment, a leaf in his hair. Behind him a giant loop of metal shivers; a great silver coiling wave, glinting in the sun, like a curl of ocean. Keith, the grubby merman, has captured it from the builders' heap and dragged it, shrieking, all the way up George's Hill Road. It will live on top of the sawn timbers that make the roof, like a roll of surf about to break.

CHAPTER 3

A girl has been murdered in Gomms Wood. A local tragedy, that is what they are calling it, that is what it is. *Local Tragedy* it said in the paper. Only weeks ago she had been in Sean's school making woollen horses with her friend Cindy. She could stand on a swing and fold her tongue in half.

'Why you so short, Sean?' she used to say, and Sean would reply, 'Why you so ugly?' He felt bad about that now. She wasn't ugly at all, he just couldn't think what else to say. It was what you said to girls, they didn't like it.

The girl was discovered by a local man walking his dog. She was folded in bracken, sparkling with maggots, with leaves in her hair. Her skin was turning mauve. The policemen came to the woods with their measuring tapes and flash photography. They arrived sombre and determined in short dark coats. They crunched through the undergrowth and put their hands in the earth. They squatted and knelt, while above them the trees whispered shhh, shhh, and the shadows drew back. The policemen left the woods and walked around the housing estates and farms. They knocked on doors and they asked people questions. Black-and-white pictures of the girl fluttered on trees; she looked surprised. *Did you see her on Friday 4 May?* the words asked those who knew their traditional ABC, and people tried to remember. But even if he had known how to read, Sean couldn't recall dates or what happened on them. She was wearing red trousers and a pink top, she had a blue purse for her dinner money, coaxed the words.

There was a number to ring if you had something to say. Some people rang it. Sean wondered what they said. He had things to say, but he wasn't going to ring the number and say them, just like that. There was something he could have said, should have said, but it was too late now. Now he wanted to say things that were not about her.

He looked at the number on the trees, below the girl's amazed smile. He tried to see if her tongue was folded or unfolded, and he thought about the other things he wanted to say.

No one was arrested. Some men were questioned. Nobody knew who these men were, but there were suspicions. The locals reckoned it had to be a man who was responsible, not a woman, and the police didn't contradict them. Sean marvelled at their guessing powers. Then it was decided he was a tall man with an evil soul and a nasty past, who lived in the vicinity but not locally and worked casually or not at all. They all agreed it was not anybody they knew; they all agreed they'd know him if they saw him. Sean supposed he was as good as caught. The mothers huddled in groups. They said hanging was too good for him.

The men from the housing estates and the farms set out after dark. United for the first time, they decided to spread out over six square miles. They covered woodland, lanes, fields and streams. Their torch beams slid into ditches, troughs and coppices, dazzling hedgehogs and foxes. They shone their light wherever it would reach, crossing beams in their urgency, blinding one another. They walked four, five abreast, murmuring while they lit their cigarettes. What did they expect to find? Their beast under a blackberry bush, lurking on a bridle path, up a tree? P'raps a message, or maybe a clue? No one commented. It didn't matter. When they got home they felt like better men.

No answers came. They began to talk of other things on the high street, at the pub and at the school. The weather-streaked pictures of the girl came down and the police stopped knocking on doors and jogging people's memories. People no longer telephoned the number with something to say. Now it was time to forget.

She was buried in St Mary's Churchyard at the top of Cryers Hill Lane. Two wispy angels floated at the corners of her gravestone, watching over her, tooting their trumpets; too late, some might argue. There were no angels, musically inclined or otherwise, in Gomms Wood on 4 May 1969. There was only panic and struggle and darkness.

Later, as the men walked together in ranks, burning up the spinneys and hedgerows with their bright white lights, they would discover they could not chase the darkness away. The darkness was here to stay.

CHAPTER 4

In the autumn of 1934, Walter Brown and his friend Charles Sankey went rabbiting. The moon floated up, released by the tall trees at the edge of Gomms Wood. She went up like a helium ship; wobbled, steadied, and silvered the fields over. Sankey was an inveterate hunter before he turned Methodist. His sensitive hearing and long fingers suited him to poaching and religion both. He seemed a tall man, though he was well below six foot. His high forehead pinned his hat down low over his eyes. The pale light of his teeth revealed him in the dark.

As soon as its neck was broken Sankey loosened the rabbit's body between his fingers. Once they were limp he stroked them tenderly down their long backs, like he was easing out their souls. Death is always a surprise, even when you see it coming.

Walter and Sankey hung two nets. The moon was bright as blindness. Sankey preferred nets to snares; he didn't use gin traps, he had seen enough of those. Sometimes, when an animal had been struggling for a long time, it would get a look in its eye that told you it understood things had turned bad. In order to die you had to stop struggling. Charles Sankey had seen it so.

Walter Brown had seen things somewhat differently. He had inherited an allotment from his father. He was not a particularly keen gardener, but his father had died there, on his knees, at gooseberry level. They found him that way, knelt, slumped, a bower of berries over his head. He was buried in St Mary's Churchyard at the top of Cryers Hill Lane.

Walter's mother had found it comforting, the fact that he had expired on his knees. Walter found it unnerving. You almost never heard of people dead on their knees. Mostly people tended to die on their backs or stomachs, or sides, and feet of course, occasionally. Anyway, it took them a long time to straighten him out. After that, whenever engaged in the task of unfolding something, Walter found himself thinking queasily of his father. He avoided at all cost any situation that might require him to kneel. In church he blamed it on sciatica, though he was just eighteen years of age.

Walter had also inherited his father's lantern jaw and drooping brown eyes, and his tall slim neck with its sharp Adam's apple. Perhaps his shyness too was passed on and his habit of rubbing his cheek. Where he got his fondness for fancy words, no one could tell. While he was not passionate about fruit or vegetables, unlike his father before him, Walter did not neglect the allotment. On the contrary, he punished his ambivalence by spending long hours bending, squatting – rather than kneeling – over rhubarb, spinach and chard. The trouble with vegetables in particular was they didn't lead to anything; they were merely their awkward, mucky selves; a few vitamins for a lot of hard work. He found fruit more uplifting. But it was poetry that Walter reserved himself for. He was keen on the Romantics: Byron, Keats, Shelley, Blake, Coleridge, Wordsworth. But also John Clare, Alfred Tennyson, George Crabbe and James Clarence Mangan. He didn't own many volumes, so he borrowed extensively from the library. He reckoned the pleasure of a good poem could put a curve into a flat day.

At Sean's school they learn a brand-new type of reading and writing. Phonetic. It is an experiment. Newfangled. It's not bad. It is not the usual alphabet, it is a new one; a liar alphabet. It's modern. They had been reading *a trap for lieonz* at the time of the *Local Tragedy*. After reading they did cutting and sticking.

The light in the classroom was a pale blue reflection of the painted walls turned greenish by electric light. It made Sean feel sick. He found himself watching the others as they glued, folded, trimmed and decorated with the absorption of master engravers, but he could not persuade himself to try a sticky creation of his own. He stared through the window at the gulf of blue sky beyond the

Esso garage and the Grange Farm fields until it became a sea on which his bobbing thoughts set sail one by one, little rudderless boats, drifting and then falling over the edge of the horizon. The windows, burned by the sun, shone like shields. The smell of glue and felt-tip pens turned his head hazy, his tongue floated in his mouth. He watched the scraggy elm outside waving its bony branches backwards and forwards until he was stunned. The fur-lined drone of a faraway voice hummed through the heat, filtering into his blood, buzzing up and down his bones. This was school. Like being put to death: a lethal experimental dose.

The movement of Ann suddenly rising from her seat roused him. He watched her walk across the room, head hanging as if one of her strings were broken, languid, indifferent. Ann was fifteen months older than Sean; she was in the year above, but the two classes always did cutting and sticking together on a Tuesday. The room made him think of a boat: the blue and green, the sticky collage of wool and yarn strung in waves across the wall, the cries of the gulls from the river.

'Sean Matthews, are you with us?' It was true, he was anaesthetised; indeed he was dead, they would have to summon him with Ouija.

'Are you with us, Sean?' Determined, give her that.

Sean felt his dazed self pushing through a froth of blur and underwater sound. A girl's giggle rushed up on his left as he surfaced and managed to focus, at last, on Miss Day and her urgent question.

Young Miss Day: there she was, there was her soft worried face with just a hint of approaching indignance, her sheaf of hair twisted over one shoulder, her arms folded patiently or impatiently (Sean couldn't tell) across her chest, across the pinafore of a summer dress that revealed her long, freckled knees and bow-shaped calves. Miss Day wore dresses that tricked you into supposing she was a child too. It was confusing. The dresses were short, with puffed sleeves or smocking or bows, and she allowed her conker-coloured hair to spill down over her shoulders the way mermaids do when luring men to their deaths. She can't have been that much older than Sean's brother, Ty. She liked to yawn and rub her eyes and smooth her dress as if she'd awoken all of a sudden in Wonderland. It swayed you. First you thought she was on your side, a child still in her own heart, then she'd surprise you with her exasperation, some scornful remark, and you'd realise she was just a grown-up after all.

Miss Day liked to dash about with the kids in the playground, that was her thing; football, rounders or tag, she reckoned herself a bit of an athlete, a bit of a huntress, blowing on her little whistle, slicing up and down on her long knees. She'd throw her lustrous hair behind her for the wind to unravel, and all the boys would stare and run into each other. Mr Stone, vice-head, found

27

the trilling of that little whistle irresistible. It brought him like the call of a conch shell from whatever smoky corner he had wrapped himself in. Mr Stone wasn't the only one. You would catch Miss Day leaning in the staffroom doorway with Mr Turner or Mr Price or the teacher with long hair who only came on a Wednesday. She was no longer your friend on these occasions, you would find that out. You might say something as you slunk glumly by, *Hello, Miss*, for instance, and she'd pull an eyebrow up at Mr Whoever and look at you without replying, and you'd see that her eyes were cold and speckled as a lizard's.

'Hello? Are you with us?'

'Yes, Miss, sorry, Miss,' Sean replied.

'Nice to have you back on earth, Sean.' Miss Day spoke cheerily like she meant it.

Sean brightened. It was a good thing to say, clever. It was what you said to returning astronauts. Wur.

There were words on the blackboard. Miss Day suspected Sean might like to read them out. The air was smoky with chalk dust, as if writing them had started a fire. Sean looked at them warily.

'yʊ lʊk egʒactly liek θrɛɛ dɪrty œld maŋgold wurzelʐ. gœ aloŋ at wuns and woʃh yʊr fæseʐ.'

Sean stared. He narrowed his genius eye.

'You look exactly like,' he said boldly, before pausing momentarily to check Miss Day's face for indignation. 'Three dirty old mangold wurzels. Go along at once and wash your faces.'

Miss Day nodded. 'And why were their faces dirty, Sean? Did they tumble into the river?' A rumble of laughter. 'Did they fall head-first into a cow-pat?' More laughter, louder. Jason Smith forcing it out, still going after the others had stopped. Sean too was rocking happily in his chair. Miss Day was funny for a woman, very.

'OK, Sean. This one please.'

ᚦhe ies ænjel gæv ᚦhe bɔi a snœbaull. whie dœn't yѡ pѡt a plaŋk ov wѡd across it and mæk it intѡ ʃhѡꞩ.

'The ice angel gave the boy a snowball.' Sean turned triumphantly towards the girl giggler on his left. 'Why don't you put a plank of wood across it and make it into shoes.'

'And the next?' Miss Day chirruped. Sean filled his lungs again, for under water, for deep space.

tѡ mæk a snœman yѡ aulwæꞩ neeḑ snœ, cœl for ieꞩ, a carot nœꞩ and tѡ branꞔheꞩ.

'To make a snowman you always need snow, coal for eyes, a carrot nose and two branches.' Easy. Peasy. Pudding. Pie.

'Good boy, Sean.'

Sean grinned at his hands. gѡd bɔi ʃhaurn. gѡd bɔi ʃhaurn. Sean glanced about proudly.

'Who would like to read the next part? Jason? Wendy?' Miss Day pointed at the words with her long finger.

when ꟙhæ got back tꞷ ꟙhe pond ꟙhæ found it woꙅ just a drie hœl agæn. aull ꟙhe wauter had sœkt awæ. it woꙅ disappointiŋ. ꟙhæ ran back tꞷ ꟙhe kitꞔhen but ꟙhær woꙅ timmy'ꙅ muꟙher, moppiŋ ꟙhe flor. 'not in heɛr,' ʃhɛe sed.

'but wɛe'r mækiŋ a pond. wɛe'v dug a speʃhial hœl for it.'

'Off you go, Jonathan. Good boy.'

CHAPTER 5

The dead girl had marks on her legs. Sean heard his mother say it to his father while she was submerging something in the kitchen sink. Sean was lurking in the hall, prodding the air bubbles that were gathering beneath the wallpaper around the doorway. Upstairs meanwhile, concoctions gurgled in the airing cupboard, all of them carefully organised and linked by rubber tubing – nameless liquids that lay still until they frothed and furred over with bitter-smelling scurf. Home-made beer. You could hear the hiss and bubble as it fermented in the buckets.

The dead girl had marks on her legs. Sean felt his skin cool. He waited, hunched out of sight, for more. His father said, 'What kind of marks?' Exactly the right question to ask. When his mum didn't reply, Sean pressed his face into the wall, flattening an air bubble between his eyes, waiting for the words to float out; hoping they would not be horrible: hoping they would be.

'Dunno,' she said. 'Sort of shapes, symbols, Chinese maybe.'

Nothing Chinese had ever happened in Cryers

Hill, maybe not even in the whole of Buckinghamshire. Sean's frown mirrored his father's on the other side of the wall.

'Chinese?' His dad spoke it low, as though it intrigued him, unlikely as it sounded.

'Or Japanese, you know, Oriental.'

'Oriental?'

'Or Arabic maybe, Egyptian, I don't know.'

'Well, make your mind up.'

Sean's dad hated surprises, secrets, uncertainties, things on tenterhooks. He preferred Jim Reeves singing 'I Love You Because', and whisky and soda and Embassy No.3 He had a good head of hair, Gordon Matthews did. He had quick blue eyes and a nose that had been broken twice.

Sean thought of the James Bond film he'd seen in High Wycombe. The baddies were narrow-eyed villains from exotic countries with horrible scars and cruel ambitions. They wore collarless tunics or a fez or an eyepatch and their weaponry was underhand and nasty, boomerang blades, sharks, that sort of thing. Sean couldn't fathom what such a person would be doing in Cryers Hill.

His mother, Cathleen, had a selection of wigs upstairs in contrasting styles. They were kept in a box labelled 'Cathleen Matthews'. Unknown to her, Sean had tried them all on over the years. Now her voice had grown shrill.

'Janet Davis said it was scribble and Colleen from the semis said it was symbols. Although someone,

I can't remember who, said the police said it was something foreign.'

'A foreigner?'

They fell quiet. A foreigner. They waited, perhaps for a sound, as though, even now, the perpetrator of this exotic tattoo, this mysterious character of inexact provenance – this foreigner – was at large, spying or stealing or whatever it was foreigners did. They listened. Maybe listening hard would reveal fancy foreign footsteps picking their way around the Hillman Avengers and communal bins. Sean had heard that a great many foreigners were unable to read, write or speak English at all. They came from countries that were far away and generally strange in their outlook. Never mind that there were two men up there on the moon, the moon didn't count as foreign. You could see it every night for a start and sometimes during the day. It hung over the estate like an old friend, like leaving the landing light on, reassuring, not like the Congo or Ceylon or even Halifax. The men on the moon were Neil and Buzz and everyone knew their faces; if they were to turn up at the post office, or pop in for a quick half at the White Lion, no one would bat an eyelid. They were everyone's heroes, they were locals in everyone's local, and they had seen off the Russians good and proper. They had described their small steps and giant leaps with poetic polish, and the whole world heard it spoken in the English language and so now it was official. The moon was an

English-speaking planet, which made it practically British.

True, the people opposite went to the Costa Brava every year and Sean's dad had visited Rotterdam, and yes, they were saving up to go to Gibraltar since Sean's brother hadn't managed to win a single family holiday competition with his foolproof genius eye, not even the one in Bournemouth, but still. Foreign was far away and strange, foreign was not to be trusted, foreign was foreign.

Finally his father said, 'Enoch was right.'

Sean was inclined to suppose this had to be someone from work, or the Bible.

'I worry about him.' His mother this time.

This was the thing about grown-up conversation: it was like a game, you had to fill in the gaps. This was why they talked so much; they gave away clues, nothing more, you had to do the rest yourself, it wasn't easy. Often the real meaning was the thing that was not said at all. Sometimes the thing that was said was simply not true. Even the adults themselves struggled to understand one another. You could hear them any day of the week, bewildered as the next man: What's that supposed to mean? I never said that. You're putting words into my mouth. What the hell are you on about? Am I making myself clear? No one knew what anybody meant. The whole thing was a minefield of trip-wires and unexploded word bombs, of meanings, half-meanings and non-meanings. You had to get in between the words, a bit like the liar alphabet.

'He's not managing.'

Tough one. Sean waited. It was an utterly mysterious remark. Who was Enoch? Why wasn't he managing? Did he know the foreigner? The one who had killed the girl?

'Don't start. He'll be all right.' His dad. You had to pick out all the liar words.

'See if his teacher agrees with you then.' His mother's voice spiralling upwards again, his dad winding her tighter with his big key.

'Young girl like that? Just out of school herself, what does she know?'

'She knows her skirts are too short.'

His dad threw back his head and laughed. A joke. Someone wore a skirt. Enoch?

'Oh, I know *you* don't mind.'

'Any beer in that fridge?'

The key in her back twists a final inch. Now she was fully wound.

'I know what you're after, Gordon Anthony Matthews.'

Now she was clockwork. The words came whirring, while her feet rushed her to every drawer and cupboard in the kitchen.

'Cath, Cath. You don't even know the capital of Poland. Don't kid yourself.'

'Oh, that's right, I forgot. Your name's Albert Einstein.'

'Don't get your knickers in a twist, bloody hell. Can't a man make a joke?'

'Ho. Ho. Ho.'

'Little Raquel Welch number moved in at twenty-nine, I see.'

The fridge door slammed. A pause while Gordon cocked his head.

'What did she want then, the lady teacher?'

'What do you think she wanted?'

'I haven't got a crystal ball, Cath. Have I got a crystal ball?'

'A child could see it, Gor.'

'Are you trying to make me look stupid?'

Sean closed his eyes. What the bludyell were they saying? Now something else happened. Now his dad was angry.

'I saw that! Thank you kindly. I saw that! Cheeky cow.'

Whatever it was his mother had done, she was doing it again.

'It's called innuendo, Cath. It begins with an i.'

Women did things with their faces, complicated things. His dad reckoned he had it all figured out. *Have you ever watched a pair of pigeons on a roof, Sean?* Gor enjoyed natural history. *Have you? It'll tell you everything you need to know about the mating game.* His dad had learned to read the signals. A woman closing her eyes could mean you were a fool, a bore, a liar; or it could mean she loved you but couldn't say it; or it could mean she was having a bit on the side. This particular phrase cropped up regularly in Gor's conversation. Whatever his mother had done with her face it would have likely been fleeting, but his dad had learned to read the smallest messages in faces, especially his wife's.

'What do you know about Einstein, Cath?'

It was frustrating, the silence. Sean too wanted to know about Einstein. He needed to know whether he was connected to Enoch, whether the clues to this whole exchange lay in these two names. Still nothing.

'I'm waiting, Cath.'

Sean waited too. This was women all over. His dad had explained it more than once. They carried on their backs an invisible shell, he said. From time to time, usually without warning, a woman retreats inside her shell and will not come out. Sean had been amazed by this, though even in his stunned consideration of it, he realised he could recall examples and saw with clarity that it was true. Why would they want to do that? His dad seemed none the wiser on this. Because they can, was all he came up with. He said it sadly, without conviction, and Sean thought of witches and princes.

'You don't know a bloody thing about Einstein!'

Sean thought he couldn't blame his father for being upset. She had introduced this other person, called him by a funny name, and now refused to reveal who this other person was.

'I asked a simple question, Cath, a simple question.'

Silence. His mother had entered her shell. Neither he nor his father could winkle her out

37

now. Bobbing in the silence were Chinese symbols, a dead girl, Bond villains, Miss Day, a foreigner and someone called Enoch. Sean flattened another wallpaper bubble with his teeth. His father burped. It had impact where the words had none. It was a sound that said, That's the end of it, like a bell.

Sean thought, what if the sun burns out? What if I become possessed by an evil spirit? What if an alien ship lands? And, what if I accidentally eat poison? Sean thought whatifs a lot. There were a lot of whatifs to think about. If you tried for the rest of your life you wouldn't get through all the whatifs that could be. These questions pressed down on Sean whether he liked it or not. He thought maybe this was why mad people were mad. This could mean that madness was just around the corner. What if people turned mad and didn't know it? What if half the world were, in fact, mad? What if these questions and all the others spun you about until you were rotating inside a vortex of whatifs? What then?

CHAPTER 6

Since boyhood Walter Brown had tried to imagine the girl who would one day be his own. He tried to conjure her from the hawthorn hedge and stile. He daydreamed and nightdreamed her. Eventually he gave her gold hair and called her Cissie. At night he felt the whisper of her breath and the arch of her back. He decided she would be happy as Larry and love him all the time. He upset himself over how she would suffer at his funeral. He pictured her clinging and crying by his grave, while the mourners shook their heads at the pity of it all.

He thought about her when the rain was coming down and when the wind pushed him home, through the fields, from school. He thought about her when the heat of the coals in the teatime fire made his eyes smart and when the sun stroked down his back in the morning. Sometimes he wondered if thinking about her this much might bring her, just from the force of wanting and the pull of his imaginings.

So he waited for her but she didn't come. While he waited for the Cissie he'd made up in his head, he practised talking to live girls. He tried Mary Hatt.

'I saw a man get his head stove in once.'

These were the first words Mary Hatt spoke to Walter Brown in the yard at Cryers Hill village school. Walter nodded politely and tried not to look at her face for fear this would release a whole chain of events. In contrast to her elder sister, the graceful Isabel, Mary Hatt carried herself carelessly and released her thoughts directly from her mouth, without censorship or consideration. In 1930 this was not regarded as a desirable attribute in a girl.

'Yes,' she continued good-humouredly, 'kicked him when he was turned. His brains went in a bucket.'

Walter struggled to come up with a suitable reply. Mary did so for him.

'Never mind,' she said.

Walter could not think of a single thing to say. He stared at the slates and waited for time to move on.

'Mind you, I seen worse than that,' she continued pleasantly.

He listened to her shoe scraping the stone, her breath go in and out of her open mouth, loud as Doug Shaw's breeding bull.

'I'm sure you have.'

'I have.'

He was done for, he suspected. He didn't know why he thought that.

'Which d'you want to hear about?'

'None. Thank you.'

'Well. So, one had his arm off from a scythe and another one got his whole head taked off by a Marshall engine at threshing time. Dogs drunk all the blood off the ground. His legs went on all right, like a chicken's, trying to run.'

And she laughed a startled, good-natured laugh as if this were not so terrible as it sounded. Walter was grateful for the laugh that wiped from his mind the poor man's scrabbling legs. Now at least they wouldn't have to stand there in silent contemplation of the wretched fellow, headless as a Christmas bird, running everywhere and nowhere at all.

He looked at her and felt the shock of her bold blunt stare. When he looked away her face remained like an imprint on his eye, her wind-tangled hair and jumble of teeth, so that he saw it over everything, the Victorian brickwork, the drain gulleys, the sky.

'Something in there?' she asked, as he pressed his finger against his eyelid.

'Gone now,' he replied, not daring to glance again.

'Give it a rub then.'

He obeyed for something to do.

'My grandad had a glass eye he could take out. He swallowed it once, playing the fool.'

'Oh.'

'He got it back. Came out his rear, covered in plop.'

41

'Oh.'

'Yes. So, cheerio then.'

Walter stood there a while after she'd gone. 'Cheerio.' He didn't trust himself to think or move; almost as though *his* head too had come clean off his shoulders and *his* legs wanted to dash nowhere at all. Here then was Mary Hatt. True enough it was to say she was no Cissie.

Sankey and Walter stand together at the old gate on the Four Ashes road. They lean their backs to the valley view. Behind them are the forested hills, sharply angled farmland and flowing sky. They smoke. Walter is forbidden to light up at home until he is twenty-one. Sankey too is unable to smoke his pipe at his lodgings. The old gate on the Four Ashes road lay between their respective addresses. If it was raining or inclement they would shelter in Town Wood or retire to the White Lion. They will speak with each and everyone who happens along. Just now it is the road sweeper, Saul, trimming the banks and verges, carrying his mole traps – a shilling he would get for a good pelt, rats too. He was surprisingly effective with his catapult and lead balls. A menace rats were, in the feed rooms, corn ricks; Saul earned his fresh milk and cheese.

One year Saul got himself chased into the pond by wasps. He still talks about it. Chased him a good quarter-mile. A million of them he said there were afterwards, showing off his red swellings. 'Your arithmetic's off,' Sid Perfect informed him. Sid Perfect was an excellent darts player. He could tell you how many you needed and how best to score them before the last dart had landed. He was good at predictions. He could tell a woman whether she should expect twins. He could tell a person they were going to die a violent death. He was never wrong.

A million, Saul insisted again. He got upset about it. I'm no liar, he said. I know one million wasps when I see them. And he punched Tommy King in the head to prove it.

Walter sees the cattle on the hill have raised their heads. More curious than a cat, a cow. Tommy Castle said that. A natural with cattle he was. Something about those who nursed a grief a long time, made them good around animals, economical with their movements. Excellent with cattle, Tommy, in spite of his old age; milk yield never better anyhow. If you ask him about the war with the Boer he'll tell you. Go on, ask Tommy, they used to say. And he did tell, even to a very small boy, which Walter was at the time. Tommy's grief was over the mothers and babies, the ones who were starved, put in camps, fenced in like you would for animals. Tommy heard them crying still, here in the Chilterns. He couldn't stand it. He kept to himself after that war. They were removed, he said, the ones who had died, to make room for more Boer mothers and their babies to come and starve and cry and wait to die. The English this was, Tommy said, who did it, the British Army. Walter, who was just a boy then, didn't believe him.

Walter and Sankey lean and smoke.

'Here, I have a good one for you, Walt.'

'Ready and able.'

'Why is a kingfisher blue?'

'Why is a kingfisher blue?'

'That's it.'

'So that he may attract the lady kingfishers.'

Sankey waits. 'How did you come by that?'

'A little knowledge of the avian kingdom goes a long way.'

'Well, it is wrong. A kingfisher's plumage, my friend, is as blue as Our Saviour's eyes. An exact replication of the colour, in order that mankind may know what it is to be looked upon by the Light of the World.'

'God help us, Sank.'

'I'll drink to that.'

'A jar of ale will cure the ailment with no name.'

'You read my mind just then, Walter.'

Walter places two halves of ale before Sankey and slides into the chair beside him. Now that they are here at the Royal Standard he finds he is happy to taste the bitter froth on his tongue and half listen to the gargles of chatter filtering through the smoke.

'This is a marvellous day,' Sankey remarks.

Walter says nothing. He does not wish to respond, fearing it is the introduction to a long, tortuous discourse. After a pause Walter fills his pipe and strikes a match and soon they are both shrouded by a dense fog.

A man enters with a cringing collie around his ankles. He nods and crosses to the bar.

Sankey raises his glass. 'You could join me, I suppose, at the church room if you so wished.'

The collie slips into the shadow beneath a table. It makes Walter think of stoats. Walter does not want to go to the church room. Sankey is always rooting about for a conversion. He does not reply. That is the end of that then.

From stoats Walter's thoughts drift towards ferrets. He fancied a ferret as a boy, but his mother would not tolerate one in the house. He suggested it could sleep outside in a kennel, to which she replied, 'Are you deaf?'

'Do you like ferrets then, Sank?'

Sankey looks hard at his drink while he decides. 'No. They bite and they smell, Walt. Canaries are nice.'

'They may give a playful nip.'

'They can draw blood.'

'Only if they're upset.'

'You can't upset a canary, they are a stable bird, Walt.'

'Not if a cat is about.'

'Morning, Jim. No, but generally.'

'I don't like the twittering.'

'They don't twitter, they sing. Good as any nightingale.'

'I'll take your word for it.'

'You should. Canaries are the ticket.'

'I'm not a bird man.'

'No, well. You might consider it, Walt.'

'So you say.'

'I do.'

'I shall sleep on it.'

'Good, then. Hello, John. That'll put hairs on your chest.'

'If you say so.'

'I do say, Walt. I do.'

CHAPTER 7

The hill that gave Cryers Hill its name could indeed make you cry. If you stood at the summit where the sky arched and the clouds raced and you turned to face the wind, your cheeks would be streaked in seconds. No one could withstand it. If you stood there you wept. Sean stood there a lot. It wasn't bad, the way the wind pulled at you, tugged you as if you were important. He ran along the ridge, where the trees were bent almost to the ground, until tears ran down his neck and pooled inside his ears. He fell against the hill and let the wind pulverise him. He watched the clouds rolling like tumbleweed, and the birds trying to fly, swiped away like paper bags.

Here was a hill for heroes. Girls didn't like it by and large; the wind made them scream, excepting Ann, who screamed for no one. Ann would stand at the highest point like a buccaneer, blinded by tears, showing her teeth. She understood perfectly well the heroics of hilltops.

It was said there were soldiers buried in the hill. It was said that during the Civil War the injured ones were carried to the top. There, with Hughenden

Valley below them and the wind of judgement above, Royalists and Roundheads alike bled to death. Their cries could be heard in the hamlets in the valley and around. This, some say, is how the village came to be known as Cryers Hill. Sean believed it must be true, and sometimes thought he heard voices in the wind.

A child was buried here too, the locals said. A hundred years after the Civil War an infant was struck down in the night by an avenging angel, and subsequently buried on the hill by her mother to be closer to God. The story was if you stood on the hill under a full moon on the exact avenging angel date, you would hear the child sing.

Sean heard no singing today, but he could see a man about five hundred yards away, standing alone below the crooked limb of a great tree. The man was staring out towards the valley. He was clothed, so Sean deduced he could not be the streaker. Why on earth did people stare into valleys? Sean tried it to see. Green. Green. Green. The End. There was nothing there! And still he was staring. Where was his dog anyway? Why would a man walk around without a dog? Ann would know. Ann would ask him. *Scuse me, Mister. What you staring at, Mister?* She would narrow her knavish eyes. It was possible Ann was not supposed to live on earth with everyone else. More than once Sean had seen her thrown into the clouds. She would be on her garden swing and he would hide by the fence, waiting. He recalled her rising into the sky, hair afloat, the shreds of her voice coming at him in ribbons, like the dead infant's song. He thought then she was born to float or fly.

One way or another Sean was used to looking up to Ann. She spiralled through his head at night and swung in and out of his waking thoughts, even when she was standing right beside him. Ann. Anna. Like that hymn Sean once heard, Who's Anna? Who's Anna? Who's Anna in the highest? *Ooh, Miss!* Sean would put his hand up because he knew the answer to that one. At night, as he fell asleep, he saw her swim across a blank sky, unhurried, long-necked, like a swan. The man is gone. Sean is amazed. He must have taken his eye off the ball. This is how it goes.

Sean appears from nowhere, treading slow-motion steps past the diggers. He has set his heart on space travel. For a week, he has been wearing a cement-sack helmet with holes cut for his eyes, and now he's upgraded to a plastic fish tank. Sun dazzles bounce off his aquarium head, which is square instead of round as it should be, but it was a matter of limited choice. Seen through the plastic, his face is determined. Every time he moves his head the thing slides about, but he is growing used to it and hardly notices the clunks around his temples and ears.

He watched them, the astronauts, bouncing across the television screen and back again, their voices bursting in their helmets against the ping and hiss of satellite static. He stared at the line of fossil-grey footprints in the moon dust, and at the American flag they'd planted, its reds and blues faded to BBC black and white. But mostly he stared at the surface of the moon, which looked a lot like their front garden, a lot of dirt and dust, waiting for turf.

The fish tank makes his voice exotically different, resonating from the bottom of a deep bell jar. Ann begins to treat him with a new respect. Some of the older kids laugh but this does not seem to affect Sean; on the contrary, he has grown fearless and debonair. The builders have left cylindrical sheaths of ribbed plastic lying around, packaging from piping and plumbing ducts. Sean wraps a length around his neck for an oxygen tube, a blue one that swings around his knees. It is perfect. Ann is finding it harder to say inconsequential things to him; the paraphernalia he wears is intimidating. Mostly he cannot hear what she is saying anyway, and she is losing the will to repeat herself. For Sean the aquarium helmet is an agreeable barrier between him and the world and now between he and she. It leaves him alone with the songs of the universe, the thoughts of an intergalactic traveller.

He struggles up behind her to the summit of a brick mountain, sweating and gasping inside his tank, watching while she springs nimbly ahead. It is higher than he anticipated. His thoughts are orange, blue, orange, blue, as he looks down, up, down, up, bricks, sky, bricks. There is no breeze to lift her skirt, Sean notices. The sound of his panting reminds him of something but he can't think what. His breaths temporarily mist up the tank so that he cannot see, clearing just in time for him to take another step before his next breath mists everything over again. He is suffocating; sweat runs down his neck and tickles around his ribs. The sound of his swallowing is unnaturally loud. A spaceman does not mind this. A spaceman does not complain, not even when his stomach floats into his mouth and his brain falls out of his shoes.

She is already there, brisk and thoughtless as an Alpine goat. The climb was tough but necessary. Ann points out to Sean that he will have to get used to high altitudes and he may as well start now. She mentions too that the brick mountain will make a man of him. 'It'll make a man of you,' she confirms, hands on her hips, glancing dismally at his muffin knees. 'It'll make a proper man of you.'

CHAPTER 8

The day Walter went alone to the woodland pond, he went to think his thoughts and catch a fish, if he was lucky. He lay down with his rod for a rest. All his thoughts and naggings tipped out of his head and he was left with a lovely blankness and the mew of a bunting.

He saw his girl swimming there. She wasn't his girl then, but he knew she would be. He was nineteen when he knew. He watched her floating and saw how white her skin was in the green water, her belly, her breasts, her pond-tangled hair. A naked girl. Then she turned over like an otter and dived down. She did not come up again. Walter ran to the edge of the water. He crashed through the reeds and stood panting at his own dirty reflection. He panicked. He pulled off his boots and socks, knowing all the time that he could not swim even if he wanted to. Finally he shouted out her name.

She was sixteen when he decided. She came up out of the water, green as a mermaid, a few feet from his face, streaming with water and duckweed, and roaring with mocking laughter. She wasn't gold-haired or loving or happy as Larry. She was no Cissie. She kept a mouthful of curses behind her crowd of teeth and a great shout of a laugh that narrowed her eyes to nothing. Walter fell in love with Mary Hatt. This was before. Later they would say, poor Walter Brown. He never really had a chance.

Sean and Ann sleep in one of the splintery bedrooms of a half-finished house. It smells of soft wood and wind. There is no roof, but in spite of this Sean is compelled to watch the sky through the empty window frame. He sees tufts of cloud and an aeroplane sail by. A breeze comes up the stairs from the hall and whirls around them and up and out where the roof should be. They are forbidden to do this. Children are not allowed in the incompleted houses; they have all been warned, but there are no workmen about today, no foreman, no one. Sean listens out for murderers or streakers. He wonders what exactly he would do if a murderer strolled in now, rolling his eyes and gnashing his teeth. Kung fu? Bruce Lee would probably never come to Buckinghamshire. If he did he would go to High Wycombe for the bright lights, or Amersham.

Nobody knows they are here in the unfinished bedroom of an incomplete house in a nameless cul-de-sac. You can bury people in cement. Duncan Drew said that. Sean wonders whether anybody will be looking for them, calling out their names. Unlikely. This is Sunday and all the parents will be sitting bare-legged in their stony gardens. The bell from the church clangs; imploring them to come up the hill in their shorts and flip-flops, so that the Good Shepherd can help them with their stony lives.

Sean notices that Ann is still asleep. Now it is he alone who knows they are lying in a pretend, dust-blown bedroom, roofless and illicit. He tries to imagine they are married and this is their real-life bedroom, with wallpaper, slippers and a nice carpet. He rolls over to his Mrs Wife and pulls her hand from her mouth. Her lips are cracked and dry and slightly apart. He touches her thigh and finds it surprisingly cool and hard, and then she shifts, 'P'sof,' and turns away from him.

They have a dog, he decides, like everyone on the estate, a big one, quite vicious, and a fast car that blows white smoke. He is much taller in his married-man self, and other men are afraid of him. He can punch too, but not women. He can kick dogs, they cower when he's around. No animal would ever dare bite him nor any person bully him or call him names like titch, spaz or mongol. All the girls love him, every single one. Ann will have to get over this. He is famous because he plays for Leeds, and he saved someone's life. He knows Bobby Charlton. When he was in the army they won the war; he's got medals to prove it. He could kill someone with his bare hands if he had to, if he felt like it. You can kill people with your bare hands, actually, it's very straightforward, his dad says. 'One squeeze, I could do the lot of you and afford a new car,' and they'd all laugh then. He was quite funny, his dad.

Sean can't really think of anything else. He decides to wake Ann, then changes his mind. She will be annoyed. He can feel dust in his nose, in his mouth. He creaks down the stairs, out through the raw-rimmed hole that is waiting for a door, across the dirt that is not yet a garden. He is a few yards along the ragged bit of road when her voice falls from the sky.

'Spaz!'

She is leaning through the empty window frame, and when he turns and looks up he is surprised at how nice-looking the whole thing is in spite of everything: her, the storybook house, the breeze in her hair. She holds up his tank and tube and then she chucks them through the hole.

'You're a spaz. What are you?'

They land in the dirt of the not-yet garden, his helmet and his oxygen pipe, his essentials for inter-galactic voyaging, his armour and his last breath.

'A spaz,' he replies.

The zigzag maze of estate paths, alleys and passages all meet up eventually and tip tunnel-travellers into the playground of the local primary school. Twice a day the tunnels are clogged with traipsing children. Twice a day the wails, moans and screams are more suggestive of asylum inmates than children learning their reading and writing.

Reading and writing is taught at Cryers Hill Primary School as at any other school, but unlike any other school they learn it differently. 'Ground-*breaking*,' Mrs Jackson had said at assembly, and Sean pictured the earth splitting while they all tumbled screaming into the cracks with the almost-houses, diggers and builders' huts. This was a new, modern way to read and write, modern as space flight. Children would learn to read faster and write quicker, like instant potato and Angel Delight – just add water – it would happen in a flash with no inconvenient old-fashioned waiting around.

'Front-*runners*,' Mrs Jackson said on the morning they were all informed.

Sean was proud to be in an experiment; not everyone could say the same, and besides, it would prepare him for a lifetime in space, where everything is new, exciting and uncertain. What's more, this experiment was official, authorised, and they were the lucky few. The government had decreed it, the actual Prime Minister himself. And they, Cryers Hill Primary, were going to be one of the schools in the south-east to embrace and implement the latest methods devised by the godfather of this modernising new experiment, Sir James Pitman. Sir! As though he were come on a white horse, clad in armour. Sir James! Bringer of words, lancer of old alphabets.

Like a brilliant cure for a tired old disease, ITA is spreading across the country: Newcastle, Hartlepool, Liverpool, Wales. In fact it is so important it is going to America and Australia as well. Soon the children who are upside down on the other side of the planet will be reading the same books as Sean in the same instantaneous way.

The experiment is called ITA. Or, ie tee æ, in the experimental vernacular. Sean's teacher, Miss Day, calls it *funetic*, as though it is a huge laugh. She says she is a *funetic fan* and Sean thinks that whatever that is, he is one too. Miss Day explains how lucky they all are to be learning the ITA alphabet, to be taught to read and write using phonetics, instead of ploughing through months of struggle and confusion as they try to learn the traditional alphabet, to read traditional books and write traditional words. Miss Day says 'traditional' as though it is a sad, pathetic thing to be, and Sean agrees that whatever it is, it's rubbish.

Miss Day says reading and writing and arithmetic are extremely difficult. When faced with them at school young children generally struggle. They cry, she explains. Some of them cry for years. Miss Day knows this for a fact because she has had to teach these poor tearful weepers herself. It's very sad, she admits. Sean and his friends are lucky, she says beamingly. They have been saved by Sir James and his modern ITA. They will learn to read and write in record time with no tears. Then, once they are experts at phonetic reading and writing, around the age of eight, they will be *changed. Changeover* is painless. They need to be *changed* at this age so that they can read and write in traditional alphabet the same as all the other poor tearful sods in the world – just like that, ɛɛʒy pɛɛʒy pʊdiŋ It is like magic, except that it is real. It is a miracle. It is going to change ðhe hœl edyʊcæʃhon sistem in ostrælia and ðhe uenieted stæts and iŋland and scotland and wælʒ.

Ann had a surprisingly snazzy laugh for a person who didn't blink. It was the cause of everything in the first place, the thing that bedazzled Sean, caught him unawares and now it was too late, he had his head through the wire. It grabbed him still. She laughed with her head back and her eyes closed and her mouth fallen open, like someone under a water fountain. Sometimes she had to hold on to something, as if laughing could knock you off your feet. Sometimes the thing she held on to was Sean, and this produced in him a sense of responsibility, of incumbence, as if he were a priest or a tree or some other immovable object. She didn't laugh often. You had to keep your eye on the ball.

Sean had not heard of anyone laughing in space. Smiling yes. But laughing? Space was not a laughing matter, you were not supposed to muck about. You couldn't just bounce up and down and go *Wur.*

Sean kept a newspaper photograph of the pre-flight Neil Armstrong and Buzz Aldrin in his pocket. He examined every detail, each grainy little truth: the two men, their faces free of helmets, grinning proudly out of the turtleneck rims of their spacesuits. For certain Sean Matthews would have grinned proudly too if it were he they were catapulting into the sky, high into the black unknown for the sake of all mankind, his country's flag in his pocket and Planet Earth's own God up there patiently waiting for him. He might well have grinned.

It amazed Sean that dogs, rats, monkeys and chimpanzees had all gone into space before mankind. It was all here in a book called *Space*, with pre-flight photographs of the animals in their capsules. Laika, once a mongrel, now the *Sputnik* space dog, showed her best doggy grin for the cameras. There was even a woman called Valentina Tereshkova. Sean had thought women were not allowed in space.

Sean sat at the bottom of the stairs reading this book. Well, not reading exactly, but looking at the pictures and guessing at words. Truth was it wasn't his book at all, but a library book which should have been returned by now. Inside, he found the moon, disappointingly grey and crumbly-looking, and pictures of the cosmonaut Yuri Gagarin, Laika, the *Sputnik* space dog, Ed White adrift on his silver cord, *Luna 9*, *Apollo 8*, and John Glenn inside the *Friendship 7*. Sean pointed things out to himself that he would later come to know by heart: Alexei Leonov, William Anders, *Apollo* command module. There were rockets exploding off launchpads and astronauts ecstatically afloat across the pages. Sean stared at the universe, or a corner of it; a fixed blackness, spangled with stars and planets and a pinkish haze to the right. He spoke the names he had heard of. Milky Way, Pluto, Venus, Saturn, Mars. This was good, this. He could talk about the cosmos all day, like bloody Patrick Moore.

At the book's centre were some photographs of what looked like white bone pushing through black. When you looked harder you saw the bone was perfectly curved like something ceramic and swirled with a dazzling blue. Sean stared. It was the most beautiful picture in the book. He knew it was Earth. You didn't have to read words in order to recognise your home.

CHAPTER 9

Walter Brown worked for the Water Company in Wycombe. He rode his bicycle there most days as it was no more than five miles away, though it was hilly on the way back, thickening his calves as each year passed. He had worked his way up from office boy and was satisfied that these days he could call himself office clerk, having put in three blameless years.

The work was relatively undemanding, though Walter discovered he tolerated it quite well. He appreciated the routine, and the anticipation of unwrapping his sandwiches or bursting on to the high street for a quick lunchtime walk, with the opportunity to visit the library or purchase tobacco or check his watch against the Town Hall clock. Lately, though, he felt himself becoming increasingly restless. The repetitive elements, the indexing, filing, stamping, he minded less owing to the existence of the immense horse-chestnut tree that grew, almost to the roof, beside the building. The tree filled the upper windows with its tentacle-spread of mature branches, a sight that mesmerised Walter throughout the seasons, whether they were black-frosted in winter or blossoming, green-laden or aflame around Michaelmas time. He stared, pen poised, until the tree had mapped itself like circuitry into his brain.

Walter had composed three odes to the tree, though he no longer bothered with the first two. Ideally he would have preferred to begin forcefully with 'Great oak!' and felt keenly the frustration of finding himself unable to, faced as he was with a horse chestnut and nothing to be done about it.

Sylvia Pusey worked as a secretary at the Water Company. Walter had not really noticed her until one day she touched his arm on the stairs and said, 'You can take me to Hughenden Park for the botany if you like.' Walter hesitated then, to be sure he had heard correctly, and he had hesitated ever since where Sylvia was concerned. She was a perfectly nice girl, pretty enough, pleasant, obliging, with nice brown hair, who held no extremist views about anything. But Walter felt only a kind of blankness when he looked at her. She produced in him something inert, disinclined. Walter's mother, on the other hand, took a shine to Sylvia.

Walter lived with his mother, Hilda Brown, in one of the red-brick semis built in 1908 on Valley Road. Hilda Brown pointed out to Walter that Sylvia was a good, ordinary, polite girl; pretty, but not too pretty, educated but not too educated. He would be a fool to look a gift horse in the mouth, she said.

Hilda Brown was always having to point things out to people. She thought if she didn't point things out, the whole world would go entirely around the bend. The man next door, for example, kept cages of yellow and blue birds, referred to by him as buggery guards, and occupied himself strangely, at night, in the back garden. He shouted out habitually in his sleep and his wife had grown nervous as a hare. Hilda knew he had fought in the Boer War, but she did not consider this an excuse. He preferred birds to people, that much was obvious. She kept Walter away from him.

Walter's father, Frank Brown, had worked at the Town Hall. It was generally supposed that he had helped arrange Walter's appointment at the Water Company. Unless you were very idle indeed, he used to say, you would have a job for life, unlike those who were laid off during difficult times and could not know what on earth was coming next, or how they would feed their families.

Walter understood it was important to know what on earth was coming next, but he couldn't bring himself to fear for his future the way everybody else did. The day he had discovered his father kneeling before the gooseberries with his face in the dirt, he had known he was going to go about things differently. To expire suddenly on your knees, while not ideal, was preferable to dying lingeringly in a bed, anyone could see that. But

Walter remained troubled by the memory of his father's body – the weight, the dampness, the yawning oval of his sour-smelling mouth.

Walter's father had managed to escape the first war by dint of his age. He was forty-three when Walter was born and forty-five by the time conscription came. Invalided soldiers and hearsay brought the facts home to him, and Frank Brown became fretful about the good fortune that had spared him. Bad luck seemed more likely, and this particular fortuity haunted him for the rest of his life.

Walter's grandfather too had worked at Wycombe Town Hall, *worked his way up*, was how Hilda put it; a dynasty of hard-working clerks, the Browns. Walter was born in their little house on Penn Road in Hazlemere where they all lived, three generations of clerks together, until Walter's father got a mortgage and they moved to one of the smart, newly built houses that was to remain his home until the day of his great departing.

As a boy Walter had known the woods as well as his own two hands. Still, Mary Hatt had a talent for hiding. He found her at last in Millfield Wood, up an elm, straddling a low branch. He had to shout, then she screamed and spat at him for frightening her. Now she would not come down. All right then, she would come down if he chased her, that was fair.

Walter had chased Mary many times. He had

stopped enjoying it, truth be told, now he was nineteen, but Mary was a creature of persistent habit and one of anything was never enough. Mary liked any sort of game or lark. Hide-and-seek was all right, but best of all she liked games involving stealth and surprise. 'Boo' was her first word. One time she chased the man come to do the steam cultivator all the way up to Provost Spinney, laughing like a bear all the way. She had a great burst of a laugh – she could let it off like a missile and it would catch up with you no matter how fast you ran.

He had agreed to her request and chased her again. Now she had disappeared. Walter stopped and caught his breath and waited for her to jump out or scream or pelt him from behind, but she didn't come. He sat down on a bulging tree root and wondered what would happen to him if it turned out he had lost her. He rested his long chin in his hand. He considered the thrashing he would get from her father, the hiding from his mother, p'raps others, p'raps all the mothers and fathers, p'raps they would line up with belts, canes and horsewhips. There would be nothing left of him by the time they were finished. They would have him arrested. Mr Looker, the policeman, would ask him where he lived, though he knew it perfectly well; he would ask it in his gloomiest tone. He would be guilty of something, of every-thing. He would go to prison. Walter hung his head. His father had once said, 'Look after nature,

Walt, and nature will look after you.' This seemed a tragically sad thing to Walter now; he couldn't think why.

It was several minutes before she threw down her shoe. It bounced, heel down, off the top his head and rolled into the moss. Now he would thrash her himself and see how she liked that. But when he looked up it was not Mary he saw, it was something else – a nymph perhaps, a thing that dwelt in a forest, and there it stood, on a branch, casual, as if this were not at all strange. 'Mary?' he said and she smiled back, though Walter would never be able to recollect this smile his whole life long, because it was her breasts he was concentrating on, her naked breasts to be precise, the only breasts he had ever seen, the only breasts he had ever thought about wanting to see. And all his boyhood dreams he hadn't yet dreamed and all his boyhood wishes he hadn't yet wished came true instantaneously, and somewhere in a darkened corner of Walter's head a star exploded.

'What y'starin' at then?'

Walter didn't answer. It was a complicated question.

'Do you like me then?'

There was no point in Walter trying to speak, so he didn't. Instead he sank to his knees, like a hind when the shot takes him cleanly, like his own poor father at the soft arrival of his death.

★ ★ ★

66

Sid Perfect and his friend, the Methodist Charles Sankey, had once made their living poaching. Sankey was from Lyme Regis. Something tragic had happened to him, though nobody could remember what exactly. The pair were dab hands with long nets, purse nets, gate nets. Like fishermen on dry land they could haul in rabbit, hare or game bird. On a weekend they would visit the White Horse and lose their sea legs altogether. You could see them pitching about like a couple of rubber pirates, tipping and falling, storm-tossed, until finally they would each vomit up a song and hit the deck.

Sankey used to join Sidney Perfect on well-lit nights with nets and spade. Everyone admired Perfect's ferrets. He had jills mainly, rather than dogs. They used to flush out scores of rabbits for Sankey to pop when they worked as a team. Sometimes they were in trouble over it and at other times a farmer would be only too grateful to get the rabbit numbers down before his crops were ravaged. Always an excellent shot, Sankey, but since he found God he had laid down his weapon and taken up The Word. Now he wouldn't hurt a fly, or a wasp, even as those very wasps devastated the orchards. Time was when a farmer would be only too glad of a team like Sankey and Perfect: rats, rabbits, pigeons, moles – a shilling per skin they got for mole pelts – even sparrows, a flock of a thousand or more might settle on a field of wheat and do for it. On a moonlit night the contrasting wide and narrow silhouettes of Sankey and Perfect with ferrets, purse nets and spade were as familiar in the nocturnal landscape as bats or barn owls.

Charles Sankey, meanwhile, had pretensions to preaching. He had never received any type of formal instruction, or even informal welcome, from any church in the parish of Hughenden or elsewhere. He had become a Methodist in Lyme Regis in 1922. He chose the Methodists because they seemed a cheery bunch compared to the other denominations. He knew nothing about it, but he liked the songs. He worshipped locally at the Widmer End Mission Hall. He made an occasional nuisance of himself, particularly where preacher Harry Blagdon was concerned. He was never without his hymnal, *Sacred Songs and Solos*, which he carried about him, though there wasn't a hymn in there he didn't know by heart. 'I know one thousand, one hundred and thirty-nine hymns by heart' – this is what he claimed and no one suggested putting it to the test. One day, out of love for God and clerical ambition for himself, Sankey gave up ale. Though it made him sorrowful to do so, he emerged a better, cleaner, godlier man. He took his large, kindly face, with its lumpy nose and dome of a forehead, to house, woodland, farm, anywhere they did not serve ale. He walked spryly, up on his toes, in any direction salvation was required and blessings prayed for. A few were charmed by his melancholy tone, friendly advice, and quick intelligent eyes that threw glances and squeezed together when he smiled. He was not too holy for jokes or sponge cake, and his long pale hands rested warmly on the palms of those in need or trouble.

Harry Blagdon, however, was the official lay preacher. He walked many miles on his circuit to Bourne End, Lacey Green, Flackwell Heath and Bledlow Ridge, and was envied by Charles Sankey, who begrudged him every step of his mission, every handshake, every cup of tea with parkin slice. At first Sankey had attempted a friendship, walking alongside him, sometimes all the way to Little Missenden, always joining him in worshipful singing as they travelled through sleet and rain and wind. But at every destination it was Father Harry they hurried out to greet, Father Harry who must come in after such a long journey and wash and get warm and take tea with cake, Father Harry who must suffer the fussing attentions of the womenfolk and the mindful solicitude of the men. It wasn't just the tea breads – Sankey could hear the jab of piano keys and bursts of song from inside the houses as he waited outside, he could hear the women's voices and the respectful silence that fell as the preacher spoke.

Sankey reckoned God was as much in his heart as in Harry's and He guided his tongue as mindfully too, but nobody else seemed to see it that way, and particularly not Father Harry as he handed

Sankey his hat to hold while he comforted a grieving woman with unusually beautiful hair.

One day Sankey had his shotgun by him as he hoped to take a bird or two at dawn at the Hughenden estate before anyone else was about. A bright disc of sun had hung itself over St Mary's Church, the place it auspiciously began each day with the melting of the churchyard dew. Then there it was: Harry's black hat skimming the hedge, a phlegmy version of 'The Lord Taketh Care of Me', and before he was able to give it careful consideration, Sankey found that he had fired.

The shot was not accurate. And though Sankey knew he had not actually killed the preacher this time, he felt sufficiently afraid of himself, of what he might do next, to run away and hide in a lightning tree until noon. He hid the gun in a dry ditch where nettles grew, until it was safe to retrieve it.

Father Harry Blagdon suffered no physical injury other than mortal fright, which repaired well enough after the ministrations of local ladies, and was aided ably by generous amounts of tea, perhaps gin, and cake. Afterwards, however, Harry's story grew tall with telling until only those closest to God were able to believe it. These enrichments (garnishings you might say), sprinkled upon the truth to better explain to his flock the everyday miracles performed by God, were not in Harry's mind in any way related to actual sinful untruths. In any case he told the story, richly embroidered, for many years to come. He had been walking by Millfield Wood, he pronounced, when a blackened creature more than ten feet high with terrible sharpened horns appeared before him. Father Harry knew right away it was the Devil. He preached the word to the beast until, terrified, it turned on its hairy hocks and ran. And though it took a swipe or two at the preacher, brave Father Harry pursued it, chasing it back into the woods with its tail on fire.

Father Harry Blagdon was a celebrated hit after that. Sankey had inadvertently boosted Blagdon's reputation and spoiled his only opportunity for apprenticeship. Blagdon's circuit increased as his reputation grew. His triumphs over the beast meant he became increasingly in demand across South Bucks. Who was to say there was not another beast lurking? It was not possible to search every copse, every spinney, each stretch of woodland. Who would protect the good people of Hughenden? Who would flush the beast from the woods, so the people of the parish could sleep soundly in their beds?

CHAPTER 10

If he is to enter deep space, Sean must practise being weightless. They walk, Sean and Ann, to the pond by Cockshoot Wood and he throws himself in. Ann waits for him to surface. She hurls in a stone to get his attention but there is no sign of him. She waits, bored. She wonders if he has drowned.

Up he comes then, spluttering like an amateur, half strangled in his blue tubing. Ann loses interest and watches the pond for movement. The surface is grey-green and busy with insects and there is a lapping at the far end.

Legend says the Hughenden Dragon lives here, though no one has ever seen it. Though it is impossible to know what to expect, chances are it won't respond kindly to the arrival of a small trainee astronaut in its depths. The dragon had to be at least four hundred years old. One day, in its youth probably, it was said to have frightened a farm girl as she collected water and the girl's neighbours hatched a plan to kill it. The story was well known locally. It was decided the girl would sit at the water's edge, tempting it to the surface, and when it appeared they would leap out from behind briars and set about the serpent with axes. It was said the unfortunate creature let out piteous cries. A woman and a baby were swallowed by a dragon from this very same pond some years after; that is the rumour. It remains unclear whether the original creature had survived or if another was in residence. Nobody took any chances, all the same, until eventually a lack of fresh occurrences faded the collective memory and turned the tales into local legend.

No one on the new Gabbett housing estate knows anything of tales, rumours or legends. On the dust-blown estate there is no collective memory. But for the long-term residents the dragon is a source of civic pride these days, not every village had one after all. At the Village Association it had become their very own heritage item, their motif, and nobody thought to be fearful, not now in the twentieth century, what with two blokes hoofing about on the moon and a nuclear reactor just a few miles up the A40.

Sean paddles frantically towards the bank, his chin held high out of the water, destreamlining him, turning his eyes wild; green stuff slimes his hair. It is doubtful at this stage that he will ever manage to break free of the Earth's gravitational field to find himself orbiting around anything other than his own imagination. He scrabbles at the bank, strangled by tubing, tearing at pond rushes, while Ann closes her eyes against the sun.

She knows it is best not to interfere with his preliminary training. She senses this would be detrimental in the long run; sometimes you have to be cruel to be kind. She holds out her palms instead to the butterflies tumbling around the tall reeds. A small blue one lands on her thumb and she calls out to Sean to look and see. She sidles over, cupping her other hand over it. 'Look! Look! It likes me, see?' Sean has managed to get himself on to the bank, and is wet and dazed and wrapped in blue tube like an alien birth. He is on his back, gazing up at Ann through his slimed fringe. 'Ahh, look, Sean, look.' Sean stares up at the inverted vision of her bare legs and softly astonished face, at her curled hands, and the bright blue butterfly growing out of her thumb. 'Ahh, look. I love you, do you love me?' she asks the insect. 'It loves me, look.' And Sean looks and sees. But he loved her first, he loved her before the butterfly, he loves her more than any insect ever could; he loves her so much he cannot speak to tell her.

Glow-worms aren't worms at all. This is a demented lie. You can see them at Dancers End, by the railway embankment. They hang from bushes, bricks and ferns in long glittering chains, twinkling like Woolworths. The chains quiver when the air moves. The same wisp of air carries the call of the evensong bell from the church at Kingshill and the bark of the dog fox in Gomms

Wood. It occurs to Sean that these are magic things, like stars and storms and meteorites.

Stars die all the time. People don't think of it. They look up and they see them twinkling in the night sky and they think because they can see them that they are there, but they are not, not always. Sean has learned this recently. His brother Ty read it out for thruppence. Ty's name is Craig, but everyone calls him Ty, which is short for Typhoid, which is a disease that can kill you. Their dad once said living with Craig was like living with typhoid. Sticks and stones.

Ty is twelve. He is built like a shed. He regularly lets off a jungle cry that, ordinarily, you would only ever hear Tarzan produce. He has sleepy eyes, as though he is permanently struggling to stay awake. He has a big head, like an ass, and a slack mouth. In spite of this he is considered to be gifted. He wins cereal-box competitions. For reading, Ty charges Sean sixpence per hundred words. It is likely that he cheats. He reads fast and you can hear snot around his tonsils. The words cannot stand it in his mouth; you can hear them sticking in his throat and hurrying to escape through his nose. The liar alphabet hadn't arrived in Cryers Hill when Ty was at the primary school; back in those days they did ABC the traditional way. Ty says when he was young they were beaten with straps and canes. Sean doesn't believe him. He's cribbed the stories from their dad's school-days after the war. But Ty shows him a scar on his arm and narrows his genius eye at Sean. He says the ABC alphabet is much harder to learn, they have to beat it into you, he explains. Sean should think himself lucky, he says, that he's got it so easy. Sean thinks about this.

In Sean's *Space* book there is a picture of a dying star. It resembles a salt grain on its journey over someone's left shoulder. A book will find you out things that you didn't know were true. For instance, if a ship could carry men all the way to Neptune or Pluto, they'd be dead of old age before they got there, skeletons in their seats. Space just didn't know when to stop, so it didn't. The book says people could be living on the moon by the year 2000. It says folk will go there on their holidays. Sean stares at the drawing of the rosy-faced children with buckets and spades, waving cheerily as they board a lunar rocket. Pan Am, the rocket says along its side. There are stewardesses in tight blue jumpsuits with rocket-booster chests and pillbox hats, they are pointing people through the door and laughing, as if they know perfectly bloody well that space is too big and that the twinkling stars are dead and cold, and have been all along.

The saddest thought of all is that the North Star, trusty guide, loyal friend, could be dead, has maybe been dead all this time, but we just don't know it.

'That's your lot, Spazbrain!' Ty takes his sixpence. Sean is glad. Ty takes all the air, all the light. He knows what his brother spends the money on. He knows more than people think. He has the number you are supposed to ring if you have anything to say. He keeps it in his pocket.

The book says the light from a star will shine on long after that star is dead and gone. It is a trick. It is not the only trick in life. There are things that appear to be there when they are not. It is hard to spot the difference, even if, like Ty, you narrow your genius eye.

There is a hare on the surface of the moon. Miss Day says so. She says if you look properly, you can't miss it. Sean is not surprised to discover he isn't looking properly. As far as he's concerned there is no hare there at all. All he can see is the moon-man's face, with its frightened look of surprise. Lately, though, he has seen other things on the surface of the moon, alphabet letters that made no sense, words that wind around, continuing on the dark side, so you cannot read them anyway, even if you can read.

He thinks he can make out an S and a Z, and he chills at the thought of *spaz* being up there, hung with glitter, accusing him in front of the whole planet. He has seen a running animal, a bear perhaps. And he has seen the workman's sign, the one all over the estate, the little man with his shovel dug in. He can see its shadow shape, plain as day on the moon, as though they were up there too, the red naked builders, building more almost-houses with their diggers and trucks and sacks of cement.

The moon aside, it is Martian these days on the Gabbet estate. A red dust covers every surface, blown in numerous directions by an unaccountable wind. Bricks, lava red in colour, are stacked tall and tapering as pyramids, offering their summits to a deserted sky. You can make out the kids at the top, inches from the sun, and above them the wide blue dome that hides the comings and goings of an impartial God.

Sean runs. The diesel exhaust, woodsmoke, and the dust from brick, timber and cement all threaten to blot out the sun. Sean narrows his eyes against the dirt. If there is a streaker, murderer, Enoch or serpent about today he will know about it. He has his eye on the ball. He glances at the sky. Certainly he will not be surprised to spot God's finger poking through a cloud, same as in his picture prayer book – an enormous accusing finger pointing with deadly conviction directly down at the estate. He runs past the dazzle that comes off car windscreens and wing mirrors, bright and glary as spaceships, making you think of little green men and saucers that can fly. The Martians live here, the estate residents themselves. Ordinary aliens these, slapping in and out of their front doors, mechanical and in-coherent, cheery at times, glowing red from burns caused by the fireball sun; sleepwalking to and from their cars or nodding up the hill with an empty shopping bag. Then there is the noise. Nothing prepares you for it. When the machines drive into it, the sound comes up through the ground like rounds of shelling, of artillery fire, like mortar bombs landing, until the air shatters in your face and the ground explodes beneath your feet. Sean runs through the dust to the Wilderness.

'Enter.' It is Pilo who speaks. Sean doesn't know why he has a stupid name, or indeed if it is a name. Pilo is small like Sean and thin as a cat. His teeth are set with wide gaps where his words fizz and bubble. Sean tips his head back to appear taller as he squeezes inside. Simon is talking, nobody is listening. He is explaining that murderers are often armed and hide in bushes. He tries to pace up and down but is jostled by other boys. He goes on to say that murderers are cunning and sometimes have special powers. He reckons he could catch a murderer quicker than a policeman because a murderer wouldn't suspect him, whereas he'd spot a policeman a mile away, in his helmet and all.

'Ip dip sky blue, who's it, not you.' Jaclyn Johnson is working her way methodically through everybody until she gets to the person who has done the crime.

In the grimy half-light it is hard to make out faces until your eyes adjust. Ann is lying at the back. She has leaves in her hair and a twig between her teeth; she ignores Sean. Jasper holds up a builder's dog-end, he says it is a clue. He asks everybody in turn whether they recognise it. Sean puts his hands on his hips. He spits on the ground a couple of times and swerves his eyes to see if Ann is watching him. The policeman who came to their school had removed his helmet, like a cowboy. He had stood in their classroom, making a silence with his dark uniform and heavy shoes. Sean places his feet the same wide way now for Ann to see. At school there is a number on the blackboard. You must telephone this number if you have anything to say. Or tell your teacher. *Miss Day, I have something to say*. Sean thinks he has something to say. But he has decided not to say it. The policeman said there was no reason to be frightened. Sean thinks this is probably a lie. The policeman said they would leave no stone unturned. Sean thinks this is the most beautiful thing he has ever heard.

'Coo-coo-ka-choo, Mrs Robinson, Jesus loves you more than you will know. Ho ho ho.' Sean wondered if these were the correct words. His dad had quite a good singing voice, Sean reckoned. No one else in the family seemed to notice. His mother closed her eyes as she laid each plate down around the dinner table. Sean wondered if she was praying, if it had come to this. They watched as she set her own plate down and sat down to join it without opening her eyes. Ty and Sean knew it was not their place to enquire, so they didn't.

'S'matter now?' enquired Gor, as gently as his natural impatience would allow him.

Cath opened her eyes and looked at them as

though she'd expected to find herself somewhere else.

'I'm quite happy,' she replied. 'Can't you tell? I am ecstatically happy.'

Well, that was all right then. Except somehow it wasn't. It was the game: you had to guess the liar words.

'Let battle commence,' said Gor, picking up his knife and fork. Sean wondered if this was a just-add-water meal or whether his mother had done it the old-fashioned way. Ty began to eat, expressionless, like a panda. You could put a blob in the oven nowadays and it would come out as a roast dinner with all the trimmings. The television said women should go to work because they had nothing to do at home all day; modern appliances did it all for you.

'Headache?' Gor offered. Ty and Sean looked across at their mother. Cath closed her eyes again. Her eyelids were her most effective weapon. Against her eyelids Gor's words bounced off like toy arrows. Once the lids were down, nothing could penetrate. They would have to wait. She would come out when it suited her. Sean wondered what happened behind the lids. Did she switch off? Or, was it possible she had established contact with a superior intelligence? Some sort of extraterrestrial life form perhaps, some kind of outside influence. There were a lot of alien sightings these days, many of them in Buckinghamshire and nearby Oxfordshire. You could hardly stroll down the

81

road for a paper without spotting a UFO or bumping into someone who had. Aliens were everywhere, TV, newspapers, cereal packets, people's brains. It was only a matter of time before they would be competing in the Olympics and starring in *Z Cars*.

Sean kept an eye on his mother's eyelids in case, for example, a coloured light flashed. He listened too, for beeps or buzzes that might indicate she was in radio contact. When she finally opened her eyes, he would avoid her again, just in case. Aliens could control you through eye contact, through thought control, and it was best to play safe, even with members of your own family, sometimes especially.

'Three wheels on my wagon, but I'm still rolling along.' Sean reckoned his dad was just as good at singing as Tom Jones. Women liked men who sang, his dad said. Gor was an expert on women. It was his specialist subject, along with natural history and the evolution of humankind. Sean knew this to be a fact, and he felt cringingly proud about it. When he was next to his father in the passenger seat of the car, for instance, it would come up. The fairer sex, that's what his dad called them, though there didn't appear to be anything fair about it. There were two main types of woman, his dad explained: decent girls, birds and tarts. OK, three. Only not to tell his mother he said that. Then there were the women's libbers, who

burned their bras. Gor didn't know why. Men and women, Gor expanded, were little different to how they were in prehistoric times, which was why these days women got their knickers in a twist about things. What they didn't understand, he explained, was that they were designed for child-rearing and sewing animal skins. Nowadays, he said, they all wanted jobs and driving licences and equal pay. Next thing you knew they would be sticking their noses into politics and the armed forces. It was a slippery slope. Married women were now demanding credit cards. Imagine the debt we'll be in, he gasped. Sean tried to imagine.

There was a whole language that went with women. There were women who would give you the brush-off and the cold shoulder; there were others who would give you the come-on and the once-over. Women were birds and chicks and tarts. Older ones were hags, bats and biddies. If you were a bloke you had to chat up birds or else you wouldn't get one. It was important to have good lines or else you'd never pick up a looker. You had to chat them up properly, they expected it, you couldn't just slide up and go *Wur*. Women were comparable to other things – cars and horses mainly. They had mileage and chassis and body-work and go.

'If I, as a male, approach a woman, she will be curious but intimidated,' Gor mused. Sean had seen his dad reading *The Naked Ape*. Sean had been shocked to see that it featured men and women without a stitch of clothing on the front cover and all across the back too.

'The male, Sean, is superior, the female submissive.' Gor shook his head in amazement at some of the complex things he came up with.

Sean stared straight ahead at a speck on the windscreen and wondered if it was a dead ant. He was glad, in a way, that his dad knew so much.

'A rich, varied, mysterious world, son. A rich and mysterious world.'

'Watch the ball.' This is maybe good advice for life in general, or perhaps it is not. Sean watches the ball anyway. He will not look away now, not even if there is a nuclear attack or a streaker. He does not even blink. Gor throws the ball. The ball leaves Gor's hand and arcs upward.

'Watch it.'

Sean watches it. Out of the corner of his eye he sees the sky and the yellow cranes and the orange-red brick towers, but mostly he sees the ball, turning in space, spinning towards him. Why do curved objects spin in space? Perhaps it is not a question for a spaz. The ball has already begun its descent. This is a crucial time. Sean is watching it and watching it. Who exactly is the naked ape? He must not take his eye off it. He will not take his eye off it – though his eye wants very much to look somewhere, anywhere else. How can an ape be naked?

'Move your feet!' A new instruction. He does

not want to move his feet; if he does he will take his eye off the ball. The ball is coming. It rushes up to meet him, parting the air. The ball is here. Sean closes his eyes. Too late he realises some facts: he cannot see anything; the ball has arrived; he has taken his eye off it. He hears the ball thwack as it lands behind him. It ricochets, *gedang*, off the metal garage door before it spins away, travelling across five or six not-yet gardens and beyond, into the dust and debris of advancing progress.

'You didn't watch the ball, you blockhead! You're a twit, Sean. What are you?'

Gor liked the heroes on TV. He empathised with them, their jump-cut black-and-white lives, the pressure, the temptations, the problems they had to solve within a thirty-minute episode; never a word of thanks from anybody either; all that effort, nil appreciation. He understood this. He watched them all, *Danger Man*, *The Saint*, *Adam Adamant Lives!* His muscles twitched as they sprinted and sprang and cornered villains; as they detained for questioning the haughty girls in zip-up boots – the ones with lustrous mink-coloured fringes and snappy answers – the ones he would never get to meet, though in his mind he had put them over his knee and spanked them all.

'*Two wheels on my wagon, but I'm still rolling along, Those Cherokees are after me, but I'm singing a happy song.*' You heard Gor before you saw him. The songs were always the same; a consolation to a blameless victim. '*Raindrops keep falling on me head – they keep falling.*' He felt himself Butch and Sundance both; he knew how they felt. He wished the girl with the long dark hair and the lace dress would ride towards *him* on her bicycle. He'd kiss her like Paul Newman did. He could have been a bank robber. He could have been a movie star. He could have had it all.

Sometimes on a Saturday night Gor would throw a little party at the house. 'What'll it be?' he'd ask himself as he approached the drinks cabinet with the glass-lined door panels that opened to form a cheery bar, complete with internal lighting. The drinks had beautiful names: whisky sour, Scotch and ginger, White Lady. Inside the cabinet were napkins and coasters and bar snacks. Gor would arrange a selection for himself, and fold into a triangle a fresh paper napkin. He would toss peanuts into the air and catch them in his mouth. He would toss them higher and higher, challenging himself, until they bounced off the ceiling and hit him in the eye. Gor mixed drinks that were the colour of jewels; ruby or emerald, topaz or amber concoctions that glowed and chimed with ice. Martini-Bianco-on-the-rocks. Sean thought these were beautiful words. He'd seen them on television, the Martini people, parking their boat and running on the beach. He and his father stared at the suntanned girls as they threw back their hair and knocked back their drinks. 'Whoa! Steady on, love!' Gor commented. 'Holy cow.'

Gor's party preparation would begin early in the evening. He would bathe, shave, and dress in his favourite green shirt and checked slacks. He would adopt a loose-hipped walk and a slow carniverous smile. *'I'm singing a higgity, haggity, hoggety, high. Pioneers they never say die.'*

Nobody else, as far as Sean remembered, was ever invited to Gor's parties. He enjoyed himself alone in his favourite armchair, checking the time on his gold wristwatch, in a fug of Wild Mustang cologne. Cath came once. She tried a jewel-coloured drink and tapped her finger to the music. She never came again. She stayed upstairs with her Avon catalogues. Gor didn't care. He was enough guest for any party, what did he need others for?

The record he loved to play on these nights was *Trini Lopez Live at the Cabana*, which made it sound like there were a hundred people in their front room. Like Dr Jekyll, Gor would begin a transformation that started in his clicking fingers and jerked its way up his arms until it reached his head, which would begin to twitch and peck and bob, followed by elbows, shoulders, hips and finally one bouncing leg, until off he would go like a voodoo rooster. The banging on the wall from next door followed. 'It's only eight o'clock,' he'd protest to himself, consulting the gold watch, waggling his hips. 'Bunch of squares!' he would roar at the wallpaper. 'Live a little!' The whooping and cheering of the audience on the record made it sound jolly and wild. Sean had to admit the songs were pretty good. 'When the Saints', 'What'd I Say?', 'La Bamba', 'Marianne', 'Unchain My Heart'.

> 'Marianne, oh Marianne,
> Oh, won't you marry me?'

The dancing wore him out, so Gor was obliged to settle himself down to study the record sleeve under the lamp. 'I might get tight tonight,' he liked to warn with his third drink. He would grin and wink like he was Gary Cooper, as though perhaps he might tell a friendly joke, the way Americans did, or maybe sing something, 'That's Amore', Dean Martin style. Before he went to bed he always put his Trini Lopez record back in its sleeve and switched off all the lights.

CHAPTER 11

*T*he *Collected Poems of W. H. Davies*. On the inside flap of the book jacket, Walter noted, were some interesting facts about the poet's life. He felt extravagantly belittled by these, though he continued to read them as if to hammer home his own limitations.

Mr Davies was born in 1871 at Newport, Monmouthshire. He wandered, as a young man, across the Atlantic. He set out with a companion for Klondyke, travelling as a stowaway on trains, missed his footing, and lost a leg. He came back to England and South-East London, lived in common lodging houses, peddled laces, and gradually accumulated enough money to publish a small volume of poems.

Walter was outclassed, he could see that. He was no writer, no poet, not he. He did not have nor ever would have what it takes to make the life of a poet. The thought remained, however, unlikely as it seemed, the idea of the writing life. The morning, afternoon and evening of the published poet. What did they do? Read, write. Rejoice? When did they write? After breakfast of course. When did they stop? Never. If there were even the remotest of possibilities, the merest chance of getting a collection published. A collection. Published. He would have a desk by a window. He would have pencils and tobacco. He would stop for a brief lunch. He didn't dare imagine what his own book-sleeve biography would consist of. And then he did. A right balls-up. He imagined it to punish himself for dreaming dreams in the first place.

Mr Brown was born in 1915 at Cryers Hill, Buckinghamshire. He did not wander as a young man, indeed he has barely left the South-East. Suffice to say he has not even managed to cross the English Channel. He once set out with a companion for High Wycombe. He has travelled on trains, but only ever with a purchased ticket, and though he has frequently missed his footing he continues to retain both legs. He lives with his mother, works for the Water Company, tends an allotment plot, and is gradually accumulating enough misery to rob him of his will to live.

There. Pipe dreams gone to blazes. Good riddance.

Walter sat between two pillars of poetry volumes, hands on his knees, and grief in his heart. It was not that he expected his life to be any different to any other ordinary fellow's. It was not that he felt he was owed or deserving or special. It was merely that he wished to belong to writing, to be put right by it. He wished to sit beside it through all the afternoons of his life until there were no more afternoons left, and then he would read Byron's 'Fare Thee Well', and slip off.

Walter Brown was not an educated man. Not like those young gentlemen in the cathedral towns, with their quotes, Latin and Greek, from the kind of obscure texts not found in Wycombe Lending Library. He did not even know French, apart from au revoir, and in lieu of. He did not know why he liked poetry, or why he preferred some to others, or which poems, in learned circles, were considered superior to others, or why. He only knew that a poem could redeem an afternoon in the same way unexpectedly good weather might. For a moment you could look upon the world with fondness, with wonder, and it would look back at you the selfsame way.

He had been struck, on occasion, by inspiration, though not often. He was probably not very good. He suspected this was the case, likely even to be the cause of his heartache, though many of his poems were as good as William Davies's. Weren't they? Well, perhaps not.

'You can't eat words.' His mother had been

particularly pleased with that one. She had banged the pots down, as though the statement warranted a drum roll.

'What a relief,' she had explained brightly to a neighbour. 'What a relief Walter has no talent, else what would we eat?'

Humble pie, he had thought; though he could not bring himself to dislike his mother altogether, in spite of everything. They had enjoyed many peaceful, dark Christmases, the two of them. She was a widow. She had looked after him, and his best suit, and fetched the doctor when he was ill. And she was his mother after all, and he suspected there were worse than her.

'I'm fond of you, you know,' she once admitted beside the last fireside embers. 'You're a good boy.' And he allowed her to take his hand and then astonish him when she wept into his palm.

He read her Wordsworth's 'Near Anio's stream I spied a gentle Dove'. It was worth a shot. She remained more or less impassive throughout, perhaps mildly disgusted. For her part, she was anxious that her only son took care over his good job with the Water Company. She was anxious that he should not do anything rash, that he should not spoil his life, or hers, by reading too many maudlin poems. Hilda Brown, after all, did not want things described, compared or identified, thank you. She wanted them dealt with and put away. Where possible, ignored, preferably forgotten about. The whole messy business of feeling was something she was keen to avoid. How much better to have a tidy-up and get on. Strong tea and a slice of cake repaired the majority of woes. There was the parish church for anything more serious, there was Father Blagdon; and if all else failed, there was God. Anyone who wanted to start *feeling* and then find it necessary to describe it, compare it and rhyme it with *ceiling* could go to the dogs.

'Your father showed no interest in you,' she mentioned breezily in response to Wordsworth's poem. 'He never took to you. I think he would have preferred a girl.'

As children, Walter and Mary had been taught by Miss Randall. Miss Randall had been let out of an asylum and so tended to please herself. She was a committed if unreliable teacher who was obliged to grapple with her physical tics as well as the classroom timetable. Her mouth appeared to move quicker than the words she was speaking and her arms jerked up and down as though she were playing an invisible drum. Sound and movement ran against one another inside Miss Randall, seeming to produce a new law of physics in her girlish body. The overall effect left the children spellbound. Words came out in triplicate, stammered rows of them. It set the children laughing, and Miss Randall would have to bang bang bang on her table and fire her voice over their heads. 'Beek-wat!' Her direst affliction – her involuntary habit of letting off a short sharp scream – was tolerated with good humour, though it always made newcomers cry.

Miss Randall took little pills she kept in her bag, the click of its fastening raising all the rows of heads. Miss Randall found their interest impertinent. It vexed her that her defects should prove interesting to the children when her lessons were not. It seemed that Miss Randall's problems were all in her head.

Miss Squires, who taught the next class up, took regular complaints concerning Miss Randall to the headmistress, Cordelia Snell – who had once, famously, snubbed a bishop. Miss Randall, it was alleged, made the children wear blindfolds during their country-dancing class. This was deemed unacceptable. It encouraged concentration, Miss Randall responded, they picked up the steps quickly, it never failed. It was impractical, countered Miss Squires, irresponsible. Miss Squires wore a piece of fox fur around her neck and high-buttoned boots, and consequently her advice was always well received but never acted upon.

Miss Snell had a lazy eye and a quick right hand. The children were required to gather around her desk with their work so that she could slap the legs of anyone who submitted a poor effort without having to leave her chair. She wore a locket around her neck and her unusually long fingers made her frail hands look like wings.

Cordelia Snell, it was said, was the victim of unrequited love.

Mrs Tarbox taught the infants. She could knock you over with the back of her meatier, altogether stubbier hand while looking the other way. Around her neck hung a playground whistle that could be heard in Wycombe.

So it was that Miss Randall had failed to develop any interest in the outside world, even declining a trip to Amersham. The village school taxed her to the very borders of her hysterical best, and was all the world she could bear to tolerate. At home under lamplight and magnification she crafted intricately detailed miniatures to the steady fizz of the fire in the grate. Some of these she fashioned into brooches that proved popular at sales of works and church fêtes. Nobody could explain how a woman of such an agitated disposition, such innate jerkiness, a sufferer from not one but three different varieties of nervous disorders, could achieve such perfection.

Walter loved Mary then. As with his passion for poetry, he had not meant to. Mary Hatt was the girl nobody invited home, but cautiously admired nonetheless. For children she was thrilling to be around: feral, fearless, her head stuffed with deplorable thoughts, her mouth full of curses and higgledy teeth. Sometimes Mary got her hands walloped at the start of class before she'd had a chance to misbehave. However, the occasion when, in front of the whole class, Miss Snell fainted clean away (a light crumpling as though she had mistimed the swing of a trapeze) found Mary's hand on her head and Mary's harlequin grin above her, while the rest of them, many in howling tears, simply ran away.

Can you see the ewe with her lamb under the yew tree? They must copy it out; they must note the different spelling of U's. Mary laughed. 'There's no yew trees up in sheep pasture!' she called out. She was proud to know something. Yew trees didn't grow on hill pasture. Idiot idea that was. Daftie. Yew grew where it was sheltered, along lanes and tracks, in churchyards and gardens. 'Yew don't grow in sheep pasture!' Hurled out the side of her mouth, like you'd call to your working dog. 'That's idiot, that is.'

'Mary Hatt, you are disturbing the peace and calm of my classroom with your inanities!' Miss Randall's last word swung into the air, high over the heads of the others, and remained airborne for several seconds: mysterious, unfathomable. Mary was walloped and sent from the classroom. Miss Randall reached for the back of her chair to steady herself. She hummed the first line of 'The Morning Stirs the Sternest Heart', something musical was always good. She could feel the curiosity of the children as she tipped forwards and backwards into her spasms that she pretended were coughs. How alluring she was to them this way – defenceless, peeled open, jumping like a hare in a gin trap; how absorbed they were by her diminishing authority, her sudden inability to command them further. She would take her pill, if she was able. Up came the heads as she gulped her water. She waited, her angry chin raised, until the last head went down and the scrape of chalk resumed.

Mary had not gone far away. They could still hear her voice barrelling in the corridor, in the schoolyard, on Cryers Hill Road. She would wait for Isabel Hatt, her elder sister, who was in the class above.

'There's know-you trees up in she-pasture!' On she went beyond the hedgerow, over the road by the Widmer barns, between the squeak of chalk letters on slate.

'You know there's trees up in she pastor! Yoo-hoo!'

Walter would look for her all the way home. She was often somewhere on his route, perhaps in the woods, though he had also discovered her floating in the pond, lying in a ditch, and spreadeagled across the roof of the Grange Road Stores, shouting down unpleasantries to the aunt of the grocer below. She got lashed for that. Seven or eight slate tiles she brought tumbling with her and a lot more language. Language, mind, you wouldn't want your mother to hear, nor your daughter neither, never heard like it before, not in all the district. Many of the women claimed not to understand it, supposed it must be foreign, though each had mastered it fluently in childbirth.

Mary lay in brine after those lashings. Her mother warmed water on the stove and filled a bath with a salt rock in. Mary's sister Isabel added zinc paste from a dark glass bottle. You had to lie still long enough for the mixture to work on the abrasions. If you lay till the water was all turned pink, so much the better. Mary held in her breath then. She floated, red and white like a dappled fish, sinewy against the pain. She lay till the pink lapped, cloudy with zinc, around her ears. And Mary cried, though she did not scream, not like the first time, nor did her mother neither, for Ida had seen it all before and had lain in zinc brine herself too. She waited until the tincture did its job and Mary's cries had settled and then Ida let her thoughts slide along the floor till they reached the wall, and rested them there, in the wall, in the bricks and mortar her great-grandfather had built.

CHAPTER 12

A falcon came drifting over the estate. It came in a lunchtime lull, while the machinery lay ticking in the heat. Sean was watching Daniel Sharp crying. Daniel could cry for hours, Sean didn't mind it much. He found it diverting rather than irritating. Sometimes he patted him on the head and sometimes he just watched the tears moving the dirt around his face, and sometimes he would give him something to really cry about.

Daniel stopped crying and looked up, and this made a silence, an absolute quiet, like just before a thunderclap. Sean looked up too and there it was: a falcon, hanging in the blue on frayed wings. The boys looked up at the sky and the bird looked down at the earth. An angel, Sean thought. The bird waited and the boys waited. They held themselves still in case there might be a revelation or a message, a command even. The bird flapped its wings once, twice, and dropped like a stone. Daniel and Sean ran down the slope in between the dry ruts and channels made by the giant tyres of the diggers. The bird swooped steeply to the left and then seemed to rise again before dipping over a brick mountain and out of sight. The boys ran towards the brick mountain, they called out after it, and they were still running long after it was gone.

'We saw an angel,' Sean panted.

'How big?' Jason Smith was the expert. They had watched the sky for the rest of the day, but the bird had not returned. Now the machines were groaning again and the visitation seemed distant and unlikely.

'A bird of prey.' Jason announced it with authority. He knew all the right terms for these and suchlike. Sean and Daniel gasped. A bird of pray. A bird of pray was here. Sean goosebumped. He had known it was an angel. He had hoped for a revelation and it had come. Let us pray, the vicar always said that. Now a bird of pray had come to them. Things were bound to change.

'I've seen it before,' Jason said. 'It's a falcon. Falcons are a bird of prey. Everyone knows falcons.' Jason strolled up and down as he instructed them. He said the bird sat on a pylon by Spurlands End. It always sat there, he said; that was its perch. He said the bird's voice was loud as a scream. The boys waited, mouths slung, crouched over their knees for the message that Jason would translate for them. What did the bird want to tell them? What did the bird have to say? It only ever said one thing, Jason explained. The bird simply repeated it over and over, he confirmed. It said, 'The Martians are coming, the Martians are coming, the Martians are coming.'

Sean had to admit they were no closer to catching the killer than they were to landing on the moon. He said this to Ann because it sounded good and somehow it suggested this was her fault. When she didn't respond he leaned his arm against a tree, like a detective.

'I know where he is.' She said it plainly, same as she would say, 'P'sof, Spaz.'

Sean recalled his dad saying that the first thing to remember about women is they are all liars. 'It's just their instinct,' he explained. 'They can't help it.' Sean wondered what the second thing was.

'I've seen him.'

Sean couldn't decide how to respond. He wanted to say, 'Liar,' but he also wanted to say, 'Where?' And he also wanted to say, 'So have I,' plus, 'I love you, do you love me?' He said nothing.

'D'you know what a prick is?'

'Yes,' he lied.

'Right, well.'

Sean felt his stare growing blank and stupid; he tried to close his mouth and found he couldn't; he tried to move and found that his arm was nailed to the tree; he tried to think and found his brain would only tick over the same word: prick, prick, prick.

'Come on,' she said. She was already stamping over tree roots, dusting off her skirt as she went, confident he would be hurrying up behind her. But he was stuck to a tree, his mouth full of fear and words he didn't understand.

The problem with Typhoid is he's a genius. That's what they say. Sean has waited patiently, without irony, for evidence of this. It was true that Ty had mystical gifts when it came to Spot the Ball competitions in the newspaper. He was almost never wrong. For a while the prize money bought their dinner in the White Lion beer garden two nights a week. They won it so many times they finally had to be investigated by the competition organisers. Then Ty made it into the local paper. His big mule head took up all the photo. Sean carried it around with him. He had to ask people to read out the words 'Local,' 'Every' and 'Time' for him, but he knew 'Boy Spots Balls'. 'Local Boy Spots Balls Every Time,' it said. Then the picture of Ty, his ball-spotting little eyes squinted into slits, his mouth hanging askew, as though something more complicated than a ball had foxed him. Then it said Ty liked Cadbury's Aztec bars and James Bond, as if anyone cared. It didn't say he had a brother. That's when their parents decided he was a genius.

When finally the family was prohibited from entering Spot the Ball competitions, their dad took his eldest son to the racecourse at Newbury. The theory was if he could spot a ball, why not a horse? They set off like two men, in clean shirts, with

102

sandwiches and a flask and a roll of pound notes warming in the glove compartment. Sean was left behind with his mother and the dirty dishes, like a girl.

When Ty was concentrating, when he was getting the feeling, you weren't allowed to enter the room, speak, move or cough. If you interrupted or distracted him in any way – for instance one time Sean walked past on the front path and glanced in – you were banned from the area until further notice. Ty explained that Sean ruined his concentration just by being in the vicinity, so Sean was banished to the further reaches of the estate, to the Wilderness, while Ty worked his genius eye. They won electric hair curlers, a whisk, a petrol voucher, a bear in a sombrero and twelve pounds in cash.

'*One wheel on my wagon, but I'm still rolling along.*' Their dad had stood by the car with his hands on his hips and an enormous pair of binoculars slung around his neck, as if now it were lions and elephants they were spotting. Somewhere at the end of those dark twin tunnels lay their fortune. Ty, the predictor, the cosmic foreteller, the spotter of invisible balls, slouched towards him. He glared momentarily at the estate and threw himself into the front seat, sweating with self-importance, sunglasses perched improbably on his nose, like now he's Chan Canasta or something, like he's going to saw the car in half.

It turned out Ty had no feeling for horses or, at

Ladbrokes in High Wycombe, any feeling for grey-hounds either. There were no Tarzan cries that week. They were back to the kitchen table, ticking boxes on the football pools, sticking Green Shield Stamps and entering competitions to win holidays, cars, caravans, kitchens and cash. Ty's big time was over, but he didn't know it yet. He discovered he could hold his breath longer than anyone else in the school. Their dad timed him with a stopwatch while submerging his son's head in the sink, and subsequently wrote to the *Guinness Book of Records*, but they already had a record-holding diver from the Philippines. Sean watched Ty turning red, purple and blue in an effort to improve on his time, and reckoned one day, with any luck, he would just explode, like a freeze-dried dinner on gas mark 10, and the local paper would come round again.

It occurs to Sean with a pang of likelihood that it was him who killed the girl in Gomms Wood. The thought pulls open his mouth and leaves his eyes staring at nothing. He wonders it for ages and the more he wonders, the more he thinks he can remember doing it.

He waits at the place where he has waited many long hours for Ann to fly up over the fence on her swing. He crouches beside one of the blocks of garages. Ordinarily, she flies up around about this time of day, and he watches her face against the sky, where it belongs. But not today. She does not come out today. The garage doors are made of tin, some are already painted. A blue door squeals open and two partially dressed girls run out screaming like rabbits.

Sean thinks that if it was him who killed her, would he run away or give himself up to the police? He wonders if they would believe him. He wonders if they know it was him already. If it is true that it was him, he thinks, then this makes him a criminal. That is quite good. He wonders if maybe he should tell just one person and leave it at that. Then that wouldn't be lying. That would be more or less telling the truth and he might not get into trouble. He tries to remember. He asks himself questions, cross-examines himself. He will have to search his own room for clues, he decides. He thinks about Ann.

He likes the narrow space between the blocks of garages where you can crawl and imagine the walls closing in until you were squished, like on *Danger Man.* The wall on the left is Ann's garage wall. He kisses the bricks. He glances about but he is completely hidden here. He licks the bricks. They taste all right, like exploding sand. If he loves Ann then he will probably marry her.

ie luv yω. mareε yω. Sean carves the words with a piece of broken brick, and then he is fed up with it. He edges out sideways. Everywhere is hot and smoky with brick dust. He can see the air wobbling as if it is turning to water. There is no one about. The machines are deadly quiet, so it must be lunchtime. The men always go to their hut for their sandwiches and cigarettes and then they lie around and rub themselves like sea lions while the sun burns them the colour of the houses. Sean feels hungry. His mouth is full of brick. He decides he will walk home for some Sugar Smacks. He decides he will tell Ann he is a murderer.

CHAPTER 13

Young Mary Hatt says she has kissed one of the lads at the farriers working up Springfields way. More than this she says she kissed one of the pigman's boys while he was sleeping in a ditch. It is hard to know whether she is telling the truth. She says she will show Walter how kissing is done and if he hurries she will show him now in Gomms Wood before she is required to help with the laundering.

Walter runs so hard he expects his teeth to fall out of his head. Everything is in his way, trees, brambles, gates, a barking dog, Mrs Prior with her cousin's friend, Eileen, from Ilfracombe. Hello, young man. What a nice lad. Don't they grow. What's the hurry then? Where's the fire?

Walter had escaped from the house quick as a cat burglar, his mother's voice ringing in his ears. 'Don't you walk on my clean floor! Don't you walk on my clean floor!' And now every item in the landscape is conspiring to keep him from Gomms Wood where the rest of his life is waiting. Mary Hatt, queen of women, wait for me.

Truth is, even as the fields and hedges are blurring past, Walter remains astounded by Mary Hatt and her behaviour. Did she care nothing for her reputation? Did she care nothing about a whipping? If caught, she would be thrashed along with those boys, if they got hold of them, and any boys working for John Hatt would be instantly dismissed without pay. Something similar had happened a year or two back to the Bennion family: a few stolen kisses, and the lad in question and his family were turfed out of their tied cottage, the father jobless, the mother pregnant. They moved up Missenden way and cleared fields of stones for work.

In the wood it is as cool as a barn and the stillness makes him stop and listen. The loudest thing is the sound of his panting and the roaring of his blood in his ears. His eyes adjust to the gloom. There is a tangle of hazel clustered with nuts and he pulls one off to chew. Where is she then? There is a click from somewhere and a warbler trembles out a note. 'Mary?' His voice sounds unnaturally loud. The wood holds itself in case he calls again. Through the trees he can see the bright juicy meadow belonging to Mr Creasy. He usually puts his bull in there, a great black beast of a thing. Walter crouches to catch a glimpse of it but sees only the waving white faces of the meadowsweet. Usually when you are looking for a bull it is standing directly behind you.

'Wally Wally Wallflower,
Growing up so high.
We're all ladies,
And we shall have to die.'

Walter spins around and around but she is
nowhere to be seen.

'Except Ena Kirton,
She's no relation.
She can go and turn her back,
To all the congregation.'

He will spank her, he decides, when he finds her.
Teach her a lesson.

'Marry in September's shine,
Your living will be rich and fine.'

Mary arrives suddenly. She falls from the tree
as if she has unexpectedly lost her footing. There
is a crash of foliage and a surprisingly loud thud,
and there she is, fallen to earth, stunned, winded,
staring up at an indifferent God. Walter rushes to
her and kicks her in the calf.
'That'll teach you.'
She has no breath, only panic and surprise. Her
mouth is open though no air or words can come.
Her hands jerk at her sides. Walter stares. He has
seen a rabbit look like this; shot in the head, not
cleanly, it danced about for a time. Walter wonders

whether she is dying; he decides not. He kneels down beside her. Her hat has fallen some feet away and her blue dress is twisted up around her waist, revealing her woollen knickers and pale thighs scored with scratches all the way down to her gumboots. Her body stiffens and her teeth clench. Her face pulls to the side, as if she is travelling at high speed. Walter detects something curious; she trembles as if she were powered by the Electric Company. Her eyes slide. Walter waits. He knows to wait while she is fitting. Her face is hot when he touches it, sticky. He imagines she may die one day in more or less this way, with a crash and thud.

He bends down to kiss her. He knows he oughtn't. She tastes sour and salty and she smells of sweat, tree lichen, laundry soap. She is his own angel fallen from the sky. 'Mary Mary, quite contrary,' he tells her. She is handsome, he thinks, in spite of it all. She moves her arm quickly behind his neck. She pulls him down and astonishes him as she pushes her warm tongue all the way inside his mouth.

Walter got himself caught with his mouth open once before; head flung back, his .410 between his knees. Bird scaring was not bad employment, Walter did not mind it when he was younger. It was boring, that was all. You had to fire to keep yourself awake more than frighten the birds, but eventually, especially in good weather, you would fall asleep. The man who found him was the same man who hired him, and he let him have it hard on both ears with his fists. Walter went home deaf in one ear, reeling as if he'd just got off a boat. On Valley Road he decided he would not go directly home. He found Mary by the cow byre with a butterfly net and a tobacco pouch and showed her his reddened ears and she squeezed them to see exactly how painful they were and she laughed.

'Tell me how much you love me and all that,' she instructed.

'I'm bloody deaf. I'm telling nothing.'

Mary wrapped his head in her scarf made cold from a dip in the water trough. 'Tell me or be sorry.'

Walter closed his eyes and made up something fancy out of nowhere. Daft words. She would not ever tell him, not on your nellie, no. She would not tell him how soothing were his idiot words.

Walter and Mary walk the lane home, between the stubble fields. Most are already gleaned, with just a few women and children now left in the big field gathering the loose corn. They would keep going with their sacks until it got dark. Walter can still feel her rough kiss between his teeth. Mary is dragging her boots, singing some kind of song. Walter likes to sing too – you do when you're walking, working, worshipping – but not the way Mary sings, like a bird shot in the breast.

Sugar-beeting would start soon, a hard job, nobody liked it, but there were always plenty of lads willing for the shilling. Hilda Brown objected to her son spending all his time in the fields, but she allowed Walter to help at harvest, and he regularly earned a few coins here and there. A shilling an acre he would get for pulling up docks and half a crown for singling mangolds, which was another back-breaking task. Hilda, however, had kept a careful eye out for signs of passion in her son. His employment was waiting for him at the Water Company. His father and grandfather worked their way up. He must be ready to begin his ascent, the same. She bought him his first suit and shoes before he left school to make certain his future was set, to see off any ideas that came in the night to ruin everything. This way her boy would be steady and secure. Not for him farming, skilled labour, craftsmanship; unreliable trades, dependent on the weather or the times or a glut of customers. The Water Company needed no such encouragements.

Walter and Mary walk the dusty lane between the uncut hedges. As the rabbits scattered at the neck of the woods, Walter shot them all with his imaginary twelve-bore and Mary makes the noise of their cries. A smell of stocks and yarrow thickens the air now and there is a scent too of cut corn with a spice of horse dung. Just here a hare was killed last night, a doe. Her leverets will starve until they are finished off by the fox. The dry dust hangs high, gauzing the sun, softening the distant line of ragged elms that marks the field's boundary.

'D'you want to marry me then?'

'No,' Walter replies, not unkindly.

Mary looks behind and sees their bootprints in the dust. She stamps harder to make a better impression.

'Well, I don't care,' she says.

To take her mind off Walter's response she remembers that to find the North Star you have to first find the Plough. You follow the two stars at the end of the tip of the Plough upwards until you get to the brightest star, and that star is the North Star. A ploughman had told her that. His name was Swift. You only knew their last names. Ploughmen knew about the sky as well as the ground. Tonight she would take a look for that bright star and make a wish and then Walter had better look out. It would be a secret else it would not come true.

'Bugga you, then, Wally Wallflower. Clear off then.'

Walter looks at her, smeared with dust, stamping her feet like a baby, and he thinks, after you kiss a girl they go queer. He will remember that.

Charles Sankey had none of the old traditional skills of the local craftsmen: the bodgers, caners, polishers and cabinetmakers. He worked in one of the new automated chair factories in Wycombe – the chair shop they called it. He worked maskless in a spray booth, using methylated spirit as a solvent. When the fumes overwhelmed him he opened the door for ventilation and if that didn't work he tried a sacred song and that always did the trick. The work was not bad, he thought, a bit cold in winter, even after you got the wood burners going; when it was cold you needed to keep the doors closed and the chemical vapours would hang in the air and burn everyone's eyes and throats. You got used to the sickly smell; Sankey found smoking a cigarette helped. Of course contrariwise the chair shop was hot in summertime and then everyone boiled over chronic. Often Sankey and the others would be put on short time due to the lack of customer demand and, depending on the time of year, this would get them into the fruit orchards or fields for harvesting and clear their heads of fumes and dust.

Sankey took to cherry-picking. Fruit it was in actual fact that made this place famous. They had orchards hereabouts of apple, pear, plum; but it was cherries that made the local reputation. Little black cherries sweet enough to make your cheeks ache, known as corones, pronounced *croons*. Black juice like ink that stained your clothes something rotten. Tall as any elm those cherry trees, interbred with wild varieties until they were colossal. In a mature orchard they blotted out the sky.

The orchards improved Sankey's health every summer during the picking season. Air, sunshine, fresh fruit and, moreover, close proximity to God. The ladders took you up and up. Longer than any ladder he'd seen before in his life, they appeared tall enough to reach inside the clouds, with rungs enough to take you all the way to Heaven. They flared out wide at the bottom, funnel-like, for stability, making them look peculiar but inviting. A feller by the name of Bill Newton made them locally in Primrose Hill (he was known as Isaac by the fruit pickers, as homage to the very gravity that brought the uninitiated down off a ladder quicker than a flash).

It was two cherry pickers per ladder usually, picking different parts of the tree, smart in their waistcoats and moustaches, chattering like women in spite of there being no ground under them for several seconds.

Sankey took to it straight away. The heights didn't bother him. After two seasons he was as good as any of them. At the top of a ladder on a clear day he felt a kind of elation at the thought that he was right under God's nose, so to speak. He sang hymns and sacred songs and the other pickers joined him for the popular ones, 'Praise my Soul, the King of Heaven' and 'All People that on Earth do Dwell', and he filled his bushel basket faster for the joy the singing made inside him.

Cherry orchards had enemies same as all crops and the weather mattered to fruit like it mattered to corn, barley, hay and wheat. Heavy rain would split the cherries and they would all go bad. Everyone had an eye to the sky and a proverb made from experience. In good weather, however,

Charles Sankey was for two or three weeks in June the happiest fruit picker in the south of England. Life, however, as anyone knew, was not a bowl of cherries. The picking season would end quicker than it started. There was the cereal harvest then, but the money was better at the chair shop, so Sankey would return with his friends to the rooms that were only ever freezing or boiling, and to the invisible poison fumes.

It was said Sankey had a hymn or four for every occasion. It was said he sang in the womb and even during his own birth, whereupon his mother, terrified out of her wits, died. Indeed, she had died young and he had hardly known her, except for a small grey-brown photograph he kept in his pocket. He imagined her a kind woman, her face suggested as much in the picture. The light was all on one side of her, brightening her skin and eyes and hair so that they glowed with goodness and humility. The other side was cast in shadow. Only the small brooch on her collar had caught the camera's attention, though insufficiently to suggest what exactly it might be. Sankey had examined the photograph every day of his life. He had long ago decided the brooch was the Saviour on the Cross, and that every person had two distinct sides, light and dark.

Oh to be over yonder, In that bright land of wonder,

Where the angel voices mingle, and the angel-
harps do ring!
To be free from care and sorrow, And the
anxious, dread to-morrow,
To rest in light and sunshine in the presence
of the King!

Sankey reckoned he would have known straight off, if he'd been around then, that the Messiah was the Messiah. He found it shoddy when people argued about that. He knew what he knew. What did they know? He would have known it was the Messiah because he would have seen it in his eyes: the light. I am the Bright and Morning Star. He would have looked in his eyes and he would have known.

'Cobblers.' This was Perfect's comment. Sid Perfect was a disgrace on many levels. Sankey knew he would have to distance himself or else be pulled down with Sid into the flames. 'You don't half talk a load of claptrap, Charles Sankey. A load of old tripe, hogwash, pap and piffle.' And the others all agreed of course; well, they would, Sankey reminded himself. This was what happened to believers, the lone voice in the crowd. First off they would drown you out – the rabble – and then they would stone you. The town square or the Fish and Firkin, there was no difference. *Weary of wand'ring long, my sore heart saith, Show me thy way O Lord! Teach me thy path!*

Nobody asked him about his relationship with

Christ. A pity, because he had it all thought out. He had contemplations and illuminations too. *I looked to Him. He looked on me. And we were one for eternity.* Sankey carved it with his penknife into the giant beech at the edge of Gomms Wood for any passing person to read and know.

CHAPTER 14

Uplands, where the long grass leans and rises like a tide. From up here you can see right across the Hughenden Valley. The pasture, waxy and sheening with lushness, is rolling. Sean hangs his face over a gate for the wind to batter, while in front of him the grass sea rushes far away to the unseen point where it tips itself silently into the valley. Beyond that, wrapped in a gauze of low cloud, another hill is rolling.

Sean climbs up on to the gate. He sits on the top bar, wobbling in the crosswind. He can see the faraway hill rising through the mist. Woodland barnacles its humpback as far as High Wycombe. In among all that forest is Hanging Wood; all the kids know it. They must have died with their heads in the clouds, those criminals long ago, dangling on their ropes. Sean had tried to strangle himself once, just to see. He'd used the bathroom light cord. He didn't think much of it. He wasn't going to do it again.

Sean wonders about the Gomms Wood girl. Don't be morbid. This is what his mother said when he talked about what happened in Gomms

Wood. 'Sean, you are so morbid,' his mother said. This didn't sound like very good English. It wasn't right to say someone or something was *so more* something than something else, was it? Sean, you are *so more* spaz. Maybe it was OK.

His mother had said it again the time he got excited about the hearse parked outside the Co-op. It was only that he wasn't ready for it. He hadn't meant to be excited, but it was so more beautiful. All that glossy black, the limousine length to accommodate the coffin, the spotlessness; you could literally see your own face looking back, that's how clean it was. Sean stared at the spade-faced undertakers, smart in their black overcoats, solemn as priests in spite of their cigarettes. He was amazed by the glazing around the hearse that provided an unobstructed view, from every angle, of the shiny handles and the words made out of flowers: MUM. RIP. FOREVER. Proper alphabet words. Sean was excited by it all. Don't be so morbid, his mother scolded again, her irritation suggesting he was more and morbid all the time.

The wind cannot make up its mind, it swings left then right, then twists and rolls. If he runs and runs, Sean thinks, he will get nowhere in particular. He will still be here in this green, there is so much of it. You can't run far enough, that's the trouble; you can't run away, the green will just follow you. England's green and pleasant land.

They had to sing about it once. Somebody important visited the school (a gloomy man in a suit, so it cannot have been the Queen). Nobody knew it, so the teachers sang it mainly. *'And did those feet'*, it began in this way, like a question, as though nobody was quite sure, *'in ancient time, Walk upon England's mountains green?'* Anyone know? No one had an answer, of course. No one cared a toss.

'Wur!' shouts Sean. The wind swipes his voice away. The view's not bad, Sean reckons. Except for the green. Too much spazzing green. He stares at the hills, clotted with cows. It occurs to him that the hills are staring back. Scenery, some people called it. Because you had seen it probably.

Sean jumps down and runs towards the valley. 'Wur!' The cows on the opposite hill raise their heads. The wind pushes him sideways, so he hurtles down on the diagonal, like a spider. He zags past the big hole filled with fridges and car doors and prams. The grass snatches his ankles, whips his legs. He tries to bring his knees up, pump his elbows in the correct manner. To run well you must develop a style. He aims himself at the hump of the distant hill. He knows if he keeps his eye on the hill, his diagonal descent will gradually become a straight line. Cricketers know this. You must keep your eye on the ball. It occurs to him there is nothing he cannot do. If he sprouts wings and flies, he will not be the least bit surprised. True fact: there is a feathered boy who flies. Sean saw a drawing of him in a book, his wings in flames. Sean stared at the picture and wondered who was the boy and why was he burning? Philip Dean didn't know either. It occurs to Sean that maybe that burning boy is in fact him. And he just doesn't know it yet. The hill is moving quicker than he is now. He speeds his legs, pushes up his chin, and he floats to the left in a funnel of green-rushing air. He is too fast, he can see that now. It is no longer possible to keep his eye on anything, not a ball or hill, because everything has become a blur, a nasty smear of colour and edge. He cannot stop or slow down. He is a missile. His excellent sprinting legs are gone and in their place are broken propellers. He is falling back to earth while the hill is falling into space. Neil Armstrong must have had to put up with this. Sean's feet finally leave the ground altogether and the earth tilts and tips him gently into the bowl of the valley. Gravity takes him. As his mouth fills up with dirt he thinks of the shiny hearse, the burning flying boy, the flowers that are also words, the men hanging on their ropes, and the song that asks, *And was Jerusalem buildèd here?* Anybody?

Mrs Roys lives in a small red-brick house that leans to one side as though it has at one time been requisitioned to support the sky. Sean has no interest in Mrs Roys or her wonky house. He delivers the leaflet about the fête through her letter box, that is all. He quite enjoys delivering. *Fête,* says the word at the top in jaunty letters. Miss Day had told him you did not pronounce it to rhyme with settee, as he had; you pronounced it faet, like that. It was French, that's why. Mrs Roys has a nice wall under a tree that grows streaming leaves, like ribbons. Sean lies on the wall to have a rest and see what it is like under the ribbon tree. It never occurs to him that anyone might come out of the house to ask what he is doing on their wall. People tended not to come out of their houses if they could help it. They were either completely out or completely in, not half and half.

Mrs Roys is white-haired and elderly. She stands on the path in her slippers, half and half, and calls out, 'Well?' as though she has already asked a question that has been left unanswered.

Sean glimpses her through the ribbon leaves and sees that she too is ribbony: long, slim, pointy around the face. She holds a jug in her hand, as if she might chuck water at him, like people do to cats.

'Well?' she repeats. Sean imagines he is in trouble. He can't remember ever having been told specifically not to lie on anyone's garden wall, but that does not mean it is all right. He sits up quickly and holds out another leaflet.

'Fate,' he says carefully, remembering it rhymes with plate, and to his surprise she takes it briskly and begins to read.

Sean slides down from the wall. He looks at her slippers and thinks that they are long and narrow for a woman. He wants to go. He wants to say, 'I better be off then,' like his dad does. But it is awkward now that she is halfway through reading the fête words and half in, half out of her house. He stares at her slippers and waits for her to release him.

'Come in,' she says. 'You can help me. Come on.'

Sean waits. He looks about. Surely he is not expected to follow her? Don't talk to strangers. This is the new rule. Don't listen to them either, or follow them indoors. Don't accept sweets from a stranger. If a stranger offers you a lift, don't get into his car. If a stranger approaches you, run away. If if if. Don't don't don't. It is a rule. Sean looks at her banana-coloured slippers and her bony calves. He follows her in. Inside, her house smells of cardboard, though it is made of brick. She has nice things, lacy bits and chinaware. There are big swirling patterns on the carpet and photographs of people who appear appalled at the unexpected sight of him. He sees a piece of cheese on a plate with a fly on it.

Mrs Roys places a large watering can under the sink tap. They wait while the water crashes in.

'My name is Mrs Roys,' she says. 'What is yours?'

Sean isn't sure if he should tell a stranger his correct name. He takes so long deciding she changes the subject.

'Are you strong?'

Sean shrugs.

'Good.'

Mrs Roys places a chair beside the sink and turns off the tap. 'Off you go then, lift it down. Best to start with the pots. Then the borders, both sides.' She waves her hand wispily towards the window, beyond which lies the back garden. 'Off you go then. Off you go.' Mrs Roys' banana slippers lead her away into the room with the staring people. Sean looks at the cheese and the fly and a drip from the tap plops into the brimming watering can.

As a matter of fact it is all right watering the plants. There is a long cat asleep on the coal bunker and a jay bird dancing about on the fence, taunting it. Sean flicks water at the bird and then the cat and they disappear. Sean stares at his reflection in Mrs Roys' windows. He puts his hand in his pocket to prove to himself he can do one-handed heavy watering. He stares and squints but all he can see in each pane of glass is a short spaz with a spout, squinting back at himself. Sean looks down at his sandals. Everything is soaked, socks, footwear, and all across his shorts, as though he has wet himself. In the palm of his hand lies the imprint of the watering-can handle. He decides it is time to say, 'Well, I better be off.' He must say it now before things get worse. He squelches towards the back door, unsure now whether he ought to knock or just go in. He stares at his reflection in the glass door panel. Wur. Spazzery. Thunderbirds are go.

'Oh, there you are. Come in.'

Ibetterbeoff. Ibetterbeoff. Ibetterbeoff.

'Did you have a little spill?'

Sean squelches behind the bananas. The fly is on the tap. The staring people are aghast. Mrs Roys hands Sean a book.

'Do you like books?'

Do not accept anything from a stranger. Do not speak to a stranger. Do not water a stranger's flower beds, pots, lawn or borders.

'Read me a page before you go. Good boy. Off you go.' Sean glances down at the book. It is a small paperback whose cover features a glamorous Scandinavian-looking couple gazing distractedly in opposite directions. Poking out from behind them is an imposing Dutch-gabled house, fringed by a menacing crowd of jagged pine trees. Sean opens the book. On the first page lies a block of words.

Saturday's child works hard for a living . . .
And so did Nurse Abigail Trent, plain and
impoverished and without hope of finding
a husband. Why did she have to fall in love
with Professor Dominic van Wijkelen, who
hated all women and Abigail in particular?

Sean stares at the words.

'My eyes aren't what they were. Just a page would be nice. Off you go.'

Sean searches for words he can recognise. He spots *And*. Mrs Roys begins to look uneasy for the first time.

'Just a paragraph perhaps.'

'And,' reads Sean. He looks up at Mrs Roys and she nods perkily back. Rudyell. He should tell her to p'sof. He should just leave. He should stop talking to strangers. Then he remembers Gor's song. He takes a breath.

'And. I'm still rolling along.' He checks her face. He scans the page. *'Them Cherokees are chasing me but I'm singing a happy song. I'm singing a higgity, haggity, hoggety, high. Pioneers they never say die. A mile up the road there's a hidden cave and we can watch those Cherokees go galloping by. "George, they're catching up to us! Get back in the wagon, woman."'*

'Good,' interrupts Mrs Roys. 'Thank you. That was nice.' Sean notices that her eyebrows, level steady before, are now masted at different heights. Other than that, Sean reckons, she seems not to have guessed that anything was wrong. Wur. Daft bat. Sean gazes at the jazzily labelled bottles of drink displayed on white lace on the corner table.

'Would you like a drink?'

'OK.'

Mrs Roys hoists herself up and the bananas take her away. Sean wonders whether his drink will have poison in it. He reckons Mrs Roys is too old to be a killer. Also, would a murderer have lace? Chinaware? Pansies in pots? Not on your life. Mrs Roys hands Sean a drink of lime. He tries it. It is tingly, nice. He drinks it all, sucking the last drips at the end, and discovers a piece of lemon bumping against his nose. It is the nicest drink he's ever had, he reckons. He must now say, 'I better be off.' It was the proper thing to say to make things final, friendly, cheery. Instead he hands back the cup wordlessly and watches the bananas convey it to the kitchen.

He glances around at the peculiar pictures on the wall. He examines a deserted lane with a wagon heaped with straw pulled by a horse; the Wild West probably. Another is just trees, hundreds of trees, and funny little men in caps balancing two at a time on circus ladders among the trees; p'raps it is the circus, in fact, because on the ground are painted wagons and horses, and the balancing men have baskets in their arms, probably for collecting money. Some pictures are photographs; a huge sideways bull for instance. Why, Sean wonders, would someone want a picture of a bull standing sideways? You couldn't even see its expression. There are lots of sideways animals: dogs, horses, pigs, and even sideways people. Then there are the photographs of longways animals, dead ones mostly, dangling from fists: birds, rabbits, giant fish. And beside them on the wall are the photographs of just fields, nothing else, with maybe one house in the valley, that's all. One of these has tiny distant cows in it, but you have to squint to see them. Sean feels sorry that all Mrs Roys has to put on her wall are these brown pictures of nothing. Still, she has the chinaware and the lacy things, and the carpet whose dizzying pattern rises up under your chin like a wave.

'Will you come and see me again?' Mrs Roys is banana-fast when she feels like it.

'OK.'

'Do you like mushrooms?'

'No.'

When Mrs Roys opens the front door the sunlight bursts in. It makes Sean think of the police. The long shadows in the hall are momentarily gone and a mist of glittering dust floats up between them. He can't be certain whether elderly people get arrested like anyone else.

He means to say goodbye, he has already decided it. But when he reaches the end of the path it is too late and he says nothing. He senses her watching him, half in, half out as usual.

'You are a very nice little boy.'

The words follow him. He feels them hanging over his head like a crowd of flies. He puts his hands in his pockets and tries, as he walks along, to think clearly how and why he now knows a woman called Mrs Roys. All along the path lie blown ribbons from the ribbon tree. It makes him think of weddings and dancing around the maypole, the way in the juniors you had to every springtime, like a twit. Then he remembers he has left all the fête leaflets at Mrs Roys' house.

CHAPTER 15

Walter has warmed the pot and brewed the tea, and arranged plates and small forks and two cotton napkins. The bread is sliced and the cake too and the watercress is washed and cut and still she does not appear. She is upstairs wasting time in order that he may become agitated. She will have succeeded if he loses his temper. He will not lose his temper, he decides, no matter that he is late for the cricket match; no matter what.

'It's going cold.' He sings it cheerily up the stairs as if it is a line from a musical revue. It betrays none of his irritation, he is certain. She does not reply. Very well. Walter pulls out his chair to sit down. He hums a tune he has not heard before. He forces it into bright quavery squirls, te-dum, tee-dee. He helps himself liberally to bread and watercress that is peppery green and chilled with droplets of water. Delicious. Ta-da, ta-dee, ti-doo. Through the window there is a burst of unclipped green, sliced at the corner by a margin of bright blue. He hears a floorboard creak. Excellent. Tra-lee, tra-la, tra-lie.

'*Walter?*'

Walter stops pretending to sing. He waits.

'Walt?' She rarely shortens his name. More often lengthens it, as in 'Walter Frederick Horace Brown you are a peculiar man, not to mention a nuisance, so you are'. His tune drains away while the food turns sour in his mouth. He will have to wait it out.

'*Walter?*' A little stronger this time, but there is no mistaking the flaunted enfeeblement.

'*Wal-ter?*'

Blast. 'Yes, Mother?'

'*Wal-ter?*'

Blast. Righto. Walter bounces out of his chair, athletic with anger. As he does so a figure bolts past the window. Walter stops. He half expects Mr Looker to follow in pursuit, or a herd of stampeding livestock. It is Charles Sankey, he knows it. It has been mentioned lately that Sankey is the object of some unpleasant rumours. Village gossips: Walter has no interest in women's clack. As he stands there, there is a knock at the door.

'Don't answer it, Walter! Who is it?'

Ah. Her frailty is flown. She is recovered, and so speedily.

'Wally?' A voice from the other side.

Walter opens the door.

'Don't call me that please, Charles.'

Sankey is glistening all over. He has pollen in his hair and is panting so hard that he cannot speak. Walter pauses only briefly before slamming the door in Sankey's face.

'Walter Frederick Horace Brown! Where do you think you're going?'

Her recovery is a miracle, she is once more entirely herself.

'Gallivanting while I sicken here alone!'

Excellent idea. Walter grabs his hat and dashes for a hurried handful of watercress in a fold of bread. When he reopens the door Sankey is still there and so Walter bundles him backwards and the door bangs a second time.

'You are a cruel, wicked person, Walter Frederick Horace! You have no backbone, no! Yes and no head, and no heart neither!' The floorboards release a discordance of cries as Mrs Brown hurries back to her thickly draped bedroom. 'You are an unpleasant child, Walter Frederick Horace Brown, and a poor son.'

Walter thinks, he will purchase tickets for *Macbeth*. The Happy Harlequinaders are performing it in Amersham. He will ask Sankey along for company. He is uncertain whether his friend is partial to theatre. Perhaps he will have to explain the text to him. He will quite enjoy that.

The Aitchy-Aitchers, as the Harlequinaders affectionately call themselves, have a fondness for performing the plays of William Shakespeare. They are a phlegmy troupe of players, whose productions you might call zesty at best, preferring as they do to remain breezily calm, genial even, during the foulest and most murderous scenes.

Threats and blackmail are issued with the utmost courtesy, in tones of ashamed politeness. Corpses are known to wink or wave, as are evil kings, despots and black-hearted schemers. Speeches are delivered with bounce or, in the case of Hilda Crane, complete bewilderment. Soliloquys strain with apology and grimacing is encouraged. Consequently they are popular with families and ladies of a nervous disposition. As a matter of fact they are popular with just about everybody and play to a packed house every performance. Walter realises he has put a curve in his day.

Ah falcon, who are in heaven. Come back.

Sean is at the summit of a medium-sized brick tower. He scans the sky, but there are only white strings of jet vapour. The sky is enormous, it arches over him, but there is no bird in it. No falcon anyhow, just sparrows, crows and Gor's pigeons. Sean has changed colour; his legs, arms and forehead are smeared brick-orange. He kneels, arms hanging, like a hare.

A pink builder, he notices, with smoke curling out the top of his head, is carrying bricks on his shoulder in a big metal spoon. Yesterday Sean surprised a builder as he sang 'One Broken Heart For Sale' in one of the not-yet gardens.

In the distance Sean can see the edge of the sky tipping into Cockshoot Wood. Funny thing to give woodland a name of its own. All things are named in the countryside to show they belong – a pasture, a spinney, a pool of water – the merest slope might have a name or a clearing in the wood. Jack of Wadleys Spring, Hogpits Bottom, Grymsdyke, Venus Hill. The names tell you who or what once happened there, they tell you what the place is like, who farms it and whether – if you are in Devils Ley, Dead Mans Way, or Hanging Wood – you should be afraid. Spurlands End: somebody gave it a name, though nobody now could tell you why. These days it is the place where the falcon bird sits, fretting over possible Martians.

How was it Jason Smith knew bird language? It was easy to be suspicious. Nobody could tell you how. Probably, it was just a speciality, like any other, same as Gor knowing the ways of the female species. Sean realised he didn't have a speciality, unless you counted spazzery. He wanted to have one. All the men he knew had a speciality; women didn't seem to bother.

He tried a bird call. He tipped his head back and out came a wail. He couldn't tell if it was any good. He tried another, higher pitched, piping, more rabbit than bird really. It set the dogs barking below. They say there is a man at the White Lion can make pigeon noises; any sort of call you want. He has made the noises for so long now, he's started to behave like a pigeon. Everyone calls him Woody after the type he imitates. He is a little man, grey and panicky. He'd been quite a hit in his heyday, but no one seemed interested now. He sits alone, it is said, under an oak beam, twittering to himself.

Maybe the bird would never return. Maybe Sean would have to go to Spurlands End to find it. He would have to get there and then he would have to remember how to get back and he had better not get lost, in the woods or anywhere else.

Sean is walking purposefully up Windmill Lane. There is still debris outside the witch's door. The kids habitually chuck handfuls of gravel and sand as they ride by on their bikes. They throw bricks at her cat and spit on her path. It is almost certain she is a witch. Everyone says she is. They shout names after sundown, standing up on their pedals like Apaches on horseback. This wasn't the only house worth a gawp. Many people had moved in as the houses were being completed, the air inside still hazy with sawdust and reeking of paint. You would see them gazing from their kitchen windows at their mud gardens, and beyond that at the brick towers and sand piles and, in the distance, the giant orange crane that stood like a great hot dragon on the hill. Beyond that, too far to see, were the slopes of the county, still green in places where the few remaining farms peeped out. You could watch people having their tea if you wanted, before they had the chance to get curtains up. You could watch someone else's TV and hear it too through the modern Gabbett Housing walls. When the mud gardens were laid with their squares of turf, everyone sat outside and pretended they were unable to see or hear their neighbours through the chicken-wire partition.

Sean runs. The tops of the trees are knocking against one another. Where has the wind come from? It occurs to him he may have created it himself with his running.

Not everyone asked for the moon, some people are sick of it already. Fruit and Veg man looks like he couldn't care less – take it or leave it – nothing in it for him. Sean trudges past his stall on the roadside. Fruit and Veg man is squatting on his stool, shading his big walrus head under his buckled brolly, resting his lunch on his wide knees, chewing as slowly as one of the old farm's dairy herd.

Sean does not stop to look at road signs – no point. He supposes they are all right if you can read them. It was amazing actually, how people knew where they were. The streets and houses with numbers on, the roads and crossroads and bridges and roundabouts. How did they know? How could they know whether a place was there on the right or a mile away or three streets down on the left? Yes, all right, the signs; the place names on white wooden fingers that pointed north, south, east, west, for those who knew their alphabet. But come off it! How did aeroplanes know where to land and boats which way to sail? Deirdre Simpson's cat found its way home from Bury End. How the bludyell did it do that? Sean reckoned it was possible he was stupider than a cat.

CHAPTER 16

The staffroom door is open. Sean waits. He must return the class ITA reading books to Miss Day in the staffroom. It is his turn. Inside he can hear teacher voices. Teachers – they know everything; they can tell you the answer to any question in the world. Except why God moves in a mysterious way. It is possible even God doesn't know why He is moving mysteriously. Sean listens for a clue. The teachers speak his parents' language fluently; the game is harder, though, as there are more players. He will have to concentrate and narrow his genius eye.

'What I *would* say, Sarah, you know, what my concerns *are*, quite honestly, well, actually they're twofold. One is the amount of books and materials and two is the fact that pupils will repeatedly encounter *traditional* orthography out of school.'

'Yes, but at five, Jeff, they would not be reading TO at home anyway.'

'That's a good point, Jeff, actually.'

'Might I just butt in, Di?'

'I think – sorry, Barbara – just a moment please.

I think it's important to be enthusiastic at this stage, without becoming blinded to the problems.'

'I agree, Di.'

'So do I, Di.'

'Our alphabet does not know *how* to spell. Who said that?'

'No idea, Jeff. Sorry.'

'Sarah? Any idea?'

'*No*, Jeff. None of us have any idea.'

'Jeff? Barbara? If we can just keep bearing in mind that a whopping sixty per cent of English words are not spelled consistently and—'

'You are repeating yourself now. Sorry, Sarah, but you are.'

'. . . Right, well, it is significant. It *is* quite significant.'

'Mark Twain. I was, in fact, quoting Mark Twain.'

'Can I get this right, that we're not supposed to discuss transition at this stage?'

'It's *significant*, that's all.'

'There's something about transition in here somewhere.'

'Changeover.'

'What?'

'It's *changeover*, not transition.'

'Right, changeover. Personally speaking, I'm not totally *au fait* with it.'

'Don't worry about that at this stage.'

'It's a murky area.'

'I don't think it's murky, sorry.'

'Don't apologise, Barbara.'

'OK, I won't. I'm not sorry!'

'If I may check the consensus re parents?'

'Sorry?'

'Parents?'

'What about them?'

The staffroom erupts with laughter. Someone has told a joke. Sean smiles. Why did the chicken cross the road? What is black and white and red all over? What goes up and down in a lift? Sean laughs. A gooseberry. A gooseberry of course. Two of the books slip from his arms to the floor, then a third and fourth. Sean can no longer hold the books. A gooseberry in a lift! He cannot breathe for laughing. He leans his head against the wall. He clutches his stomach. The books slide and drop, one after another. A gooseberry cannot reach the buttons! A gooseberry cannot read the numbers! Sean laughs until he cries.

CHAPTER 17

The sky is bright blue and startlingly empty over the allotment, as though someone has forgotten to paint in any clouds. Out of the corner of his eye Walter sees Nobby Dean flapping about with his binding twine, talking to himself. The trouble with competition growers is they make such a song and dance about it all. It affects them eventually, the competitive spirit, they become tunnel-minded or whatever it is. Work, family, church, all down the Swanee. Nothing else matters but the dimensions of their tomatoes or artichokes. Their world boils down to a single row of beans. Nobby won't be happy until he has won prizes for all his veg and dropped down dead in the process. One day he will be found rigor-mortising beside his vines, same as Walter's own father. Old Nobby, he lived for his allotment, they will say.

In spite of everything Walter finds he is warming to cultivation. Increasingly he catches himself thinking of his runners or the goosegogs. They drift in his mind with his non-scanning rhymes and Mary's mouth and the sheening promise of his imminent future. Walt ignores the inexplicable hammer blows from Nobby's site. He can hammer all he likes, winning is not the be-all and end-all. Here in this small patch of earth and fostered green Walt can think and scan and dare to predict the good fortune that awaits him. They are perhaps related, the business of composition and cultivation. He supposes a wiser man than he would be able to explain it. A man from a cathedral town who had attended university, this sort of person supplied explanations for all sorts of enigmas; they were relied upon to do so. It was not his place to know the whys and wherefores of things. He was glad about that.

Sankey's face presents itself through a hole in the hedge, framed within in a ring of hawthorn, eyebrows raised into his hairline. Walter does his best to conceal his startlement, he does not wish to appear nervy.

'Whatsoever a man soweth, Walt, that shall he also reap.'

'What d'you think you're playing at? Made me jump.'

'Absinthe makes the heart grow fonder, Wally.'

Walter is not a drinking man but there is something to be said for a table by the fireplace on a day of the week that belongs neither to God nor employer, with a pint of ale that lasts all morning. As the sun rolls above their heads it ignites the copperware around the hearth, tinting the room rose pink. There in the low-beamed stillness of this little slanting space Walter can begin to collect his thoughts and enjoy the sound of time falling away. Here there is no mother, no task awaiting completion, no clerical duty, and only the faintest, ghostly impression of the person his father once was.

Sankey's conversation is not taxing. The subject is always the same, himself, the Almighty, and himself. In the corner, the dartboard can be glimpsed through the mists of smoke. Floating in the mists are the flat-capped heads with blood-burst cheeks and yellow teeth and their talk and grumbling laughter. One will slowly rise and aim and release his arrows in short sharp jabs. As they plunge into the rings of the dartboard Sid Perfect will say, 'What did I tell you?' And Dannel, seated by the door with his great head in his hand, will nod.

There are no women in the public houses, nor talk of women. There is talk of war, the war already fought and won. The war that surely will not come, not another. You have to be careful with such talk when Percy Evans is in, owing to his experiences in the last war. Poor unlucky Percy whom everyone calls lucky. Poor lucky Percy whose thoughts creep across the oak floor like woodworm. The new war, if it comes, will be different. Whole villages will not be emptied of their young men and boys. It could not happen a second time; they will not allow it. Poor Percy's war will not come again.

Walter reckons he'll drink to that. He raises his glass to himself and drains it.

He will walk the long way home through the wood, it being Saturday. Sankey has his rounds to do. Sankey is proud of his Saturday rounds. They are not official rounds as such, not like the preacher's visits; Sankey is no preacher, truth be told. Pesterings they are really, or, more kindly put, neighbourly visitations. He presents himself anyhow, here and there, to proffer advice and prayer, though he does no odd jobs, not usually, or manual labour, unless for a monetary donation. There are those who do not welcome him and those houses cease to exist in Sankey's mind. The only homes he registers are those where a warm pot of tea and a slice of cake or bread are offered and a piece of his home-wrought advice is gratefully received. He is godly and devout, is he not? He therefore opts to dress in black, suggestively, but stops short of the frock. Perhaps many just presume some affiliation with the Church.

For a godly person he is a good shot. Moreover, he knows how to prepare snipe, rook and eel and to always add streaky bacon with rabbit.

Sankey reminds Walter of the Sale of Work next week a couple or so miles away at the Methodist church in Great Kingshill. It will be opened by Mrs Coningsby Disraeli, OBE. There will be stalls and a bran tub and a ham tea at 4.30 p.m. for ninepence, and at 7.30 p.m. there will be a grand concert in aid of the debt reduction fund. Walter

143

remembers now. Mary will be displaying her home-made jams: damson, marrow, rhubarb. She will bring them in the cart, same as last year. Walter will take Mary and her brothers to the concert, though admission is ninepence each. There are seats for sixpence but it would appear frugal, what with his decent job, so he will bear the expense and hope there will not be any stall purchases costing more than sixpence.

Life, he decides, requires an awful lot of thinking out at times.

CHAPTER 18

'**D**'you want to see the murderer? I've seen him more than once – he likes me – d'you want to see him?'

'OK.'

They ran along the tarmac paths until the digging and drilling and thumping faded behind them. Ann had legs like rods, long and straight, without curve or irregularity. Sean thought if you fixed them on upside down no one would ever tell. Sean noticed his running style had improved. He kept a careful eye on his legs; the way his knees came up suddenly, one after the other, seemed to him not too bad, practically excellent. He suspected he might be turning into a long-distance runner. He thought how useful it would be to be able to run a very long way without stopping.

'Spaz!'

He had run into the back of her again. Her sandal had come off.

'If I've said it once I've said it a hundred times you are a spaz, Sean Matthews, what are you?'

'A spaz.'

'You are more crip than I thought.'

'Sorry.'

They ran past the stupefied cows, past the tin bath she'd once tried to drown him in and through the kissing gate where no one got kissed these days. They were almost at the place where there was once a castle. There remained a little moat and a ditch. This is a story Sean knows. He took a deep breath so he could blow her over with it. Seven hundred years ago a baron from Normandy lived here with his ten-year-old wife. It is completely true. He rode his horse, a knight in armour, a fierce lion upon his shield, with his friend Gilbert the Red. The Baron and Gilbert rode against the King, who was an idiot.

Ann was not interested in Gilbert the Red. 'Are you chewing a brick?' she enquired.

Sean had watched them coming and going around here after the girl was found in the wood. Gliding past in their Hillman Husky patrol cars, sideburns wide as television actors', ashtrays brimming, slamming doors; some of them without a uniform even. It used to be just one policeman. Local Bobby everyone called him. You could see him drifting about aimlessly from time to time, casting around for crime, gazing forlornly up and down Cryers Hill, squeaking down the deserted cul-de-sacs in his big law-enforcing shoes.

'What did he say to you?'

'Who?'

'Him.'

'That's for me to know.'

146

Truly Sean did not want to know, but you were supposed to ask, and truly he did also want to know but she would never tell him. It was typical of Ann to have befriended a dangerous criminal, Sean thought. He pictured them together, unblinking, baring their teeth, grinning like leopards. He felt jealous. He thought it was possible this could turn out to be a bad day. Bad days didn't let you know from the start, they took you by surprise same as good luck and death. Things that seem like a good idea at the time have a nasty habit of going wrong.

Sean wondered why the murderer had not killed Ann. Perhaps she unnerved him, perhaps he intended to, or perhaps he had fallen in love with her. It occurred to Sean he might be seen as a rival. The thought stopped him dead in his tracks.

'I'm not coming.'

'Good. I'll go on my own then p'sof.'

Sean watched her stamping away on her long rod legs. He saw the smudge of dirt across her flower-print bottom where she'd sat on the ground and her dark hair in rat's tails that swung over her back. He wondered if he would ever see her again.

Whatif this was the last time?

'Ann.'

'What?' He waited until she turned. She was irritated. This was the wrong time. I love you I love you I love you.

'Nothing.'

She closed her eyes with the exasperation of it all.

'Spaz,' she whispered, and Sean thought he could detect some tenderness in the way she said it, softly like that.

Off she went on her rod legs. Stilt woman, off to meet her murderer in the woods.

Sean thinks the plants in Mrs Roys' garden look better since he watered them. He is pleased about that. They don't have plants on the estate. Instead of grass they have rocks and stones in the gardens. Inside Sean's house it smells of paint and cigarette smoke, but here it smells of coal and carpet and cooking. What is she cooking?

Her embroidery lies on the chair; the old lady is sewing a picture. Sean didn't know you could sew pictures. He bends down to study it. The picture is of fairies and flowers. Fairies! A bit crip. Ann would say so. Ann would like it here, though she would pretend not to. Sean sits on the settee for a rest. It's lovely and soft and spattered with flowers. It makes you sigh to sit on it. A dismayed photograph watches him from the table, while Mrs Roys' newspaper swoons to the floor.

She is upstairs; she seemed quite pleased to see him. He stood on the doorstep in a blast of fiery sunlight. He told her he had forgotten his leaflets, and in he came to the dust-blurred hallway. She said she had something for him. A ball she said. A ball? Sean wonders if it is a trick and really she is up to something else. Like what? He couldn't think. It had once belonged to her son, she said.

It had not entered Sean's head that Mrs Roys might be a mother. Maybe her son was among the photograph faces. He wondered what he was called, this son, but did not ask in case she said something like Oswald.

Now Sean wonders if he ought to find out more about the son. He did not wish to upset Mrs Roys but it is important to leave no stone unturned. And where was this son now? This Oswald. Strolling about in dense woodland on the off chance he may come across an unsuspecting child? Sprinting across Widmer field, stark naked except for shoes?

A church bell chimes somewhere. Sean allows it to lull him and soon all the froth in his head settles.

'Sorry to have kept you. Here it is!'

Mrs Roys is offering Sean a large lumpy-looking egg. He is speechless. He takes it. It is brown and dimpled and fantastically heavy. Sean has never seen anything like it before. He wonders if she went upstairs and laid it herself. He doesn't know what it is, but it is not a ball. He hasn't the heart to tell her. He says, thank you very much, instead. She seems pleased. He notices then that she is wearing her coat and hat.

'I won't be long. Just to the shop. You can play with the ball in the garden if you like. You could water the pots for me.'

And off she goes, the goose that laid the big brown egg. Sean stands there holding the thing, like a boy in a fairy tale. Someone at school said that women have eggs inside them, loads, and Sean was horrified. He knows it is not true, but still.

Every time it bounces the egg goes off at an unexpected angle, and when you kick it it curves madly like a boomerang. It dives into the shrub pots and jackknifes under the hedge. It is like chasing a small escaped pig. More than this it has laces on one side, like a shoe. Sean feels sorry for it. He leaves it hiding beneath a wire chair and goes indoors.

Inside Mrs Roys' house is not like the inside of other houses. Her furniture is old, from another time, and everywhere there are things made of enamel, silver, crystal and gold that ting and ping and alter in the light. At home all they have are three smoked-glass cats on the mantelpiece. Here there are things from dreams and stories and faraway places. Sean holds up oddments to examine in the sunlight. He finds a large waxy cone with a tassel that is decorated with picture mountains; he pops it on his head. There are chests and tables and drawers made of wood that smell a hundred years old. Cautiously, then carelessly, Sean begins to open the drawers and bureaus. Mostly they are full of things that do not interest him: fabric and cloth wrapped in tissue, placemats, keys, maps, leather-bound notebooks. But sometimes there is something interesting like coins, or silver pencils in a decorative box, or more photographs of the sort of strangers you are not supposed to talk to. After a while Sean begins to lose the will to continue. He is tired, mildly dizzy. He notices a pebble lying inside an opened bureau. The bureau is narrow and upright and orderly, like a little man in uniform, and smells of sand and something metal. The pebble is smooth and dark and beautiful. It is laced around with white lines, like threads. He reminds himself that he must leave no stone unturned, that Ann will blink and throw her arms around him when he solves the murder, that he will no longer be spaz. Sean puts it in his pocket and continues. There are little drawers within the bureau, a row of them. It is his solemn duty to open them, to find out the truth. Inside each drawer are bundles of paper, tied with ribbon. Sean is unsure what they are, except that they appear almost identical and are numerous and fill all the drawers and are therefore perhaps important in some way. Eeny meeny miney mo. The chosen drawer gives up its bundle. Sean closes the remaining drawers and lids and replaces the doilies and ornaments that he has moved. Clutching the bundle, he stands for a moment, to think. He has forgotten he has a cone on his head. Thunderbirds are go, you spaz. He thinks it is possible things have taken a turn for the better. He thinks he does not want to see Mrs Roys when she returns. He thinks he will go. He thinks it is possible he is almost solving a crime. Wur.

The wood is dim at this time of day, murky brown as the lake. The hills begin to drag the sun behind them until they brood darkly over the valley. Once upon a time Lady Godiva rode here.

Sean scans for movement beyond the purplish trees. He skirts around the edge of the wood, listening to the sounds it makes. Chink and tac tac tac and the mysterious call of a flute. There is a bird which sings like a flute but Sean can't remember its name. The sun lies low, orange hot, turning the air copper-coloured. Sean runs, trailing a stem of willow grass in his mouth. He stops every now and then to listen. In his game he is a warrior astride his horse, a dagger in his teeth. From any other perspective an observer would have seen a disorganised bird in short trousers, building a nest at the wrong time of year.

Sean runs on. Showers were becoming popular these days, he thinks. Showers were the modern alternative to a bath. His mother wanted a shower. In response Gor had asked her a question. The question was: *Do you think I am made of money?* Sean had reckoned the answer was: *No.* But his mother said nothing at all. She just walked away clockwork-fast to begin a silence that lasted three days.

You have to stand still in a shower. When Sean stands still all the whatifs come. He wonders whether this is something you just grow out of, or whether the adults too find themselves standing around in their lives thinking whatif whatif whatif.

Sean places the paper bundles from Mrs Roys' house under two house bricks inside their

152

garage. The loops of writing are still visible, poking out. Sean adds another brick and then another. He steps back to admire it. He has constructed a mini brick mountain: he is pleased. No one will ever guess that real alphabet words are hiding under bricks, that he is nearly solving a crime, or that he has a secret friend who is as old as the hills and lives in a wonky house.

Sean runs to the tip. Behind him trail all his thoughts; too slow to catch him, they drift and float away. Sean loves the way his body runs. He loves the way his plimsolls land, the way they do it on their own. He bends over as far as he can to watch his legs going round.

By the overgrown stile Sean checks over his shoulder to see whether he is being followed. He must keep his eye on the ball. Then it occurs to him that maybe *he* is the ball. That maybe someone has their eye on him. He is amazed he has not thought of this before.

The tip is supposed to be a load of old rubbish, but the truth is it is brimful of excellent things. Things you would never find all in one shop. In any case you can sit on top of the tip when there is no one else around, evenings especially, and apart from a bit of a view you have warmth too. The tip is always warm, it gives off its own heat. Sean feels chatty at the tip. It is being around all those things, it makes you talkative. He can be master and commander of the conversation and the tip never disagrees, though he suspects it listens, so that is all right.

You never know what you will find. Sean has discovered theatre seats (whole rows), staircases, surgical waste (including syringes and examination tables), baths (including taps) and a wheelchair. There are wigs, guitars, stuffed animals, an enormous distorting mirror, artificial limbs and, of course, lots of rubbish. He had a go in the wheelchair and it was quite good. Once you got the hang of it you could do laps around the tip, you could turn and reverse and zigzag. If you were tired after that, you could nod off in it. If you put a wig on no one would know it was you.

It wasn't just Sean at the tip, the seagulls liked it too. Sean wonders why they are not at the sea. They fall screaming from the sky on to the rubbish, where they strut stiffly about, pugnacious and self-important, inspecting the rubbish sideways with their flat fishy eyes. The birds hang about all day, wheeling circles with the sun on their backs. You get used to the noise, it's no good minding it. Their shrieking becomes the sound of the tip, as if it were the same thing. Sean closes his eyes and the gulls turn into babies, wailing as they tumble out of their prams.

'No wheels on my wagon, but I'm still rolling along. Bloody stink in here. Holy cow. Is it you?'

'No.' A pointless lie. Even Sean can smell himself.

He meant to wash when he came in; he'd forgotten. He sniffs his hands. They smell leafy at first and then you get the bird shit, metal and waste that make your eyes water. Gordon wrinkles his nose. 'You bloody pong, you do.' And he swings out to report it.

'He pongs.'

'What?'

'He pongs! He pongs! He pongs!'

Sean moves to the sink to rinse his hands. His dad reacted badly to certain smells, which was why they couldn't have a dog. He liked nice smells, aftershave, cologne, soap. He would sniff himself and, if he thought he required it, apply more Tai Winds for Men.

The water flashes in the light and Sean thinks about the saints and the way they always look so worn out, and also how there was never a speck of dirt to be seen on any of them. Maybe there was a connection. Saint or sinner, you couldn't leave your washing out around here. His mother had stopped saying that, he realised. She used to say it every day. They had used to say prayers. They had used to be Catholic, but now they couldn't be bothered. It was his mother who had taken them to church. 'At least there are some believers left in this house,' she said. She spoke it piously, but you could still hear the anger poking through. His dad just laughed. His pointed his index finger at Sean and sang, *'I'm a believer, I couldn't leave her if I tried.'*

Cath wasn't in a mood for singing. She fought him with silence instead. She always won.

The training for Avon representatives was brief but intense. Cath had decided this was the answer to all her prayers. Door-to-door selling. It was popular, easy, glamorous, well paid. It would get her out of the house and into other people's houses. Doreen would teach her how. Doreen could turn hours into minutes with her smooth creamy Avon-lipped persuasion. She had a face made out of candy colours, pretty as a sweetshop, and she'd cooed and coaxed Cath out of four pounds six shillings, and stirred her tea for her in return. While Doreen counted out the money (including the coins) to check it was the correct amount, Cath noted that her hair had been piled on top of her head in an enviably laborious construction, like a giant honeycomb. Carefully selected strands had been teased out and curled to make helter-skelter rides for ants. She was beautiful, Cath thought. Everything would be lovely if she could become more like Doreen. Cath thought she would very much like to have a sweetshop face and Avon talk and helter-skelter hair.

Each night Cath opened her Avon boxes. She liked to touch the products, though she didn't intend using them. She couldn't imagine ringing the doorbells; she didn't trust people to let her in. Perhaps she would ring the bell and run away, she thought, like a child. How could she ask for money? She was too shy. She would give the stuff away for free. She'd go to prison. She wouldn't be able to sell it in prison either. She was quite unsuited to it. No one would buy anything. Ding-dong. The chimes rang in her head, sweet bells to the devoted. Ding-dong, the sound of freedom, the promise of escape, a siren call. She would practise and rehearse and prepare, as Doreen had shown her. She knew the products and the prices and the free gifts and the special offers. She knew to smile and cock her head and sit with her knees to the side, never crossed. She knew to hold the product up in the air as it was being discussed, like a third party, a VIP guest. She knew to place her other hand under the product, as though offering it a little chair, as a sale drew closer. And she knew to say: *You are the woman we have designed this season's range for.* If she practised then maybe one day the bells would ring for her.

CHAPTER 19

Walter did not dare to take his poems too seriously. That all changed one harvest festival when Ginny Hall read out a poem called 'Abundance'. Walter had been astonished to hear the vicar announce that she had written it herself. He hadn't realised any old nobody could write poetry and then read it out, just like that, in front of people, and at harvest festival, and in church. He had supposed there would be guidelines, strict controls, rules drawn up by the universities or societies or something. But here was Ginny delivering, in her best Sunday vowels, words she had dredged up herself, blowing them over the marrows and radishes, shrilling them up at the stained-glass figures with their staffs and shields, until their colours burst and lit the air above their heads. Everyone in their pew below felt her words on them, just as if they were from the Holy Book itself. Walter recalled only snatches of Ginny's dramatic composition now, but its disquieting sense of threat goosebumped him still. He had forgotten the start but remembered:

thy bounty grown to fulsome ripeness,
ballast gainst a fearful winter storm . . .

And

winter, aye, that cometh to tear asunder,
winter's wrath: our enemy forsworn . . .

And

that we with tender care, not flights of fancy,
may gather in the yield to stay our want.

He regarded Ginny quite differently after that. She
had previously offered no clues to suggest her poetic
leanings, though she was clearly, beneath cardigan
and raincoat, a first-rate poet. Walter had to admit
he had passed her over on almost every count. Now
he was forced to reconsider. Now he dropped his
glance when she approached and waited, in the hope
he might become infected, if it were at all conta-
gious, by her cunning way with words.

'In the crimson blush of morning, In the glitter
  of the noon,
In the midnight's gloomy darkness, Or the
  gleaming of the moon,
In the stillness of the twilight, As it shimmers in
  the sky,
We are watching, we are waiting, For the end that
  draweth nigh.'

Sankey enjoyed the sound of his singing voice. He thought it a curious thing the way music behaved beside water. Take that bit just now. Water, he suspected, was a transmitter of sorts, a mover of sound. His voice became the clanger and the dewpond the bell.

There was a magician who said he could do a trick where he appeared to walk on water. Sankey thought little of that sort of skylarking, but he wouldn't have minded a glimpse to see if the fellow could or not. There were tricks and there were miracles. This life was an extravagant trick, but coming along just in time was a genuine miracle. Sankey knew it, he could taste it behind his teeth.

Sankey was a Methodist. He knew God's love lived in a man's heart and sprang from his throat in worshipful song. He knew the road to salvation was a rocky one, and he knew that beyond the swelling flood the gates of Heaven glittered brightly, golden as the King's own ceremonial carriage.

Sankey had many favourite hymns; he found it impossible to choose between them. He reckoned that to write a hymn a man must be as clever as a politician, as pure as a bishop, and musical as sin. He marvelled at the words in the hymnal, how they arranged themselves in line beside a tune. How did they do that? Why didn't they drift apart from the musical notes? Or run on, or run out, or go bad? Who could answer? Sankey explained it to himself. *Sacred words will find their way around a venerable tune*. A chill blew under his skin at the sanctity of that remark. Where did it come from? Wise words. What were they doing inside his head? He must be patient. He must not excite himself. The still small voice of calm. *I am the light.* The still small voice. *I am the Door.* A voice. *Choose you this day whom ye will serve.* Pay attention. Attend. *Be still and know that I am God.* Sankey's hands reached to cover his mouth, one after the other, as if they did not trust it to speak. He shivered as he knelt. He tried to stop the sudden gasp of tears. He must compose himself. Simmer down. 'Help me, Father. My heart is pure. Lord God, Heavenly Father of all mankind. Creator of the universe. All things are ready – come.'

It occurred to Walter that if Miss Hall could manage original verse fit for public consumption, then so could he. Why not? Walter thought if he were to be inspired then he had better get out and let nature rouse him. All the best poets dealt with nature, it couldn't be avoided.

He found himself torn between woodland and water and so opted for a bit of both, taking the path by Millfield Wood, which led to the pond. The day was bright, occasionally darkened by fast-moving cloud, which he thought good for mood. He crept diligently along North Road, where the hay carts had left scatterings of straw, hands clasped at his back, head high, alert for any sudden displays of nature or other notable manifestations besides the twitterings of birds and water-gurgles of ditches. He paused at the drinking trough; he and Cecil Harvey used to walk under the plough horses' bellies without ducking their heads. He came upon the Tisdale woman, bucket in hand, at the corner house before she knew he was there. Her shriek startled them both, launching all the songbirds out of the trees. 'I beg your pardon, Mrs Tisdale.' But she was already gone and the door slapped shut. The birds wheeled round and resettled on their perches. A solitary bark sounded. Some guard dog, that.

As he walked poetry words rolled about in his head. The lazy guard dog suggested something. By the time he reached Four Ashes Road, Walter had it.

> I fear your dog is fearful lacking
> When it comes to security.
> We may find that hound cat-napping
> 'Neath some tree in surety.
> Some guard dog, that, Mrs Tisdale!
> Some guard dog, that.

Walter was pleased with it. Not bad. At the bend by the lower field gate he tried it again, and decided it lacked scope, ambition, finesse. It was terrible. He discarded it. Nothing would come of the second-rate guard dog. He was not a dog born for art, or guarding.

When he got home he would put the kettle on and read through his scribblings. Mostly it was poor. Cobblers, Perfect might say. *For she was ne'er the girl, Oh no, Unlike the pansy and dandelion dear.*

Wretched. Like a rhyme for a skipping game. Now he would feel cheesed off. He would erase all the pencillings. He would sink into a drift of misery, punctuated by traipsings towards the kettle and the WC. His mother would appear at five o'clock and put their dinner on, meat and gravy twice a week. Then they would sit and watch the windows darkening while they occupied themselves; he with reading volumes of verse (how these poets of note would laugh at his efforts) and she with mending and needlepoint until they each appeared reflected in their chairs, gazing back at themselves.

Mary says she wishes Walter were a painter rather than a poet because then he could paint her beauty and the world would see it and there it would stay for ever and ever, amen. A poet, she continues, is good for nothing but a few old words that nobody wants. Who wants words? People have got plenty of words of their own, haven't they? Spray, she says, that's what words are, a squirt of dirty business to be precise: poop. Poets, she scoffs; spraying their words where they're not welcome. And who would want to hang poop on their wall? Nobody, that's who.

Walter says nothing. There are no words anyhow. Only jets of shit.

Mary lies under a hornbeam with marigolds in her hair, her bare shoulder exposed. She stares boldly at him; there is a warning in her eye. Walter is angry; he paints incautiously, truthfully. He has no talent, but he puts it down, what he sees. It is difficult. The very devil to do, he thinks, to make a mark on the canvas that rings true. As he becomes absorbed the expression on Mary's face begins to sour, and her eye narrows with suspicion. She covers herself up, yawns, and rolls on to her belly. He shall not paint her this way. Bugga him and all who sail. Daftie. Men for you. P'raps she'll get someone else to do it anyhow. She mentions this to him through the quick pull of a second yawn, but Walter pays it no attention. She is going to the city, she informs him matter-of-factly. She will get out of this place if it is the last thing she does – what a poop-hole! She will go and work in a Lyons Corner House, yes, that's right. She will be a Nippy and wear a smart uniform and have proposals of marriage from proper types, toffs and all. She will eat mixed grill every day with cups of sugared tea. She will not remain here in this poop-hole. He paints on. He is still painting long after she has fallen asleep.

It is for you
The nightingale sings her song
It is for you
the celandines, anemones and woodland
    orchids throng

It is your face
that each day pulls the sun around

It is your voice
in quiet prayer that I have found

It is for you
the night-black throws her stars
for you
time ticks away her hours

For you
the oak and sycamore against the wind do
  stand
For you
the world turns
and I upon it
bowed to your command.

Walter has signed his small curly signature at the
corner of the page. Indeed, it is for her, but she
shall not have it now. She does not deserve it. It
is a few old words nobody wants, a squirt of poop,
after all.

CHAPTER 20

Sean looks at the clock and wonders if Ann is dead yet. He tries to recall what time it was when he last saw her and add up the hours in between. He remembers he cannot tell time. He sits in the bathroom with the lights off. He reckons if she is a ghost by now, she might appear to him in the dark, try to frighten him, remind him from the other side that he is spaz. He realises she will make an excellent ghost. 'Ann?' He speaks her name quietly to show respect for the departed. 'Ann?' She does not appear. 'Ann!' You cannot rush the dead.

Sean slips into the dark shadows that live inside their garage. The whine of the aluminium door doesn't give him away. The paper bundles lie waiting beneath their burial mound of bricks. Sean will start with the top one, the first beneath the ribbon bow. The paper is blue, light and sheer as moth wings. The words are made in blue ink, with small curly sweeps. They could be letters. Sean has never received a letter, so he would not like to say. He stares down at it. He wonders if it is

166

in English. He thinks probably it is. The shapes C and S are very nice, swirly. Also the G shape and the F. The Os are disappointing, not very big. He recognises words: Donkeys. Jam. On. The. Pig. Drum. Not. Lads.

If he goes slowly he can tell many parts of it. If he goes slowly he finds he can sort of read the spaz thing.

8th September 1942, M.E.F.

Dear Mary,

Well, here is a turn-up for the books. Me writing a letter to you!

The appearance of this airgraph will give the game away, as you only have to see the Censor's mark and the field post-office stamp to know I am presently on active service. I hope you won't mind my writing, only all the lads write to their girls and wives back home, so I thought I'd give it a try! Why not eh?

How are you, Mary? I heard from Mother and she mentioned things had not been easy for you and Joseph and Clem at the farm, but that it has all picked up now. I am glad to hear this. I take it Isabel is happy in Kingshill. I hope your parents are improving health-wise. What a lot of trouble this war is giving people.

Well, we are under canvas (all we need is

a bucket and spade) and so far life here in Egypt is not too bad, though it is fearfully hot during the day and the flies are a curse. As I write the wretched insects traipse over my words. When the bugle blows for the midday meal, it is the flies that invariably beat us to it! The fellows with false teeth have some trouble incidentally with the hard biscuit (they have to soak theirs in their tea).

The streets in the town near here are choked in dust, though interesting. There are wealthy-looking men on donkeys holding big white umbrellas over themselves and then to contrast there are the beggars on their haunches in the shade. The only women to be seen on the streets are the fortune tellers – and no, I have not yet had my fortune told – nor do I intend to! The shoeblacks and watch sellers are a binding nuisance.

Have you made any jam? Or cherry pie? I find myself thinking of home-cooked food. You know, a 2d bar of chocolate here is 5d. Fletcher has an upset stomach so cannot eat anything at all – probably these flies. (He gets low-spirited but he is a fine mate.) At night it is very cold and we wear our battle-dress and coats, though the moon is lovely, like a bright, pigskin drum.

Now space is getting rather short, so I

will close. Cheerio for now then. All the best, Mary.

Yours, Walter

P.S. All the lads long for mail – Please write, Mary! I should be so grateful if you did.

Sean watches the final words as they rise up from the page.

chee ri for no. al the bets. yous water. p sal the lads lon for mae. ples witer marey. water.

A miracle has happened. He can read. Sort of. Some words anyhow. The ability to read real words has come to him while he was doing other things. Easy peasy pudding pie. Does this mean there are now two alphabets in his brain? Wur. *the moon is lov lyk a big pigs kind run.* Spaz, it was peasy! Bludyell. At the beginning of the letter, by the edge of the paper, Sean sees there are numbers. He knows numbers, so he reads them out.

Gor liked to read the paper and sing a Tony Bennett song and chew peanuts all at the same time. It was how he relaxed. Sometimes he added a coloured drink or smoked a No. 3 filter-tipped as well. And so when he was relaxing he was busy with some or all of these things.

'What's one nine four two?'

Sean's father looks at him without any expression

169

for a moment, before a crease of irritation folds above his eye. 'What?'

'One nine four two?'

'What about it?'

'One nine four two.'

'What are you on about?'

'Just tell me then.'

'What? They're numbers.'

'One nine four two.'

'Some bird's phone number.'

'A bird's phone number?'

'Holy cow.'

'Can I phone it on the phone?'

'No.'

Inside a drawer in the cabinet that stands beside the smoked-glass cats, the Matthews family keep their small brown correspondence envelopes. Sean chooses a pencil from the pot and writes down the numbers just as he had seen them on the blue letter. He places the envelope in front of his father and Gor reads it out immediately like a code.

'Nineteen forty-two.'

'Nineteen. Forty. Two,' Sean repeats. It is a series of numbers which seems to exasperate his father.

'Nineteen! Forty! Two! It is a date. A date, Sean. A flaming flipping date! Nineteen forty-two. We were at war with Germany. At. War. Hitler. Goebbels. Rommel. Ruddy Nora. Cath? What's the matter with him? What do they teach him at that bloody school? The lad's a cretin. My eight-year-old son is a cretin.'

170

Nineteen. Forty. Two. It is a flaming flipping date, Sean knew that now. His mother and father were at war with Germany. Why? They had certainly never mentioned it before. He also knew cretin was proper English for spaz. This date: it could be a long-time date like the date of Jesus, or it could be sooner, like last Tuesday. Miss Day will know. She knows dates like falling off a log.

CHAPTER 21

Walter walks as if he were alone. It is no civilised sort of walk as Sankey has acquired a large black hound, a lurcher by the name of Jack, that drags him about, requiring him to lean exaggeratedly backwards as if he were on waterskis. The dog belongs to a sickly girl whom Sankey visits. Her health has deteriorated and Sankey blames himself. He suspects his prayers are feeble. He worries that his Word is not good enough, that he will not save many souls, or heal many hurts. He knows his heart is in the right place, he says, but he worries his message is tangled and impure. He has offered to care for the dog.

'Can you not control the thing, Charles? Steer it.'

'He is beginning to respond, Walt.'

The dog's shaggy spine is curved like a hoop. It swings Sankey into the trees and they disappear, though Walter can hear Charles protesting, and every now and then commanding the creature in that high voice of his. Walter thinks he may as well sermonise to the poor beast for all the good it will do.

It is a fine day and the sky is filled with long

clouds sailing in fleets. There is pennycress and foxglove in flower and bluebells in the woods, and Walter imagines there can be few better places in the world. Moreover, he is a young man ready and able to begin an interesting life, just as soon as one comes along; surely it will not be long now.

The dog is bouncing towards the sown field. Sankey jerks behind at the end of the leash. He is appealing to the creature in rising and falling cries, or perhaps he is singing, it is hard for Walter to tell. They are lost for a while as Walter skirts the trees, and then he hears another cry and catches sight of the dog streaking across the field, jagging left and right and then flying wide in an arc before disappearing over the rise. Walter waits. *As straight as an arrow, as crooked as a bow. As yellow as saffron, as black as a sloe.* Schoolboy rhymes; he could remember them all. He hears Sankey calling, 'Walter?' Walter has cause to wonder on occasions such as these what he is doing with a fellow like Charles Sankey. There were a hundred things he could occupy himself with, as many people with whom he could spend profitable time; it could give you the pip.

The fields are writhing with rabbits and the dog cannot resist. No sooner do they find it, shivering, frothing with excitement, than it is off all over again. Sankey holds him for a while, leaning on his heels, singing out his name. The moment the dog breaks away is almost a relief. It flows silently into the grass and from there moves like ribbon up the incline, like something elemental, dark and smooth as river eel. The rabbit will feel a rush of air it has never known before, a crack of bone, then nothing more.

They wait but the dog does not return. Sankey calls its name and then Walter tries, reluctantly at first, then loudly, indignantly. They call its name together; they try high voices, like choristers, until they are hot and browned off.

'A right balls-up,' Walter says finally. 'And no rabbits to show for it.'

Walter and Charles rest by the pond. The sun is high, insects are busy. The dog is gone, likely in the next county by now. It is a mystery, Sankey agrees with himself, why such a dog, when offered comfort and care and human company, would wish to run off like that, as though such benefits were to be found any old where from any old one.

'Cheer up, Charles. Never mind.'

Sankey hangs his head. 'I have no comfort for any souls, not even a poacher's hound.'

'Like I say, Sank, never mind about it.'

'Sorry to say, but I do mind, Walt.'

'Perhaps it had dementia. It looked unstable, to be frank.'

'Perhaps.'

'Right balls-up, but that's life.'

A lapping begins at the edge of the water.

'Supposed to be a creature in this water, that's the legend anyhow.'

'Nothing here but God, Walt.'

'No point in chancing it,' Walter laughs.

Sankey glances at Walter. 'Are you afraid?'

'Course not.'

'You certain, then?'

'Course.'

'Shall we swim in that case? Cool off?'

'I don't swim,' Walter replies.

'Dip your toes then, Walt. Cool off.'

'Perhaps.'

'Come on!' Sankey is on his feet, peeling off his shirt to reveal pale ropy arms. He moves with heron steps to the water's edge and Walter is surprised to see how small his feet are, how narrow his waist and how childishly bowed are his legs. 'Come on. Cool off. Are you chicken?'

Walter watches Sankey, gawky in his underwear, as he shuffles along the bank for the best spot. Perhaps he *is* chicken. He had not thought of that. Perhaps it explains everything.

Sankey launches himself, without finesse, into the water.

'Good dive, Sank,' Walter calls.

Perhaps he is chicken. That's it. Perhaps there is nothing at all waiting for him around the corner of his life. Perhaps his life will be like the absconded lurcher, unremarkably present one minute and fled to the back of beyond the next.

Sankey's head bobs up like a buoy. 'Coming in? It's lovely.' He waves to Walter before setting off across the pond. Walter forces himself to wave back.

Walter lights his pipe. The smoke curls upwards towards the beech umbrella. Tut tut tut, calls a warbler. Sankey has given up trying to swim. He stands in the water, dazed, watching the light burn off the surface. It occurs to Walter that this moment has poetic potential, though it is unlikely he has brought his pencil, let alone his notebook, and he realises this is probably why he will never amount to anything poetry-wise. William H. Davies would not have forgotten his notebook or pencil. Indeed, he would be on the third verse by now. Balls-up as usual. Silence is how he would begin his poem, with that word. *Silence.*

'We thank you, Lord,' moans Sankey from the water.

Walter closes his eyes. It was hard not to be cheesed off.

'For the gift of water to sustain, refresh and cleanse all life.'

Charles has his arms outspread, like a pigeon-chested Errol Flynn.

'Over water the Holy Spirit moved at the beginning of Creation. Through water you led the children of Israel from slavery in Egypt to freedom in the Promised Land.'

It is in this one distinct area, Walter thinks, that Sankey has come unstuck. A pity in many ways, as he has good points and makes for cheerful company at times, but on this particular theme he has conceivably, arguably, gone too far.

There would be no more silence now and it was too late to write his poem. He should have written it ten minutes ago. In this way, he thinks, all manner of poems, paintings, novellas and assorted artworks are lost to their creators, as they are interrupted by women with brooms, crying babies, freak weather, ill health and Methodists. All these faceless would-be geniuses sunk into pitiless oblivion. And he too joining them shortly, with the flockless Charles Sankey by his side. It was all he deserved, particularly if it were to prove correct that he was chicken, which of course it probably damn well would.

'In water Your son, Jesus, received the baptism of John and was anointed by the Holy Spirit as the Messiah, the Christ, to lead us from the death of sin to newness of life,' chimes Sankey, enjoying his acoustically pond-enhanced voice.

Walter remembered there was a poem by W. H. Davies called 'On Hearing Mrs Woodhouse Play the Harpsichord', which began: *We poets pride ourselves on what we feel, and not what we achieve.* Walter thought that was rather good. He had hoped to use it in conversation at some point, but so far the opportunity had not presented itself. He admired the pomposity of it, the certainty, the way it excluded all non-poets.

'Are you still chicken then, Walt?' Bright water droplets fall from Sankey's elbows, chin and ears.

'Cluck-cluck-cluck,' he says. 'Cluckety-cluck. Love-a-duck. Cluckety-cluckie-cluck.'

Sankey's clucking is intolerable. In comparison, drowning seems the lesser evil. The water is not as cold as Walter expected it to be, and his dive is no worse than his friend's. It is possible to stand up on the muddy bottom as long as you don't move towards the centre, where it is deepest and darkest. Still, Walter feels afraid. He tries to smile, to appear as though he is enjoying himself, when all he feels is fear and irritation and a sort of pity for himself. Charles splashes Walter. The splashing is worse than the clucking.

'That's enough then, Sank. That's enough now. Bugger off bugger off bugger off bugger – !'

Underwater Walter is surprised how loud air bubbles sound, how bright the sunlight is through the gloom, how strong Sankey's arm is as he holds his head under. He has feared water all his life and now here it is filling his ears and nose and eyes, squeezing his heart. He should like to swim. Mary would swim, she would go deeper and circle back and surprise Sankey, beat him at his own game. He cannot swim. Nor for that matter can he ride a horse or drive a motor car, and he's not much good with his hands either – not even with his own fruit and veg – not to mention his singing, which is off, and his piano-playing, which is terrible. He is at least a poet, remaining (as yet) undiscovered. If he drowns now will someone root out his poems and find a publisher to publish

178

them? He would like to hope that people will remark upon the fact that this talented young poet died before he had the chance to produce his finest work, drowned tragically, needlessly, suspiciously, while out swimming with an apprentice lay-preaching Methodist. Perhaps Sankey will be hanged for it. The water rushes inside Walter's ears as he comes up, and as he gasps for air he sees that Sankey is speaking mouthfuls of words, his voice a whine of piety, and the words, urgent, imploring, are rising from the water into the trees.

'. . . *confess the faith of Christ crucified. Manfully fight under his banner against sin, the world, the devil. Continue as Christ's faithful soldier and servant unto your life's end.'*

'Charles!' Walter cannot speak for coughing.

Sankey closes his eyes. He cradles Walter's head in one hand as if he were a baptised child, the flat palm of the other is pressed against his brow. He lowers his voice. 'He will come to judge the living and the dead, Walt. Accept him, accept him.'

'Christ's sake, Sank!'

'Christ claims you for his own! Receive the sign of his cross!'

Walter wonders if, in the event he is not hanged, Sankey may, at least, be institutionalised. Walter struggles. He is surprised to discover he cannot get free. He kicks and pulls at his friend, but Sankey proves considerably stronger than Walter could have estimated. Finally, Walter swings at him, catching him sharply across the cheek.

'Inherit the kingdom of God.' Sankey cries, in response.

Walter swings again, landing one on his ear.

'O father!' calls Sankey, as Walter continues to thrash. 'O father!' he cries. 'Here is a light delivered. Hallelujah! Hallelujah! Hallelujah!'

CHAPTER 22

The local children had been told they must not walk anywhere alone. Especially not the woods. They were not allowed in the woods, it was banned. Nobody took any notice. Now the estate kids visited the woodland in twos and threes or in morbidly curious groups.

The game was always the same. The boys all wanted to be the beast. Some roared and spat, some crawled with bared teeth, some dropped from branches and some staggered with rolling eyes. As one re-enactment finished so another candidate would declare himself and off it would go again. The boys were always the murderer and, one after the other, the girls were always the victim, walking along in the woods without a care in the world, a bag on her arm, sunlight flecking her shoes. Often more than one girl at a time declared herself about to die. Chorusing screams filled the woodland so that nearby herds would lift their heads from grazing. Some of these girls would alter the proper course of events, escaping or fighting their attacker to the ground, thereby creating a different ending, leaving the beast not the beauty in a bed of leaves. Most of the girls were faithful to the facts, however. Most of them fell to their knees and cried out to their mothers and died with their eyes open.

All except Sean. Sean was the only dead girl who was a live boy, the only one who wanted to. Something about this fact roused the other boys and they chased him with a new resolve. Gone was the pantomime growling and eye-rolling and in its place was feral intent. They chased him as a pack, at least seven of them. They chased him with cunning, working as a team, happy as wolves. The forgotten girls hurried after, hooting, laughing at the thought of Sean pretending to be a girl in the woods, pretending to be hunted, pretending he was important. Sean, dashing on his soft streaky legs, hoping to die with dignity.

They piled on top of him and stuffed his mouth with leaves and dirt and Sean was happy. They pulled off all his clothes and covered him with twigs and soil and he didn't mind. The boys saw that he didn't mind and so they hit him with sticks and pushed earth in his eyes. Sean had pictured himself dying well. He'd imagined himself producing an awful scream and dropping face down (the girls never did that). He suspected he could die the best. Now the boys were shouting in his ears and whipping his legs with switches. His punishment for wanting to be her, for wanting to be the hunted thing, for upsetting the natural order. Who did he think he was? Sticks and stones can break my bones, he told himself. He covered his head with his arms and drew his knees up. He considered how this sort of thing would be impossible in space. How the sticks and stones would merely float or twirl through the air, no matter how hard they were flung. He realised it would be hard to hurt someone on the moon, to break their bones or even shoot them. He imagined that if you managed it somehow their blood might hang about in globules like Christmas berries.

It wasn't bad in the woods. Once the others were gone it was peaceful. He found his socks, his other shoe. He listened for the murderer. The silence began to make him afraid. *Do not go to the woods alone. Do not talk to strangers. Do not take your eye off the ball. Do you think I am made of money?* Sean ran. As he ran he thought to himself: I can run, I can run. Sometimes when you are looking for a murderer it may turn out they are standing right behind you.

18th September 1942, M.E.F.

Dear Mary,

I hope you received my airgraph. This time I am trying an airmail letter-card.

Well, what a sky. Not an English sky I should hasten to add. It is a blue of the lapis lazuli variety (if you know lapis).

Newsflash! George Williams has just got engaged by letter. It seems to be quite the fashion to do it by letter or cable these days. How are your parents? And Joseph and Clem? What is the local news? Have you seen or heard from Sankey? I shall drop another line to Mother, though it would be so kind of you if you could pay her a visit sometime. She did, in fact, mention that Isabel is expecting. What jolly news.

There are many types of lizard here, Mary. For instance there are two chameleons who sit on the ration wagon's backboard chains and catch flies on their tongues – I think you would like them. Fletch has called them Monty and Rommel, what a wag. Sandstorms blow up here without any warning, real whirlwinds they are. Of course this is the reason why camels have the ability to close their nostrils.

We are allowed out on evening leave, so Bob Henderson and I went on a walk. After 3 miles we found an Egyptian canteen. It cost us a small fortune! Whatever money you put down, you hardly ever receive change. A small tin of pineapples is 5/- and a pen is 2/-. Well, when you consider our salary of 30/- (less one and a quarter piastres lost on rate of exchange) someone is doing well, but it is not us! Moreover, Bob and I got ourselves lost on our return and arrived back rather pooped.

Well, darling, everyone thinks we now

have Jerry on the run. (The Italians don't count any more – they are poor fish.) You'd be amazed to see all the stuff left behind by Jerry and the Italians – vehicle parts, chairs, tables, pans, stoves, ammunition, old planes, tanks, tins, helmets, clothing, boxes of cigarettes (rain-soaked, unsmokeable!) – all left lying on the desert sands. And the harbour nearby is full of half-sunken ships. By the way, the Greeks are nice – polite and kindly disposed. Odd how they all seem to have fillings in their teeth.

I could eat some allotment peas now, and perhaps one of your potato pies. We have stewed bully and biscuits at night and sometimes cold bully during the day – a bit monotonous, I'm sure you'll agree. These letter-cards are rather short on space, aren't they? So I'll close now. I am thinking of you. Cheerio. God bless you. Please write, Mary!

Yours, Walter xx

P.S. You are beautiful.

soll cloes now. chee ri. o.god be less yoo. ples witer maryi. yous water.

This was a good letter. This letter he liked. *dear mary, dear mary. yurs waltr. yurs waltr xx.* This was Sean's favourite letter. He carefully replaced the bricks.

CHAPTER 23

If Walter wanted a kiss before his eighteenth birthday he would have to take Mary to the orchards in April, when the cherry blossom was thick and the sweet smell made you gag. He took her in May as it turned out, just as the blossoms were falling in the orchards. They lay under the trees and watched the flowers as they came down until they were smothered, snowbound as two polar explorers.

'Give us a kiss then.'

'Not likely.'

Mary Hatt was not a formal girl, it was one of her charms. Walter couldn't understand which part of his approach was off the mark. If he spoke pretty words, she would just laugh.

'Give us a kiss. Just one. Go on.'

'Not on your nelly, Wally-Walt.'

'I think you may have a mean streak, Mary Ann Hatt.'

'Stick it in your pipe and smoke it. Ha ha ha.'

A ball of blossom landed in Walter's eye. He could not understand why anyone, William Shakespeare included, would write sonnets in praise of the female sex. They seemed to him a petty, single-minded lot, the two he knew at any rate. For his part, he decided, he would stick to nature and, when the chance came, travel. He thought if another war were to come along and if he were called upon to do his duty, she might live to regret her decision to leave him unkissed in the snow blossom. Perhaps one day she would weep at his grave, perhaps there, on her knees, she would beg his forgiveness, and perhaps she would never, ever forgive herself and die a lonely spinster.

'Give us a kiss or I'll spank you.'

'Spank me then.'

Walter came up on one elbow to decide.

'Well? Hurry up. I haven't got all day, Walter Wallflower, unlike some layabout buggas.'

'If I spank you, will you kiss me?'

'You shall have to wait and see.'

This was no good at all. Walter Brown had hoped Mary Hatt would love him ferociously. He had hoped she would be grateful for his attention and that she might throw her arms around his neck and kiss him and tell him what a clever and handsome feller he really was. He would love her back, naturally. He thought this kind of thing would probably be perfectly all right.

Mary Hatt had no plans of this type. Mary had pictured herself marrying a sturdy, wealthy man like the ones in her sister's magazines. Someone who would drive her to the racecourse in his long-nosed car. She liked the idea of servants and gardeners and how she would laugh at them. But Mary had miscalculated. She had not anticipated falling in love with Walter Brown, indeed she had reckoned him faintly ridiculous in some departments, namely the department of poop-poetry and fancy whatnottery. Words and more words, not as valuable as water or timber or land or the muck that did wonders for crops. *You don't know nothing about blood and muck, Walter Brown.* Fancy words did wonders for no one, not even the fancy-worder himself, as who would want a load of words? He ought to be falling in love with her and she ought to be laughing at him, not the other way round. How had it become the other ways about? It was too late now. Bugga the back of it. He thought a lot of himself too these days. His talk had got bigger and bigger until it hardly could fit inside his mouth. Lately he reckoned he was too good for this place and lately she had begun wondering if he was right. She kept something of his in her pocket, folded up. She thought it was rubbish but she had been reading it more and more frequently.

Here is a daisy chain for your hair,
Here is gingerbread I won you at the fair.
Apple blossom, cherry blossom, peach blossom,
  pear,
Come beside the water, find her swimming
  there.

Walter's fancy words; even she had become susceptible.

Walter had thought to visit George Osbourne, who lived in an ivy-wrapped red-brick house by the smithy's old forge. He would show him five of his poems and hope he might receive a positive response. George had had his poem 'Lepidoptera' published in the church magazine, and another, 'The Cinnabar', published in the *Bucks Gazette* Poets Corner. He was the only published poet Walter had ever met. Walter considered him an interesting personality. George was a collector of butterflies and moths, but also of birds' eggs and occasional lizards. He was keen on ballroom dancing, though had to borrow partners, as his wife had been fatally hit by a tram in her twenties, and consequently there were no children.

George retired early from his accountancy firm in High Wycombe due, it was said, to lung problems caused by the poison fumes he breathed when preparing the killing bottles for his entomology. Not to be put off, however, he continued signing for his cyanide at the chemist, and announced he would be grateful to be buried with his collections like an Egyptian. Nobody paid any attention to that.

He had recently acquired an unusual specimen, he claimed. The death's-head hawkmoth was the largest moth in Britain, a rare find indeed, and so Walter had two good reasons to visit.

On the inside George's house was neat and immaculately ordered, as though he had a pinafored woman tucked away in his collections too. On almost every wall hung the delicately framed corpses of winged insects. The butterflies in particular magnified the stillness in the house, their gaudy colours brightening the dull browns of the sitting room. The clock on the mantelpiece counted down the minutes with an ostentatious ticking, as if it were logging this living death for some important purpose. As if, Walter fancied, at some preordained moment the hour would chime and all the butterflies would simultaneously reanimate and burst from their glass cases to swarm in a blaze of colour. How he wished they would. How pitiful they looked, he decided, in their categorised rows; how unremarkable in such vast numbers.

'Cake, Walter?' George was an attentive host. No less than three types of sliced cake fanned in a pleasing spiral across the plate and the tea was strong and very hot. Walter found he could relax and let his thoughts drift. George never minded a pause or a dismal observation. If you preferred to be gloomy or distant, that was all right with him. He would continue to rush for your refill, scoop up your crumbs, and chuckle at your frailest swing at humour. He would proceed as though you were a credit to the afternoon, as though he were indeed fortunate to have you in his second armchair.

The moth was very large indeed, Walter noted, almost a shrew. It made him squeamish to look at it, pinned through the thorax, splayed and stretched. He thought, startlingly, of the Messiah in his agony. He stared at its furred face, the dusty wings, and found he could not meet George's eye for a moment.

He was almost sure, George was explaining, that it was a death's-head, but he was going to write to the Society to be certain. It required authenticating, he explained. Words bubbled out of his mouth in a froth of excitement. 'Walter,' he said, 'a young man like you should have a pastime. A hobby is an excellent way to organise your mind. Pick the right thing and you won't know yourself. You're only half a man without a passion, son.'

Walter thought of his father on his knees to his root vegetables, and of Sankey bowed before God. He pictured George piercing the hearts of lepidoptera with a pin, and staking down their wings. He smiled and, producing the poems from his jacket, said, 'I have brought these for you to see, George.'

George sat with the poems for some time. He read each one twice, sniffing irritably when he got to the end. Finally he handed them back to Walter without meeting his eye, and Walter's heart sank. George put his hand to his jaw and stared towards the window. Walter waited. He began to think bringing the poems had been a mistake.

'They're good,' said George, quietly.

'Oh?' replied Walter, unable to hide the bounce of excitement in his voice.

'Yes,' continued George. 'But they are unlikely to be published.'

'Oh.'

George turned towards Walter. He was smiling warmly now. 'They are, how shall I put it? They are good, Walter, you have talent, certainly. But.' George wrung his hands as though he must now express some complicated truth in such a way that a simple soul like Walter would understand. 'Talent is not enough, Walt.'

'It's not?'

'No, Walt. Talent is a beginning. You have purchased your first killing bottles and rudiments and now you must discover whether you can capture any decent specimens and, moreover, display them to Society standard. They possess pep, I accept. *Joie de vivre* let us call it. Also an attractive melancholy. Some pleasant rhymes. But they lack originality, technique, expertise. They are, in a word, amateur, Walt. There is work to be done.' George beamed. He had warmed himself up with this advice. He had quelled his fears, allayed his suspicions that his young friend possessed a superior gift. He had destroyed Walter's hopes. He felt buoyant, peckish.

'Thank you, George. I'm obliged.'

George swung an arm around Walter's shoulder and fixed him with a friendly grimace. 'Any time, Walt, any time.'

George's moth collection was kept in another room. Moths are nocturnal, he confided, his commiserating arm still curled up on Walt's shoulder.

The room containing the collection was north-facing, cool and grey and filled by a large oval dining table, covered partially by a cloth at one end, and laid with two places. For lunch there was beetroot and cress and steak-and-kidney pudding. George swooped down with his fork. Another clock ticked faintly, sporadically, as if it wasn't much bothered about the o'clock. George began to talk animatedly with his mouth full: 'A moth, you see, must be trapped at night with treacle. A tree trunk will do the job; daub your chosen tree, then use a torch to choose from the dozens that are stuck all over the bark. Many of the more common varieties you will already have in your collection, so it pays off to take your time, to inspect thoroughly; likewise you can miss a real treat if you're not careful.' Swoop.

The clock pinged the hour, though Walter saw it was already a quarter past by his watch. Ping ping ping. On it went like a child, insistent, inaccurate, ping ping, on and girlishly on. Walter thought of Mary.

Piri-iri-ig-dum, do-man-wee,
My love is a sailor on the sea.
Piri-iri-ig-dum, do-man-wee,
If he do not return, I'll marry thee.

'A moth,' George said conspiratorially, 'is distinguished from a butterfly by the absence of a knob on the end of the antennae.'

As though silenced by George's pronouncement, the clock stopped pinging.

'Fortunately,' he went on, 'there are somewhere in the region of one hundred thousand species, so there is plenty enough to keep you occupied for a lifetime.'

After lunch there were a few minutes remaining in which to look at the eggs. George's egg collection stretched back to his boyhood. They lay cold as stones in a glass display case. They too possessed a strange defiled stillness that left Walter feeling gloomy. As he looked at them, speckled, dappled, in creams and browns and blues – colours that remained as pretty as they had been before George got his hands on them – Walter wondered whether in fact the gulf between him and his friend was as great as he imagined.

Sensing Walter's attention wandering, George blew his nose abruptly. Did he think he might fancy eggs? As he folded away his handkerchief, he raised a finger. As with moths, there were rules with egg collecting. George explained them: 'Do not, Walter, take more than one egg from a nest. And do not take more than two eggs from one species – excepting, of course, for vermin. Moreover, an egg must be correctly blown – that is, have its contents removed.' George offered to lend Walter his own blow-pipes if he ever fancied a go at eggs in the future. Did he think he might fancy having a go in the future? Walter thought, yes, he probably, almost certainly, assuredly would have a go, yes. In the future.

George offered Walter his consoling arm again as he bid him goodbye at the door. 'Good luck with any future attempts!' was his parting commiseration. Walter had replaced the poems in the inside pocket of his jacket. George reached out and tapped them with his finger, three prods on Walter's heart.

Though he took the long way, Walter walked home quickly. He disliked himself thoroughly; he couldn't say why. It occurred to him he ought to be lying under glass with the eggs, inert, cold, his innards all sucked out. Was he ashamed? Probably. How could he have imagined he was a poet? Dead insects were simpler, that was evident, cheerier too, no doubt. Right balls-up. The truth of it, he suspected, was that there was no difference between George and himself, none. George with his moths and eggs, and he with his words, and the selfsame business of pinning them down for others to admire; it was all a vanity. Each man thought himself a god. Mary was right. It was a squirt of poop, all in all.

CHAPTER 24

The sound starts as his head goes under. The lonely sound of the satellite ping bounces over the crackling static. Once he is fully submerged it fills his head, loud and clear. Now, even if they shout and bang on the door he will not hear them.

Delta zero mac. This is a good one. Delta one. The Eagle has landed.

Sean is rationed to one bath a week due to his habit of filling the bath to the very top, thereby emptying the hot-water tank, so he is resolved to make the most of it. He turns his head below the surface to adjust his soap-on-a-rope breathing apparatus. His helmet, recognisable to other members of the family as his mother's transparent shower cap, billows as it fills up. *Ping.* Bubbles blow from Sean's mouth. *I have opened the hatch.* His hair floats inside his helmet. He submerges his blue breathing tube. *Ping. Receiving you. I am exiting lunar module, Columbia.*

As he rotates, Sean uncoils the dressing-gown belt around his waist that attaches him to the lunar module, to avoid becoming entangled. The last

196

bubbles escape from his mouth. He stares up. He has no air left. He places the blue tube in his mouth and breathes. The other end of it swings over the bath mat. He can breathe. *Ping*.

He can open and close his eyes, he can smile, he can breathe, he can think and he can dream. Thunderbirds are go, you spaz. Perfect happiness. He can hang about like a gas, bothering no one, feeling nothing. If he had freeze-dried food he'd never have to leave the bathroom.

Delta Houston. This is an A1. Sean is turning again. Slow slow. He is keen to watch the progress of a plastic soap dish as it floats by; here comes a toothbrush. He smiles, sending tiny bubbles from the tube. He looks up through the water at the shower head high up on the wall and raises his thumb to it. His breathing is loud in his ears. He is unaware of the slops of water escaping over the top of the bath, waterfalling on to the carpet.

That's one small step for man. Ping. He rolls with his knees tucked up. *One giant. Ping. Leap for mankind. Delta one, we copy you.*

Sean is unaware that a controller has begun his ascent, that even now he is approaching the lunar module and that Sean will be required to respond immediately to new commands from the control room. He is oblivious and weightless and orbiting. Unaware that ground control has issued a final warning. Unaware that he is about to suffer the consequences. *Ping*. He is aware at last. He suspects there may be a malfunction. There is an

197

unidentified object visible through the porthole. He jerks up, sending more water into the atmosphere. *I copy you, Control. I copy you. Er, Houston, I think we may have a problem.*

'Do you want a leathering?'

'No.'

'Do you want a leathering?'

'No.'

'You're asking for a leathering, young man. Bloody well asking for it! You are a cretin. What are you?'

'A cretin.'

'You are a stupid, stupid little boy. What are you?'

'Stupid.'

'Do you think I want to redecorate this house?'

Careful. A trick question.

'Well?'

'Um.'

'You dumb bloody kids. What if no one was here? What if you flooded the whole ruddy house?'

Whatif, whatif, whatif. The controller leaves quickly, too quickly. You get the bends at that pace. You cannot lose your temper in space, the doors will not slam. You cannot fling open the hatch and demand, *Whatif!* Space will give no answer. Space does not care about your whatifs. In space there is only *So what?*

Sean has a great long stick. He is hitting the estate with it: the bricks, the houses, the almost-paths, the tyres of the lorries. It makes a loud cracking noise that makes you want to do it again. 'Oi! Little sod you!' A red builder with a roly-poly tummy and a square mouth, brick-shaped. He is burned all over, even his ears and his eyelids. He is coming for him. Sean thwacks his lorry with the stick one more time, gives him the V-sign and runs.

'I'll break your bloody little arms,' shouts Brick Man. Sticks and stones, sticks and stones, sticks and stones will break my bones.

Sean runs down the echo tunnel, flushing out a trio of wiry dogs, and out on to Shepherds Lane, where the residents have lush little lawns with pansy borders and nets up at the windows. Sean wonders why it is bones are white. Why not a dark colour? Like navy.

The houses look cheery here, stuffed with families and furniture and coyly veiled at the windows to discourage nosy parkers like Sean from peering in on their secret lives. He peers anyway. There is a solitary car parked in the street, a blue Ford Consul. The tarmac road curves proudly around it. Sean stops to look. He presses his face against the window, burning his nose, to see the shiny seats and wide Saturn ring of the steering wheel. He breathes in the rainwater smell of the glass and lets his fingers burn on the hot metal door. To drive your own car was a step up in the world, to park it in your own garage was another step. A house was a step. These were the steps you made until you hit your head on the ceiling of life, which meant you'd reached the top. The people who lived in Mary's Mead, outside Wycombe, had reached the top. They had double garages, big gardens and (it was rumoured) swimming pools, so they had definitely reached the top.

Top people. Rich people. Fatheads, Gor called them. You would have thought they should be called flatheads, but it wasn't prudent to challenge Gor.

At Fray Bentos there were men above Sean's dad. At work you were either over or under somebody. Gor worked under these superior Fray Bentos men. Sean pictured a kind of tower into which the men were stuffed, under, over, under, over, each in his own cubbyhole, each both above and below another. Everybody wanted to go up, even Gor, everybody wanted to become a fathead. The Fray Bentos fatheads received special treats like cars or cash, the same as cereal-box competition winners. Gor wanted treats too: cars, cash, holidays, the special fathead parking spot in the company car park, not to mention the executive fathead Christmas lunch. Not everyone attended the executive Christmas lunch; that was the idea, you had to be an executive. Executive perks. These were the words that tortured Gor. He spoke them nervously as if they might conjure something holy, or unholy. He spoke them wistfully too; they made his eyes widen and his mouth tighten. Even when separated, the words held their command over Sean's dad. 'Perk' or 'executive', singly, could produce the same effect.

Elvis, according to Ty, had thirty-two cars, mostly sedans and Corvettes. Sean had no idea how Ty knew that. Elvis had got to the top. He was, if you like, a fathead. He had gone through the ceiling of life and burst through the roof, but he still sang 'Heartbreak Hotel' as though nothing was going right at all.

Sean runs across Foxes Field. You are an executive runner, he tells himself; perky. When Sean is running he pulls the grass and the wind and the sky with him. *Top. Executive. Fathead. Perk.* You had to get the rhythm. When he is running, he is not afraid.

Ann is not dead. Sean is both relieved and disappointed. She says, 'Wotcha, Spaz,' as though everything is completely normal. Her knees are orange with brick dust and her hairband is dirty. Sean points these things out and she stares over his head. Women do this, his dad explained it. Not explained exactly, but he mentioned it. No one could explain it as a matter of fact, not even scientists. A woman's mind is a mysterious terrain, his dad said, not for mortal men to fathom. Even women themselves didn't understand their minds, so it was no good asking them. Sean wondered, if there was a woman scientist one day, would she understand her own mind? A rhetorical question as it turned out.

'Women and science don't mix,' his dad informed him.

So Ann doesn't care about dust and dirt today. She cared last Tuesday when she asked Sean to bury her in builder's sand and then violently changed her mind. She may well care tomorrow because tomorrow is another place, disconnected from today. Women like to change their minds and then change them back. This was something Sean could sympathise with, he required no explanation for the mind-changing part. Being a woman, Sean thought, probably wasn't so bad. There was only one drawback as he saw it: women weren't allowed in space. This was a major drawback and he pitied them on account of it.

Ann has finished staring over Sean's head and now she is walking determinedly away from him. She is heading for the brick mountain. It is infuriating, the way she just does things without discussing them first. He hurries after, watching his feet to see how quick they can go. Sometimes he watches his face in the hall mirror to see if he can catch it doing something. This is pointless, things don't happen while you look at them. *Watch the ball* is a good example. He reckons his face does all kinds of things behind his back. 'A watched pot never boils,' his dad said. His grandmother had said it before him. She was from Newport. Sean thinks that if someone had been watching in Gomms Wood that day, really looking hard, perhaps a child would not be dead. Things happen, he decides, when you take your eye off the ball.

Ann is standing at the foot of the brick mountain. The mysterious wind lifts her hair and presses her dress against her bones.

'You can look.' Sean hands her a thin blue letter. 'It's from mista waltr, see. I got them off Mrs Roys.'

Ann stares at the swirly blue words. 'This is rubbish. Put it in the dustbin.'

'It's not. I read it.'

'You can't read, you nasty little liar!'

'She gave me a fizzy drink and a giant egg.'

'Liar liar liar liar.'

'She has got banana feet.'

'Yur a spaz liar, Sean Matthews.'

'It's true.'

'I wasn't born yesterday, was I?'

Sean pushes the letter into his pocket. *Women are controlled by the cycles of the moon, son. There's nothing we can do about it.*

'Climb.'

Sean looks up at the cliff face of brick, the faraway summit touching the blue.

'P'sof.'

'Climb, Sean.'

'Climb yourself.'

The mysterious wind whips a piece of hair across Ann's face. She doesn't pull it away. Sean can see the stain on her neck from the day before and the bruise on her arm that won't go.

'Spaz spaz spaz. Horrible little liar spaz. Do as you're told.'

'P'sof.'

'I see.' And she is gone. Off on her rod legs. Good riddance. That's what she would have said. Good riddance to bad rubbish. Sean can't be bothered to say it. The wind is nice, it blows away the dust, the smell of cement. It blows away Ann. 'Goodbye.' She stops and turns to say it, her arms are folded. She has to shout. Her hair blows into her mouth. 'You won't see me again. Goodbye, Spaz. Good riddance to bad rubbish.' And she whirls round and takes off again.

'Bye.' Sean doesn't mind if she hears it or not.

There is a tune playing, not exactly a tune. It is the wind in the plumbing pipes, the same three notes really.

The brick mountains are strong, he realises. The wind presses against them, but the mountain is too strong for the wind. You have to admire the bricks, the way they hold together, their strength. Sean looks up again. The sky is swaying at the top; its blueness makes the bricks redder and their redness makes the sky bluer. Sean begins to climb.

CHAPTER 25

Pyuu-pyuu-peeoo. The gold plover is always sad. Walter could remember a long trail of gold plover over Escourt Farm, crying like little girls. The grey plover looks on the bright side, pee-oo-wee, like a man calling his dog. You get to know them, buntings, skylarks, linnets. Four thousand house martins lifted out of a field beside The Harrow as Walter cycled home last week and as he tipped his head back to take in the sight his bicycle dawdled into the ditch. Today Walter can hear the chak-chak-chak of the red-backed shrike and somewhere about is a song thrush, *throstle*, they call him, letting off a gruellingly complicated song.

The Sale of Work was to be held in the schoolroom and was due to commence at 2.30 p.m. Mrs Brown had set off walking as she could no longer cycle up the hills. Walter was therefore free of the scoldings he would have received for overfilling/underfilling her cycle tyres, not cleaning the frame and failing to mend her bell. It meant he would arrive early. He considered riding on and circling back and he considered riding on and never returning at all. Instead he parked up neatly within a row of cycles, before discovering a gaggle of circuit ministers flapping over the imminent arrival of Mrs Coningsby Disraeli, OBE.

Charles Sankey was tolerated by the ministers so long as he worked harder than anyone else. He was arranging the trestle tables and chairs and helping prepare the stalls and fill the bran tub. Walter thought he had never seen him happier.

'Lend us a hand with this, Walt, grab hold. When's Mary coming?'

These village events always enjoyed a good turnout, though nobody had much money to spend these days. They would come from Holmer Green, Hazlemere, Wycombe, Naphill. Last year there was a man from Denmark.

'Lay it down, Walt, good man. Fancy a smoke? Shall I have a look-out for Mary?'

Mary came swaying up the hill in her best hat and print dress fastened at the front by her mother's peacock brooch. She clomped in her heels up Cryers Hill Road, under the great green bursts of beech and sycamore. She hurried as fast as she dare without running, calling out to those she recognised, chivvying her brothers traipsing behind her. Other girls arrived in groups or in twos and threes, arm in arm, weaving around the prams and carts and darting children. Most were accompanied by older women, but Mary clomped alone, one hand on her hat, the other swinging her bag, as if she were still a gawky child. If she would only find a way of adapting herself, Walter thought. There were things Mary did, styles of behaviour, that charmed him in private and embarrassed him in public. If only she would imitate the other girls' behaviour now and then.

Sankey stepped out to greet her.

'Mary,' he breathed, as she swayed past him.

'Wally Wallflower,' she said. 'Fancy seeing you then,' and she yanked his cap over his eyes.

Mrs Coningsby Disraeli, OBE, is wearing a large hat consisting mainly of feathers. At her bosom is a ruff of lace out of which sprout two dark pink velvet roses, complete with leaves. There are pearls around her neck and more pearls swing cheerily from her ears when she speaks. She speaks for rather a long time, about the village and the valley, the people who live here, their fortitude, talents, skills, their resilience in the face of economic adversity, their cheerful outlook, their way of life, which she refers to as 'our way of life'. She waves her glove towards the stalls and mentions her astonishment at the depth and range of talent in such a small rural community, commending the ministers and members of the church charity committees and everyone who pulls together during times such as these. She says she is proud to be a member of such a community, hip hip hooray. She declares the Sale of Works open and receives a burst of applause.

Walter stands with his hands in his pockets while his mother, Mary, Sankey and the others look at tapestry purses and fabric fans. The local ladies have turned out in force in their best hats and glass beads and their chatter rises right up to the tin roof. Sankey has been helping with the bran tub and even makes an announcement in his high voice, making some of the girls giggle. He is flushed with self-importance and keeps rushing up to apologise to Walter – 'Sorry Walt, I can't stop' – before whisking himself away again. Walter trails, like a little boy, after the women. His mother tolerates Mary's presence in public. She hopes her patience and goodwill towards Mary Hatt will be read as confidence in her belief that, in the end, the day will be hers: her son will be sensible and marry Sylvia.

The women are interested in the needlecraft and crochetwork, and also the two stalls devoted one to lace and the other to beaded items. They chatter without pause and Walter is overawed at their ability to both speak and listen at the same time. He knows when women get together plots are hatched. His mother purchases a hook-rug needle and Mary, he notes, buys a needlepoint pattern featuring the words *We Mourn Our Loss*.

At the bran tub Mary wins a necklace made of oval yellow beads and frightens Walter with her shriek of delight. The ham tea costs ninepence each and Walter is obliged to pay for his mother's and Mary's and her brother Joseph's as well as his own. To cap it all, Sankey, who is not entitled to a free tea, as he is not officially considered a circuit minister, presents himself as parched, starved and gasping, and Walter is obliged, grudgingly, to buy his tea too.

'This afternoon has been a great success!' Sankey declares over his cup, as though he is transformed into Mrs Coningsby Disraeli herself. 'Everybody says so,' he confirms.

Walter can't help feeling it has been expensive and diverting in a tedious way, though there is still the evening concert to come.

Walter watches Mary laugh at the ventriloquist's doll in the Children's Corner. She puts her hands on her hips and flashes her higgledy teeth. Walter suspects that when a man is deeply in love he is most likely unable to see anything derelict in the world at all.

Walter is becoming uncomfortable in his suit, such is the heat rising inside the Methodist chapel tonight. He squirms his feet inside his shoes and tries to swallow into his dry throat. The room is packed to the rafters for the Grand Concert, though Walter supposes there is not too much grand about it really, though it is well attended. His knee is pressed agreeably against Mary's. His mother sits on Walter's left. He did not want to bring her, but there it is. He told her she would not enjoy it, and so now he has proved himself right. She is stony-faced, though there is a glitter in her eye, which Walter suspects may be burgeoning psychosis. He hates himself for repeating, 'All right, Mother?' To which she bobs her head smartly once, as if to limit the amount of energy she expends on him.

Layers of smoke drift over the combed and curled

heads of the audience and the smell of smoke combines with the pong of mothballs, jasmine eau de cologne and the faint bitterness of sweat.

A man who has been introduced as Eric is playing the violin. Walter is aware of the sound of a dog barking outside. Sankey, he notices, is swaying slightly to the tune the violin is playing and each time he does so he knocks against the felt hat of the lady on his right. Mary is sitting bolt upright with her mouth open and her hands clasped at her breastbone. Well, there's a turn-up for the books. Walter had no idea she appreciated music, he thought she merely tolerated it for the lark of a good saucy song. It was irritating, the thought that she might respond sympathetically to music while referring to his poetry as poop.

A woman has arrived beside Eric and received a big cheer. She has a powdery face and a tall blue feather on her head. Walter wonders whether it is a man. Mary nudges him sharply in the ribs.

'See look, Mrs Deacon!'

Not a man, though Walter still does not recognise this person. The draper is called Deacon; it must be his wife, or his mother. Mrs Deacon sings 'On the Sunny Side of the Street'. Mary bounces up and down slightly and so, Walter notices, does Sankey. Then Mrs Deacon sings 'Stormy Weather', and everyone sways as if they are on board ship, except for Walter and his mother. Mrs Deacon sings mainly of the weather; it makes her feather tremble. She finishes up with 'When I'm Calling You'. It isn't very good, which is a pity because she was doing reasonably well up to then. She clears her throat several times during the song and rises on her toes to reach the high notes as if they are up on a shelf. She receives a jolly good ovation anyway and off goes her feather again.

There is a long queue at the tea stall during the interval. Walter has barely sipped his and scalded his lips when it is time to go back in and sit down. His mother says, 'Mind my coat! Mind my shoe!' He is cheesed off with Sankey and Mary who stand leaning on the bran tub laughing like a couple of sailors. Sankey is dressed in an unlikely ensemble of black and white items, including a stiff-collar shirt. He looks ridiculous, like a bank clerk at a funeral, except that his bowler is dusty and faded and discoloured at the back. What on earth are they laughing at?

Back in the church room it is a little cooler, though the audience are somewhat chattier. As they settle a drift of pipe smoke rises and the ladies fan themselves with their programmes. A man introduced as Frank 'Frankie' Frost is next. He has a blacked-up face and startlingly white hands with which he occasionally strums a banjo. He sings 'Lily of Laguna', followed by 'Little Dolly Daydream', and he receives a standing ovation. Only Hilda Brown remains in her seat, obliging Walter to remain beside her in his, while every body in the room gets to their feet. Somebody behind them shouts 'Bravo!', which causes Mary to honk with laughter.

Finally, a group of people sidle on to stand beside Frankie Frost. The four women are dressed in matching blue velvet gowns and there are two more sleek gentlemen in tuxedos and of course Frankie, whose paint-caked face begins to look silly suddenly, surrounded by such elegance. One of the women is greying, but the others have plump, pretty faces and glossy hair arranged in thick brown curls. A bespectacled male singer begins. The light winks in one lens then the other. The others join in:

> Oh, Susanna,
> Oh don't you cry for me
> For I come from Alabama
> With my banjo on my knee

They sing in different registers, like the variations in a single colour. Walter thinks it is the most beautiful thing he has ever heard. He feels his skin shiver and the hair on his neck move. They sing the harmonies slowly like a lament for a while and then Frankie Cake-Face lays into his banjo, making it sound speeded-up, like Charlie Chaplin running after a train. It is a sound like pure joy. It makes Walter want to leap to his feet and whoop and shout, but of course he doesn't. He sits perfectly still with his hands laid in his lap, heavy as two stones, and a slow tear in his eye.

CHAPTER 26

Miss Day holds the page as though it were made of water. She scoops her palms to make a bowl for it to lie in. As they stare, the blue mothwing letter trembles. Sean watches Miss Day's eyes as they follow the words. Invisible lines tow her gaze across row after row. Sean thinks this is a thing even more lovely than Ann raising her animal face against the Cryers Hill wind. Sometimes Miss Day's lips move with the words, and at the end of each row her eyes return, both at the same time, to the beginning of the next row, ready to begin the journey across. Hundreds of little journeys are undertaken by Miss Day's eyes across the blue. Maybe it is thousands, it is hard to pin down a thousand. Keith at school said it was what millionaires had. It occurs to Sean that now he almost knows how to read, his eyes must be going across too. He thinks he would like to watch his own eyes go across the way Miss Day's do. He wants to do everything the same as Miss Day. He decides on the spot that if Miss Day dies, he will throw himself into the pond without his breathing tube. There.

'These are very precious, Sean.'

Wur. 'I know, Miss.'

'Your grandfather has a very nice hand.'

'Yes, Miss.'

'Do your parents know you have brought these to school?'

'Yes, Miss.'

Miss Day looks carefully at Sean.

'No, Miss.'

Miss Day folds the letter in her hand as though it were made of air, as though she were miming it. 'These are nice family treasures, Sean. Do you understand?'

'Yes, Miss.'

'They must be kept in a safe place, because in the future, Sean, people will want to see them and read them. Your children, perhaps your children's children. And so for the time being these letters must be put away safely. Give them to your mum and dad for safe keeping, all right, Sean?'

'Yes, Miss.'

'Do you promise me?'

'Yes, Miss.'

'OK then. All right then, Sean.'

Sean walks home with a light head. It is because I can nearly-read, he thinks. The words are growing in my brain, like the wallpaper bubbles. Perhaps this will create a black hole inside my head. Inside Miss Day's head, on the other hand, must surely be meteors and exploding supernovas. *Your children, your children's children's children.* This is typical of Miss Day. It was how she looked at the world, through a very long telescope so that she could see things that were far away, that had not even happened yet, that might never even happen at all. Miss Day would merely suspect them into being. It didn't matter that they never happened in a month of Sundays. Miss Day was full to the brim of whatifs. If you could imagine something, it was already a half-truth – from a whatif to a when.

For instance, Sean could not imagine Mrs Roys hurting a child, though he could see her wearing goggles. More importantly, why worry about children who weren't being born yet? This is a whatif for a loon. If she were not careful this kind of thinking would send Miss Day off her rocker.

Sean did not want to see telescope worlds, faraway things that might come along. He wanted to see planets in their proper places and the blue marble Earth, swirled with white, turning cheerfully on its axis. He wanted to hang in the black inside his silver capsule and wave at it. Yoohoo.

Besides, the end of the world was coming, the man on television said so. We were shortly going to be blown up by an asteroid. Even the vicar did not deny it. What good are letters when an asteroid is coming? Answer that, Miss Day.

PS You are beautiful.

Sean did not know what to expect. He had vaguely thought that *changeover* might involve darkness, or perhaps conversely, light, and that there might be a chant or a clap of noise or a cheer. But *changeover* offered none of these things. *Changeover* was the same as before, only worse.

'OK. Right. Next one. Sean?'

Oliver thought that lions were like cats. 'They always fall on their feet,' he said. When the trap was quite finished the three little funny ones climbed up into the tree so that they could watch the lion cub when he came along and fell into the trap.

Sean mashed his hands together and lowered his head down on top of the words in the hope they might suddenly become recognisable closer up. Somebody had come along and mixed up all the letters he had known perfectly well yesterday so that he no longer recognised them today. This was *changeover*. Some of the words, or parts of words, remained untouched, while others had been blown up and reassembled by a sightless troll.

'Oliver thog. that lie onz. werie lickie cats.'

Sean checked Miss Day's face. Not her cheeriest one. Odd, because he had read the words exactly as they were written. He glanced back at the words in case they had changed themselves. No, they were the same.

He had read them very well, hadn't he? Sean

raised his eyebrows at Miss Day. *Very good, Sean? Good boy, Sean?*

'No? OK,' says Miss Day. 'Who can tell me what the sentence says? Steven? Julia? No, Sean, you've had your try. Anybody? Nobody?'

The moon swung teasingly high over his head, perfectly round in a blue daylight sky, watchful yet coolly impartial. Sean couldn't take his eyes off it. He crouched, waiting patiently at the top of a brick pile, until he was sure that it had moved a little to the right. At the other side of the sky the sun was burning blithely away. From the top of the brick mountain Sean could see far across the estate. He watched the other kids beneath him and felt pleased when he realised how insignificant they appeared. He didn't care if he never came down. Up here everything was just right. Up here there was nothing to puzzle over.

The space age they called it. It was now. Sean knew that one day he would be living on the moon and Earth would be small, like Beaconsfield, and the world would be space and space would be home. Aeroplanes would be rockets and clothes would be spacesuits and food would be drink (just add water). He couldn't wait for then. He wished and hoped for then. How marvellous it would be, you couldn't even imagine it. This world would seem lousy and plain; people would laugh about it, same as they laughed now at the farmers' boys with their dirt-splattered cows. In the space age everything will be just right and there'll be no trouble or wars or dying or bad news. There'll be happiness and clothes made from silver threads and you will see anyone you want to see from a beep machine in your pocket, and if your pet dies you will be able to make another one, exactly the same. He wished it was then now.

He lay down on his back and looked up at the giant sky. He scanned for the merest evidence of God, but there was only a small glinty aeroplane in the distance, silently chalking its white line across. Blue, as any astronaut will tell you, is the colour of home. From up there in the black, the Earth shines bright as a jewel. Ip dip sky blue, who's it, not you. Sean saw blue but he thought about black. The colour of magic and mystery and cold, cold space. Hung with a zillion planets, some hot and gassy and some bright as Christmas and circled with coloured hoops and stars and flashes of gold. Some dark and dead and waiting. He thinks by the time he is an astronaut he will be bouncing on planets far beyond the moon. His very own left foot might step, before anyone else's, on Venus, Mercury, Mars. And then he would have to think of words – true words – as good as Neil's. *Ping.*

Sean reckoned he would not labour on the farms around here, not in a million years. He'd have a nice job more like; get paid lots of money so he could buy a red roofless car. He'd seen exactly the kind of man he wanted to be in High Wycombe.

Straight from school and into their brand new suits, narrow ties, wide sideburns. He liked the way they walked, with their hands in their pockets and shoulders up. He would be like them, he reckoned. You wouldn't catch them working on farms, standing around in the fields. Not bludwell likely. He'd seen them go to the pub instead to have their ploughman's lunches and their Embassy Filter-Tipped.

'Spaz!'

Don't move. She can't see you from there. Cheeky cow. Women have no patience, it is a plain fact. It is why they nag nag nag and yak yak yak. Gor said if you give them an inch, they take a mile. Perhaps this is why they are not allowed in space.

Vivid imaginations were not considered an asset. Children were befuddled, everyone knew that. Your only hope was to pay attention to the adults. If you didn't pay proper attention your life would explode with you inside it, and any chance of a happy future would be flung, along with the debris you allowed yourself to be distracted by, to the furthermost corners of the earth. It was called throwing your life away, it was a shocking waste, and daydreamers were the worst offenders.

Sean was one of those prone to imaginings, everybody said so. You're imagining things, they said. It's all in your head. It was true that he could see things in his head without closing his eyes. He could conceive thoughts and visions he didn't recognise as his own, including words he wasn't sure he understood. It was time-consuming and demanded that he spent hours of class-time listening to the stuff in his head and overseeing the flickering pictures as they presented themselves, rather than paying attention.

There were penalties for dreaming; these varied and were often accompanied by dire warnings of a life wasted, come to nothing and gone to hell. This was because a child left to the mess and whimsy of its own brain would warp itself and those around it in the end. Warped people were inconvenient and unstable, they were not team players, they did not make good neighbours, you would not want to employ one. To live with your head in the clouds was thought of as a misfortune, like a gammy leg or a cleft palate, something requiring correction. Sean knew he was a dreamer even before he had been accused. Once he was identified as one of these unfortunates, he found himself charged with it daily. He lived in cloud cuckoo land, they said, he was not all there, he was away with the fairies, arrived from another planet. Sean learned that dreaming was of no practical use to anyone, least of all the dreamer; it was, he discovered, something to rid yourself of as quickly as possible.

Ann has taken up knitting. It is incredible that she knits, Sean thinks, while a murderer strolls in the woods. She has two thick white needles, like bones, and a ball of orange wool. She has knitted something maybe big enough for an insect to wear, Sean thinks. It is ragged and sloping, and you can see right through parts of it. Sean decides to say nothing. He watches carefully though for mistakes, or for signs of genius; above all he waits for her to give up.

Knitting has lent Ann a new piety; an air of devoutness hangs about her now that crushes Sean. The more she knits, the more saintly she becomes. There is no situation that doesn't demand the fetching out of her woolly new fetish. It has come between them, the knitting. Sean is undecided as to what to do just yet, so he bides his time and waits. He keeps a careful eye on the thing, as if Ann is knitting a big orange answer right there under their noses. There is a system with the wool. The needle must first poke itself in, then the wool is required to loop over before the needle slides through the other side and finally comes out again. In, over, through, and out. She mouths it to herself. He hates the way the needles point at him; point, point, point, spaz, spaz, spaz. He wants to have a go but she won't let him and she won't teach him how to do it either. He stares at her fingers, trying to pick up the sequencing, willing hers to fail, wishing it would all unravel so he could have her back again.

She knits beside the pond while he experiences zero gravity at the bottom of it. He can still see the orange of the wool, hear the click, click, click of the needles, even down here in the slimy dark. The water is cold at first, then you don't feel it. His breathing tube is an unqualified success, allowing him to remain under for long periods if necessary, though he hates the brushing of reeds and God-knows-what against his legs; he doesn't want to look or feel, he doesn't want to see or hear or know anything at all. When he comes up for air it is the flash of orange wool among the green sedge that catches his eye first. She doesn't even look up, not even when he splashes extra loud. He thinks a knitting needle could be a very dangerous thing. He wonders how long he would have to drown for before she noticed. Would she, for instance, finish her row first? He pictures himself floating, dead, while she clacks away on the bank.

He remembered his dad saying, 'A woman's attention span in minutes is less than her shoe size.' He couldn't make head or tail of that. His mind just filled up brown and dead like the pond water when he tried. Nevertheless, he sensed it didn't apply where Ann was concerned, clickety-clack.

Beneath the water the noise in his head just stopped, leaving only heartbeat and dark and weightlessness. You get used to it, the astronauts said. You get used to feeling your heart in your mouth and your brain in your feet, and not knowing if you're the right way up or not. On TV they said the Soviet cosmonauts trained in giant water tanks, and Sean gasped to think he was doing the same.

Nobody knew what the Americans did; it was secret. The space race they called it, as if everybody were ready steady go in their rocket ships.

The underwater plants reached up to touch him. When his feet found the bottom where it was shallow, he sent up clouds of silt as he panicked. He didn't want to know about the bottom, with its slime and stones and secrets. He didn't want to feel things that were in the pond and he didn't want the things to feel him either. They would leave one another alone, the pond and he. *Laid to rest*. He had heard those words spoken. He liked them. Some words made things better, like *leave no stone unturned*.

As he surfaced, Sean felt certain that she was gone. Sure enough, there was no sign of her or her orange flag. He looked up at the jet trails graffitied all over the holiday sky; they seemed to suggest just about everybody except him had buggered off.

As he climbed out Sean found himself overwhelmed by a furious, self-pitying grief. He opened his mouth to shout but only a squeak came out, the sound of which made him cry bitter tears for himself. After tears there was only anger left. He snatched at the reeds that grew in spiky clumps around the pond, though they resisted and fought back, cutting his palms and squealing their own fibrous protests. He tossed them behind him and they landed and drifted across the water. He trudged home. Though the sun was high, he remained soaked through. The birdsong seemed unusually loud, almost deafening, as if each bird had commandeered a megaphone for the job.

Ann was sitting on the wall by the school path at the bottom of George's Hill Road with a clot of other nitwit girls. Sean gathered himself, rearranged his walk, whistled something tuneless. She was throwing her orange rag about under everyone's noses, counting her stitches, showing off. The others were bent over it, looking up as they saw Sean approaching. He swung his tube and pretended not to see them until the last minute and then he had to make a pantomime of being all surprised. He overdid it, fakery wasn't his strength. Anyway, the girls laughed and so, encouraged, he laughed too. 'I never knew it was you lot, I never knew it,' shaking his head at the miracle of not knowing it. This made the girls laugh more and Sean thought things were going rather well, not too bad anyway, so he loosened his tubing and began to swing it in a big arc over his head. That shut them up; now they couldn't care less about stink knitting.

If you swung it hard enough the tube would make a weird noise, a bit like blowing in a bottle, ghostly, like something uncanny. You had to spread your feet and rotate it like a lassoo to get it going, and that's what Sean did, and it was this that collapsed the girls again. He heard them all right, but he reckoned the noise when it came would shush them, so he swung as hard as he could. Now the girls were clutching each other and laughing the way most people cried, with twisty faces and no breathing. Sean closed his eyes for concentration and prayed for the noise to come. But the girls' laughter was the only sound, snortier and gaspier, on and on.

Then the noise came. For a moment everything was just right. The sound pushed the air apart and hung there. Everyone was quiet, even the megaphone birds. It was just the noise calling, like the end of the world, and Sean's arms whirling wildly in left-handed circles, as if he were a human clock spinning backwards through time all the way to the beginning. Then they started, and it was hard to say who began because very quickly it was all the girls and their chant went: 'Spaz. Spaz. Spaz. Spaz.' Accompanied gradually by a stamp of feet and clatter of handclaps.

Sean heard the words and they seemed to fall in a loop with the revolutions of the tube until they were the same thing. And this, in a way, was fine for a while. Girls were watching, girls were clapping. If it wasn't for the S word this would be the greatest day of his life so far. Maybe for this reason, maybe to diminish the word, to spoil its impact, Sean began to chant it too.

By this stage you could hardly hear the tube noise over the Spaz chorus. The word had whipped up a spell, and it was expanding. It floated above their heads and mushroomed out towards the almost-houses and the Church of the Good Shepherd on the hill. Spaz Spaz Spaz Spaz. It bubbled and frothed and grew bigger and bigger until it hung with the dust in a dome over the estate.

Sean didn't feel his fingers release the tube, but he watched it go sailing over his head. He saw it twisting as it travelled, like one of the Dewell gang's sorry-faced adders. He walked away while the tube was still airborne. He was on the other side of the road by the time it landed. He discovered he no longer cared. What was the use of a breathing tube when you didn't deserve to live. It wasn't a question because he already knew the answer, and anyway who would he ask? The clappers and the stampers? The trick teachers with their liar alphabet? The smoky policemen in their short raincoats?

The word followed him. More chanters arrived. They came at a charge, hair flying, mouths stretched, tiddlers galloping at the back. A whole battalion of snot-faced spazzes, smeared and wild with shouting, coursing around Larkspur Way, surging up the hill. The word rained down on Sean like Lothian's arrows. He didn't want to think about whether Ann was there or not, coasting sideways in her crab run, baring her teeth, shaking her fist of knitting. He hoped she had stayed behind on the wall, finishing another row of stitches. Sean ran. He did his best style and pumped his arms. Free of his breathing apparatus, he could move as fast as the taller boys.

He panted in time with his strides. *Top. Executive. Fathead. Perk.* He headed for the farm beyond the hill, the other side of Watchet Lane. He could see an arch of light on the horizon, pink-tipped, like dragon fire, falling over the busy A-road to Great Missenden. He sprinted for it.

Sean unwrapped the next letter in the same way Miss Day had, in flourishes, with careful fingers. This one had a different flaming flipping date. Once again Sean found he could sort of read bits. Again there were some words sticking out, good ones. These were: clem. tank. sad. mo. sold. perky. lark. bell. sting. The words he didn't recognise melted away.

14th October 1942, M.E.F.

Dear Mary,
    What a joy to receive your letter! You mustn't apologise for it, Mary. It has made me very happy because, though short, it conveys a real sense of home. It was lovely to hear some news, though of course I was sad to hear that your parents remain unwell. I am sure Joseph will manage where he is, and try not to worry about Clem – at least he is not landed in a tank. I am glad to hear that Isabel's husband has found work at Naphill.
    I had thirty hours' leave last weekend and

227

went to a town some miles away, which made a nice change. A few of us went to an Arab picture house, which shows a different picture each night for about 1/-, not bad, and anyhow while I was there in town, I had my photo taken. Shall I send you one? I can't tell if it is good or bad. I shall leave you to be the judge! Speaking of which, I should so much love to have a photograph of you, Mary.

By the way, I met an Australian lecturer and writer yesterday. I did enjoy that. He was forty and had been wounded three times. I wonder if, one day, he will write about all this. I should write about it (if I were he) without a doubt.

We had a parade today and some big chappie came to speak to us. Two and three-quarter hours in the heat – several young and sporty types fainted. The M.O. advises Eno's fruit salts each morning and foot powder too.

I was interested to hear that the iron-monger has sold his business. How did the tomatoes do? Here they manage three crops in a season! How did the beans turn out with that wretched blackfly? I was glad to hear about the harvest this year. You seem to have done exceptionally well, considering. You sound very pleased about all the land girls and the commotion they cause.

Quite a lark, by the sound of it. Are there many flowers this year? In Alexandria the flower shops are crammed with roses and chrysanthemums – some an astonishing deep blue hue. You know how perky and confident a robin is in England? Well, here they are shy, always hiding. There are lots of wagtails too and plover-type birds and various types of hawk.

Did you know scorpions commit suicide? If caught in an impossible situation, it stings itself and dies instantly.

I almost forgot, there is a chap here, Frank Miller, who was born in Hazlemere! I thought the name rang some sort of bell. Please write when you get the chance. Everyone here is writing to their girls and wives. Are you my girl? I have told the others you are! Well, I must close. We are never still. Always moving on. Cheerio. Please remember me to people.

Yours, Walter xx

P.S. Hope you are able to get your shoes in next quota.

Sean liked the letters more and more. He reread the words he could understand. The others lay temptingly out of reach, fuzzy and peculiar. Still, you could build pictures: *tank enos green MO wagtalls plovertip wivers waltr. too crossis. yoo get yur shoos. nex qoota. nex qoota.* A neck scooter? There remained many mysterious unknowable things. *A rich, varied, mysterious world, son.* A mystery was meant to be solved, Sean knew that. Like the creature in the pond and the girl in the woods and the true alphabet beginning with ABC.

CHAPTER 27

'I spy with my little eye something that begins with M.'

'Myself,' grins Sankey.

'Don't be daft.'

'Marjoram,' says Walter, narrowing his eye.

'Where?' demands Mary.

'By the stile.'

'Not that, anyhow.'

'May Day parade,' suggests Sankey.

'*May Day parade*?' Walter sounds irritable. 'Where, pray, do you spy one of those?'

'I spy it in my mind's eye.'

'Play properly, Sank, or else clear off.'

Walter, Mary and Charles Sankey stop for a rest at the top of the hill, where meadowsweet, clover and heartsease grow. The wind sweeps off their hats and Mary chases after them, dipping and laughing after each as it blows along the cowslip bank. The cloud above them is stretched fleecy thin and the long grass is combed sideways in the breeze.

'Who says you may not spy articles in your mind's eye?'

'Come on. It's obvious.'

'Says who?'

'Muntjac. Muntjac? Muntjac!'

'Pride comes before a fall, Wally Wallflower.'

Sankey fancies a quick prayer, but he does not want the others to think he is all God God God, so he forgoes it. He takes out his tobacco instead.

'Where d'you reckon this baccy was grown then?'

'America of course. They have plantations, don't they, like cotton.'

Mary takes out her sampler: *Mary Hatt is my name. And with my needle mark the same. And by this you all may see. What care I take with embroidery.*

'America. There's the place for your preaching, Sank. I reckon you'd get a warm welcome there, I do. They like their worshipping, I hear. And I hear they like their grub and they aren't afraid of hard work to boot.'

'Well then. How do you know so much about it?'

'I must have picked it up, mustn't I?'

'Must've.'

Mary sings.

'Bishop Bishop Barnabee,
Tell me when my wedding shall be.
If it be tomorrow day,
Open your wings and fly away.'

She screams as her captured butterfly takes flight from her hands. She looks around. 'Did you see? I shall be married! I shall be married soon!'

'Now who's daft, eh?' Walter asks Sankey. Then

he calls out to Mary: 'That's a good bit of news then!' Only to find Sankey is watching him with a plain face and no hint of a smile. Pitysake, Walter thinks to himself, if you can't have a joke, dear me.

'Look out, else it'll be you I'm marrying!' Mary slaps Walter's cap on to his head. She tosses Sankey's bowler to him and he lunges to catch it.

'Good throw,' he says. 'And a good catch by me.'

'You've reminded me,' says Walter. 'They asked me to try out for the Hughenden eleven.'

'Bit of a cricketer are you now? enquires Sankey.

'I get by.'

'Well, if they need a bowler, you might say I'm your man.'

'You? A bowler?' Walter is amused.

'Do not mock, young man, unless you have good evidence for contradicting me.' Sankey adjusts his jacket and sniffs.

'Right then. Fair enough. Let's put it to the test.' Walter is already on his feet.

'Without a ball, Walt? Without bats? Do we bowl air, is that it?' Sankey and Mary laugh together. Mary laughs longest.

'Bowlair!' she shrieks, pointing at Sankey's head. 'You could bowl with a bowlair hat!'

'No, Mary,' Sankey laughs back. 'It is you who are the Hatt! Ha! Do you get that one? You who are the Hatt! Ha ha! Walt! Did you hear that? She said –'

'Yes, yes, I heard it.'

'Yes! And I said, It is you who are the Hatt! Ha ha!'

'And don't you call me a Mad Hatter, Charles Sankey!'

'Ha ha ha ha ha!'

'Right.' Walter has gathered some stones. He waits impatiently beside them. Sankey gasps.

'Ha ha, oh-dear-oh-dear, ha!'

Walter waits until he has their attention. He has a voice borrowed off the wireless: 'The first man bowls against the wind towards the valley. Here I have made a mark. The second man bowls next, and so on. The umpire then – I would thank you to stop grinning like an idiot please, umpire – will judge who is the winner based on points awarded for individual skill and style. Yes?'

'Yes.'

'Aye aye, sir.'

'Right. I shall bowl first. Umpire?'

Mary scrambles to her feet and hurries towards Walter.

'No, no, back, back. Over there. Stand over there.'

Mary trots backwards. Walter chooses a stone from the pile, examines it, and walks away, loosening his right arm as he goes, holding up a finger to the wind. When he is ready he turns to face the valley. He tucks the stone under his chin and waits. Mary looks at Sankey and grins. A beat and then Walter bolts forward with great long spider strides. As he nears the spot he unravels his arm as if he might very well step off the hill and float right over

234

the valley. Instead, he releases the stone in an arcing motion that starts in his shoulder, curls through, and fires the stone out of his hand. They stand and watch it sail into the valley. Over the greenness it goes, turning slowly in the empty sky.

'I can improve on that,' mentions Walter as the stone sinks out of sight, but still they wait as though they are hoping to hear the sound of the thud as it lands far below. The wind is the only sound, and then Mary's volley of handclaps.

Sankey tears towards the bowler's mark as if he has no intention of remaining on the hill a second longer. He has removed his glasses and it is possible he cannot see the mark, the valley, or the point at which his feet will leave the ground. As he releases the stone Mary shouts a great cheer, and the stone and cheer are launched together into the void as Charles stumbles blindly out of sight.

Mary claps and calls out, 'Sank! Sank! He is gone for a burton!'

Walter laughs. The silly fool has indeed rolled himself down the hill. Walter is the winner. 'Hip hip!' he calls and answers himself, 'hooray!' They will have to go looking for Sankey. They will doubtless find him on his back somewhere, in maudlin conversation with himself, or communing with his long-suffering God.

'What a twerp, eh?' But Mary is not where she stood a moment ago either. She lies on the ground, stiffened, trembling, swallowing her tongue. Walter hurries to her. He knows what to do. Mary's mother,

Ida Hatt, showed him, never once taking her eye off him as she demonstrated, leaving him feeling oddly culpable somehow, as though she doubted he would be spending any more polite time with her daughter now. It made him resolute, that suspicion that he lacked character, lacked pluck. They would see – her mother, his mother, and the others – what he was made of. They would see his bold heart, his steady hand and his poet's soul.

Walter did stray once, however, aged eighteen, while Mary was still at school. He watched her elder sister as she rode one of the Home Farm shires from the field. The sun had fallen behind the line of oaks that formed the boundary to the lower field, turning them black and scorching the sky over Spurlands End. He knew her well of course, but on this particular day Walter watched Isabel lay herself down along the broad back of the saddleless horse, so that she could watch the sky changing colour. She swung her legs to the motion of its walk, urging it on with a click of her tongue. Her hair, he noticed, fell down its flank.

There were stalls and country dancing and fancy dress when he saw her again at the Silver Jubilee celebrations held at Home Farm. Isabel was got up as Britannia. She was dancing 'Hey, Boys, Up Go We' and she clapped and stamped and picked up her dress. Walter stared until she smiled at him. When he got home he wrote:

Sunset tows her through the green,
On warm-breathed horses, like a queen,
Her feet shall tap the steps of time,
Her name shall follow, like a rhyme.

He wrote her name, *Isabel Hatt*, in small slanting letters on the envelope and imagined her opening it. He spoke his own words back to himself as he thought of her reading them. He wondered whether perhaps he ought to have written her something jollier, lighter, something amusing. It was too late. He reassured himself with the thought, borrowed from somewhere, that girls like lovelorn language and the men who speak it; and, given a choice, they would rather take a man who knew how to speak it than a man who could not.

He was wrong. Her words to him were not unkind, not complicated either. She said, 'I'm going with another boy, Walter.'

And that was that.

By the end of the week Walter discovered his feelings had changed somewhat. When he saw Isabel at the farm he was civil and she smiled sympathetically back.

'Well, well, Walter, I know you want to kiss me.' So said Mary Hatt. 'You don't love me like you should, but you will,' she said, her face side on, suspicious and satisfied both. 'I know you,' she added. 'Daft boy.' And she was right, about everything.

CHAPTER 28

Mr Denner emptied a bag of blood-stringed eyeballs on to his desk. 'Dissection,' he announced. He spoke it out in pieces as if he'd cut up the word too. To Sean it sounded like a threat. *Die sex Sean.*

You had to go and pick out an eyeball and cut it up and that was it: dissection. Before you broke up for the holidays you had to cut something up, it was part of your edyɷcæʃhon. The eyeballs had once belonged to cows. Sean looked at them spilled on the desk, staring out in all directions. He wondered if they were the cows from Grange Farm. Whether these eyeballs had looked across the Hughenden Valley or the uplands by the Four Ashes road. He wondered whether these eyeballs had watched him as he'd rushed past on his way to Gomms Wood or the tip at Widmer End. Were these the cows he'd V-signed? The ones who had watched him moonwalk in the mud? You had to team up, a younger one with an older one. He shuffled miserably forward in the queue for an eye, sickened at the thought of the task ahead. Some of the class were shrieky with excitement.

Even Mr Denner was springy on his toes. Eye after eye was claimed and carried away. 'Urgghhh!' cried the girls. Mr Denner handed out the little scalpels, one per table, and began his mantra. 'Quiet. Quiet. Don't be silly. When I say so. Put it down. Are you deaf? When I say so. *When*. I say so. Michael Millard. I won't tell you again. Quiet Quiet. Quiet Quiet.' Mr Denner sounded like one of the wading birds at the pond.

The eyeball was sticky. It trailed a pink and red thread. Sean wondered where all the other bits of the cow had gone. Into the picture boxes probably. The picture boxes contained granules that could turn themselves into dinners fit for a king. You could see the picture food on the box, glistening under candlelight: Beef Romana, it would say, or Chow Mein. When you shook the box it sounded like gravel. 'Fancy foreign,' his dad called it; 'Accelerated freeze-dried,' his mother corrected him, as if you could buckle up inside it and take off. This was astronaut food for earthlings; cubes and powder that could turn themselves into Scotch Broth or Spanish Paella.

Perhaps bits of the cows were spread for miles. It would take months to gather up all the pieces, reunite them, and anyway who would want to? Sean realised he did. He wanted to rebuild at least one cow. The eye gazed forlornly up at him. Where are all the cow's thoughts? Its memories? It was dreadful, the way the eye stared. He rolled it over so it stared instead at Mr Denner, the eyeball-gatherer, the pond-wader, whose fault all this was. Quiet Quiet Quiet.

There is a man behind the cricket pavilion. A cricketer? Sean watches him. He is alone, and as far as Sean understands it, cricketers usually operate in teams. The man is very still. He has disobeyed the sign that says 'Keep Off the Grass'. An interesting situation, Sean realises. People who disobey signs are exotic and rare and don't live in Cryers Hill. It is hard to imagine what, if anything, has caught his attention. He stands as though he sees nothing at all, like the brown-suited mannequins in the windows of Lord John in High Wycombe, frozen in their fight-or-flight poses. And another thing: the man is not wearing white; it is therefore unlikely he is here for cricketing reasons. His trousers disappear into his boots and his hat is pulled down over his eyes. He is the same colours as the hedges and the road. The man moves his hand; or maybe, Sean realises, he is just imagining that it moves. The man remains so impossibly still, your mind begins to play tricks. Best thing is to look away and blink and start again. Sean does this. The man is the same.

Sean thinks this could maybe go on for years. He shouts, 'Wur!' He can't believe he has done this. He dives for cover. He tries to mask himself behind the fence, then he scrabbles behind the cow parsley. What did you do that for? He doesn't know, he can't tell himself. 'Wur,' he says again, to himself. He still can't understand it. He feels afraid. What if the man heard him? Maybe the man didn't hear him. What if the man is coming for him? What if he gets into trouble? Whatif whatif whatif. He is going to have to look, to see if the man heard him. To see if he is still there.

Sean forces himself up so he can just see over the top of the cow parsley. The man is gone. There is just the hedge, the sky, the Keep Off the Grass sign and the cricket pavilion gawping at him through its childishly square windows. Rudyell, where's the man gone? Sean gets up and moves out from behind the parsley. Maybe the man will reappear if he stands where he was before. He feels cheated now. This is a good day going wrong. Small things can pull a day out of shape.

There is a mob of crows in the great oak, like miniature vampires, flapping about, darkening the afternoon. Sean wishes he could throw a stone, but they are too high. He throws a stone anyway, and it hits the Keep Off the Grass sign. Sean walks to the path, across the grass, beneath the giant tree, under the birds cackling. He decides that when he is grown up he will shoot crows, like farmers. Did farmers shoot crows? He didn't know any farmers to ask. He would shoot them anyway. Four and twenty blackbirds baked in a pie. What was that? A rhyme? What was it doing in his head? Who would want to eat a blackbird?

Sean lies in bed and thinks about the man. Who can he be? He is not from the estate. He is a local. Local yokels his dad calls them. Anyone who is not an estate resident is a local yokel. They are easily upset, according to Gordon. He says one night they'll come round with their pitchforks and dogs to burn down the estate and hound the residents out of the village. Sean wonders if they will have to fight them. He realises they have no weaponry other than Lothian's bow and his mother's eyelids. 'Have no fear of southern pansies,' Gor advises. It occurs to Sean that if angry yokels did come round with pitchforks and flaming torches Gor might enjoy it.

The man is a local yokel then, probably. He likely had yokel stuff on his mind, yokel stuff to do. There was a boy at school, Samuel. His dad was a farmer and his mother a farmer's wife, so they were a bit locally yokelly. The farm had gone wrong and they had no money for anything, which was why Samuel's trousers stopped above his ankles. One of their teachers, young Mr Turner, said soon there would be no farms left at all. He said it was an absolute disgrace. He said it quietly and then he turned red in the face. Mr Turner was always embarrassing himself with remarks. 'Commuter housing,' he said scornfully, reddening deeper, the colour of meat. He tried to stop himself making more remarks. He put his hand against his mouth, he clamped his teeth together, sometimes he shut his eyes, trying to switch himself off. Nobody cared about his remarks, but everyone liked to watch him having one of his red-heads. The subject didn't vary: 'This government; this country; no going back; spinning in their graves, what do you lot care?' Until he took himself off, yanked himself through the door. His punishment is a self-imposed frogmarch around the playground and an eye-burning cigarette to smoke. The class watch from the window. Sometimes you could think there were several people living inside Mr Turner and he was embarrassed by them all. He turned so red you thought his head would burst. The slightest thing brought it on: speaking, smiling, eye contact, playing guitar. He liked to play guitar. He blushed high into his sandy hairline until he looked like a haystack set ablaze.

There were two Mr Turners at school, an older and a younger. Old Mr Turner was somebody else entirely. He never turned red even when he should. Old Mr Turner had springy white hair and a tanned potato face, so they called him Tate. He taught the older children. He bounced along with his hands in his pockets. Mr Turner's hands lived permanently in his trouser pockets. They ferreted busily about for hours and only came out in an emergency, like falling down the stairs. The children sniggered at him when he sat in the classroom, pockets bulging, and they laughed as he swayed across the playground, a spring of hair adrift in the wind. If a football crossed his path he'd, quite unexpectedly, go after it, though the hands would not budge. He could sea-horse along at surprising speed after a ball. It was said his hands were in his pockets far too often. It was said that when his hands were in his pockets they were up to no good.

'Rome wasn't built in a day.' This was Gor's considered answer to a question. The question was: *When will the police catch the man?* Talking was a game of riddles, Sean can see that now. He thinks he will go and look for the cricket-pavilion man. This way he will leave no stone unturned. He will take his breathing tube. He will wear his helmet for protection.

CHAPTER 29

Walter suspects something peculiar must have happened during the Hughenden Fruit and Flower Show in aid of the church clothing club. Nothing had come on well enough at the allotment to enter, but he had got there early to compete in the flat races. He wore his father's canvas tennis shoes and indeed had won the second race in them. He had gone looking for Mary so that he might enjoy a boast. Mary was at the Comic Dog Show and had seen nothing of his heroic dash.

'Daft. Anyone can run,' she pointed out. They stood together for a while watching a pair of terriers in bonnets and matinee jackets pushing a doll's pram containing a Jack Russell in a beret. Walter couldn't help feeling downcast. She did this. You could be William Wordsworth, you could write 'Daffodils', for instance, and she would say it was just blooms, a lot of old daffs. He joined the applause for the dogs. Mary was talking, explaining.

''S'arder if you're an animal. They don't know nothing about it, do they?'

She wanted to see the Baby Show next. More bug-eyed creatures in bonnets and bibs.

'They're just babies,' Walter reminded her waspishly.

'Wally-Walt, they're not *just* babies, they're the me-s and you-s in this valley for tomorrow and after.'

This was another deeply irritating thing about Mary Hatt. She could trump you with an observation. She could make a remark she was in no position to make. She would make them when you least expected. Loving Mary Hatt was complicated and difficult; not loving Mary Hatt was complicated and difficult.

The babies all looked the same to Walter but Mary was transfixed. She laughed and pointed and cooed, and when she got close enough she squeezed their pudgy hands and wobbled her head until they laughed.

'Look, Walt! Oh, look at this bonny boy! Ha ha.'

Walter took her hand. Mary put her head on his shoulder.

'Married within the year!' Mrs Bates said, pointing at them, fanning herself, raising her voice. 'If these two aren't married within the year I shall want to know why!' Embarrassed, Walter dropped Mary's hand and everyone heckled and cheered.

Aside from all the fruit and flowers on display, there were refreshments for sale. Walter and Mary sat beneath the trees to drink ginger beer and eat fruit bread. Before long they were joined by

Sankey, carrying a cherry cake in a cloth as though it were the King's own crown.

'I was looking for you,' he said.

'Well, now you have found us,' replied Walter. 'Let's have a look at that cake then.'

'Mrs Ford baked it. She charged me five bob.'

'She saw you coming, Sank.'

'Is that so? You won't be laughing once you've tried it.'

Walter realised he must have fallen asleep when he awoke to discover himself alone in the cool shadow of the giant tree. Mary and Sankey were gone; the cherry-cake cloth was folded neatly on the flattened grass where they had sat.

Walter took himself off to view the fruit and flowers. He noted some good specimens and admired the winners in the various categories, particularly the dahlias, sweet peas and roses, and the displays of beautiful Black Heart cherries, Laxton's gages and yellow speckled Williams' pears.

During the sack race Walter skirted the boundary of the field. There were some fine oak trees there and an old ditch that had become a stream full of tadpoles and minnows. There appeared no sign of either Mary or Sankey. Where had they got to?

During the bowling for a pig, which Mary always enjoyed, Walter crossed to the other boundary. The hedges were clogged with nests and lush with creeping roses and wild honeysuckle. He lit his pipe. The shouts and cheers from the crowd drifted over. Mary Mary, quite contrary. Sometimes he thought p'raps he ought to simply marry Sylvia, the butcher's daughter, and have done with it. Perhaps then things would be straightforward instead of tangled. But then he thought of her father's shop, with its hooks and heads and hooves and how he really would be trapped then, hooked and hung like a bacon pig for the rest of his life. The clatter of distant applause roused him. There was the ladies' three-legged and ladies' skittles coming up and he knew Mary would not want to miss them. He walked back towards the crowd.

'Where are your raspberries this year then?' Harry Dugden was a committed competition grower and Walter always did his best to avoid conversation with him, as it was only another type of competition in itself.

'Nothing come up this year, Harry.'

'Nothing? Bit of care and attention. Raspberry is kinder nor the damson is. Now, my harvest better than last. Seen my roseberries? Bit o' muck helps. You want to point on next year. I seen your friend there staring like scissors.'

'Where? Where did you see her?'

'Ah. I'll lay a bob on ye and she. No harvest? Ha!'

Walter turned to walk away.

'In the birch coppice. I saw her.'

Walter considered returning to the hedge where he'd left his bicycle. Might as well clear off home. Then again.

The copse of birch and hazel lay to the east of the field. Walter couldn't imagine why Mary would be there, though he knew somehow that she was. A slight incline tipped him towards the woodland, hurrying him at a quicker pace than he wanted to go, suggestive of urgency when he wished to display nonchalance. As he entered the copse, a mistle thrush burst out, rattling its alarm call over his head. Walter stood for a moment within the trees, listening to the accordion tune that had started in the field behind him until his eyes adjusted to the gloom. He stepped only a couple of paces and there she was on the ground, grinning up at him.

'Wally Wally Wallflower,' she said through her jumble of teeth.

'What are you doing there?' he asked stupidly.

'Looking for buried gold.'

A twig broke behind her. There was somebody else there, hidden behind the brush and fern. Walter yearned to be somewhere, anywhere else. He turned, dismayed, acutely embarrassed, and hurried away. He bumped himself and tore some ivy as he went.

'Walt! Walt! Walt!'

Walter ran up the incline towards the noise and music. He deserved this, thoroughly. He wondered why he felt so distressed, so queasy. She was following him, making everything worse, calling his name. Now the whole village would know. Walter made for the small tent where Fred and Len Page were selling their home-brewed beer to any man old enough to drink. Walter bought a small one and downed it. Not bad, foam like soapsuds across the top, but otherwise not bad. He bought another and lit his pipe, which was the only way to stand the intensity of the smoke inside the tent. Mary could not follow him here; it was gentlemen only. Mary could go to hell.

'Well, well, Walter Brown. Anything to tell of Wycombe town?' John Roach had a slow, careful speaking style that Walter found reassuring. Roach had been head carter in his heyday; he sat in pubs and tents and fields and told his leisurely stories through a fleece of smoke.

As they spoke, a team for tug of war was identified. And two teams it was that finally emerged like the Devil's own smithies wrapped in smoke, red-eyed and shirtless. Walter reckoned, with the powers invested in him by the home brew, that he would know at a glance who had snapped the twig in the birch coppice. He caught sight of Mary with her dress hitched up around her knees. She was in a line-up of local girls all flashing their legs for the Ladies' Ankle Show. She was turning this way and that, posing, laughing like a drain. Just now Walter felt he could pull a ropeful of men from here to Derbyshire. They spat on their palms and checked to see the ladies were watching. Stanley Gunn positioned the middle of the rope on its mark and counted them in: one, two, three, heave!'

Far away down the rope Walter saw the thin, curved comma of Sankey's body. He watched his face strain as he pulled his pigeon weight for the opposing team – *heave, heave* – and he realised (though he stood under a boiled sun, full of beer suds, and could not know anything for certain) that there was a devil's chance Charles Sankey was responsible for the broken twig and everything that followed. As their ale-soaked team pulled Sankey's mob over the line, Walter found himself wondering whether he might break his friend's nose and defame his God and perhaps never speak with him again.

Hilda Brown scrubbed, dusted, sluiced, beat and polished seven days a week. This was what she did. She suspected it was all right to do the silver on a Sunday in spite of what it said in Exodus 20: verses 1–17. She did all these things just the same as her mother had done, aided here and there by an innovation, like washing detergent or a carpet sweeper. Laundry on a Monday, baking on a Thursday. She did the windows in all weathers, particularly at the front. A clean house was a clean soul, something to be proud of. Locally Hilda was admired for her inability to stop cleaning. It was her badge of honour. In spite of this, it gave her little or no satisfaction. The baking, perhaps she enjoyed that, and the redisplayed silver when it was all done and ready to blind anyone who entered, none of the rest. 'This house will kill me,' she liked to warn. 'Sooner or later,' was her murmured calculation, while casting a critical eye over the china and glass, as though she didn't want the house to hear. 'It will run me into the ground. You will come home one day to find me lying here dead.'

'I don't know why you bother,' Walter commented. 'It's just us two.'

'I'm only doing the necessaries as it is,' she responded icily. 'Do less and idle in squalor.' She said it proudly; she was a martyr. She had won that round. Just so.

He thought if overwork was killing her, then underuse was doing for him. He neither liked nor disliked his job; while realising he was fortunate to have it, he would not have objected to a circumstance which removed it entirely from his life. Likewise his cricket, rabbiting, the allotment too. He would keep his two pints of ale a week and his books of poetry. The rest could go to the Devil. He was ashamed to admit it, but he suspected he was a poet born. And what was wrong with that? He wished he had a close friend his own age who shared his passion, but he was unlike any of the other local boys he'd grown up with. They all seemed content with their lives, their apprenticeships, their fathers' footsteps; long ago he had stopped trying to pretend he was one of them. The fledgling shopkeepers, farmers, farriers, clergymen, craftsmen and orchard foremen – none as far as Walter could see had any reservations about their predefined roles or sought to question them. It was just him, the malcontent, the sole misshape, the glitch in the machine.

It was entirely possible, he decided, that he was the only twenty-year-old poet in England, Scotland, Ireland and Wales. If there were another, he mused, '*but one other,*' then I should put my arm around his shoulder, and he would put his arm around mine. Walter leaned against a giant beech. This was what poets did, they leaned against towering trees; only farmers and shepherds leaned on gates. And he consoled himself with the thought that in a hundred years people might know his name and admire his stanzas. Surely he would travel far and wide, he wished more than anything for this. He would compose verses to celebrate things the crowd around here would never see, never dream of seeing. How small their lives were, how repetitive and narrow. Apart from crops, livestock, seasons, weather, what was there? You could expect the odd fayre or sale, funerals and births, the odd bloody accident with a horse or bull or machine and the nocturnal gin-trap screams. And the green of course. The green would always be there. You could grow tired of it as a matter of fact. Walter found himself longing instead for desert, fjord and mountain pass.

CHAPTER 30

Sean saw the figures every day, standing in the unfinished houses. Like Ann, Sean noticed, they had taught themselves not to blink. They stood gazing out of the gaps that would one day be windows and doors, across the dust-crater landscape that was home. They stood in the naked roofs, leaning against timbers, or staring up the hill towards the church. Motionless, expressionless, each gazed out in its own lonely direction. They paid no attention to Sean, even when he threw a stone at them, even as it ricocheted off the rafters or clattered down the stairs beside them: the figures never moved a muscle, never turned their heads to look.

The figures could make themselves disappear. When Sean crept up, they were gone by the time he got there. If he blinked, if he looked twice, they would be gone, just like that, revealing themselves on closer inspection to be merely a flap of tarpaulin, an abandoned hod, a huddle of planks with numbers on, tied with twine.

They can read my mind, he thought, and turn themselves into wood and stone. No one else could see the figures. Sean didn't understand why they would not appear for Ann, who shared personal characteristics with them and would not have been afraid. But though she stared till brick-dust tears ran down, they would not come. Sean could not hide his disappointment. He threw bigger and bigger missiles at them and finally refused to look at them any more. They were not people, he told himself; they were not real people.

They started to talk. Just hums and ticks initially, then words, and finally strings of words, and often all at once. He pressed his fingers in his ears and blah-blahed so as not to hear them. He said a prayer to make them stop. They went quiet for a while after that. Then one morning they began to sing *There's a hole in my bucket, dear Liza, dear Liza.* The sound was beautiful, like seraphs or mermaids, it rose up into the dust-bowl sky. Sean ran away. He ran until he could no longer hear singing or see bricks or taste dust.

He sat on a farmer's gate and thought three things. That love was hard, that life was harder, and that God seemed not remotely fussed either way. He felt no wiser for thinking these things. The things that you thought did not make you clever, he knew this. Reading, writing, arithmetic made you clever. Knowing answers, knowing how to spell them. It was certainly not clever to question the answers, or argue with the facts, this was not clever at all. And you didn't want to know too many answers or else you would be too clever by half. It was all right to be a clever dick, but you didn't want to be a proper little clever dick. Are you trying to be clever, Sean Matthews? No. Godnose.

The cows stopped chewing. They stared, affronted, scandalised, in Sean's direction. What was it with cows? Why was everything incomprehensible to them? Matter-of-fact things like a boy, a streaker, or a milk float left them stumped, and yet they knew if it was going to rain after lunch.

If there were no answers in his head then what was there? Rubbish probably, like off the tip. Bits and bobs: a load of scrapings and buckled prams. Best thing was to keep your mouth shut in case a bit of peel or wheel poked out and then everyone would know. Sean thought he would sit on the gate and fire off some arrows, perhaps at the cows, and wait for the streaker.

No streaker came. They did not come every day of course, they did other things. They had days off probably. Sean tried to imagine what they did on such days. Streaking – maybe streaking was what they did on their days off? Of course. He had it all backwards. He couldn't think of the sort of job a streaker might have. Lifeguard? He would not give up. He would catch his streaker. It was just a matter of time.

Sean remembered then that Miss Day's first name was Shara, which, like her hair, was beautiful, a thing from the *Arabian Nights*. Sean thought it was the most beautiful word he'd ever heard; he thought how well it went with Sean: ʃhaɾa and ʃhauɾn For ever. He wished he could write it everywhere for people to see, like the spray words at the bus shelter. Miss Day had said to Gor, 'Call me Shara, please,' and Gor had carefully mispronounced it, twice, to demonstrate his disapproval of such names.

In fact, Miss Day was from Amersham and her real name was Sarah. She had moved the h. Plucked it from the back and placed it at the front, where it promised sunsets, horsemen and spontaneous happenstance. This was what happened when you moved a letter; things went differently. Sean wondered if anyone else had ever moved a letter to somewhere else in their name. He had thought you weren't allowed.

During the nuclear-attack drill at school, Sean recalled, you had to put your arms over your head and get on the floor under the tables. You could see the girls' knickers and you could watch Miss Day's freckled legs scissoring past as she taped up the windows, the groove of her calf muscle curving out against the long straight bone of her shin. You could listen to the metronome tap of her heels and her cheerful voice that swooped up and down like a garden swing. Sean hoped there would be another nuclear-attack drill soon. After all, you couldn't be too careful.

For every grain of sand on earth, there are a million stars in space. Sean couldn't remember if this was the truth or a song, or whether he'd just made it up. He thought, if it were true, then it would be impossible for anyone ever to count all the stars, astronaut or not. He considered how terrible it would be, having reached three million thousand, whatsit and something, for an astronaut to suddenly lose count. This was what training was all about; not making mistakes. You couldn't let your mind wander off. You couldn't start thinking about whatifs or God or girls.

23rd December 1942, M.E.F.

Dear Mary,

Well, we have arrived at Tobruk, fearfully dirty and weary. Libya is much nicer than Egypt, Mary. The air is better and you lose the flat desert and gain miles of farmsteads, white with fire ovens outside. The ground seems fertile, a deep brown-red sand. There are fig trees and beautiful wild flowers in the rocks.

We found Benghazi abandoned, a shambles, just a few ragtag Libyans left. We are eating the tinned Jerry foods, they are rather good.

There was an air raid last night and we brought a plane down – all very exciting while it lasted. It dropped like a red-hot coal on fire. We are camped on the battleground. Half-sunken ships litter the small distant harbour. In an air raid Jerry flares look like Japanese lanterns in the sky.

Fletcher has an ear abscess. M.O. says one of his eardrums has gone. There is miles of mined ground, each bang reminds you of them. I wonder where our next place will be? A transit camp some say. The word is we are going to El Duba via Bang el Arab. We rarely stay in one place long. Our troop sergeant is in hospital as he is severely burned. Arthur has boils like many others. I am taking Yeastvite to avoid them.

Guess what? We have all been saving 2d a week towards Christmas, so we can buy some extras. Me and the lads have been digging a table in the sand, with a trench all around, and petrol tins filled with sand for chairs – all ready for Christmas Day. We have 4 turkeys, a piece of pork, an orange, 2 bottles of beer, and 50 cigs. If the wind keeps down it will be a treat for us all!

I wish I could be there with you to hear the church bells ringing. I'll bet they sound sweet as ever. Merry Christmas, Mary. And a Happy New Year.

God bless you. Cheerio for now.
Yours, Walter xx

P.S. You won't believe me, but there is a word in Arabic: Hatt. Yes, truly. It means: Bring me. And so my dearest, hats off to that! And hatt home soon.

Sean reckons he will write letters one day. Maybe he will just copy out waltrs. Sean has a plan. It has formed in his head while he was doing other things. He must have narrowed his genius eye. Wur.

CHAPTER 31

A flock of at least a thousand sparrows rises off a field of wheat. Walter stops to watch. Pests they were to farmers, though not as bad as pigeons. Hard to credit the way a flock of birds can move together, like fish in a shoal, funny. This was a habit peculiar to fish and birds, and certain herd animals, but it was not in men's nature to stick together this way. The military had to train it into their recruits. Here on this lane at the right time of year you could pick blackberries and loganberries, fill a basket if you liked. Plenty of fruit on the ground in the orchards off Coombe Lane too. No one need starve around here, not like those in the cities, the unemployed. Walter read the newspaper, he knew about the cities, the shipbuilding, the unemployment, and the rise of an Austrian corporal named Adolf Hitler.

Here on the left was the acreage set aside for swede and turnip, waiting to be flat-hoed and singled, and further on lay the field set aside for the cattle-feed mangolds. Soon they would start on these, hoes tied with binder twine to their cycle crossbars. A rainbird calls. Rain is coming, you know it if you hear the green woodpecker laugh, though rain is nothing to laugh about before harvest. A proper rainstorm will flatten a field of corn and money a farmer thought was in his pocket is suddenly there no more.

If you are downwind, around this corner you will often see hares boxing in the meadow; all for a doe of course. Walter has been known to watch the bucks kick and jump until he is too tired and hungry to watch them any longer. Leverets came in early spring, he knew that. He had seen them, newly born, running with their mothers. Open-eyed they were at birth, with glossy coats. A hare can snap the wire in a man-made snare with his kicking; better, some think, to tangle him in a gate net: though when you hear him scuffle you'd better be quick to chop him hard and break his neck. That is what Sankey said, and he should know. If you must strike him twice, get on with it. He added that, as if he didn't expect for a moment that Walter would be any good.

Walter has seen the hare man. He works alone with a dog. He carries a dead hare by its ears, and Walter wondered about that until he mentioned it to Mary. 'Daftie. You want blood in his belly, don't you, for soup.' And he felt like a twerp then, for asking.

There is a time to go out after rabbit and hare, Sankey says. Wait for a moonlit sky that shows you cloud, but not the lines on your palm. And breeze that sounds like surf in the trees.

They were ploughing with tractors around here nowadays. John Dean, known as Jondy, said the iron seat hurt his rear chronic, even through a sack of straw. His father had been a first-class ploughman and won plenty of competitions in his day. The birds still followed the plough, horse or tractor, they weren't fussed. They hung like gulls above a trawler, settling noisily on each swell of soil, floating to the next, levitating in the breeze. Starlings, rooks, chaffinches, green- finches, black-headed gulls, the pied wagtails at the back, dipping and bobbing like busy waiters. In the old days a ploughman would have dragged these birds up and down a field all day and the next too. Two horses you needed around here for a single furrow, because of the soil, the inclines. After ploughing came cultivating with a grubber, then harrowing, then rolling. Nothing ever finished, it only kept on turning over like the clay earth itself. No time to stand by and say, well, here am I, an important man. Weather was important, more like. Reducing vermin was important. Disease was important: don't get any. No individual man or woman, unless they had station, could call themselves important here. It was the place itself carried all the importance for everyone; in the chalk-flecked soil, in the ruts, hills, valleys, woods.

Walter pushes through the broom and giant cow parsley, snagging his sleeve on the barbed wire he declined to notice. Good piece of corduroy gone to nothing. He'd thought corduroy was robust, like India rubber. There is a thin violet light, swallows dipping in the valley and a spark of orange over the foundry. Dairymen would be finished. Nearby a thrush squeezes out a tune. *It is for you the nightingale sings her song.* Somehow he misses her company when she is elsewhere. It is mysterious. I love you, Mary Hatt. It sounds cheerful. He will not say it though, not yet. Along with the hills and farms she will still be here tomorrow. His life lies stretched out before him and he does not want to shorten it by racing on ahead and missing the good parts.

Sankey, meanwhile, was returning from a house call; a widow with three unmarried daughters in Naphill who was losing her sight. She had a son too, a farm labourer who, finding himself injured, had been sacked while owed a month's salary. Sankey read to the widow from Revelation and offered a buoyant prayer, but it was the Agricultural Labourers' Union and the Central Wages Board the family really needed over a well-meaning Methodist in a bowler hat.

Em and Eff Rackstraw always wore the same black coats their long-dead mother had made them. Em, tall and stooped, would add a set of jet beads around her neck, while Eff, short and dumpy, preferred a piece of rabbit fur at her throat. Em and Eff had never married. They always walked in single file, one behind the other, no matter how much space was available. They drifted along, their coats dark against the snowy blitz of fruit-tree blossom whirling in the wind. Walter considered that one day they would make an excellent pair of ghosts. It occurred to him then that perhaps they were ghosts already; never having heard either one speak, never having received more than a nodded greeting, he realised this was entirely possible. He waited until they had floated away into the blossom blizzard before he fetched his notebook:

> Through the foam of winter snow
> Beyond the raging gale
> Two sisters tread a glassy path
> Their passing leaves no trail.

> Twin spectres,

His mother startled him. 'I'm not sure you want to be doodling away at your age, Walter. Ham is on the table, the pot is warmed. There are those who would say it is just childish.'

Walter folded the notebook away. 'Which it is, very,' she added. 'Bread and butter?' The pencil fell from his hand and as he bent to retrieve it he was overwhelmed by a sense that it was pointless to straighten up. Perhaps he would lie here for the rest of his life, inexplicably paralysed. What a pity, they would say. His poems were excellent.

'Your father had dreams.' His mother said this as though dreams were haemorrhoids. She helped herself to bread and butter and made a bell-ringing session out of stirring her tea.

'Dreams are for children and cripples,' she said through her mouthful. 'A young man such as yourself cannot gad about dreaming. People will think you peculiar.'

Walter declined to answer, it was his only hope of dignity. He chewed his bread and butter with his mouth closed and stirred his tea without releasing a single chime.

His mother blinked towards the window and swallowed noisily. 'The trouble with dreamers is they think themselves more important than other people,' she said. 'As if dreams were food on the table and shoes on feet.' She took a scoop of black cherry jam from the pot and licked her finger. 'Don't be led astray by fancies, son. It's only vanity. Vanity will lead you a merry dance and leave you penniless in the end, mark my words.'

'Not all writers are penniless, you know.' Walter spoke it with as much pitying condescension as he could muster. Even as he said it he thought of William H. Davies, known as the tramp poet by many, referred to as such in poetry publications. His mother drained her teacup.

'I dare say,' she replied, 'there are some that have family money. Don't throw your life away on fancies.'

CHAPTER 32

The day had started badly. Sean had stood staring outside Ann's house until she came out and then they walked to the top of the hill by the church. Sean had a plan, but before he had the chance to boast of it to Ann, things began to slide. Some boys were hanging around, breaking things. One of them, with long arms and hair in his eyes, threw some gravel at Sean. He did it to impress Ann, Sean suspected. Ann smiled at the boy, a sort of grateful smile it was, as though something had been understood. Sean was not supposed to see the smile, it was for the boy only. A thought popped into Sean's head; it was about an animal who ate her babies, a turtle was it? A mouse? He tried to remember.

Now all the boys were throwing gravel. Sean put his hands in his pockets and pretended not to notice. A mouse? It could have been a mouse. The gravel stung, so he walked away towards the church, pretending to look at it, examining its cement corners as though he'd never seen it before, craning his neck to get a better view of the bell and iron cross that he saw every day, same as he saw the sky and the moon and his own smeary hands. The boys threw more gravel. It rained down like freak weather, as though all of Sean's bad luck had turned into a thousand sharp teeth. Ow. Yes, it was a mouse and she ate all her babies, that was it. There were tears in his throat now, rudyell. Don't cry Spaz all right don't cry you spazzing squirt. He thought of Ann's smile to the boy, the way it slid, like something submerging. The stones were stinging through his clothes, bouncing off his skull. He watched them landing and rolling as if they were alive; it made him think of insects. Sean ran. Some gravel followed, like a killer swarm, and then stopped. Sean ran on. The sound of his plimsolls, ack, ack, ack, was like a machine, like a long-distance runner: he loved this sound.

At the bottom of Campion Road Sean sees Rob Boyles sitting on the kerb with his chin on his knees. Beside him lies a long stick. Rob Boyles has trouble saying his name and other words. Sean reckoned 'Rob' was simple enough to say. 'Boyles', what could be difficult about that? Sean slows down.

'RobBoylesRobBoylesRobBoyles.' Sean says it aloud with his chin high, so that the words fall down mockingly on Rob's head. Well, what did he expect?

Sean waits but Rob does not look up. A breeze pulls the dust on the tarmac towards them. It gives off a fine spray as it moves, and then the breeze pushes it back again, like a tide. Sean looks at the stick. Rob lifts it and lays it across his knees. The heat presses them deeper into the tar.

Sean is transfixed by the top of Rob's head. In his hair are dozens of red crusts where he has picked and scratched and bled. Some crusts have oozed into others, forming larger ones that look like volcanic lava. Across his scalp there are lumps, bumps and craters. Rob looks up. Sean puts his hands on his hips so that Rob will see a runner standing there, tall and strong, with no time for this sort of thing. Rob sees Sean's helmet of yellow hair blazing under a noon-day sun.

'I was wondering where that was.' Sean kicks the stick with his toe.

It is a fine stick, dark and heavy and kinked at its middle, suggestive of a rifle.

'Mine.' Rob says the word perfectly well, though he knows the stick no longer belongs to him. He speaks the word to the stick, without eye contact, so that Sean knows he can take it without a fight, and so he does, examining it carefully first and then raising it to his shoulder.

'I've been looking for that stick.'

Rob knows better than to call a liar a liar. I am a long-distance runner, thinks Sean. I am Danger Man. I've got a stick.

'OK, Spaz? Cheerio then.' And he raps Rob smartly on the head with the gnarled end.

Over the course of two hundred yards the day

269

has improved immensely. Sean runs, ack, ack, ack, his stick on his shoulder and a plan in his head. This day is turning out all right. He has survived gravel and now he has a stick. Out there are murderers, streakers, water serpents and loons. He will hunt them down and return a hero. They will clap, cheer, everyone. They will pat his back, shake his hand. Girls will rest their heads upon his shoulder. The flash from the newspaper camera will dazzle his eyes, and Ann will kiss his lips.

Sean lies on his back in the long grass. In his head he has saved the world from myriad threats and now he is tired. He has his plan, but he must rest first. The grass is so tall that Sean has disappeared. He listens to the hiss of breeze moving towards him and the scrape and click of insects. He can see nothing but pointed blade tips and the broad sky.

He wonders when he will get to the bottom of Ann. 'You'll never get to the bottom of a female,' his dad told him. 'Women are bottomless pits.'

Nevertheless there have been some improvements lately, this cannot be denied. As Andy Williams himself sings, 'Love is a Many Splendoured Thing.'

There cannot be a man in the moon, Sean realises as he dozes off, because if there were the astronauts would have found him there. It was just a tale, like Father Christmas, a fib, like the liar alphabet.

Things change while you sleep. When Sean wakes he discovers the sun has swung itself into the wood and is busy burning up the trees. The sky above him has grown burrs of wispy cloud and the high grass no longer burns but is dingy and cold. Sean has a feeling he has missed something important. He examines his hands for a nail to chew. He wonders if anyone has died while he's been asleep. It is possible.

He hears a scream. He waits in case the scream is in his head. The scream comes again and this time it shushes the birds. Sean buries his head in the grass. Who would scream and why? There is only one answer and here he is alone, drowsy, with no nails left to bite. No more screams come. A single bird begins a tentative song, a burbling tune with excessive tremolo. Sean reckons there is a story about a child fallen asleep in a cornfield who gets chopped up by a combine harvester. He stands up.

'Spaz!'

It is her voice. She is by the elm trees in Foxes Field, her hair flying from running. Even from here he can see she is grinning. Bludyell. Sean lifts his stick rifle and aims. She is coming; her elbows float above the tall grass and her mouth is speaking. About him probably, about spazzery. Sean cannot hear the words. He shoots. Bang bang pop pop you're dead I'm not.

> Marry Ann,
> Oh marry Ann,
> Oh won't you *Bang*! *Gotcha*!
> marry me?

Here she comes walking and talking. By the time she arrives she will have stopped all that. She will be watchful and will not blink. Ann would make an excellent dead girl. And she'll say nothing at all, except 'Spaz'. Reminding him, like that. Then she'll take over. She'll pocket his afternoon and all his thinking thoughts and it will become her afternoon, her grass, her sky, all hers. She will take his stick and he will fall in behind her and follow like a child, like a naked ape.

He hates her. He should hit her with the stick and that would be that. If it were a gun, this stick, he would shoot her, yes he would. He would shoot her all over, like in that film, but mostly he would shoot her smile off, that would be first. He would shoot the smile right off her face, leave it lying in the grass. Shooting was nothing to laugh about.

'Where'f you bin?'

'That's for me to know.'

Ann falls down in the grass, like he has already shot her. He checks in case there is blood. It is possible to do things without knowing you've done them, like when his mother clouts him over the head for something he did earlier, or his dad clouts him for something he did not do at all. Or sometimes his mother will arrive in a room and not know why she is there. Why am I here? she will say. And nobody will be able to tell her. Out she will go again to try and discover. Sometimes she never discovers why and it just goes down as another one of life's mysteries.

Ann lies in the grass. Her mouth is slightly open and she is staring at the sky as though something significant is about to happen there. Sean reckons if aliens were about to land then Ann would know about it. They would inform her in advance. He follows her gaze. The cloud has formed in loops, like a giant net. Sean imagines that Ann will almost certainly become a spy when she grows up. Spies can spear you with poison umbrellas; there was one in the newspaper.

Ann closes her eyes. Gor says the female skull is smaller than the male. This is due to the fact that the male brain is larger than the female brain. Sean lies down beside Ann. If he has the bigger brain then why is she so difficult to understand? He knows she knows it all. The sun bakes them into the ground like fossils. Sean closes his eyes and feels the earth whip beneath them. Maybe they will be discovered here in a thousand years, their bones grown into the hill, like those fish bones in rocks. Maybe they will go in a museum and people will say, Oh look, a girl and a spaz.

'Would you rather burn to death or drown?'

Sean tries to think. 'Drown.'

'Me too.'

There is a quiet then. Sean wonders with dread if God is writing it down.

'Would you rather be dead or crippled?'

'Dunno. Crippled.'

He speaks quickly and quietly in the hope that an Almighty God, even one with sonic hearing,

273

won't catch it. This is just talking anyway, chatting for heaven's sake. Surely He doesn't expect people to mean every little idle thing they say.

'Anyway, you can kiss me if you want, I don't mind.'

Sean waits. This is the kind of thing his brain does in spare moments. Voices that sound real that are only in his head, thoughts that run amok and turn themselves into remarks, laughter, screams.

'Well, hurry up.'

There is still no hard evidence that Ann is actually speaking.

'Where then?' Clever. A way of testing.

'What on the lips stupid bludyell Sean, you're so spaz.'

It is really happening. She actually spoke the kiss words. Maybe there will be an alien invasion after all. It is the only thing weirder than this. Here is a thing: *The male and the female Homo sapiens are behaviourally unique on earth.* Gor had pronounced it. It had tumbled out of his mouth like one of the estate bricks and lay on the floor for everyone to step over. Except for Gor, they couldn't care less about such things in their house. Gor liked to potter about in evolutionary science the same way other men liked to potter about in sheds, or tinker with cars. Gor pottered and tinkered with his apemen and his bones in Africa and his pigeons on aerials. It pops into Sean's head now, the Homo sapiens thing. Time to be uniquely Homo sapiens, hurry up. On the lips, stupid.

He feels air pressing on his eyelids, on the top of his skull, squeezing his heart. A loop of it has found its way inside his stomach and is pulling up a drink he's forgotten he's had. It is hard to know which way is up and which is down.

'Go on then.'

'I am.'

'Well, hurry up.'

'I am.'

It is possible this will be his one and only chance. He has to keep his eye on the ball, that's all. A small step, a giant leap, he can do it. He has begun his descent. There were no second chances over the Sea of Tranquillity, they just had to put it down, Neil and Buzz, in front of the whole world. There is that bird again, the one who sounds as if it is warbling through water. The trees and the grass turn to water too, rippling and rushing, filling his ears with trick sounds. The sun is burning the back of his head as his lips touch hers; he thinks maybe there will be a scorch there later, or a word.

She closes her eyes just before, he sees them close, twin hatches, as his kiss arrives on her mouth. Not a kiss, a landing. Once he is there he gives up. He waits on her lips as if someone has pulled the wind-up key out of his back. There is no more information, there are no clues about where to go from here. The warbly bird sings on. He can feel Ann's teeth and the lap of her tongue. Her tongue is cooler than his; it hurries around his own limpid one, making him think of sock puppets. A sock puppet? I'll give you a bloody sock puppet in a minute. He is aware that his body is doing things by itself now while his large brain looks on in astonishment. He feels his hips hard against hers and heat inside his bones. He can feel her sigh; it raises him up at least an inch and he thinks, oh God, now she will roll her eyes, yes of course, and laugh, and he will be the biggest spaz who ever fell on a girl's lips. But instead she breathes out a long gasp. And when she opens her eyes she says, 'Sean, do you love me?'

January 1943, M.E.F.

My dearest Mary,

I hope this finds you well and not too chilly there at home. Those land girls must be wishing they were tucked up inside a munitions factory by now! I was relieved to hear that John is thoroughly improved. The increased herd, being useful, as you say, has put him right.

I am dug well in, as there is a smell of death on the air. Jerry is really trying to trouble us and bombs are dropping all over the place. The Colonel came and there has been action all day. The big push has started. We had a church service on the sand today, which was good. Then we found some Jerry food which we ate; it was delicious. There is a lot of night-strafing. A little kiddie has just been buried nearby (bomb blast), such a little mound.

A huge pile of post has come in! Will I be lucky?

Later:

Exceptionally lucky as it turns out, as I have three letters. Best of all one from you, also one from Mother, and one from Uncle Gerald. Well, I am very proud to think of you training hard at Valley Road Garage. A mechanic! Are they lucky to have you? I should say so! It sounds as though you are learning fast, Mary. Soon you will be a first-class mechanic – what a turn-up for the books. True to say this war is doing strange things to the world.

The winter cauliflowers sound all well and good, a credit to you, and not easy to grow. You say the beetroots are small but healthy. Did you give them any salt? Manure will enrich the soil, but you will have to be careful in applying it as it burns so.

A Shakespearean storm earlier: sand everywhere, thunder, wind, lightning. It gives you the pip. One of ours was killed in a booby trap this afternoon. He thought he'd found a battery and picked it up – it exploded, leaving him in pieces. We're told repeatedly not to pick up things of course.

Not much of a New Year for him. Everywhere smells of shot, shell and corpse – and everywhere lie the discarded implements of battle. Here and there are crosses (Australian, English, German graves) all entangled – apart in life, together in death.

Sorry to be so down and dreary, Mary. My head appears to be in a brain muddle for some reason and I don't want to put you off with my ramblings. I've been in the dumps but everything is OK now.

I can't remember whether I mentioned I found a jar containing a set of false teeth and a scorpion? Also, did I tell you I saw *In the Navy* with Abbott and Costello, in Alexandria? Anyhow, I killed a rat beside my bed last night.

I have no more light to write by.

Ana mamnoon lak for being you. I think of you all the time.

Yours, Walter xx

P.S. Did you receive my photo I sent you? Perhaps you are too polite to comment on it. Oh dear! Well, the dust and heat do make us all appear jaded.

CHAPTER 33

Harry Styles owns the brick foundry. He has no sons, though he does have a cine camera. There is a sign up outside the Grove Road Stores. It says:

To the Village Residents: You are Invited to Gather at this Spot at 9 o'clock on Saturday the 14th of June for the Purpose of a Village Photograph. Attendance is Optional. Filming by Harry Styles and his Cine Camera.

Harry Styles is a cine-photography enthusiast. He taught himself to use the camera and is now quite adept. In the beginning he filmed only the works at the foundry, reel after reel of black-and-white furnace heat, leaping sparks and faces gathered around a cigarette. Then he filmed each of his daughters as they came along, his dogs, and his hunting horse. Now he films things that don't belong to him, ordinary village things: children, arguments, bicycles and the sawing down of the diseased tree at Scratch Corner. Nobody has escaped the sleek eye of his mysteriously glassy contraption. He will film man, beast, machine and weather without a thought for who will want to watch this stuff.

There are those who do not wish to be filmed and some who reckon they will remonstrate with Mr Styles when he points his camera at them and their private business. Nobody does, however. Once they see Mr Styles with the thing to his eye and realise it is busy noting the best and worst of their attributes, manners and all, they soon come round. Most people smile, or pretend to. And there is a good deal of last-minute spit-licking and smoothing down. Everyone knows that appearance tells a story, and demeanour too. The camera will judge in an instant; it will identify the decent from the not-quite-so-decent and those from the God-awfully indecent. All in all the appearance of the cine camera is apt to produce the best in the residents of Cryers Hill, even as they are proclaiming not the slightest interest in the thing.

Harry Styles manages to carry his camera, his tripod and his lunch on his bicycle. He films the farrier in his dark, smoky forge. He films the plough horses leaning into the hills as they work. All ploughmen talk to their horses, some sing. A good horseman never has a problem with his team, he knows them better than his own family. A straight furrow is something to be proud of, true enough; nobody wants to look back and see a wavering furrow. A straight furrow is that man's mark on the land; it may as well have been his own name there for all to see.

Harry Styles films these plough teams as they criss-cross the hills. He thinks it a pity he has no way of recording sound, because he considers that one day – what with tractors taking over – the ploughmen's songs might get forgotten along with the hiss of wheat as it is cut, the jangle of harness and the chink of stones on the harrow. Harry is tolerated in the fields, ignored more accurately. But ignored is what a film-maker hopes to be, and Harry can often be seen walking backwards or sideways on the tracks and lanes while the giant horses wade towards him. He films in any weather. The snow-draped landscape looks very well, he thinks, on his black-and-white film, and he gets himself out to film winter feeding, as well as children tobogganing on hemp sacks or sliding on frozen cowponds. He films at dawn as the carters lead their steamy-breathed horses into the mists that cling to the churches and farms. He films geese running down Windmill Lane, foraging white sows getting dirty in a winter field and the cowman tapping the dairy herds in for milking. Perhaps, though, his personal favourites are the films he takes of people. He has spools of farm labourers squinting through cigarette smoke towards the camera, talking-talking, never taking their eyes off the lens – laughing suddenly at a gibe; then the farrier in his apron, stock-still, jaw locked, arms hanging motionless at his sides, as if the slightest movement will spoil the film. There is Mrs Hurst taking her apron off for the camera while Dukes, the butcher, hurriedly puts his on. Then the Walker girls skipping with a long rope,

Fred and Ernest Evans riding the same bicycle, Albert Hodge with the milk wagon and Albert Tilbury with the bread wagon, toddlers crying while their mothers laugh and little Archibald Perkins drinking from the horse trough. These are the films he loves best, the people that he has known for years held fleetingly in a wink of time.

He has tried hard not to favour one area of village life over another, or any particular inhabitant over their neighbours. For example, last evening he viewed some footage of the lay preacher, Harry Blagdon, and the fellow not of this parish, him from the Dorset coast in the bowler hat who found God while out poaching and makes Samaritan visits to the sick. Harry watched while the fellow tipped back his bowler and chattered as if the camera could hear him. Off came the spectacles next, while the chap grinned like a fool. A bit of a clown. Somewhere there is some film of his friend, the young man who lives with his mother, Brown. Some say the son did not earn his position at the Water Company in Wycombe. Walter Brown, that's it. Some say he loves Farmer Hatt's youngest daughter, Mary. Some say he composes poetry; inferior quality, Mrs Williams said of it. He is a sensitive-looking young man, bashful. Harry watched young Brown straighten his cap, take out his pipe, and wait – as if he were a man of note: an explorer you might be led to believe, or a writer.

Meanwhile, Harry has allowed himself to develop a penchant for girls on bicycles. His favourite of these is the Stevens girl, Edna, and her friend, the young Mary Hatt, riding their bicycles past the lush verges around the corner at Four Ashes. He had been obliged, on that occasion, to rush out and stop them and ask whether they would mind riding around again for the camera and they had laughingly agreed to reappear at the sound of Harry's signal, which as it happened was a duck whistle. On the film you see a butter-haired Edna Stevens first, cycling prettily past the stocks and foxgloves, her strong, freckled calves going round, followed by Mary Hatt, racked with laughter, losing her cloche to the breeze so that her hair streaks her face as she goes; and as she passes her face turns to the lens so that you see her rakish laugh and slanting eyes and silent words that she calls out to the camera before she is gone in a blur.

Harry Styles habitually threw up a sheet at home to view his footage. He had used to arrange chairs in two neat rows, but the number of family members attending viewings dwindled, and eventually the formal dining room became a lonely cinema for one. No other member of the family could understand what Harry saw in the repeated viewings of the black-and-white places and faces they saw every day – in colour. But Harry saw something. And what he saw kept him gazing up at the illuminated sheet most evenings, while other family members continued to wonder why he bothered. What he saw, it's fair to say, was time. Tick-tock. What he gazed at were the legs and ticking arms of a moving clock.

CHAPTER 34

'Don't tell me you're still sweet on poor Mary. Poor girl. They run in families, you know, these afflictions.'

Walter did his best to ignore his mother. He busied himself with the apples, slicing his irritation into long coils of peel that ran and ran and eventually dropped into the kitchen bucket.

'Your great-uncle Herbert knew a lunatic once, in Oxfordshire I believe. Quite good pals they were for a time.'

Walter thought the apple peels were beautiful in their way. Coiling like that, spiralling on and on as they went.

'It all ended in misery of course, these things always do. The lunatic was removed to an asylum and Herbert got all upset about it. Your great-grandmother, God rest her soul, was very relieved. Well, anything could have happened after all. They say these things get passed on.'

Inside the bucket the peel was turning brown and sour.

'Your father was a strange man. Don't get me wrong, he was decent and good – I was no fool when it came to boys – but he had peculiar sides, Walter. Which I will not go into. Very peculiar indeed.'

Walter found himself concentrating on the *crex crex* of a corncrake in the field. She did this sometimes, delivered a sample, a titbit of something that promised to be surprising, revelatory, and then made a show of silencing herself.

'There's no easy path through marriage, son, take my word for it. It's all sacrifice and I should know. You don't know the first thing about it, not the first thing. Ha!'

'Right, that should do,' Walter said briskly. He stood up. He bent briefly to lift the basket of apples on to the table. He had intended to do them all; there was a good third left, but if he continued she would go on and he wanted her to stop.

'What about those, then? Aren't you doing those? Too sour for the table, they are.'

He had grown used to thinking on his feet; second nature these hurried lies were now. 'I promised the Denholms some, Ma, promised them yesterday.'

'Did you?' She picked her tooth with her fingernail and eyed him carefully.

'Can't let them down.'

'Not too much pride in that family, is there? Never too proud for charity.'

'I offered the apples, Ma. I can't let them down.'

'Funny woman she is. I reckon she's got a jealous streak. Always wanted a son, that's what they say anyway, I wouldn't know. She asks after you, always did. Never a good word about her daughters, mind. Begrudged me you, I think. I do think that.'

'I'll take these now before they sit down to their tea. I said I would.'

'Well, let her try and raise a son and see how she manages. Promised, did you? It's no picnic raising a lad, you know! I told her that once. People always think they could be better off. When did you promise her then?'

'What?'

'When did you promise her the apples?'

'I didn't promise. I just said I would take some round, you know, offer some because we had a surplus, that's all.'

'Well, she wouldn't know what *surplus* means, Walter.'

'Well, she knows what apples means, doesn't she? So I'm taking some round, Ma, and that's an end to it.'

'Oh, well, it's nothing to do with me. These are your private arrangements with Mrs Denholm, and I'm sure it's none of my business. Be sure to let me know if you sell the house or join the Foreign Legion.'

'I don't know what you're talking about. I'll get these round.'

'Your funny ways are all from your father's side. And your temper. You men have the life of Riley compared to us women, not that you have to worry.'

★   ★   ★

Sankey is on the lookout for signs. The Good Lord sends His messages whither which way, and it is important not to be looking in the wrong direction when He sends a sacred signal.

Mr Palmer, Sankey notices, is standing at the front window looking out. This is the corner cottage on Grange Road, so there is no gate or garden at the front and consequently the window is almost on the road. There is a postbox in the wall beside the window. Mr Palmer stands there, sentry-like, at all hours. He has a full white moustache, hinting at possible past heroism. He is a cripple, so he leans on a stick. Anybody wishing to post a letter must face Mr Palmer through the window glass. There are those who would rather not, and they post their letters after dark. It is as if the village letters are posted directly into Mr Palmer's sitting room. His disposition – aged, frail, exhausted – is suggestive of him having read them all.

Sankey touches his hat and Mr Palmer nods. Something about the way Mr Palmer stands there alone causes Sankey to recall that a man had walked off a cliff at Pevensey Bay. Yes, he'd seen the headline. *Pevensey Man's Fatal Clifftop Tumble*, it said. Quite a tongue-twister, quite a mouthful for the wireless newscaster. He supposes the chap hadn't thought about that when he threw himself off. Perhaps, thinks Sankey, he could have helped the fellow, guided him back to the fold. Bit of a hike to Pevensey, mind you. The chap will know comfort in the arms of Jesus by now. *I will give you rest. Come thou, for there is peace.*

If he is to commit himself one day to the job of village preacher, Sankey muses, then he will require a bicycle. There is a shop nearby in Hazlemere, *J. W. Money: Cycle and motor repairs: Phono and record stores: Cycles built of BSA Fittings.* Mr J. W. Money knew a thing or two about enterprise. Sankey stands at his shop window almost every day in order to enjoy the items displayed there. Mr Money had the agency for Sunbeam cycles. He could build any manner of cycle, including motorised ones, in his shed on Brimmers Hill. He had successfully constructed a motorised contraption like a backwards tricycle, with the pair of wheels at the front and single behind. Behind the saddle perched a smart leather bag for small items and at the front, between the mudguards, was a comfortable-looking armchair complete with footrest. If approaching head-on with a passenger, the impression given was of two people in a single easy chair, one growing out of the top of the other. Sankey pictured Mary in it. He would ride behind her, steering, amusing her with stories. A Bible and a hymnal would fit nicely inside the leather bag, and they would not struggle up a single hill but, due to the engine, only laugh and sing 'Do Believe!' into the wind. Together they would guide and save and enlighten across the Chilterns and beyond. Together they would enter the golden gates of Heaven and be ecstatically deafened by the flutes, lutes and lullabies of angels.

Mary likes muffins, Sankey remembers. She likes them toasted on a coal fire. The muffin man always came down Grove Road on a Saturday with his tray on his head, swinging his bell. Sankey decides he will buy her a muffin; where's the harm in that?

CHAPTER 35

There is a photograph of a man in Mrs Roys' house. It stands on the table in a metal frame among a small crowd of other faces in similar frames. This man does not appear offended, as some of the faces do, at the sight of an untidy boy in their midst, but seems instead to be amused and enquiring and youthfully alert. Sean sees the man is staring directly at him, unlike some of the subjects, who present their profiles to the camera as they gaze contemplatively away. The man is wearing uniform. A soldier? *My darling Mary. I shall have to close.* Sean touches the edge of the metal frame; it is smooth and cold. He has been listening to Mrs Roys in the kitchen, pouring the lime-fizzed drink that probably isn't poisoned. Now she is here, unsure momentarily where to set down the tray, each banana slipper pointing in a different direction, while she smiles apologetically.

'Oh yes,' she says, on seeing the frame repositioned, Sean's fingers at its corner. 'Do you like soldiers?'

'No,' Sean replies.

'Oh.'

'I like astronauts.'

'I see. Yes, of course. Shall we have our drinks?'

Sean and Mrs Roys sit in companionable silence while the shrubs wobble in the breeze outside. Sean tries not to slurp. Ann will believe him eventually: *Her name is Mrs Roys, she has banana feet, she gives me tingly drinks, she has photographs, I have to do important jobs.*

'What do you think of the moon landings?'

Mrs Roys' question surprises all the objects in the room. Sean's ice cube crashes inside his glass. He sees the fireplace gawping in disbelief. No one has asked him this question before. This is his starter for ten, his heart's desire. Sentences line up in his mouth: about Neil, about Buzz, about *Eagle* and the lunar module and the Sea of Tranquillity.

''S'all right.'

Sean wonders why she is so interested. If he was a detective he would know. What could an old woman want with the moon? Godnose. He slurps his ice cube. It was hard to think straight in someone else's house. Think, you spaz.

'I was born in 1913. If you'd talked about men on the moon in those days you would be assumed to be pretty queer.'

Sean says nothing. He is not in a position to agree or disagree. She has said numbers. It is a date when you say numbers, like 1942. A flaming flipping date.

'Turns out we had rather poor imaginations, don't you think? I mean, you have only got to look at television now, haven't you? Petroleum changed everything. And of course the war. And industry, not forgetting that.'

Sean wonders what the bludyell she's saying. He recognises some of it. Television. War. Is he supposed to talk now? Sean glances at her.

'Of course you're far too young to understand. Silly me. What do you know of it all?'

There, she agrees that you are a spaz. She knows you know nothing. Daft bat. He knows plenty. He has the number to ring. He knows stuff she doesn't know. Stuff that would blow her out of her bananas. Well, must be off. Why won't he say it? Just say it. He speaks, finally.

'Nineteen forty-two.'

'What's that?'

Sean gets up to leave. Mustbeoff mustbeoff. He turns to look at the photograph and the face of the soldier gazes genially back. He wishes he could have that picture in its cool metal frame. At home they don't have photographs in frames. He can hear Mrs Roys speaking.

'That man's name is Walter Brown.'

I know I know I know I know.

'He was born here too. They lived on Valley Road, he and his mother. What was her name? Nice man. He loved the woods. He used to catch rabbits, he and his bowler-hatted chum. And he loved the dewponds.'

292

Sean feels his mouth filling up with things to say.

'Poor man,' Mrs Roys sighs.

None of the things in Sean's mouth have made it out yet. He looks at her.

'Poor Walter,' she says.

Sean nods as though he knows what she means. mista waltr. The man who has written the blue letters which Sean is nearly-reading. mista waltr. If the soldier man is mista waltr then Mrs Roys must be mary hat. There, he has left no stone unturned. *For your information*, this is what Ann says. Well, *for your information* he is a detective, almost. Wur.

'Poor Walter.'

She has drifted away in her face, gone off. Sean glances at the limp bananas on the end of her legs. He feels ashamed of himself, embarrassed for her. He shouldn't be here. You are not allowed to talk to strangers. You are not supposed to water their pots or sit on their settees or make them sad or steal their things. He will be in big trouble.

'Walter couldn't swim a stroke,' Mrs Roys pipes suddenly. 'Although he loved a girl who could.' And now her sadness is gone, just like that. Mrs Roys is too quick for him, Sean decides. She looks at him brightly and winks.

'Are you mary hat?'

Mrs Roys doesn't move or blink or speak, even after the question has completely dissolved in the air and there is nothing left to fill the space between them. Sean wonders whether he will have to wait here until he grows taller before he gets an answer. Or whether Mrs Roys is bewitched or has turned to stone.

His mother told him once that if something really awful happened and he needed help, he should call 999. He can't recall seeing a telephone here at Mrs Roys' house.

He wonders if he should ask the mary hat question again, or just go home, or call 999. He wonders if he should say, *Get back in the wagon, woman*. Or what.

'No,' she says at last. 'I'm Isabel.'

The world is mad, Sean can see that now. He is not prepared for a person called 'is a bell'. He has no plan now, or sensible reply.

'I am Isabel Hatt. My sister's name is Mary Hatt.'

Sean would like to kill himself, or at least run away. What is he supposed to do? Nobody mentioned a sister. What is he doing in Mary Hatt's sister's house? He is a thief and a spaz and a weirdo.

'How do you know my sister's name?'

Wur.

'Do you know something about my sister? Did your parents, your grandparents know her? Have your family lived here a long time?'

Wur. Wur. Wur.

'You're a funny one, aren't you?'

'I've got to go home now.' Spaz spaz spaz. Say it properly, *I must be off*.

'Yes. Off you go. Good boy. Do you like puzzles?'
'No.'

The sunlight is there on the front step again, waiting. It hurls itself over them as the door swings open and they are dazzled momentarily by the brightness.

'Ta-ta, then.'

Sean is not altogether used to being hugged. He doesn't much like it. Mrs Roys hugs him now. She seems to like it. Being hugged by an elderly person is not as nice as you're supposed to pretend it is. You are closer to death in those arms. When they squeeze tight you suspect they may take you with them, off to the place the dead people go. You must resist and you do. And then you are petitioned for a kiss.

'Your leaflets!' she remembers. And the bananas march her out. He had completely forgotten about the leaflets. Fête. That's what the leaflets said. That was why he was here.

Sean runs. Here he is again in the place where he lives, running. Not running, sprinting. He pumps his arms. Executive strides; rhythmical: Weirdo. Murderer. Madman. Spaz. Weirdo. Murderer. Madman. Spaz.

9th February 1943, M.E.F.

Dearest Mary,
    It's been a while since your last letter. I hope you are well and not working too hard.

295

I hope John and Ida are in good spirits, and Isabel too over there in Kingshill. Any news of Clem? Or Joseph?

Well, Mary, in Tripoli I saw Monty take the salute at the march past – a moving experience. The cathedral and promenade there are lovely. The shops were mostly closed, but I enjoyed the change. Arthur's ear is troubling him again. At night the sky is vivid red, shading to the palest salmon pink. I saw a film in Castle Benito, though the light came through the shrapnel holes and faded the picture somewhat. Jerry still raids constantly, lighting up the night sky until it is bright as day. Churchill is in Tripoli tomorrow. This means we now have to salute when we are there and we cannot go into the town if there are stains on our suits. Am entirely fed up with army biscuits. What we would give for some bread!

Later:

Arthur has been touching the top of the tent with his head and now rain is coming in. However, we found a tin of Australian peaches and one of corned beef – we ate the lot. I bought you a book of views in Tripoli as Arthur and I went around the Arab and Turkish quarters. And I now have two school exercise books that I obtained in town, which I am using for letter-writing as I can now fill several sides! I bought a fountain pen too. I hope I am allowed to send them to you.

Later:

Arthur has to go into hospital in Tripoli. He is worried about it of course. One hundred per cent bullshit here, if you will pardon the expression, though now we're allowed to wear shorts without woollen hose. I have eaten a tin of sardines. On the move again.

Later:

Tripoli has just been bombed and the lovely promenade was hit slap-bang in the centre. All the hospitals are being emptied and Arthur has been moved. We have passed through Zavia, Sabrate – wooded country – and you can see the blue Mediterranean. We camped on sandhills among blue flowers like primroses. Now we are in Tunisia after going through Bengardane. Rooney is a very greedy fellow over rations. I cannot understand him.

Beneath this sand there is heavy chalk rock. It's the very devil digging in and we have had plenty of action call-outs. While we were laughing over something at the Command Post, a squadron leader was killed – shot in the head. Typhus has broken out in places.

Apparently people at home think we are having marvellous food. Please, Mary, tell them not to be so silly. At most we have 15 biscuits a day and teas are thin. Yes, we had turkey and pork for Christmas, true, but under what conditions? And it was only part-cooked.

Later:

Today I saw a bird drawn backwards by the dropping of a Jerry bomb, then hurled forward by our guns. Odd, what you notice. We have a night guard of 15 instead of 6 now and different passwords each day.

Later:

We have moved on. We are now near the American and South African armies – there are double guards everywhere. No vegetation here at all – just sand and beetles. I watched a most beautiful caterpillar yesterday as our tanks were broken through and we hurriedly moved a mine back (being bombed 3 times as we did so). A major and 2 men were killed. The raids are sharp and quick. I called your name as I lay in the dirt. On 7th March Gunner Douglas Smith was killed with Harry Mills, Jack Davies and 8 others. A bomb hit 30 yards from me. We have made a wooden cross for Doug's grave. All the dead men have correspondence that has just arrived. We prayed a bit at Doug's grave.

Later:

We have been badly strafed and Stuka-bombed. It was deafening and would have sorted out Arthur's other ear if he had been with us. Gunner John Butler died in hospital and Bdr Gray is still shell-shocked – really stunned he is, only half here. We had a march today and were inspected of all things! Hard to believe while men are dying all around.

1700 hrs:

We are arrived at a fort in a range of hills. So much action we can't dig in till morning. Hard stone beneath, so you can only go in about one foot. You have to hold hard against the terrific attack barrage, otherwise it begins to get to you, easy to feel demoralised. It is hot and I have had no proper sleep for a week. Bert Jones has had his arm off.

Our shadows on the sand in the moonlight look grotesque. Guns and Bofors pop. I found a dead snake and we heard some news on the wireless. Terribly low Kitty Hawks overhead. Please let there be a letter from you tomorrow. Do you care for me,

Mary? God knows I care for you. Sweet dreams.

Yours, Walter xx

A cat has been cemented on Lilac Drive, at the top of the estate, where the new, more expensive houses gloat condescendingly down on the others. Everybody is asking, what cat? Is it dead? A woman with a tissue up her sleeve said, 'Was it done deliberately?' She said it accusingly, with her chin tilted, as if she suspected it was. Sean knows it was done deliberately, only a spaz would think otherwise. What kind of self-regarding cat would have an accident involving cement. And besides, there was concrete evidence. That's what Gor said. He said it over and over until he'd spoken it to every single person on the estate. 'Concrete evidence,' tipping his head back and groaning with laughter, while everyone looked at his fillings. The rumour is that a cat fell asleep in the sun on drying concrete and awoke to discover itself stuck fast. Adam swears it is true. One of the parents said, 'Pity it wasn't one of the bloody kids,' and got a big laugh. This, surely, proved that dogs were cleverer than cats. The dogs didn't have a problem with wet cement. They ran straight over it, pock-marking its surface with every imaginable style of print. Likewise the kids knew you had to ride your bike over it quickly, trailing rattlesnake patterns across people's nearly-patios for all time.

The cement-cat episode drew kids up to Lilac

Drive. They hung about and stared at the windows, hoping for a glimpse of something, anything: policemen, grief, fur. A few of them peered into a sun-filled, roofless house. It was unpainted inside and sweet with the smell of split wood. It was hard not to be impressed, upstairs and down. These had an extra small bedroom and, mysteriously, an extra toilet in the hall; perhaps in case two people needed to go at exactly the same time. There were doors at the back that opened onto a little patio, as well as a mud patch waiting for turf. They had creosote fencing instead of chicken wire. Charlie wrote a phonetic obscenity on the window frame and biro'd a huge pair of tits on the wall. Dean did a crap in an unplumbed toilet he found waiting outside on the path.

The houses at the top were the land developer's stroke of genius. They sold quickly and the new occupants named them after unspoilt moors in the Chilterns on pieces of varnished wood. From the carefully appointed windows they could observe the cheaper houses below, descending in their wildflower cul-de-sacs.

Nothing remained of the cement cat. There was nothing to see. Probably it was not even true. Sean left the others. He preferred to be by himself on the days when Ann did not fly up over the fence on her swing. He would go to the modern church. Maybe a modern miracle might happen.

How come they killed Jesus? That was his

thinking thought. It didn't make any sense. You can't kill Danger Man. And why did he let them? Why didn't he just zap them or beam himself up or turn himself into an eagle? Sean wondered if the wooden cross they made Jesus carry was as heavy as it looked. He looked for something to put on his back. He spied an empty box of Daz with a dark stain on it. He remembered the voice on the television said Daz had blue energy that could drive out stains, although there was another washing powder that could actually eat dirt. Even he couldn't manage that.

He filled the box with stones and swung it on to his shoulders. It felt good to walk with the heavy box, it made you stoop like a persecuted man. He wished someone could see him right now, stooping and staggering.

CHURCH OF THE GOOD SHEPHERD, the sign informed anyone who could read. This was once sheep country, it was true. Once this hill would have been grazed by Southdowns all year round. Sean stared at the other words on the sign. JESUS LOVES YOU. Soon, he thought, when he was *changed*, he would read out those sign words. Sean set down his heavy box of Daz on one of the turf squares that was piled up waiting to be holy lawn.

In spite of its name, the Church of the Good Shepherd was self-consciously modern. The concrete bell tower consisted of two geometric interlocking slabs that left the church bell open to the elements on all sides. An average wind could ring the bell without difficulty and a storm would have it tolling all night like the end of the world had come. There were six tall church windows, thin as slits and hung inside with modish vertical blinds. The church had been completed before the water supply, some said. Local committees and town planners congratulated themselves. Gabbett Housing had a cheese and wine evening. It was considered proper that these new commuter families with their young children should arrive in their overloaded Hillman Sedans with their city ways and kidney-shaped dressing tables, to the summoning chime of a Christian bell. They could rest secure in the knowledge that whatever troubles, large or small, befell them, their village church (a church on a hill no less, meticulously designed to blend in style and tone with the estate) was there with new Cyril Lord carpet, co-ordinating cushions, and two Sunday-morning services. Sean tried the door, it was locked. He peered through the windows at the rows of blue chairs and the appliquéd wall hangings of aghast-looking shepherds surrounded by their hand-stitched, satin-horned flocks. It was a light, airy room, barely like a church at all, with a noticeboard, leaflet stand, and even a sideboard at the back housing a kettle, tea and coffee, for when the occasion demanded. It looked cosy and inviting compared to the annihilated shells of the unfinished houses.

Rev Davis is in charge at the Church of the Good

Shepherd. That is what people call him. Encased in sandals are his long white toes, stroked with hair. This is the first thing you notice if you are a child. The theme continues up, even when he is off duty, through his bell-sleeved smock shirt and the tormented smile that is full of chestnut beard and the tumbles of John the Baptist hair. The Rev is a huge fan of the Messiah, you can tell. He looks up skywards to the Divine Father for inspiration, and down at the ground for effect. A right *poofter*, is how Gor described him. *A right fruit and nut cake*, he always added, laughing out loud at himself.

As a matter of fact there were those who had already begun attending the Sunday-morning services, though most of the newly arrived families, Sean noticed, preferred to unfold wire chairs in their garden and read the newspaper. The tolling bell did not call them from their rest, not even for a free cup of coffee and a biscuit. The Good Shepherd was offering nothing they really wanted, truth be told. They had forgiven themselves their sins and renewed their flagging spirits at the White Lion the night before. Now they wanted some peace and quiet on a lawn chair, even while the grass turf remained undelivered (though none of them seemed to mind), even as they sank lower and lower, along with their uncleansed souls, into the chalk and clay-bound earth.

It is cool in the woods and quiet as a crypt. This is where Ann likes to hide, to play tricks. She wanders off and hopes to scare him. You must be careful with your noise, the snap of a twig rings out like a rifle crack. Sean bows his head and creeps along, while above him birds call out their warnings. Spears of sunlight come down through the gaps in the forest canopy, like Lothian's arrows, hot and gold and sending up dust, like smoke.

Sean thinks he will see if he can start a flame. He kneels down to make a bushman's fire. There was a programme he saw on television. The bushmen were long and slender and moved deftly as hunting cats. Their hair was curled close to their heads and they had small, smiling, crinkled faces, like old ladies. They knew how to make fire with two sticks: *far*, the television voice said. *They have no need of matches when it comes to making a far.* Sean gives up on his. His two sticks won't co-operate and have never seen a bushman, much less a far.

This is where she hid last time. His dad was right. The female species are a strange law unto themselves, *bottomless pits*.

'Ann?' he calls.

Above him a warbler adjusts his song and a general shushing flows through the trees. Sean sees a line of words. They are growing on the bark of a tree with the lichen and moss. He stares. *I looked to Him. He looked on me. And we were one for eternity.* Tree words. Tree talk. What does a tree know? Not the liar alphabet. Sean hopes the tree cannot read and write. Holy cow. Where would that leave him? What if he were stupider than a tree?

Sean thinks about the story-children who fell asleep in the woods. He struggles to remember their names. They are in an illustrated book of fairy tales he had been given once. He remembers looking at the wispy watercolour pictures, at the pale pinks of their fingers and toes, the blue spill of sky, and the watery greens and reds of their clothes. The book is not phonetic, so he is still peering at the pictures now, trying to figure it out while the words lie uselessly about. Somebody fell asleep, anyway, and paid the price. What was the price? He didn't know. Something bad, it always was. He will wait one more minute for Ann – however long that is.

Sean is asleep beside a bramble thicket. Click. The trees stop their shushing. Through the fug of sleep Sean can feel the eye on him, the all-observing lens of the forest. Click. Every forest has an eye. He wonders if it watched him trying to make fire, being a spaz.

He thinks he will go now. She always says she will count to twenty. Then she does not bother to come and find him. Liar. Liar. As he gets to his feet, something in the forest moves with him, shadows drift. He hears another click, and then again, like a person tutting. Where are the birds? The wood holds itself still. Is he awake? Is he dreaming? Dreamers eat pie in the sky. They live on cloud nine. They throw their lives away. They don't listen. They get knocked down on zebra crossings, tumble into manholes. They float off the earth.

There is a rustling in the treetops. One tree and then the next and then the one beside it, as though something were moving quickly from one to the other. A creature? Sean thinks it would most probably be a creature. A dreadful one offers itself to his mind's eye. A thing with liquid bones and teeth like pins, who knows his name, who speaks it with a creature's hiss. He has heard his name spoken this way before, this way but with a curl at the end, same as when someone asks you a question, so that the hiss gave way to a cry, *Sean?* And the cry was all in the N at the end, so the call was, *Seaner?*

Sean is running. It might not be a dreadful creature, he tells himself, it might just be a squirrel or a pigeon. But he runs anyway, and as he runs he thinks he is sick of running. He hopes he is sleeping. He hopes he is sleep-running. This would explain the colours that move and bleed against one another as if they can't decide, and the ground that rolls like water. Stop the dream. He must stop the dream.

He is running without clothes. The dream will not stop. He is naked as Pan, with a straight back and startled face. Something else is running, he doesn't know what, nor whether behind or in front. Something burns and he feels the heat of it on his skin. He runs hard, straining the hoops of his ribs. Sensation is gone from his feet, as if he dashes on hooves now. The eye watches him, he knows it. It halts him between strides, frame by frame, looking, checking. It can speed you up, slow you down, and erase you completely. The figures are here. Some are in groups, some are alone. He tries to avoid them, to swerve, he tries not to look. They are hushed as Sean bursts past. Though he is moving at speed he feels sluggish. Is he being chased? Is he the chaser? No clue comes. He sees someone, just a flash. A girl, he thinks he knows her. She is curled up with her back to him, and he frightens her then, rushing up. He should have crept quietly. He does know her. He ought not to have frightened her. She turns and screams and that is when he sees that her flesh is almost gone and her body is liquid, like something spilled, and her bones are small and springy. She is frightened and so she screams and her teeth are long and sharp as knives, though her tears come down like any other girl's.

Sean runs away, but her voice follows. *Sean! Seaner!* she cries. He does not want to stop. *Seaner!* He runs for the edge of the wood, towards the fields and paths and home. And as he runs he sees that the thing that is on fire, is burning, is him.

CHAPTER 36

Sean watches his mum as she wipes something from her fingers with a kitchen cloth. She stares out of the window as she does this, at the dirt and diggers and garage roofs. It could have been anything on her fingers, grease, salt or some other bitter thing. It could have been blood; no one would pay any attention. She is not speaking today. Today she will be starring in her own silent film. The other members of the cast are left to wander haplessly in and out of her scenes. Their job is to ruin her performance, deliver poor lines from some other script, spoil everything; at this they prove impeccable.

Sean senses her silences are a punishment of some sort, for what he can't be sure. There are things that upset her, things you couldn't imagine would ever upset anybody; things like eating and laughing at the same time, jumping on or off furniture (unless the house was on fire), shouting (unless the house was on fire); running is another, but then so is dragging your feet. Sean had once tried to match her silence with one of his own. He too made his own dramatic film without words.

He too stared and slumped and swiped at things with a limp cloth. At her approach he would fall aside like a wretch and let his mouth hang and his arm swing like an empty sleeve. Rather than capture her attention, it swiftly caught on as a competitive sport in the family. Gor, having noted with a narrow eye that elaborately executed mute battles were taking place around him, felt himself excluded and was quick to respond. To everyone's surprise, he suddenly struck himself dumb one night during *The Avengers* and didn't speak again for almost a week. A record. An unbeatable achievement in their household. One Cathleen couldn't hope to challenge in spite of her experience. Together they went about their silent business in the house, sitting like three speak-no-evil monkeys around the Sunday-lunch table while Ty pulled out his eyelashes and groaned tunelessly through advertisement jingles. His Tarzan calls (more awful than ever when released into the silence) made Sean think of a jungle gone badly wrong, where the animals behaved freakishly, where roaring machines dug holes for the trees to fall into.

If Ty noticed the silent tournament taking place he didn't bother participating. Gor was therefore, unarguably, the winner, and did not need to button up ever again.

Sean and Ann are walking backwards up George's Hill Road for something to do. It is not as easy as it looks. Sean has developed a rhythm. He uses his arms as oars, he bends his knees; he goes off at tangents nevertheless. It is surprisingly difficult. Ann does well for a while. She creeps backwards with her hands in her pockets, she hums, she scolds. 'Spaz! Spaz! Crine out loud!' She has stopped now. Going backwards has made her sick and she is lying on the new tarmac pavement with grit in her hair. Sean bends over her to tell her about the grit and the ants and the tar that is on her dress. Ann lies there. It starts to become strange that she is lying there. *Women don't behave like you or I, they are influenced by the moon.* Sean pulls on her arm, but she won't get up. He sits on the kerbstone. The tar stinks, it makes you dizzy. There was a story, Sean thinks, a true one, about a horse who wouldn't get up and they had to shoot it. He tells it to Ann. She won't get up, she says, because she is bored, bored of him, bored of life, bored. She is going to get a different boyfriend this afternoon and anyway he is not her boyfriend, never was, never will be. Then they are quiet. Sean thinks about the streaker. There is more to streaking, he suspects, than meets the eye. If the streaker and the murderer turn out to be the same person it is possible he will be the first of his kind. Sean wonders if this could mean more will follow, or perhaps he would remain unique, a local legend, like the water serpent. P'raps they will have to change the name of the wood. P'raps one day Four Ashes will become Three Streakers.

Ann has closed her eyes. She is very white against the black tar pavement. It is possible she has died of boredom. It's not so silly, somebody somewhere must have once, else why would people say it? Sean pulls at her dress.

'Oi.' He watches the ants around her head; one of them hauling itself on to a strand of hair.

'Oi.'

She opens one eye, but it does not look at him.

'P'sof, Spaz.'

Sean wishes he could tell her something shocking and fantastic. He wishes he could say something that would electrocute her body, make her bounce up and look at him with two big unblinking eyeballs. Her mouth is closed. It is small and warm and full of commands. He wishes she would gasp and cry and flop against him, and kiss him with that mouth.

Ann has a long red scratch on her calf, he notices, curling at the end like the letter L. Sean follows it down to the dirty ruff of her sock. By the time he gets there he has made up his mind. He bends over her to speak into her ear.

'I'm going away for a long time.' Sean rubs his nose. 'I'm going now. Must be off. Don't tell anyone.' She closes her eye. She doesn't reply. 'See y'later,' Sean says. He stands on some ants beside her ear and then he is gone. When he is at the bottom of the hill he turns and calls back, 'Alligator!' But the wind pushes the word over his head so she does not hear.

20th February 1943, M.E.F.

Darling Mary,

I am thrilled with the photograph of you. What a good one it is. I keep looking at it over and over again. I have shown it around, I hope you don't mind, but I thought it was such a good one of you. I was pleased to see the lane behind you and the old beeches. I also enjoyed hearing about your film-star moment on Clem's bicycle. I'm not surprised old Styles still has his cine camera on the go, in particular when a pretty girl rides by. I should like to see that cine film one day, so I would. I have a picture of it in my mind and that will have to do for now.

We passed some white anemones, like a wondrous fall of snow, and I thought of home and of you. And then we came across a spread of wild flowers: miniaturised snapdragons, primroses, delphiniums and daisies. I gathered a few to press inside this letter.

The Italians and Jerries have left their dugouts filthy and soiled. They leave notes: 'Hope we find this clean when we come back.' It makes you sick.

The big news is that Churchill has visited and stayed near to us. He received a great welcome. A pithy remark of his was: 'If you are asked what you did in the war, all you need to say is you belonged to the desert army.'

Soon Rommel's Panzer army will be extinct. I remember a while back meeting a pilot and he said, 'What mob are you?' I told him and his reply was, 'Steak meat, eh? Damn that for a game.' And we always thank our lucky stars we are on the ground!

We have anchored our bivvies with tons of boulders. There is no water available. My uniform is dirty and full of holes and I have a beard and worn-out boots.

Later:

We're out of smokes and have pinched some food and cooked a cosmopolitan meal: Jerry stew, Italian tomatoes and English chips – very appetising.

Later:

Jerry attacks again and again. I was almost blown up trying to shave with spit in my bivvy this morning. Brigadier Lucas paid us a visit. We hope to be in Tripoli by the 17th. There are lorries burning everywhere along our route and we're knocking out tanks galore as we go. When we are stopped by Jerry tanks in a sand pocket, we disperse. Every man for himself then! A Spitfire came down nearby. The pilot only had a broken shoulder. We are filthy and hot. I am not allowed to say too much.

Later:

We have found a well in a lovely village, but there are many booby traps left by Jerry. We found a wine vat today with millions of gallons in. We had a sing-song and every single man in our brigade got drunk. A welcome break after travelling over 1,600 miles of desert. We see dogfights every day. Jerry is losing lots. The knocked-out Jerry and Italian vehicles have pin-ups of cinema actresses. You forget that they are human. We all have to be vaccinated again. Well, I'd better close. I look at your picture every day.

Two days later:

We went to a draughty place for a picture show yesterday. First there was a VD picture – the frankest I have ever seen. Then a Judy Garland musical. I have seen the brothels, Mary, but it is not for me. The women have two rooms usually; one to dance and talk, and one for their work. It costs 22 piastres, which is handed to an old woman at the door, and five or ten minutes later the woman is out again beseeching new customers. Most of the lads have tried it. I find I am not interested.

Later:

We captured the aerodrome before the Italians had time to move – about 200 planes. I am going on leave to Tripoli on Saturday with Arthur. I ate pomegranate and monkey nuts for tea today. I had better get this off to you, Mary. I look at your picture all the time. You are getting lovelier by the day. Are you my girl? Please say yes! Have you written? Well, cheerio for now.

Yours, Walter xx

It is a small shed. It stands in the playing field that is utilised by the school on one day of the year only, for their chaotic summer-term running races. Sean stands on a plastic bucket to see through the web-laced window. There is equipment, machinery, tools. He casts his eye over the blades and oily black chains. The door is locked, fastened by a padlock that is heavy as a stone. As he selects a brick, Sean has to steady himself. He is a thief today, a criminal. This is quite good. It is a masterful plan. His breathing comes in rushes and his skin prickles with cold in spite of the sunlight. He must keep his eye on the ball. He must remain calm so as not to unduly affect his aim. You do not go all the way to the moon only to turn spaz when you get there. If Neil had turned spaz over the Sea of Tranquillity things might have been very different.

Sean pulls himself tall, takes a few paces back,

rushes the same paces forward again and releases the brick. He keeps his eye on the window and the brick sails from his hand that is guided by his eye into the glass, which parts perfectly. There is a crash, a thud, then a slow tinkle of pieces as they drop into the lawnmower on the other side. The tinkling sounds festive. The world is silent for a moment. The trees, grass, sky, all wait. Nothing bad happens. Two-four-six-eight who do we appreciate? Sean is looking at a black hole. It is magnificent. It deserves a name. Holey. He has made it be there, it was not there before. Holey holey holey. It is one of the greatest holes in the world. Sean thinks he would like to make some more holes, honest to God. Sean picks up a piece of the broken glass and looks through it at the world. Everything is slightly different. He holds it up to the sky for a cloud to pass through. Ann will be amazed, perhaps she will blink. Sean Matthews, you're my hero. Sean imagines it, the words pressed between her lips. Girls like broken glass. Sean doesn't know why. He remembers how all the girls crowded around Nigel Drake the time he broke the bay window of an almost-house on Harebell Walk; hung round him like horseflies, swaying up and down the hill with him for days, giggling and whispering and laughing at nothing. It was mysterious. Sean was nonplussed and waited for an answer. The only clue was the glass.

Now he has broken glass of his own. He begins to gather the pieces to show Ann and the others.

It would be useful to have a pot to put them in, or an envelope, but he only has pockets, so he fills both pockets with jags of window. He can feel their sharpness against his legs. He knocks against the heavy padlock as he straightens up. No padlock in the world can keep him out, ha. No match for his aim, for his Holey. He kicks the door – it whines scornfully as it falls open. Sean hesitates while he thinks everything through. The shed. It was open all the time.

Inside dust is rising and floating towards the door like smoke. The door was open, he could have stolen something without smashing the window. But now he has broken glass, which is better. Sean steps into the falling dust. It is hard to choose; there are cutters, scythes, saws, twine, pegs, paint, bicycle tyres. There are tins of nails too, a line-marker, a box of hammers and chisels, drills. It is difficult to want one thing more than another. He tries the rhyme. Eeny meeny miney mo. He doesn't want the broom. He tries the rhyme again.

CHAPTER 37

'Wally Wallflower, YOU ugly bugga, this is your last chance to marry me.'

She said it five days before her fifteenth birthday in the middle of the cornfield, far from the lane, surrounded by men who worked for her father, some of whom had guns to shoot the rabbits as they fled from the corn.

'I'd like to think about it.'

The harvest holidays were hot and dry and went on for a hundred years, though you never got any older. Everyone helped at harvest time unless they were infirm or insane. At school they lined up and shrieked 'Gather in the Sheaves' to a piano accompaniment, before bolting as hard as they could go for the fields. This was Walter's last schoolboy harvest, as by St Matthew's Day he would be working as an office boy in Wycombe, and happy too to miss the winter grind of sugar-beeting. Harvest in the shires was no small thing. A lad who was willing was allowed to do a man's work and find himself treated like a man too, and if you worked hard you might even get paid something. It was a time to grow up and taste your first beer and your first tobacco and work until your back broke.

The teams of horses, two to each binder, have already started in the cornfield after the hand-reapers, who began yesterday. A straggly troupe are hanging on the gate: Ernest Wright is by Walter's elbow and Eddie Redrup next to him with Bertie King, who is yawning great wide groans. Edna Stevens, Betsy Newell and Mary Hatt are making daisy chains while they wait for Mrs Hatt and Mrs Stevens to arrive with breakfast in the cart. Eddie is smoking a lumpy cigarette and boasting about his mole traps and all the rookeries his father shot in spring. Walter takes his fag off him and puts it between his own teeth. 'Cooked rook stinks,' he says.

'Twerp, we don't eat 'em,' Eddie replies.

Some of these boys would habitually raid birds' nests. They would stamp on any baby birds, especially sparrows, which they earned money from as they were a pest to farmers, along with pigeons. Rats too they killed with catapults for the farmers, a penny or maybe tuppence per tail. As a matter of fact they killed anything they could, whether it was a pest to farmers or not. Killing was natural to country boys in 1931.

No sign of Charles Sankey from Lyme Regis. He will be on God's business. God's business my hat! This is what Walter's mother said. Walter waited for her proverb to follow. 'Him and that Perfect man. One bush can never hide two thieves.'

Walter swings his legs over the gate and thinks, if harvest is not God's business, then whose is it?

'Get down off that gate sharp!'

A scythesman in waistcoat and cap finishes opening up the standing corn in the awkward corners where the binder cannot go. He leans slightly and swings his sickle. From Walter's position, the scythesman's progress suggests a lonely raftsman adrift on a high yellow sea. Naturally Walter does not have his notebook to write that down. In his notebook he collects interesting facts, remarkable observations, and amusements. He is susceptible to remarkable observations: he suspects he was born like it. He forgets to carry his notebook most days. He reckons all his best observations are blowing across Buckinghamshire with the corn stubble. He looks at Mary Hatt in her beret, daisy chains around her neck. Worrisome Wally Wallflower Woebetide you When you go. That's what she says to him these days, as if she's turned gypsy.

The scythesmen, horsemen, all the harvest men seem to possess unknowable wisdoms about unimaginable things. Things Walter does not have in his notebook. He watches the men working, talking, making their quick remarks and asides. He studies them for information, hoping to catch something that will release their secret code, help him understand. He catches one of them saying, 'She said, I'll give you a go in a minute, and I said a minute's too long!' And they all laugh. What

321

is funny about that? It is perplexing, as horses and dogs appear to understand them perfectly well.

Compared to these unfathomably skilled workers, Walter feels he and the others are no more than a pile of idiots. This was borne out when George Rouse smashed his leg riding on the hay elevator, while his brother fell off a wheat stack, hit his head and fell asleep for a month. Another time little Sidney Wood lost one and a half fingers in the feed-masher.

A man called Bailey arrives with his son; the corners of Bailey's mouth are flecked with white. They are on hard times and he has lost whatever job he thought he had. They have walked from Winchmore Hill looking for harvest work. Another family have walked from Beamond End. They stand away from everyone else, and the father wears his cap down to hide his eyes and does not speak a word. Walter wonders if he is a farmer gone to nothing.

Walter likes to be around the working horses, masked in their leather blinkers, jangling, creaking in their harness. He likes to touch their hot, damp necks and feel their giant bony heads searching his pockets for apples. 'Warkon gowarn,' the horseman says, and his hands and voice are quick and he knows exactly what must happen and Walter wishes he were a ploughman, just for today, and could drive his chariot up and down till dark.

Walter walks away with Eddie's smoke. It tastes good. He watches the sails on the binders turning like miniature windmills and the horses climbing, and far down the field, between the distant hedgerows by the giant oaks, he sees a black bowler gliding. Man of God, my hat. By the end of the day that bowler will be covered in straw.

The way it was done was you all had to go after the binder and gather the corn sheaves into stooks, six sheaves per stook, grain at the top, butts on the ground. If you hadn't done stooking before you got your arms scratched, even while the straw was still green. Everybody did it, men and girls. Mary was fast and efficient and made remarks about the other helpers as she went; personal comments about this one, that one: 'No help but hindrance. Dear me – look at *her*.'

Walter was picked to do rabbits. It was not a girl's job. You arrived with your stick and you hit the rabbits as they ran out from the standing corn as the binders approached – bashed them on the head. Any injured ones were finished off when they were gathered up. Fetched a reasonable price when you had as many as this, 6d or even up to a shilling each, which added up of course. By this stage the field would be running with them, and all the lads would be bringing their sticks down over and over as if they were hand-threshing. Thump thump thump. Rabbit heads broke surprisingly easily. You lost count of how many you had done. Some froze with panic and waited while you did them. Walter found he couldn't ignore the corn dust and clatter of the binders and the raw burn of the sun on his neck, but after a while he stopped seeing the pulp from the burst heads. You just kept bringing your stick down. Those who escaped the sticks would run into the guns. Walter didn't know Sankey had arranged to be a gun. How has he managed it? The other guns are farm men and Mary's brothers, Joseph and Clem. It is true he is a good shot, but to have someone who is neither family nor employee enjoying himself in this way? He has finagled himself. Walter feels childishly jealous. The guns are in a potentially dangerous corner; there are stookers, lads, horses and ploughmen moving continually about. A gun must shoot away from the corn as the rabbits flee for their burrows without killing any person or working horse.

'Keeping you busy, Walt?' Sankey has become sardonic with a .410 on his arm. He addresses the head carter differently. 'Sorry to be late. I've been up Langley's at Spurlands End.' It is a given there will be nothing more said. William Fountain's family have farmed at Langley's for years. He had taken it over as a young man, but the farm had been in trouble like so many others, and last month he went bankrupt. Yesterday he hanged himself in the feed barn.

Walter notices Sankey's walk is different. It is something, he thinks, a godly man who shoots like a demon.

Walter is behind the south hedge relieving himself when Mary appears, startling him. She says nothing at all, but walks deliberately up, takes hold of his face and kisses him on the mouth. Her mouth and fingers are hot and sticky and she tastes of salt and something sour. Walter thinks some girls might be put off by the rabbit blood on his shirt. He listens to the guns popping. He thinks about the pounding his own head will receive if they are seen by anyone.

'There now,' she says. 'Huh. Daft bugga.' He watches her go and he thinks there is not enough room in his notebook for this particular subject.

As the light begins to fade they stop work. The air cools, darkens mauve, and the clouds of midges bring swifts and swallows diving from a pink-lit sky. It will be the same again tomorrow and the next day. There is a stooked field of wheat ready for carting tomorrow; but the church bell must ring three times before they cart today's oats for ricking, else they'll not be ready. Only God knows how many dry days are left. Nobody wants to hear the rainbird sing at this time of year. A storm now would be disastrous.

Grub is always good on harvest nights and mothers' curfews do not exist. There is stewed pork and broad beans or rabbit pie with salt pork, cheese pudding, cherry cake, cherry pie and beer that was brewed in March, as well as cowslip or rhubarb wine. The harvest men clash mugs and begin slowly to change shape. By the end of the night they are bendy as if they had no bones at all, but by next morning they are completely upright again, quick and efficient on their usual skeletons, teasing their fellows about their bonelessness the night before.

Walter and Sankey walk home draped in rabbits. It is dark but the moon curves over the great field, silvering the crop over. Clouds drift, veiling the stars, silent as icebergs. Sankey's shoulders are all fur as though he is Mrs Disraeli from the big house. Walt watches the soft heads swinging on his back. He is fuzzy with drink. He can feel beer bubbles gurgling inside him. His own rabbits are heavy to carry ungutted. His hands are sticky with blood and as he walks their skulls bump against his legs. He has two for his mother. She will say, 'Not on my clean table.' He will have to leave them in the sink and she will say, 'Don't walk on my floor.'

Something ghostly flaps over the lower field. A barn owl hunting leisurely up the boundary hedge. 'Who?' it asks, a quaver in its question. This – like a coin in the slot of a penny marionette – jerks Sankey into the first verse of 'Gather the Reapers Home'.

Walter is not afraid of nocturnal shrieks; you hear cries at night from snares and gin traps and again in the early morning. Walter doesn't care for trapping, but he is keen to shoot. Sankey is odd about teaching him, coy. Walter reckons Sankey's relationship with God is more complicated than most. His singing is beginning to get on Walter's nerves.

Just past the war memorial they bid one another goodnight. At seventeen Walter is the same height as Sankey but finds himself struggling to lift his chin high enough to make eye contact. He hears Sankey laugh. 'Look out whose bed you fall into!' Walter opens his mouth to reply, but catches sight of something over Sankey's shoulder instead. He looks again. A man is it, standing there in the shadow of the houses?

'Thrust in thy sickle and reap,' says Sankey, 'for the harvest of the earth is ripe.'

Standing alone beside the ditch. A man in uniform is it? Is he waiting there?

'See the soldier, Sank?'

'Walt, Walt, Walt. The harvest is truly plenteous; but the labourers are few!'

Walter is afraid. 'I see him, behind. See, Sank? Look.'

Sankey places a hand on Walter's shoulder. His singing is soft and as high as a boy's: 'Throw out the lifeline across the dark wave, there is a brother whom someone should save.'

'Take a look there!' Walter hisses.

Sankey winks at his friend as he turns. He blocks Walter's view, so that Walter has to step around him. It is not possible, thinks young Walter Brown, it is too peculiar, this. He looks again and sees that the soldier is gone. There is only the dark tree with the moon in its branches. There is nobody there at all.

★   ★   ★

Walter suspected that inspiration was eluding him. It was necessary to pin a poem down as they were flighty things. Walter narrowed his eye at the sky, the weather, the girls in the bakery; all conspired against him. Whenever he felt himself assailed by doubt he returned to the volumes of poetry written by other people. He noted that the esteemed William H. Davies had written a poem entitled 'The Rainbow', whose first line went: *Rainbows are lovely things*. He felt his confidence returning at this. Here was something he could have written himself. It was the other poets, the geniuses, particularly the B brigade: the Brookes, Brownings, Burnses, Byrons, these were the ones you had to watch out for, these were the fellers who made you feel a fool with their hollows, heights and haywains, their naked crags and solitary hills. It is this mob who will crush you with their cache of shadowy banks, leaf-blown churchyards, stippled rivers, icicled minarets, lighted moons, close-wrapped fogs and blaz'd twilights. Take the wind from your sails before you even get started.

Of all the Romantic poets, Walter thought he loved Shelley the best. He couldn't say why. For his dreamer's heart perhaps. Walter suspected he and Percy Shelley were made of the same fibre. He would have liked to have shaken his hand: 'Mr Shelley, how do you do, sir. Walter Brown.' With dreaming must come faraway lands, because that was the way of dreams. A kind of transport, dreaming was.

Besides, a writer, a poet, must travel to see and know the world of which he writes, surely. A poet could not remain all his life in the south-east of England. He might *return* to the south-east of England, but that is different. Truly, Walter told himself, if he was ever going to write anything of note, he would have to cross an ocean, perhaps two. He would have to devise his own heartfelt notions, and set them down, well lettered, for the cogitation of others. This is not as easy as it sounds.

Walter Brown filled two notebooks with his poetry. He loved to feel their weight, as though the poems themselves had made the notebooks heavier. And the words did have weight, he knew that, and characters all their own. Sometimes the words could be bidden and sometimes not. Walter did not understand how this worked, he only knew that on some days he opened a notebook and no words would come. Other days they came slowly, grudgingly, in the wrong order. It occurred to Walter that a poet who wished to write of home would do so better if he simply left. He opened his notebook and tried again:

> Let not the songbird fail:
> She travels from Africa,
> the bold, intrepid nightingale.
>
> Her gentle songs do ne'er betray
> her will to conquer squall and storm;

until, at last, her darkest night gives way
to bright and hopeful dawn.

Keats to Rome. Byron to Malta. Shelley to
Switzerland. Wordsworth to France. At night
Walter dreamed of deserts with wide golden tides
rolling like ocean waves. And hillsides of olive
groves, blooming with wildflowers, tinkling with
the sound of goat bells. He dreamed of a fjord,
high as a building, and himself at its crest with
his pipe and his pen, and his beard (for he would
grow one) frosted and his cheekbones mauve.
And he dreamed of a volcano that burned away
his clothes and, as he fell into its furnace centre,
he dreamed that her voice was calling him. And he
dreamed that he died there, burned to ash, and
he saw them clearly – his teeth and his pipe and
his sturdy pen – in the dust before the snow began
to fall, and they were covered over then, flake by
flake, as though by the laying of thousands of tiny
cold wreaths.

'And what will you live on, thin air?'
It was not for Walter Brown to explain to his
mother that a poet must eat and sleep where he
can, and not bother too much about his animal
needs.
'Or perhaps you will eat your words, young man.
Ha! Imagine, if we all lived by our fancies, where
would it lead?' Her laugh squeezed her till her
eyes watered. 'Nothing, my son, not coal in the

grate, food on the table, or roof overhead, is materialised from a young man's whimsy, or where would we be?' The laugh is replaced by a quiet, threatening formality. And a warning stare. 'Hard work puts things in their place, Walter Frederick Horace Brown, and don't you forget it.'

That night Walter dreamed he found Mary in his loop snare. She was naked and he shot her. She screamed and kicked like a doe. Her eyes watched him as they filmed over. He was looking at her breasts, rose-brown tipped and mottled with cold. He wondered if he should skin her. God Almighty. The next morning he could not look at himself in the mirror to shave. The previous night he had dreamed her arms grew longer and longer until she could tap him on the shoulder from half a mile away. *Wally Wally Wallflower, growing up so high.*

Serpent or no serpent, the water pool by Cockshoot Wood is Sankey's favourite pond. In this July heat it is a dark oasis, trembling with insect life. He is standing in it up to his neck for there is no one about – man, woman or meddler – to pass comment or demand that he remove himself. Folk are far too willing to interfere when they should be minding their own business. Today at any rate he is alone save for a family of little grebe and the occasional startled flap of woodpigeon.

'What shall I do to be saved? When the pleas-
ures of youth are all fled:
And the friends I have loved from the earth are
removed,
And I weep o'er the graves of the dead?'

The song skates across the water and rises up into
the hornbeam trees.

Sankey wonders whether it is Tuesday or
Wednesday. If it is Tuesday he will collect his
paraffin from Grove Road. If he forgets he will
have no light or heat tonight and moreover he is
intending to cook an egg and piece of mutton for
his supper. Perfect would be in his cups by now,
or attempting to lighten his load; game birds were
two shillings these days. A bird would be nice,
roasted with thyme. *Behold*, he muses, to take his
mind off food, *here is Light. Here in this sanctuary
I have seen thee.* Sankey raises his arms and notes
how brightly the drips of water glitter. *My soul
waiteth upon Him, From Him cometh my salvation.*
Sankey closes his eyes. He smiles. Everything is
splendid. In his heart is comfort and everlasting
love. Here is the Almighty, here in the pond, and
in everything reflected therein, thereof.

'*My soul thirsteth for thee, my flesh longeth for thee
in a dry and thirsty land, where no water is. To see
thy power and thy glory, so as I have seen thee in the
sanctuary. Because thy loving kindness is better than
life, my lips shall praise thee, now and for ever. Amen.*'

Sankey opens his eyes. A conversation would be

nice. Young Walter will be busy in Wycombe. The Water Company must keep the water flowing or else. God shall wipe away all tears from their eyes, Walt. At evening time it shall be light.

When at last the sun sinks behind the Chilterns' widest hill, he wades out and lays himself down on the bank. His head is filled with colour as he shivers. A marvellous feeling this, better than any food or lust or winnings or fiery drink; gone now was his paraffin, his egg and his mutton chop.

'Behold, I stand at the door and knock!' Sankey calls up at the navy sky, darkening now with night cloud, for at last he knows that only He is his rock, his salvation, his defence. I shall not be greatly moved, he thinks. And falls asleep.

Sankey had only one real memory of his mother. The rest was a wash of longing and some hotch-potch pictures his mind had constructed for comfort. His real memory though, like the photo-graph in his pocket, was a bright living thing. It remained in his mind sleeping or waking and some-times drifted into view uninvited as he engaged in conversation or cut firewood or assisted Father Blagdon. In this real memory she is bending down to him. Behind her the sunlight is so dazzling it is hard for the young Charles to focus, but he can make out eyes, lips, teeth, revealed by her widening smile – the smile she has for him. She is talking, but he doesn't understand what she is saying. He doesn't care because he has the best part, the golden light of her attention, the evidence of her delight in him, and the cool softness of her hand on the back of his neck. He remembers her touch on his neck, on his head; it is sacramental, merciful, it is laid there to bless him, forgive him, protect him, it is laid there still. He looks up at her, into her brightness, and here, blinding him, is the love he dreams of now and has dreamed of always. He would like to say a prayer to that love but can think of none, save for the one he learned on her knee: *Mary, Mother, all the day, Close beside thee let me stay. Keep me pure from sinful stain, Till the night return again.*

Close beside thee. Let me stay. Though he had spoken it morning and night like a good boy, no amount of praying had kept her. He had padded around her sickbed restlessly, counting her fingers, humming the hymn he knew, and when he grew sleepy he stood at her shoulder and rested his cheek on her arm. When she finally went away she did so quiet as a bird, though she had resisted for several weeks because she worried for her boy.

'My poor Charlie,' she said to her friend Evelyn. 'What'll happen to him?'

He saw her face. She was asleep. My boy, my darling boy, my darling little boy. These were her words. She said them whether she was dying or not. She held his face in her hands and he watched her tears make their long journey to her pillow. She stared at him as if to remember his face. She would have to wait a long time perhaps until he arrived at the gates. She would be waiting. They would be reunited then. My boy, my darling boy. I shall wait for you.

When she died she said nothing at all. Charles ran to her bedside to show her his stone in the shape of a shield and found she had slipped away.

Evelyn did her best with Mary's boy. 'Oh dear,' Charles commented. It was all he would say. Nobody could get any other words from him, not even a prayer. It upset the older ladies, the pity of it, until finally it was the ladies themselves that required comforting. Evelyn did her best, she dressed, bathed and held him, and still he continued: 'Oh dear. Oh dear. Oh dear.' Evie thought, well, it will soon stop after a day or two, but it did not. After a while, her charity used up, it began to grate on her.

He had no memory of his mother's funeral. He could not be altogether sure whether he had been there, buttoned up in a dark coat, or not. He went to live with the draper's widow, whose own children were almost grown, and there he settled down and did his lessons at school and, once he learned to read, attended to the two books in the house, the Holy Bible and Ira Sankey's *Sacred Songs and Solos*. He visited his mother's grave in his short trousers, long trousers, and finally in his working boots. As he learned them he sang her the hymns from the book, though it was breezy at the churchyard on the hill. And this way Charles Collins became Sankey, or Charles Sankey for formal occasions, after the revivalist Ira Sankey's collection of hymns and sacred songs. They christened him in the schoolyard and it remained. A name his own mother would not recognise.

Mary Hatt and Walter Brown were married in Gomms Wood by Charles Sankey around the time of Mary's seventeenth birthday. They placed their hands on the Holy Bible and exchanged flowers for rings. They sang 'Jesus, Beloved of My Heart'. Sankey had not intended to marry them but found himself, to his astonishment, offering to do so the day they discovered him close by, behind a holly bush with a ladies' hand mirror. He offered to charge them nothing – owing, he said, to the fact of his being an apprentice preacher at this stage. Walter and Mary saw no reason to refuse. It was a fine blowy day and Sankey had his Holy Book with him and everyone loved a wedding, so. More than this he volunteered to share his good tobacco afterwards.

During the ceremony, as Sankey drifted, directionless, between sermon, homily, advice and admonishment, he fancied he felt the heat of God on them, all three. He found the spell of his own words deeply moving as he blessed the happy couple, blessed the day, blessed the cathedral of birch, beech and oak in which they stood, and blessed himself.

'You have gone off the topic,' Walter Brown pointed out impatiently, but Sankey had inspired himself with a blizzard of wisdoms. Some considerable time passed before Mary and Walter were able to find themselves conjoined by God. Afterwards they shared the pipe tobacco Sankey had been saving, and Walter was violently ill over his shoes.

God's men, men of God. What Sankey wouldn't give to be counted among them. He wished he had learned more about reading and writing. He wished he could wear the collar and the wide-brimmed hat and that way be a salve and a salvation to the people who would come to him. The men of the cloth; it was they with all the answers and the final say, they with the power and glory for ever and ever, Amen.

'A great and powerful wind tore the mountains apart and shattered the rocks before the Lord, but the Lord was not in the wind. After the wind there was an earthquake, but the Lord was not in the earthquake. After the earthquake came a fire, but the Lord was not in the fire. And after the fire came a gentle whisper.'

Sankey's voice drifts thinly out of him. He has always had a high voice, like a girl. Something was coming, he knew that now. The trumpet would sound. He was ready for the labour, for the Light. Difficult to find his preaching voice, to practise, with this cough. Sankey reckons it is walking up these hills that's done it. That and the damp in winter.

When he began to lose his appetite he suspected

it was the Lord, lightening his load to ready him for action. No good being a slowcoach when it came to God's own work. Others said it was the wood dust at the chair factory (worse than the solvents some said) that got inside the workers' throats and lungs. These were exotic woods imported from Africa. Some of the men developed chronic headaches and asthma and some of these men suspected a connection, but they were reassured by their own good doctor, Dr Summer, who could not confirm any link whatsoever between the imported wood and the symptoms.

One day in the near future, during a time of turbulence in Europe that could not yet be imagined, it would be noted that the men in the area who were dying of throat and nasal cancers had, at one time or another, all worked at the chair shops.

CHAPTER 38

The line-marker makes no comment, it just draws the line. Sean discovers that it is very satisfying to draw a line and walk away. Sean draws the line. So long as the wheel is turning the paint pours itself in a careful stripe. It pours steadily, consistently. The smell of the paint, Sean thinks, is how the space shuttle must smell: new, fresh, white, scientific. Where Sean goes, the line goes. Sean is God. The line-marker squeaks with each revolution, it is the sound of progress. It dictates the rhythm of Sean's steps, so that each is perfectly synchronised with the other. The line-marker leads him, as if it knows where it would prefer to go. He follows it across Windmill Lane, down the path skirting Lower Field at Widmer Farm, where the nettles are taller than him, past the tin bath where insects float and down North Road for a while. At the sound of a car the line-marker hurries him behind a tree until it is safe. It is, however, a giveaway, the way the paint stops suddenly beside a large object. Peep-peep, off he goes again. Sean thinks this is the best thing he has ever done in his life. He is making his mark on earth. Here and there he stops and listens, waits for trouble. But there is only the chattering of birds and the constancy of the lonely fireball sun.

At the top of Cryers Hill Lane he takes a rest. Behind him the line stretches all the way down to Bottom Farm. It waggles a bit between the giant chestnuts, where he had looked over his shoulder to see behind him, and there is a deviation to the side further down, by the house with the low roof, where he had craned his neck for a glimpse of the old codger who lived there without electricity, and it had made him swerve. In spite of these lapses the line runs down the hill like a line on a map, jinking a little as map lines do, but swift and purposeful, as if it knows where it's going. Certainly it will lead him back; this line would lead anyone, it is a good line. There were lines on the stones in the classroom collection drawer; wispy they were, like feathers. Sean told the teacher that he did not know what they were. Bones, Miss Day replied. Yes, they are of course bones. Fossils, she said, to be precise. Miss Day is always precise, she never takes her eye off the ball. Miss Day told the whole class then, announced in her best sing-song voice, that the markings on the fossil stones were the bones of the dead. No one believed her for a second, but it was a good reply.

26th March 1943, M.E.F.

My dear Mary,

I received your letter! You don't seem to have had much frost this year, kiddie? It sounds as though your farm girls are doing well enough, despite John's fears! How I wish I could have enjoyed some of that stewed rhubarb with you. Try not to worry about Clem, I am sure he is settling down wherever he is. Two of our guns are now out of action and I no longer have time to attend a church service. There are lots of skylarks here. I found 2 babies in a nest on the ground – hardly feathered. I pray they will survive. I wish you could see the huge beetles here. You know, these Italian cigarettes make a poor smoke.

Sad to say but Bert Jones has died. I had spoken of you to him many times, and he told me of his adored wife and sister-in-law. Gunner Horner has been taken away with overheated mastoid.

There are plenty of tortoises here. If you pick them up, they pee down your arm. Would you believe I've just brushed 100 ants off this letter. By the way, I have enclosed a few wildflower seeds in order that you should plant them and perhaps we shall see the same pretty plants each day. There is a limit on letters and I am therefore using my school exercise books to make longer letters and hope the sheets do not run out too soon.

One of our fellows has not heard from his wife for five months. We have just heard Smith was taken prisoner.

Later (April):

We now have a hen. When we stop we tip it out of the lorry and it potters around and we feed it. It lays about 3 eggs a week. A funny thing, Sinclair was a bully during training and now he is a jelly. A good driver, but goes to pieces in action these days. Do not work too hard (though I know how gladsome harvest time can be when it comes).

Ted Jarvis wrote to his wife suggesting the name Eric for their new son. She has called him Keith. It is too dark to write more.

Later:

We found a donkey almost buried under the sand, so we dug it out and it staggered to its feet. We poured some of our water ration down it and it revived and wandered off.

Later:

At last! A wireless! Bertha Willmott is singing 'Nellie Dean' on it and all the boys are singing. It's just been reported that

'Rommel has left Africa'. We were hoping to take him prisoner.

The natives at Mahadia cannot believe we've come all the way overland from Egypt. They seem to think we have come from the skies by magic.

The Yanks receive such wonderful parcels from home, gee. Every luxury you can imagine. They think the Tommies have a hard time. The cockney lads make good pals, though they talk the hind legs off a donkey. The New Zealander, it has to be said, has a heart of gold.

We moved on at 0500 hrs through gold and mauve dog daisies. Monty is hugely popular. He has the one hundred per cent trust of everyone. We tickle the scorpions with grass and they sting themselves to death.

Later:

The 15th Panzers have surrendered! It is 130 degrees in the shade. I have a Jerry foxhole lined with hay, which is alive with field mice. Very comfortable. I met Zeb, a Slovak soldier. He talked me into the ground. We have 3 days' leave in Cairo.

1800 hrs:

We went to Benghazi but there was nothing open. Came back along the coast road – miles of nothing except locusts. I enclose a

pressed red flower from one of the blossoming trees. Watermelons are 1/3- each
here. The slices are so wide they wet your
ears. We are still on the road. Many of the
lads have been ill with septic sores; some
have pleurisy or influenza, so now we're
being granted 7 days' leave in Cairo – the
first lot go tomorrow. I feel so alone sometimes. I made friends with a native who
spoke good English. His wee eight-year-old
daughter had rings in her ears and nose.

I wish I could be a writer. I dare say poet
is out of the question, but always I want to
write, write, write. My thoughts are of you.

(Soon it will be your birthday, now that
it is May.)

Shed helah. Allah yeb mek feek.

Ma assalamah,

Walter xx

Sean holds the letter up so that the sun shines
through it. Wur. He doesn't mind that he cannot
read the words. He can see his fingers through
the paper, then his whole splayed hand. He
presses the letter against his face and smells. He
decides he will tell Miss Day he is *changeover'd*
from a letter. He doesn't care that it's a lie. Now
he can nearly-read p'raps she will hug him again.
P'raps when she hugs him he will tell her what
he knows.

★　　★　　★

At school they don't sing hymns or say prayers. Perhaps because it is not modern, Sean thinks. They sing 'Lord of the Dance' and 'Kumbaya', and 'Them Bones, Them Bones, Them Dry Bones', with Mr Turner on guitar. Mr Turner likes to strum with his fingernails, hitting the strings hard, turning his face beetroot. He slaps a rhythm on the wood too, and bobs his head like a pop star, making the girls giggle.

Hymns and prayers are for church. Sean suspected it would be pointless to pray in a prefab. Proper prayers needed gold, hush and the chink of a collection box or else they would not go all the way up; they would hover and drift. Proper hymns and prayers needed stained glass and the swish of a dome-headed priest, whose entrance would roll the eyes of the Saints.

Girls seemed to know lots of songs, all the words, the correct tunes. They sang together like thrushes; they liked to glimpse one another and sing through their smiles. It was a secret code, invisible as radar; a boy would understand nothing. A boy would rather not sing at all, unless it was a good dirty song and everyone cheered. A boy would stare at the ceiling and mouth nearly-words, and if he saw another boy smiling his way, he'd know someone had farted.

Sean wears his brother's shoes. They are too big and too beautiful; black suede with pointed toes. Shoes you might solve a crime in. Not actual suede but lookalike suede, synthetic. Anything synthetic is sophisticated. The girl with the lazy eye in Barratt Shoes said so. She said it didn't stain and it didn't smell. It was modern. She finished talking and her lazy eye slid off up the wall, across the plastic boots and handbags.

Ty bought the modern synthetic shoes there and then. He counted his money. Sean watched her good eye roll as the cash came down. When the till pinged, the drawer flew into her stomach and her eye floated off again. These were shoes you would see on *Top of the Pops*, on the shuffling feet of Cliff or Ringo. These shoes had panache, that's what Ty said. God knows how he knew that.

Ty walked so fast Sean had to run to keep up. They sat down in the bus shelter and Ty put them on. He made Sean carry his old ones in the box. On the bus Ty put his feet up on the back of the seat in front so they could watch the shoes all the way home.

Sean clops past the garages at the back of Ann's house. He gazes at the shoes as they lead him where they will. If Ty finds out that Sean is wearing the brand-new modern synthetic suede shoes, he will kill him. Ty wasn't going to find out.

Sean waits by the fence to see if she will fly up. Nothing. He continues up the hill to the Wilderness. Not many there, just spaz tiddlers: Tim, Eg, Gerald and a toddler, naked except for a gun holster. Where is everyone? His shoes have been spotted. The toddler comes and squats to inspect them.

'They're too big,' Gerald accuses, pointing at them like he is the shoe police, but Sean is already busy flopping back to the road.

'Spaz, they an't mine,' Sean explains, brash on account of the toddler.

'Because you stoled a person's shoes!' Tim is startled by the speed of his deduction.

'Spaz, I loaned 'em, geddit?'

The shoes are harder to control off the tarmac. Sean claws his toes.

'*Whose* shoes wan't they?' demands Tim, alarmed.

'They're too *big*,' Gerald insists, pointing them out to the aghast toddler. Sean throws his hands on his hips like Ty does.

'Holy cow. These are modern shoes costing two pounds four shilling. Synthetic *not* suede you spaz. *Pan* ash, see? Now p'sof.'

He almost gets the hang of the shoes on Hawbush Road. It is a flip-flop technique, pinching and relaxing your toes at the right moment, rotating your hips.

His older brother had a thing about Hawbush Road. 'Hawbush, geddit?' Typhoid had said. 'D'you geddit? *Hawbush*!' And he thrashed himself laughing. 'Geddit?' Sean told everyone. He didn't get it either, but they rolled off chairs laughing just the same, even the girls. Sean twinkled up at Miss Day. '*Haw bush*, Miss, d'you geddit!' He was sent home. His dad knocked him against the TV with his swinging arm. *Deputy Dawg* was on. He got sent to his room with no dinner. They had to

347

apologise to Miss Day together, Sean and his dad. Gor did the talking.

What do you say to the lady teacher?

Sean still didn't get it.

Modern shoes were not an everyday sight around Cryers Hill. It was not a with-it place like London or High Wycombe. Never mind that the word *GROOVY* was scrawled in the bus shelter. Who were they kidding?

Hello, lamp post, what you knowing? Glad to see your flowers growing. Songs flew out of the builders' transistor radios all day, loud as the drilling. You didn't talk to lamp posts around here unless you were the village loon, and then people knew to avert their eyes.

Sean puts his hands on his hips and clops like a horseless cowboy. Some of the builders, he notices, are watching. He tries not to cringe, he forces his legs to swing, his body to sway. He wants to call out something funny, clever. All he can think of is *Hawbush, geddit?*

He arrives at the skeleton frames of the newest houses at the top of the hill. Up here a desert wind whips the sand into your eyes. The houses make unfamiliar noises; they crack and hum and moan like injured souls when the wind flies into their pipes. *Columbia, this is Houston, over. Ping. Houston, Roger, we copy and we're standing by for your e.t.d.* Sean floats; it is harder in a wind. *Ping.* He claws his toes and the shoes come with him. Ropes of dust twirl, spraying fine particles into his eyes;

sheets of plastic snap and the houses moan. *This is Houston, loud and clear. OK, Neil. Ping. We can see you coming down the ladder now. Roger, Houston. Ping. We copy you.* Sean pauses beside some freshly laid cement. When it is dry it will be a patio. Patios are the latest thing, everybody wants one. The smaller houses, Sean's included, don't have one. One day a family will sit right here on their fashionable garden chairs (plastic weave in get-ahead colours that last a lifetime) and they will celebrate their patio-ownership. A patio is stylish and with-it. A patio is for people who aspire to cocktails. A patio means you are somebody. Sean doubts, with a conviction that surprises him, that he will ever be the owner of a patio. The first step is indeed a small step, and though he cannot pretend it is for all mankind or anything, in terms off soothing his troubled, patioless soul it seems to do the trick. There is something satisfying about the sight of a panache shoe standing on an almost-patio. Here is a wearer of modern shoes relaxing on his new terrace. If only Ann were here to see this.

Moon dust smells just like wet ashes. Neil Armstrong says so. To Neil Armstrong, up on high where the angels float, right there under God's nose, moon dust smelling like wet ashes is bloody marvellous, and the whole world agrees with him. Moondust. Wetash. Panash. Maybe all beautiful words are connected.

It's creepy, the quiet. The builders must be on a break. Sean looks up through the grit at the wooden joists fanning out like dinosaur ribs to make the gabled roofs; torn plastic flaps like skin at the top. The houses look wild and dangerous to Sean, herded together, a sandstorm behind them, prehistoric.

The Windsor-vowelled BBC voice remains characteristically calm; '*There he is now, putting his foot out. You can see him leaning on it.*' Sean waits calmly too, while the dust blows, while the world watches, while he makes history. *Ping.* Everyone waits while Neil thinks. *It's one small step for man.* Sean closes his eyes. *One giant leap for mankind.* Neil has spoken, amen. He is still speaking, wur. *The surface is fine and powdery. Ping. I can pick it up loosely with my toe.* Except it isn't loose, it isn't powdery. Sean attempts to lift a foot. For a terrible moment, like when someone forgets to speak on television, nothing happens. The shoe remains stuck to the fashionable patio, while somewhere across the estate a chainsaw cries a great wail of dismay. Then, as fear turns to panic, Sean crouches so that he can grasp hold of his knee and pull harder, wrench the bastard, so that the shoe is finally, suddenly, stickily, released. He stares at the footprint left behind. Here he once stood in a magnificent shoe. Sean woz ere. The village could remember it for ever, like Neil on the moon, like the baby on the hill, like the girl in the wood. Sean is history, the print makes it so. He looks up at the vacant sky and sees one lonely aeroplane, tiny as a pin, hanging in the heavens. Ah farther.

The walk back is complicated. The sun is high, and with each step, as the machinery groans, the shoe gets heavier. Sean reminds himself he will feel this way upon returning to Earth. The BBC voice pronounced: '*Neil Armstrong's footprints will remain on the surface of the moon, undisturbed, for millions of years.*' Truthfully, that is what the television said. It is because there is no wind on the moon. They are there now, Neil's feet. It is hard not to be impressed. They will always be there, in a hundred years, in a thousand, in a minute, for ever. Sean watches the cemented panache shoe as it swings its small steps. He is as good as dead; Ty will make it so. You can't make a giant leap in a concrete shoe. Sean wonders if anyone ever said that.

'Are you going to the village-hall film?' he asks anyone, everyone.

'What for?'

'Dunno. Why not? Might be good.'

'Nah. What for?'

There are posters up announcing the screening tonight at the village hall. Sean cannot imagine why anyone would want to go. It is not a proper film like *The Pink Panther* or *Dracula*. It is bits and bobs as far as he can tell, like your Aunty Noreen's holiday snaps. It sounds like rubbish. He thinks he will go. He wonders if the murderer will be there, sitting at the back.

'Are *you* going?' he asks his dad.

'Village *hall*?' His dad repeats it as if each word

is foreign, incomprehensible. Sean begins to explain, translate. Gor interrupts with, 'Take your mother.'

Sean does not want to take his mother. He cannot be sure what effect the village hall will have on her. She might lock herself behind her eyelids and not come out.

Ann was an altogether more complicated proposition. Sean would have to be on his mettle. He employed a decoy for his opener.

'I'm not going tonight, are you?'

'Where?'

'Village hall.'

'Why?'

'See that *film*.'

'It's rubbish.'

'I know. Might not be.'

'Stupid it's spazzes from the olden days who lived round here, that's all, you crip.'

'I know, that's what I said.'

It costs two bob to see the rubbish film at the village hall.

'My dad's coming, he's paying,' Sean explains to the hair-lacquered women on the door. He gets in free. There are plastic chairs and a tea urn and some giant plates of iced biscuits. Sean takes a handful of the biscuits and sits down at the end of a row. There is a white rectangle on the wall and everybody sits down and stares at it. It is old people mostly.

A man everyone calls Mr Deacon is fussing

about with the projector. His fringe is stuck to his forehead and inside his square spectacles his fishy eyes are sliding, panicking, while his mouth complains about something in little gasps.

Finally the lights go out and a cheer goes up that sounds so joyful it makes Sean laugh out loud. A bright light burns on to the white rectangle and the room is silent. A flash, a flicker, a face, then it's gone. The lights go on. A groan. Sean looks around. This is quite good so far. A younger group has arrived, older than Sean. They clomp to the front row and sit down. They look embarrassed. They nudge each other and cackle like strange birds. A few families have arrived. Sean waves to their neighbours. They are with another family and they don't wave back. Sean wonders if he goes to get some more biscuits, will someone take his seat? The room is quite full now, the biscuits will be gone. Maybe the biscuits are all gone already. Darkness. Another cheer, loud. In the front row a frantic outbreak of nudging and squirming. The beam of light burns through the dust on to the white rectangle. Dark flecks begin to jostle there. The youths in the front row dart their arms up into the light to make rude shadow-shapes on the screen. Sean laughs and claps. A crowd of bobbing V-signs clogs the screen. Sean is glad he came. He will tell the others.

'Sit down!' some of the adults are shouting. As they call out to the front row a face flickers on to the screen. The room begins to quieten. It is the face of a man. He is staring into the lens of the camera. Nothing else. He blinks a few times, that's it. He gazes out at the village-hall audience and they gaze back. The film bounces on the screen, but nobody complains or makes a tutting noise. Sean looks at the man, at his shirt collar and the space between his teeth. The man is talking again, chatterbox. He's wearing a funny round black hat, like the Homepride Flour men. There is no sound except for the whirring and occasional clack-clack of the projector. The man smiles suddenly, mouths something, and the audience laughs self-consciously. The man in the film is laughing too now, amused perhaps by his own remark, and the audience laughs a little more easily. The man is taking something from his pocket. He puts them on. Spectacles. Is he going to read? Could they read in the olden days? Probably. Probably they are cleverer. Nowadays they are thick but taller. His dad said that. True alphabet, liar alphabet, which? The man is still talking. He is reading out from a black book. He closes it and holds it up for the camera to see. Some people might be able to work out what he is saying, Sean thinks. Deaf people can see words on people's lips. He reckons if he was deaf he'd at least be able to do that. He glances around. The faces beside him are grey-lit, impassive. Hard to tell if it's a good film or not. The man removes his specs, grins, and is gone. There is a murmur of laughter in the audience. Specman. Wur.

Another man now, younger. This man is wearing a cap. He takes it off and puts it back on and he smiles. He has a long sad face, even when he's smiling. He takes something from his pocket. A pipe! Ha! He puts it between his teeth. Everyone is laughing now in the village hall. Ha ha ha! The finger-shadows go up again on the screen, giving the man rabbit ears. The man poses with his pipe while the fingers get ruder. He is gone. I know you. Pipeman. Now on screen, a group of children are running down a lane towards the village-hall audience. Wur.

28th July 1943, M.E.F.

My dearest Mary,

I was delighted to hear that Isabel had a baby boy! William is a fine name. And you are become an aunt! I hope this finds you well. Are you looking forward to your birthday? How I wish I was there to wish you many happy returns. I try not to think of the hedgerows at home coming into flower – here is just sand, heat, fleas, bugs.

Also, I have had a gippy tummy, typical of this place! Lime juice is the only thing I can drink. When you order a drink in Cairo you have all kinds of bits included. Lots of the lads are going ill – septic sores, bladder trouble, flu. At the moment I can see two sparrowhawks flying about. We went 10 miles beyond Tobruk (oh the blueness) then Whadi la Knif – wild, rocky, steep – on through Bazleaze and Toor Pass. We hear Mussolini is no longer in charge. I hope it's true.

Sgt Dove and I talk for hours at a time. We discuss everything from philosophical matters to the strange varieties you find in the animal kingdom. I have been reading *The Insect Man*. Did you know certain types have 8 eyes and females eat the males after marriage? The other day we found a sultan lying on the sand. On to Burat.

Later:
The water is salty, the ground stony to sleep on, but lovely lilies abound. My bivvy is under date palms. The dates hang in bunches like walnuts. Now we are in the 10th Corps of the 8th Army. There are boy bird-scarers here for the crops (takes me back). The boys yell out each time a bird flies overhead, so the birds therefore rarely settle.

We are by the sea and bathe every day now (I am quite the Esther Williams lately). Sadly one of the boys who bathed at night was drowned. You have to be careful. I do not swim out ever. Another fellow of ours accidentally offended an officer and was punished severely. He was told to nail a can to a post – but there was no post there. Then he was ridiculed and humiliated. The tragicomedy of the army!

Later:

The bivvies are small and unbearable in the summer heat. The officers have shade rigged up and drink rum and cognac. You wouldn't believe the queues for meals – 8,000 men waiting at each meal. It smacks of poor organisation and inefficiency. I saw two ships blow up at sea today. Our letters are passed in for censoring at 9 a.m., so I'll close now and get this one off. Lots of mail is stolen before it reaches us, alas. Please remember me to everyone. Cheerio and keep smiling. Did anyone ever tell you you're beautiful? They have now, darling.

Yours, Walter xxx

P.S. Some of the lads found Bert Jones's grave and came to tell me so that I could let his wife know. It is beautifully kept, they say, and one of them took a photo of it for her.

P.P.S. The shooting stars at night make me think of home. I can't think why.

CHAPTER 39

Farmer John Hatt, father of Mary Hatt, has had to let some of his dairymen go and his head carter is unhappy, they say. It is not clear how much longer he will be able to go on. He is not alone. Stanley Smith's farm has fields lying fallow and his herd is already depleted; it will not be long for him. His sons are working on farms as far away as Penn Street. He is waiting for someone to make him an offer. No one has. Already people are speaking of the old days – stockmen preparing for show, local growers in competition, ploughing matches, that sort of thing. Bill Woods was finished off last year by the harvest storm. No warning either, a fine week previous, then the heaviest rainstorm of the year, a real burster, flattening most of his corn to the ground. John had got his in only a couple of days earlier. He had jokingly asked Bill when he was going to stop admiring his and get on with it and Bill had laughed heartily because it was a very decent-looking crop indeed. No one really saw Bill again after that. The word was he had troubles to start with and the storm finished him off quickly.

The rain continued all week and anyone with corn out suffered, including another farm that went under at Naphill.

Next thing is a cow has slipped her calf at a farm not six miles away. John will wait to hear, but if another goes the same way, he will know what to expect. It has happened before. It's possible to lose an entire herd this way. He was a young man at the time and in those days with application you could recover and restock. These days an outbreak was about the end of the matter. John put goats in with the herd, three billies, and hoped for the best. He left the praying to Mrs Hatt – she was in charge of prayers and second chances.

Young Mary Hatt on the other hand had little time for prayers. What was the point of praying for a few dead calves? Animals were always busy getting born and killed, it's what they did. Animals were blood and muck and trouble, and if you want your living from them, get used to it. Her father had said it to her as soon as she could walk in her first boots, and she had taken pleasure in rattling it off ever since with just the right air of grim-faced conviction.

Mary couldn't understand her father's squeamishness when it came to laying men off. Dairymen, ploughmen, pigmen, carters, there was no shortage of them, let them go and come and never mind about it. After all, it was not as though they were going to vanish off the face of the earth for ever.

Sometimes, she reckoned, a man's no good for

his own advice. One day, when the farm belonged to her brothers, as it eventually would, she would give a hand, get it done proper and decent, and then they would see. She would show everyone a thing or two about blood and muck.

Cattle didn't move her anyhow; matter of fact, Mary was fondest of pigs. As a girl it had been her job to watch over them as they grazed for corn ears in the harvested stubble, a job that kept you standing as the stubble was sharp, and a lie-down in a corn stook would earn you a walloping. Though they could be affectionate, she admired more their lack of sentimentality and bent for enjoying themselves. 'A pig has a knowing for enjoyments,' she said. 'They are partial to a lark.'

Like many, she disliked the back-breaking field-work: planting, hoeing, singling and most of the hand-picking (except for peas, which she didn't mind because at least you could sit and clack with the other women). The rest you could keep, the beets, mangels, onions, cabbages, sprouts, spuds and all – in particular on a finger-cold day – keep the buggers.

Harvest time though, now that was different. The way the scythesmen swung their sickles made hand-reaping look restful, though it was no such thing. Like boatmen they swayed through a standing tow of corn; the rhythm, like a weave loom, would make you drift. John Brock threw his sandwiches ahead of him and scythed towards them to keep himself travelling.

Mary's other partiality was reserved for Lyons Corner Houses. She had never in her life visited a Lyons Corner House, but she knew they existed. She had spied a photograph in a magazine. At any of these establishments you could order from a Lyons Corner House menu. One of their waitresses, a Nippy, would serve you. Lyons Nippies were famous. They were smartly dressed in immaculate uniforms that were sewn together with a particular scarlet thread, and beautiful as film stars. If you lost a button the replacement had to be secured with replica red cotton. Mary had never heard of anything so extravagant, so stylish. There were things Mary had in mind, like Lyons Corner Houses, private things, personal. *It is for you the nightingale sings her song.* She had found it in his pocket the night he wrapped his jacket around her shoulders to keep out the cold. He loved her, now she knew it. She wasn't telling. Not on your nelly, no. She would wait for him to go down on one knee.

CHAPTER 40

Sean asks one of the builders when the estate will be finished, please.

'In a month of Sundays,' he replies pleasantly, and grins.

'Ta,' says Sean.

Sean is pleased. He will pass this on.

He goes past the White Lion and stares at the Wag-Wanton Mummers grouped around one of the tables outside on the grass. Five of them anyway, one is missing. Perhaps one of the Daves. The Wag-Wanton Mummers are Brian Ross, Charlie Cross, Dave Pritchard, Dave Waddle, Dave Atkins and Dave Hodge. They are all talking at once and one of them, possibly a Dave, is saying, 'May God strike me down if I'm lying.'

Sean stares because they'd heard that Mummers went back as far as the thirteenth century, maybe even further. But they looked surprisingly young in fact, with their side partings, big square spectacles and open-necked shirts. He watches them grinning into their beer, blowing smoke over one another's heads. They like to accuse each other in loud mocking voices and smack the table with the palms of their hands. If two of them say something at the same time, they shake hands vigorously or embrace. Sean thinks they are strange and magical, like leprechauns. He wonders whether God *would* strike one of the Daves down.

Peep peep peep. Sean pauses when he gets to the lane. Here is the old church and the war memorial. He parks the line-marker beside the stile under a sycamore. You can't take a line-marker into a churchyard and start drawing lines around the dead, it is bad luck. Nor anywhere near a war memorial neither. He knows this because once when he sat on the little stone step at the memorial's base, his father pulled him up by his collar, by the scruff of the neck, like you would a rabbit.

'Show some bloody respect for these lads who got themselves killed for you,' his father had said. He sounded upset.

Sean had become interested in the memorial after that. He had had no idea any lads had got themselves killed, especially not for him. Why would anyone get killed for someone they had never met? There were no clues in the names. *Stanley Collins. Archibald Dean. Albert Evans. Edward Evans. Herbert Evans.* On and on they went; brothers, cousins, sons. Sean looks at all the names, unrecognisable in their spelling, unfamiliar in their sounds. He searches for his own name, but it is not there.

Inside the church it is cool and still. The air is tinged with green and watery thin. Above his head

Sean sees coloured windows in reds and golds; men with shields, with staffs, men on their knees. Far down beyond the altar, where Sean is too afraid to go, the Messiah is still dying on the cross.

In the church it smells of rain and sand, as though it has stood here for all time like the Pyramids, before housing estates or line-markers or astronauts. In the corner are hymn books and flowers. There is a stone font and Sean tries to imagine what it is for. A giant gold lectern, draped in tassels, supports a giant book, partly read. When he looks away, Sean feels, the carvings adjust themselves. He places the hot-pressed daisy inside his hand into the long wooden palm of St Peter.

People sang in churches, he knew that. Plus the vicar was in charge. Sean touches a pew. It is lovely in the church, he thinks. He is amazed it isn't full of people eating their sandwiches, or having a sit. Inside the pew there are little cushions stitched in clashing colours. This is nice. Being here is like waiting for something good to happen.

'Ooooh!' Sean calls. His voice sets off. It travels all around the church. Up to the windows, down to the nave, around the Holy Virgin praying in the corner, over the heads of the wooden cherubs, across the robes of John the Baptist and back to him, four times bigger.

'Aaaah!' Off it went. Then he doesn't do it any more in case a vicar guard flies out. Inside the church there is a stone tablet on the wall, bearing the names of more lads who got themselves killed for Sean Matthews. Sean deduces these are not the same lads as those outside. Still he does not see his own name, though he moves his finger carefully across the ones he can reach.

Robert Riley. Jack Robson. Kenneth Sanderson. Charles Sankey.

He reckons he should say a prayer, but realises he doesn't know any. Godsake. There are things that get said at weddings and funerals and when a man lands on the moon. Sean wishes he had the knack of those words. Then he thinks if he stands very still and stares at his shoes, the way they used to in church in the days when they could still be bothered, this might do for the lads behind the stone who got themselves killed for him. Then he goes outside to collect his line-marker.

17th September 1943

Dearest Mary,

Sorry not to have written for a while. It has been rather a busy time. I felt so weary when we finally left this part of the world. We were loaded like horses and were dead-beat by the time we marched down to the docks. On board ship the bunks were full, so I slept on deck.

The Italian landing, when it came, was hard. Frankly, you were either alert or dead. Five of ours were killed by a flame-thrower. Bob Davis was also killed and Sgt White and Lt Bass have been wounded. There were long-range snipers everywhere and warships out at sea sending screaming shells. At night we lay on the swampy ground (no cover, just face nets and gloves) and the mosquitoes were unbelievably numerous, adding to the misery. Somehow we slept well, even with all the guns banging away, and the rations were good, even providing cigs and chocolate. Everywhere about were ripe tomatoes, either hanging or harvested in piles, squashed, rotting – we grew sick of them.

It is a fearsome thing to see an artillery barrage creeping nearer and nearer to you. It takes all your strength to stay put. One minute you're chatting to the fellow beside you, and the next he is peppered over with holes.

Sometimes our planes came from over the sea, bombed Jerry and quickly flew back. We always seemed to be straining our eyes upward to the Apennine tops. Eventually we grew so weary we became sort of listless over the shells and bombs and the mud dragging, sucking you down. Anyhow, we stuck it. For some reason no thought of retreat ever entered our heads. The few poor simple folk from the hills were very kind – scared of course. The situation was either we were going into the sea or Jerry was going back.

Eventually – slowly, slowly – Jerry went back. Now we are waiting – waiting – for what? God knows! All day shooting, bombing, killing, and now in the quiet moments the mosquitoes surge in.

Vickers is hysterical and in the hospital tent. I may have some sort of fever. I feel vaguely wretched. Last night in the dark each fellow as he lay on his blanket sang a song. One fellow sang a song his little girl had taught him, 'God Bless My Daddy'. It made us all feel quite softie. Sorry to go on.

Are you well, Mary? I still have your photo. I was afraid it would get damaged, but luckily you remain lovely, smiling up at me through it all.

I have been vomiting, I do not know why. At this stage I feel the vomiting is worse than the shelling.

I have to close, I wish I didn't. You are the most beautiful girl on God's earth. How lucky I am to have found you. You have lit up my life more than you will ever know. God bless you and keep you always.

Yours, Walter xx

Sean folds the letter into his pocket. He has no idea how far he has gone. He stops and glances back and there is the paint, perfect and precise, no matter how it squiggles or doubles back. Wet paint is a beautiful thing, he decides. He loves everything about it, the smell, the way it moves, the different colours. He wishes he had discovered paint before, but at least it is not too late. This is the best summer he's ever had, partly because of paint. Left or right here? Sean cannot decide. Eeny meeny miney mo.

CHAPTER 41

Sean keeps very still, same as you would for a deer. There is no deer, however. There is a man. He is in the woods. He just stands there as though this is normal. He has something in his hand. Sean waits, while the paint drips, for the man to say or do something reassuring. Adults do odd things sometimes and there's no point panicking; like when Mandy Day tried nude sunbathing on strips of tinfoil, or the time his own father pushed their car around the corner in his pyjamas so the engine wouldn't make a noise.

What is a man doing alone in a wood? He should be at work. He should be trying to be an executive, a fathead. He should be thinking about his perks. Men in woods. Good or bad? Men who spend time in woods: lumberjack, murderer, lumberjack. Sean has never heard the word 'bodger'. He has no idea bodgers worked in beech woods or that this was their county, or that they had crafted Windsor chairs in the area for two hundred years. But the birds are all songless, because they know as well as Sean knows, bodger or not, that a man is standing aimlessly in the woods. If he dies today, Sean wonders, will he become famous like the dead girl? The man is moving. Rudyell. Bludyell. Sean thinks of two things. First, that he does not want to die. Second: Is the eye watching? Is God watching? Does anyone have their eye on the ball?

The man is looking at the ground. The line. Now Sean understands. The man has followed the paint line. The man has followed him from wherever it was he discovered the line.

The man is looking at Sean. It is too late to hide now, you spaz. Sean swallows instead of breathing. He can hear his own heart and the sound makes him want to cry. He pushes his fingers in his mouth to stop himself crying. What would his mum say? What would his dad say? A man in a wood. *A man in a wood is superior to a woman in a wood, though it is she who will display first to the male.* Sean can smell dirt and dead trees and wind. He wants to run, but his legs have switched themselves off, they will not run: they are filled instead with sand and fag butts. The guardian angel that lives inside him is panicking to get out, he can feel her struggling against his ribs. She doesn't want to die alone in the woods, neither does he. He would rather have a hundred years of whatifs, a thousand. This is a whatif become a whatnow. It's no good crying. Our Father . . . He can't remember the rest. The man is talking. He is talking to Sean. The wood is green and gold, the light is pushing up and high above the blue sky

370

is pressing down. Is that the sound of the man speaking? Is he saying something? He is saying, 'Good afternoon,' like that.

'Good afternoon.' There, he said it again. He is standing next to Sean now.

'Good afternoon,' the man repeats.

Sean doesn't look at him. If he doesn't look maybe he'll go away.

'Hello,' Sean replies. You can change your mind. Girls do. Best to be polite. They are standing underneath a beech tree. The tree has stood here for hundreds of years. Maybe, Sean thinks, he will have to stand here hundreds of years before the man goes away.

'Looking for your trap?'

What? What did he say?

'Pardon what?'

'Looking for your trap?'

Licking Fear Trapped? *What?* What did he say?

'No,' Sean replies.

'What you trapping?'

What? God*sake.*

'Dunno,' Sean says.

'Eh? Birds you after?'

Birds? What, like chicks? *If you fancy a bird, offer her your seat, light her cigarette, ask her name. Birds like to yak.*

'Rabbit?' the man tries.

Sean tries to think. P'sof. P'sof spazspaz-spazspaz. His brain won't co-operate. A rabbit hangs in front of Sean's face, a dead one. It is brown and long and smooth and dead. The man is holding it. Sean says, 'P'sof, spaz.'

'Eh?'

'P'sof.'

The man lowers the rabbit. It hangs by his side.

'Plenty about if you want 'em.'

Sean turns to look at the man. He has done it now, it is too late, he has looked at him and the man is looking back. It is a long face, spiky with new beard, pale lips with spit between them. Sean knows this face. The face smiles. Sean does not want to say the man's name. He cannot say it. He doesn't want to see any more.

'What's that you say?'

'Nothing.'

The man's shoes are quite shiny. *I saw a man in the woods. He was wearing quite shiny shoes.* Sean feels the man's hand on his head, resting there like a cap.

'You're a good lad. A fine lad, you are. Am I right? I can tell. Can I see your contraption?'

Bludyell. Rudyell. The man begins to move. Bludyell rudyell beggarman thief. Sean is running. The line-marker makes a small noise as it falls. He hears the man call after him.

'Come back, sonny.'

As he runs Sean wonders how long it will be before the paint begins to ooze out over the ground. Sean bursts between the trees. He thinks the man is not following, but he is too afraid to look. Running is about rhythm. See me run. Catch me if you can. Spaz talking spaz talk. Weirdo-man.

Sean pumps his elbows. His technique is too jerky for style points, but his speed is undeniably quick. The image of a hare falls into his mind, the way they zag away from danger, the way they flatten on corners. He watches the landmarks that he knows well spin past him. He must be a blur, he thinks. Nobody could get a target on him now, with an arrow, with a gun, nobody, not even the eye. He runs for his life until he reaches the estate. Words fly up with his feet. Weirdo. Spaz. Madman. Murderer. Weirdo. Spaz. Madman. Murderer.

Once he is there, everything seems entirely normal; diggers, kids, dogs, the mushroom cloud of dirt. Sean slows down only to find he cannot walk properly. Gone are the bones, joints and muscle from his legs and in their place is liquid rubber. Each leg squirms and shivers and flaps itself down like a fin. He has become a fish. This is what happens when you meddle. There is surely a fable about this, most likely in the real alphabet, and so now he is paying the price for lying, stealing, meddling and spazzery.

Two giggling girls in hairbands and flower-print dresses put down what they're doing to stare at him. Sean flippers his legs towards them. They approach cautiously, hands on hips like a pair of drudges, to inspect, comment and laugh.

'I've seen the murderer. I've seen the murderer!' Sean informs them. He buckles and sways a little. 'I've seen the murderer. He's in the wood!' Both girls stop, open their mouths and scream.

'Wait! I've seen him! Wait!'

But they are gone, run to their mothers who will hear it all but understand nothing.

Sean sinks to the kerb. He sits and watches his legs bounce, as though each is dancing to its own private tune. He thinks of Ann. He will wait for her to come out. She will believe him, she will know it is true from his rubber leg fins. She will come with him and together they will capture the shiny-shoed murderer in the woods.

CHAPTER 42

Whether or not Mary Hatt was pretty Walter could not tell. As she grew she changed. Her hair: this was dark and had a look as though the wind had been at it. It suited her, this weathered hair – rolls and ribbons would have made her plain. Her mouth: surly, but curled ready for laughing – at him, mostly. Her eyes. A poet would pay attention here. Green-grey. A poetic soul would think of water, of depths. Walter did. (The left eye may drift independently, though not always, during a seizure.) Her skin: pale, lashed with freckles under each eye. Her body. Place of havoc. Wide crescents of sweat in the armpits of her blouse. Girlish breasts. A sailor's swagger.

His first kiss from her cherry mouth was at cherry-picking time, he remembered that. Her lips were stained black from the juice, a patch as big as a bruise that reached up to her cheek on one side; her teeth were purple and she tasted of jam. Walter Brown, who was just a lad then, kissed her harder than he meant to. Once he had started he found he couldn't stop; he put it down to the cherries. She didn't seem to mind. 'Wally, Woolly,' she said to him as though she were concussed. He had had no idea at all that kissing was as grand as this. He kissed her again to make her stop it, and then he just kissed her harder and harder until she was completely silent.

Nowadays their mouths taste of tree bark and woodsmoke. They kiss in the woods. It is the only way. They press against the loosening boundaries of their clothes. It is armour they require now, iron and steel, not buttons, if they are to be kept apart. She bites his lip; there, that's for *you*, you bugga. And he takes her hand gently and presses it towards his belly, while she laughs at his pleading.

The wood keeps their secret, while overhead the sky hurries by. The sun slips imperceptibly to the right for a better view, its hot eye agog. It shrinks their shadows, lengthens them and wipes them clean away.

At the farm there is a barn, foggy with dust, sweet with the smell of hay, clover, flax. There is a single opening in the roof, where God's light pours in, and corners that are dark and gummy with age. Walter can hear the skittering of rats as he kisses her, and the cracks and creaks of the old beams. The gloom makes him bold, but Mary Hatt is no fool. She pushes him hard so that he teeters backwards, almost to the floor.

'Steady on,' she gasps. 'Stupid bugga.'

He looks at her dumbly.

'Wait your turn,' she says, a hint of a whine. And

so Walter waits, like one of the Home Farm bullocks, with his wet breathing and standing heavy on his spread hooves. Mary Hatt knows to make him wait. She is her own best protector, though there are few who might suspect as much.

'Wally, Wally, Wallflower,' she coos. 'When you are washing at the tub, think of me with every rub.'

And Walter's head drops, as the heads of large livestock are prone to do, while Mary Hatt raises the hem of her wool skirt to expose one pale, sturdy leg.

'If the water be ever so hot.'

At the top of this leg Walter sees broad knickers that are white, laundered grey, with thick bindings. If the slaughterman were to arrive now with his firing bolt, Walter would take it between the eyes and go down heavy and unsuspecting as any poor bugger bull.

'*If* the water be ever so hot . . .' Up goes the skirt. He stares at her drawers bunching thickly over her belly, the sketch of dark hair crescenting the top of her thigh. 'Lather away and forget me not.' She raises her eyebrows, juts her chin, and drops her skirt in a single movement.

Walter Brown is deeply in love.

Summer's green has crested all the hills
and grown across my heart a kind of moss.
Sorrel and field pansy bind your hair
While blackbird sings his song of loss.

Pity the muntjac, fallow and roe,
they flee phantoms you cannot see,
Pity the red-back shrike
who sails alone
in a wide celestial sea.

Walter closes his notebook. He has sickened himself with poetry. He is no good, he is not good enough. He doesn't wish to write any more for the time being. There must be an end to what a thing is like and how it compares to another thing and whether it scans or not. He would like to look at the world dumbly, he decides, without judgement or expectation, like an ox. There, he has done it again.

There are more pressing things to worry about besides. God is at His mysterious ways hereabouts. He is moving things around and knocking people askew. He is flattening barley and sickening livestock. He has struck with a bolt a God-fearing, humble man and ruined a farmer and an innocent girl. There are men on the lanes these days; labourers, farmers, those who have lost their livings as the farms go under. They are walking to find work where they may. Some walk into the next counties and beyond and some never come back. Walter himself does not know if he is coming or going, whether they are all individually or collectively going to Hell.

Moreover, there is a rumour that says they want to build houses at Four Ashes, lots of them.

Grange Farm would go, also Terriers Farm, Rockall and Widmer Farms, and the ancient dew ponds too, not to mention Cockshoot Wood and all the fields and low grazing hills from Widmer End to Terriers, some 350 acres.

Who is they? They are known locally as the Powers That Be, as if they are implacable pagan gods. In reality they are a collection of men from cities and towns and other shires with no chalk in their soil. They are sometimes known as Planners, but their proper name is Developers; this is the correct terminology, the name they have given themselves. The Developer, like any other raptor in the valley, helps himself. Not for him the extended tedium of consultation, deliberation, collaboration. Naturally, he tells it differently. In his version the valley will not survive without him. In his version he is keen to be helpful, to engineer advancement where none has so far been made, to foster progress, expansion, to broaden, augment, restyle and refine. As if an overdue evolution must now take place and he, the single-breasted midwife, trained to facilitate and deliver, will take charge. Areas flagged for development are renamed: H5. H9. H7.

'We are planning for fifty years ahead, not five,' the Developers declare loftily. As though the view from their high horse affords them telescopic vistas of the future that no mere local could begin to visualise or comprehend.

Sid Perfect predicts that one day houses and

factories will replace every last field and orchard in the Hughenden Valley. Everyone had a good laugh at him over that, and a few cheered at the prospect of a regular paid job in that case, and a decent roof to live under. Sid Perfect is never wrong.

If the Developers come it will be the end of Cryers Hill and Widmer End and Hazlemere. Dorrie Penn said that. Now everybody is saying it. 'And it'll be the end of me and you,' she added, 'and my lot and your lot too.' Dorrie Penn made sure she got everybody upset over it. She had long ago discovered that other people's upset soothed her own, was like a tonic to her. 'And don't think they will care to remember the way it was, they won't. People like you and me don't end up recorded, there'll be no books or CinemaScope about it, no; only the graveyards here and what has been writ on the stones.' Dorrie had a cheery few days after that.

But soon the talk moved on to other things. The Developers did no developing for the time being that year or the next and soon it was all forgotten. The talk of approaching war put paid to it. The woodland, farms, dew ponds and grazing land were safe from development for now, because somewhere in a smoky room in Munich the foundations for a brand-new development led by Adolf Hitler and his Nazi Party were taking shape.

CHAPTER 43

'I've seen him. I know who he is.' There, he has said it.

Ann looks at Sean. She doesn't blink, but she cocks her head.

'Liar.'

'Not.'

'Liar.'

This was a thing about Ann, hers was the last word, her decision was always final. Sean continued anyway, though the protest in his voice was gone.

'He had a rabbit, a dead one. Reckon he's foreign, so there.'

'I see,' she said, rolling her eyes.

Sean thought p'raps he should push her down, sit on her. Instead he said, 'It's true, you better believe it. And I know his name.'

'What then?'

'Not telling.'

Ann enjoyed rolling her eyes these days, it was her new thing. Sean thought soon they might roll right out of her head and land in her lap, like the cows' eyes.

'Sean Matthews, you are a little liar.'

You could push a person so far. You could push a person too far.

'Liar liar pants on fire. Sean Matthews, where d'you think you're going?'

He didn't know, he didn't care. He had not yet made an executive decision.

Sean could see there were no kids like him in the Gabbett's Housing brochure. Only bright sketches of children in red knee socks strolling under cherry-blossom trees, not to mention grass and shrubs and a smartly dressed woman with a dachshund waving at a handsome man driving a Ford Zodiac Estate. It was not supposed to be a landscape of mud and dust and cement and sand filled with tribes of dirty kids. There was none of that in the brochure. Where were the packs of running dogs? Apart from the dachshund, there was only a white Scottie in a tartan jacket. And a shiny-shoed murderer in the woods? No sign of him. Perhaps they were on their way: the cherry-blossom trees, the grass and shrubs, and everything else. Perhaps they were just around the corner.

18th December 1943, C.M.F.

Dearest Mary,

I am sorry it has been such a long time since I was last able to write. Please forgive me. I hope you were not too worried. I had developed a case of jaundice and had to be hospitalised near Karnos, back in North Africa. Afterwards they diagnosed me as suffering with nerves. Having lost my exercise books, somehow I couldn't bring myself to write a letter, no other type of paper seemed suitable. I am so sorry. I feel better lately, though I was not at any stage before now aware of feeling nervy at all.

I'm afraid Bob Charles got badly shot up. I did my best, we all did, telling him it was not serious, telling him he'd be back home in time for New Year and so on, while he lay squirming, poor fella. He died of course.

I'm afraid Naples was terribly badly knocked about. I am writing this in the lorry. Everywhere is a quagmire outside. We await the din of the guns in the dark. I hear we are moving again, so I will say goodnight now and finish this later as my rigged light is poor. Cheerio, my darling girl.

Later:

Somerset has gone to Naples for a few days' rest and has loaned me his bivvy. Would you believe it, he has a carpet in here – filched from somewhere. Guns are going off all over. Everything is all right as long as our guns keep quiet. If ours go off the light is blasted out and everything in the bivvy dances about as if by magic. Jerry rakes the place with shellfire and, apart from casualties, lots of the lads lose all their kit. It is 6.30 p.m. and there is a new moon. Soto bene. Buona fortuna. Arriverderce. (I am speaking in Italian.)

Later:

We have not washed or shaved. The icy wind blew my grub out of my hand and knocked me over. Lots of the lads are sleeping in caves in the banks. We feel like Arctic explorers. Funny, after all the excess heat and the trouble that gave us. In the caves is a woman living with 4 kiddies between 3 and 10 years old. They have made their way from Jerry lines and are destitute. The kiddies watch us hungrily – they never beg, just watch each mouthful we eat with big, wondering eyes. Who can eat? I can't without giving them some. No stockings or shoes – bits of cloth bind their feet. How they got across the mountain amid a sea of shelling we do not know. Motherhood is tigerish and extraordinary.

Also, we had a new lad with us. When Jerry last shelled us he was too terrified to come out of his bivvy. He was found dead in it hours later. Poor young chap. For the next few months it will be all snow, hail and ice – so different to the desert.

Well, I had better close. Keep smiling, Mary. Remember me to everyone. I have written twice to Mother – she is a plucky old bird it turns out. I am looking at your picture. You are the loveliest girl in the world. God keep you safe.

Yours, always, Walter xx

Sean had to stay after school and write out 'ie must not tel lies,' one hundred times. He didn't know if he'd reached a hundred. He stopped when his pencil lead snapped. The teacher reading the newspaper didn't count them. Sean told all the kids he saw on the way home that he'd written a thousand.

Sean had told Miss Day that his mother was dying of typhoid. He didn't know why he said it. Except in a way it was true; his brother was making their mother miserable with his great big head and disgusting habits. Anyway it was too late now. The school had told his parents.

'You're a right little liar,' his mother said.

His dad told him, 'Don't lie to the lady teachers.' And then, 'Brainless little sod, what are you?'

Later on when his dad was soft and sleepy in his armchair watching *Oh Brother!* starring Derek Nimmo, Sean mentioned that it was the teacher who was a liar not him, as he had only meant that Ty was driving his mum around the bend. But this too was a lie. Typhoid was the only deadly disease Sean had heard of.

Gor swung a slap that landed on the back of Sean's neck, a dull thud of meat and bone that tipped the room over and kept his head at an angle all the next day. But it didn't matter what kind of disease was not killing his mother, because Miss Day had put her arms around Sean as soon as he delivered the typhoid news, and he had breathed her in and told her what he knew: everything.

In truth Sean was not the only fibber. Especially since the girl died in Gomms Wood. Now there were stories growing taller each day, in the playground, at the launderette, in the queue for a tint and blow-dry at Faith's Creations. The small forked tongues, the ones belonging to the playground kids, the ones waiting to speak the words of service engineers, supermarket tellers, depot managers and town planners, these tongues were busy too, whispering and falsifying, wailing and rumour-mongering around the classroom huts; quick to judge, slow to pardon, but always tirelessly at it in their toytown court of no appeal.

Sean had always liked to watch the boys in the playground whipping themselves into the air, you could even see them from the road, above the fence, popping up like salmon. People on passing buses would turn their heads. And the girls, the way they would all lace themselves together in a herringbone weave of elbows; they could move great distances like that, plaited in a chain, cooperating, compacted, like something nature was about to unleash.

At the height of its torment the village saw murderers at every creosoted corner. The woman at the post office and the manager from the bank found themselves leaning confidentially left and right all day till you wondered why they were called upright citizens at all. Everybody had an opinion to voice over a Campari and an Embassy Tipped Virginia in their almost-house and not-yet garden. To cheer himself up, Sean opened two letters in one day.

10th January 1944, C.M.F.

Dearest Mary,

Well, Monty has left the 8th. We're still in the 8th, though attached to the 5th. I saw Abbott and Costello in *Who Done It?* at the cinema last night – amusing. There are hungry priests here with burst boots tied up with strips of rag. I haven't been out of my clothes for a week now. The soles of my boots are worn through and stones play havoc with the feet. Some Douglas transport planes have arrived. Our advance position is now secure. We have Jerries behind as well as in front of us. There is a lovely full moon, it makes me think of home.

You won't believe it but in Naples young boy touts cry, 'Fish and chips!' And you are led through backstreets and eventually to a room containing a naked woman on a bed. If you look nonplussed they all cry, 'Clean! Clean!'

Three of my pals have been killed. We have to keep jumping into holes like animals. A tank fellow went beserk and had to be knocked out for his own good. Mind you, Jerry never actually discovered our company. We were in pinewoods and he kept flying over us.

Arthur Atkins trod on a mine under the snow last night. He lost his right leg and left hand and cheek. He just looked absolutely amazed and kept repeating unbelievingly, 'No foot! No foot!' and looking down as if he'd lost his wallet. It is icy cold. My right foot has chilblains, they burn and itch.

The refugees are so upsetting. They are the same to Jerry as to us and forever on the scrounge. Villages like Sessa, Mondzone and Capri are nothing but stones and dirt.

We are the most forward ack-ack in Italy and are all the time doing field shooting. It feels as though we've been with the 5th Army for some time now. I dream of roast beef, lamb with mint, steamy potatoes and horseradish.

Well, chin up, Mary. Please write. I long to hear news. Keep smiling, darling. You are the world to me. There is nothing but you.

Yours, Walter xx

Sean notes that there are only a few letters left unread. He replaces the bricks. He wishes he had more. He will have to return to Mrs Roys. He must think of some kind of excuse. He wonders if he has nearly solved a crime.

CHAPTER 44

The Dean family lived next door. Walter had been at school with Robert Dean. Robert was raised to bodging, all the men in his family were bodgers and if Robert had any opinion on it, nobody ever asked him for it. Robert's grandfather was also known as Robert Dean. He had started in the local saw pits at the age of seven. He had to sit for many hours a day on the shaving horse (his leg wrapped around to steady himself), with a spoke shave tool which he learned to work by himself. By the time he was sixteen his right leg had become permanently curved. He never mentioned it, to complain or otherwise. Being unable to read or write, having missed his schooling, his sign was a cross. Walter remembered him well; he recalled the cowboy bend of his leg, the sway as he came down the stairs and the sound of his sawdust voice. He remembered Robert's sister attempting to teach the old man to read. 'The Deans are an educated lot nowadays,' he said through the gaps in his teeth. 'I am the last who cannot tell his alphabet.'

Their house was narrow and cheery with mess.

There were kitchen smells and girls' noises and bright little pictures in every room. Walter liked it very much. He would have liked to live there and never go home. He wished he were one of the Dean children; he imagined he was, filled up with shouting, bread and gravy and loud mocking bursts of laughter. He imitated and learned to sound and feel like a little Dean. He tormented the girls and kicked the kitchen chairs and cursed his ancestors. When they flapped around their mother, he caught on to her skirt and apron too and let his head fall on her thigh and even as she walked away he left it bumping there until she peeled him off.

There was a corner of the Dean household, beside the yellow window, and this corner was a place where a terrible thing had happened.

Great-granny Martha Dean, the children's own relative, dropped her oil lamp on this spot and set fire to the carpet, table and herself. Her son James (brother to the cowboy-legged Robert) came hurrying at the sound of her screams, and he beat out the flames. His apprentice boy ran to Mr and Mrs Nash next door (the very same house Walter and his mother now lived in) crying out, 'Granny Dean is all aflare.' 'Oh Mrs Nash,' said Granny Dean as they dabbed her with oil and sweet lime, 'I am burned to death.' And indeed she was, as she died the following day.

An awful thing for anyone's great-grandmother, and particularly incongruous for the happy Deans in their cheery yellow house. Walter stared at the walls and the curls of grime on the windows. He fancied he saw the tall flames and felt their heat too. He strained to hear the screams of pain and surprise. The Dean children liked to tell and retell what had happened here in this particular place. Here on this spot poor Granny Dean fell and cried, and here on this spot too she died. Walter crammed into the corner with the Deans and bowed his head and tried to feel their loss as his own. He wished more than anything he were a Dean. He wished his great-granny had gone all aflare and burned to death in a yellow corner. He wished he lived here in this house, all chock-a-block, sardines in a tin, here with the shouting and cooking and sisters, instead of the other side of the wall where it was quiet and still; where the walls grew long shadows that crept across the rug. Where his mother sat, her mending needle dancing in and out of his clothes, while her dreams withered, one by one, and fell to the floor.

Charles Sankey has his eye on Mary. Women, he knows, cannot be close to God the way men are, it is not the way. God Himself is a man, and men are made in God's likeness. Women, though they may be gentle and diverting, at times rejuvenating, comforting and ministering, are not the ticket when it comes to all things sacred. Sankey concedes this is a pity, highly regrettable, but there it is. It is not his design. Women have complications, pains, mysteries, childbirth and so forth. Mary is different, however. He has his eye on her. He would like to know what she meant when she said, 'Mind you don't fall into the flames, Sank.' She whispered it in his ear, like a sprite, giving him a wakeful night and worry thereafter. What could she mean? He was a godly man, true, devout, sincere, anyone could see. She was having a game with him, teasing. That could mean she felt fondly about him. On the other hand, why – when he had only ever acted, thought and spoken with her best interests at heart – did she provoke him this way?

Sankey has not failed to notice that Walter and Mary spend a good deal of time together. He thought about this at work, sitting in one of his own freshly turned chairs, still blooming with the scent of beech, and through the smoke-filled lunchtime, and all over the chatter and cackle of his workmates, and over his mutton sandwich and slice of fruit cake, and he thought about it restlessly in his bed at night.

At first he couldn't be sure what he hoped to secure as he crouched behind wych hazel and waited, sometimes all evening, for a glimpse or sound of them. He couldn't put his finger on his own motive until one Thursday afternoon, when he spotted them pressed against an elm at the north end of Gomms Wood, and knew immediately that he wanted to break the poet Walter's long lantern jaw.

★   ★   ★

'Not Far, Not Far From the Kingdom' was a good one for the piano, as it contained plenty of bounce. Sankey played it with gusto, if not style, and though his command of the instrument was basic he had an arrangement of head bobs and grimaces that distracted well enough from this fact, while his pouncing hands moved up and down the keys. Walter and Mary sat together in the wing chairs, leaning in over the song sheet while the tune crashed out of the upright that had been in the Brown family three generations.

Not far, not far from the kingdom,
Yet in the shadow of sin;
How many are coming and going!
How few there are entering in!

In the kitchen, the breeze from the back door wafts laundry hanging from the ceiling dryers. As it moves it reveals Hilda Brown sitting at the table by the range with a face as long as coal irons. Carrots, potatoes and apples lie unpeeled beside her hand and she closes her eyes against the pictures playing in her head. The sound of the piano has conjured Mr Brown in her mind. Poor Mr Brown: nervy and musical, dome-headed and clergy-faced, his freckled hands sidling up and down the keyboard like two broad-clawed crabs. He could play with or without music and withheld from singing along, which allowed Mrs Brown to do so instead in a faint, chirrupy voice after a brief pantomime of shyness. Music, she said, did the heart good. The angels knew that. Mrs Brown liked angels; she had a small collection of china seraphs, complete with dainty harps and lutes, arranged upon her dressing table, and she doodled angels on slips of paper, envelopes and other scraps. Angels, she said, when you thought about it, had the best of both worlds.

Sadly there was no angel available during the scarlet fever epidemic of 1915 at the isolation hospital in Hazlemere. Here her two children, Walter and Alice Brown, were taken during the worst of the outbreak. Walter was not yet walking and appeared to have remembered nothing at all about it. Alice was just eight weeks old and she never came home again. They donated her crib and baby clothes to the church fund and, after her funeral, no more was said about it. In the Brown household angels were never mentioned, doodled or dusted again. The group on her dressing table disappeared, never to return. Walter had not asked about or even mentioned it. Hilda Brown had to assume he had entirely forgotten he had ever had a sister. It were better, she concluded, not to remind him, and better still not to remind herself. They would pick themselves up and carry on; that was the way things were soonest mended.

> Away in the dark and the danger,
> Far out in the night and the cold;

There Jesus is waiting to lead you,
So tenderly into his fold.

But Mrs Brown had not forgotten Alice, and the grief was not mended but bitterly endured. What about all those other little girls? The ones she saw every day, whose hair grew long and wavy, the ones who learned to sing and skip, the mothers' little helpers. Why should she not feel angry? Where was her bonny girl? *Where* was her Alice? Hilda Brown could not bear to remember but neither did she wish to relinquish the memory of her only daughter, more vivid with time; the soft dark crown of hair, puffs of warm breath and curling toes. And she had been careful not to love so hard again, and especially where Walter was concerned. Because when you loved in that way you had to expect they might be taken from you. And so she had been careful with Walter, because, after all, you cannot be too careful, and he had not been taken from her.

Not far, not far from the Kingdom,
'Tis only a little space;
But oh, you may still be for ever,
Shut out from yon heavenly place.

CHAPTER 45

'When the trap was quiet finished the three little funny ones climbed up into the tree so that they could watch the lion cub when he came along and fell into the trap.'

Jane Stevens is a proper little know-it-all. A weirdo. A git.

'Very good, Jane! Yes! But that's *quite*, not *quiet*, isn't it? Good. Clever girl.'

One day Jane Stevens will fall into a trap herself. Let's hope there's a good book down there for her to read. Let's hope she is down there a long time. Poor little Sean. That's what she calls him. She is freakishly tall, Jane Stevens. She has no need of the library step. Tall people think they are it. Anyway. She is a git.

'Last one, Sean.'

Oh God, wur. Sean clamps his hands over his ears, and steers his head towards the book. He has not switched his brain on. He is not ready. And she is always picking on him lately, Miss Day. He can't understand what has gone wrong between them. Before it was all precious blue letters and typhoid hugs, but now something's changed. Was it something he said? Does she like someone else?

Outside the elm jerks to and fro in a bid to attract his attention. Sean looks at it in the distant hope it may semaphore the words. A man can jump and skip on the moon, so why not?

'Sean? Are you deaf? Are your ears stuffed with cotton wool?'

Everyone laughs, even Sean. She is still funny, give her that.

There was a loud rustling and thumping going on in the lion trap and the branches were moving on the top. Tom pulled his hat down on to his nose, which made him feel braver.

'there wass a lord rust lig and Thump gongon in the leon trap.'

Genius. How is her face? Rudyell.

'the branchees wer e mauv mauv mauving On.'

'On the what, Sean?'

'the top, Miss.'

'The top, Sean.'

'tom pullered hiss hat doo dow dowern *dowern.* Dowern?'

Ann has informed Sean that she will marry someone tall called Tom. He will have long hair and a kitten on his shoulder. He will drive a red car with no roof called Triumph. They will laugh like drains and live to be a hundred. Tom will call her *my darling*. It is the love story of the century, even before it has happened. Sean hasn't got a hope in hell. No mortal man can compete with Tom. Ann has some words of comfort for Sean. They are: *You'll get over it.* She speaks the words solemnly and places her hand on his shoulder. This is the worst whatif yet. Except it is not a whatif, it is a when.

Sean walked home the long route. He hoped something would happen on the way. He didn't mind what. Nothing did. He dragged his plimsoll bag behind him like a dead animal. If you forget your dinner money you can't have your dinner at lunchtime. He forgot his dinner money once, but they let him have his dinner after all. It was meat and gravy and hot cake with sauce for afters. A two-course meal! That's what his mum called it when he first started school. She sounded astonished, indignant. Clearly someone was being cheated here, but he never worked out who.

At home they had a tea towel with words on. He couldn't tell what it said. Ty read it out for sixpence. It said: *Life is not a bowl of cherries.* When he finished reading Ty looked at Sean, as though he hadn't thought about it before. Then he chucked it and sloped off. Sean hung up the towel, and considered the cherry thing. Of course, there were cherries on stalks above the words. He hadn't recognised them. Did cherries grow on trees? He didn't ask his mum when she came in. He didn't know why. Lately she'd looked at him with mild surprise, as though she'd forgotten she had a youngest son. She had a lot on her plate, his dad said. No point adding cherries, then. His mum moved straight to the tea towel. Uncanny. She took it down and hung it back the other way: it must have been upside down. She wanted her *Life is not a bowl of cherries* the right way up in the morning. So that she could read it again and again and know.

Sean's dead plimsoll bag scraped along behind him until it was all the colours of the nearly-houses. He was not the only one who could not read the true alphabet words. Lots of them could not do it. Not including Jane Stevens, but then Jane Stevens could probably read Greek, Igloo and Australian too. Adam Jacobs seemed to read the true words without difficulty also. And Debora Duke. *I don't care*; that's what Sean told himself. But an awkward thought stuck there, in the front of his brain. It went: I am short. My girlfriend doesn't love me. I am nearly nine years old. I can't read or write. I can't float good enough for space. I live on Mars. I am spaz spaz spaz.

'Spaz!'

No, no. He is not in the mood.

'Spaz!'

She is up on the bricks, high up. There is just her face coming over the bricks and a freshly painted sky behind. She comes along at his worst moments, always, only ever at the spazziest. She is that kind of girl.

'Come up here now!'

He ignores her. It is strangely liberating. He swings his plimsoll bag over his shoulder and picks up his pace.

'Come. Up. Here. Now. *Spaz!*'

This is nice. He should have done this years ago. He picks his knees up. He is a soldier, sailor, astronaut. The rest can bugga off.

'Sean! *Please!*'

He turns, but only briefly.

'LIFE is NOT a BOWL of CHERRIES!' There. That shut her up. He stamps on. He does not look back. He leaves her there, hanging in the sky.

Ahh father,
heart in haven,
hallo . . .

He couldn't remember the rest. There was a part about bread. The one that made you float. Nimble.

19th January 1944, C.M.F.

Dearest Mary,

The Italian peasants around here are poor and diseased. Strangely, amid all this gunfire 60 per cent of the women are carrying. I gave a boy some meat, particularly as his eyes were diseased. I wonder whether he will go blind or what. He was wearing a German forage cap and he has stuck in my mind.

There are no tranquil places anywhere. It is war, plain and simple, with its long trail of horrors. There is a lot we must not write of, and lots we cannot somehow bring ourselves to write of.

We are, for now, on a farm – fairly battered. The scenery is better and the farm folk have been kind, though they're destitute. There is little room for pleasure these days, but I am quite cheerful. I think of you all each day and wonder what you are doing.

Jerry has certainly vented his spite on these Italian peasants. Here and there, written in chalk on the crumbly battle-scarred buildings are still traces of 'Duce! Duce!' But how these people hate him. Heaven knows how all this will end.

Naples was pitiful, but the locals there were knowing and cute. Here – as we go forward – we meet the country folk. They seem stunned and unable to grasp all these unpleasant happenings.

By the way, you could slide down one of the rainbows here.

Later:
We have had a good dose of rain and the ground is like slush – sticky and slippy. One never knows what to expect in sunny Italy. There is a mist above the mountain tops.

402

I keep changing pencils – sorry. I only wish I had a real black soft one. I wish I could send you some nuts and lemons. A fellow here has loaned me some ink, but none of my pens work now. Did you receive my last letter? There are no letters from you yet, though I had one from Mother. There was something I wanted to ask you, but I have forgotten what it was for the present.

I have met plenty of Yanks now. It is not always possible to get a straightforward story from them – they are mighty leg-pullers – but they are very generous with their goods.

I'm afraid lots of the local children have picked up some unholy words and without knowing what they say are cursing and swearing. It fair stuns one at times.

There are plenty of lemons and oranges on the trees – no sign of tomatoes.

So, keep smiling and happy and write! Write! Write! Remember me to everyone. Remember how I feel about you. You walk beside me, Mary.

Yours, Walter xx

Once upon a time there was a squirrel.
'Good boy, Sean, off you go. Try your best.'
Sean pointed his brain at the words. He tried with his left eye, then his right. Then both. Eye

on the ball. Eye on the ball. *Thunderbirds are go, you spaz.*

'Onkey upon a timmy the wass a skew rile.'

He looked up at Miss Day. Her face was bad. Bludyell. He checked again. That's what the words said. Sean, you spaz. But these were the words. What kind of crip words were these anyway? Written for a laugh by a monkey. What?

'A screw wile?' he tried. But still this was wrong.

He knew words. He liked words. What's happened to the monkey words?

'A skwile?' Screwing up his face as though he very much doubted it, just as much as Miss Day doubted it too. The true alphabet. helo. welcum. wur.

'This is a difficult word, isn't it, Sean?' Miss Day has been led by her chalk to the board.

Yes. Very very difficult word, Miss, bludyell. This word may be too difficult even for Miss Day. Her chalk is poised. All eyes watch the ball. All mouths open to say the chalkword. Her chalk writes. The word is, *wuns.* Oh.

'Wuns,' says everyone. 'Wuns.'

Miss Day writes. wuns upon a tiem ꝥhær woꙅ a skwirel.

Oh. ' wuns upon a tiem ꝥhær woꙅ a skwirel.' Everyone says it now with relief. Oh. Sean checks the changeover words. But they still say, *Onkey upon a timmy the wass a skew rile.*

Changeover is a good word for it. The days when you could read and write are *over.* It is time for

404

Class 4 to cry themselves stupid, like Miss Day said. This will make a *change*. That was clever, one word made from two things. Sean hadn't known you could do that. He wanted to put his hand up. He wanted to say, *Miss, Miss, changeover's got two things in it*. And maybe she'd say, gʊd bɔi, ʃhaʊrn. But he didn't. She is talking again. Maybe she is still talking. Changeover. Wur.

'*SEAN!*'

'Yesmiss!'

'Do I have to say it all again?'

'Nomiss, yesmiss!'

'Then stop wasting everybody's time and read out the next sentence.'

They went down to the lion trap but there was nobody there except a squirrel who was using it to store his nuts in.

Sean stared at the words. Black and white. Easy and peasy. They were laid out in code. You had to know the code to get the ever-changing neverending inexplicable shapes. Black and white, it should be easy.

'OK, Sean. Never mind. Jane?'

Jane Stevens. Soon they will have to cut a hole in the ceiling for her head. She opens her mouth like a sparrow.

'ʃhæ went dɔun tʊ ʃhe lieon–trap,' she reads.

She does read well, give her that. Lispy. Nice. No pauses, much.

'ʃhær wɒʐ nœbody ʃhær eksept a skwirrel hʊ wɒʐ ueʐiɳ it tʊ stor hiʐ nuts in.'

She can read true words. She knows the code. She is a git.

'OK, good, Jane. Very nice, thank you. Sean?'

Godnose.

'Would you like to finish the very last sentence for Jane?'

No. 'Yesmiss.'

'Good boy. Off you go. From timmy'ꙅ muꝥer woꙅ biꙅy ieroniŋ. OK?'

Timmy's mother was busy ironing. 'Oh dear, it's you, is it?' she said. 'What's the matter now?'

'Sean?'

Black and white. Easy and peasy. Laid out in code. You had to know the code. You had to get the ever-changing never-ending inexplicable shapes. Black and white, it should be easy. There are more than fifty thousand galaxies in space. These are only words. Why couldn't he read them? whie? ꝥeeꙅ ar œnly wurdꙅ. sœ whie? cum on. ꝥeeꙅ ar œnly wurdꙅ, ʃhaurn, not galakseeꙅ. ꝥæ ar œnly bludee wurdꙅ after aull.

CHAPTER 46

Walter and Mary walk clockwise around the cricket green in Montague's Meadow. Walter would have preferred to go to the woods, but Mary insisted. He walks with his hands at his back, ignoring the sunset over the pavilion and the cruising dragonflies. He inspects the grass instead with forensic interest. Mary hums a tune.

'Don't you know any others?' he asks.

Mary blows in his ear. 'Wait your turn.'

He will end up on his knees in his father's allotment, he thinks. He has known it always. It is waiting for him, that scene, as it waited for his father, as it will wait for his son when he comes. It is a dark and certain shape, and a tunnel of time will lead him there. If he does not leave soon, the pattern will not be broken.

Mary is lunging at dragonflies. She trips about, hands outstretched, spinning left and right. She chants:

'The first butterfly you see
cut off its head across your knee.

Bury the head beneath a stone
and lots of money you will own.'

Walter has reached the bench; he sits down to watch her. Now that he has decided he feels better. Each thing he studies now, the shadowed green, the insects, the sunset, Mary, each is loaded with significance. These are the things he will leave behind. These are the things he will learn to love.

Walter and Sankey walk up Deadman's Hill, where the line of elm has stood guard for hundreds of years. Walter has his .410 on his arm, and they have two rabbits apiece. Walter has not broken his friend's nose or defamed his God after all. He has forgiven him instead. Sankey, by turn, has not broken his friend's lantern jaw either. Walter reckons Sankey is a child when it comes to matters of the heart. Sankey reckons Walter is a child when it comes to matters of the heart.

Sankey says his knee is paining him on account of Edna Green's bicycle, which he felt obliged to ride after she had kindly offered it for his Saturday rounds, but is, he explains, not fit for human usage.

They stop at the gate to watch the view below them. On winter mornings mist and cloud gather in the valley and smoke up the woodland like a forest fire. Today the sun has glazed all the green hillside, coppice and pasture and pulls the birds into busy patterns across the sky. They stand for a time before Walter speaks.

'I've been considering trying my luck in the city.'

'There's none too many jobs.'

'No, but I could try my luck.'

'What is there to see except motor cars?'

'I don't know. See what I can see. P'raps fate has a surprise in store.'

Sankey is quiet for a while.

'Restless legs, that's your trouble.'

'Most likely.'

'Restless legs.'

It could have been the storm that did it. Sankey suspected as much. Storms had a way of redesigning what was assumed to be permanent. The good Lord had sent storms since the beginning of time for the purpose of rearranging, redefining.

Sankey would not have been at Sladmore Farm for a start were it not for the storm, but there he was among the ruins of the two-hundred-year-old oak tree, which had been hit by a lightning bolt and shattered into thousands of pieces. A pity as it was a great old tree, the pride of Cryers Hill, and had survived being hit by both a truck and a motor car, as well as a fire in the nearby barn. Moreover, the ghost of a child skipped around it at night, and her songs could be heard from the outbuildings. Now the tree was gone. Only half its charred trunk remained, revealing ropy cables at its core. Above, it has been cross-sectioned, leaving spliced upper branches to sway and creak flimsily in the breeze, like the mast and rigging of a stricken boat. Folk are arriving to take firewood and souvenirs. Sankey ties up a bundle of good sticks for his stove and listens as people discuss the tree. They remember how it was spared in the last big storm before the war; they agree the pity of it all; they thank their fortune things were not worse, that they suffered no more than the heads off their nasturtiums. Morning, Sankey, they say. No, none of us got a wink, not one wink of sleep. Still. Alive to tell the tale, they say.

Not everyone is alive to tell the tale. The facts are gathering on Dorrie Penn's tongue. She lives next door to Mr Looker, so she has heard it from the horse's mouth. Sankey hears it now hushing around him. The Pages' cottage on Boss Lane near Gomms Wood has been hit and gutted by the lightning. Tom Page was asleep in his bed and most likely knew nothing about it. Poor Tom. His son George was killed at Passchendaele and his wife, George's mother, died quietly afterwards from grief. She turned her face to the wall. That's what Dorrie Penn said. After her boy was killed in Belgium she turned her face to the wall.

All the men in the Page family go to violent ends it was said. This sounds unlikely until you think it through: two fires, a flood, war, a fall from a rick, a firearm incident, a bolting horse incident, war, a lightning bolt. Not a single Page man now remained to face his fate. All had been wiped away, one after another. There was a nephew, somebody pointed out. He had moved to the New Forest. A quietening then while everyone considered the kind of untimely death he might expect there.

Sankey sees Mary Hatt. She is walking away. He hadn't noticed her at the lightning tree, but sees her now plain as day with her piece of wood in hand. He follows her. He means to call out to her, but thinks he will catch up with her first. She walks with small steps like a child or a nun. In spite of this, oddly, he finds himself lagging behind.

By the time he crosses Cryers Hill Lane into the woodland he has lost sight of her. He runs, pausing only to be sure there is not another direction she may have taken. He is a hundred yards down the path before he finds her. She is lying on her side, tipped over like a clockwork toy.

'Mary?' The sound of her name in his mouth makes him stumble; it is a word belonging to prayer.

'Mary?'

She is fallen across the path, her feet in the shade. Her eyes are open and so Sankey speaks again. 'Mary?' But she does not respond or look at him, but only stares, not at him, not at anything; her eyes are dull as if she were blind or deceased. She is gone from herself, this is how it seems.

'Mary?' Sankey whispers it as though she were asleep. Do not wake the dead, he thinks, and no. 531 from *Sacred Songs* balloons up in him in spite of everything. *In the shadow of the rock, let me rest, let me rest.*

Sankey kneels beside her. He is tempted to touch her forehead, to stroke her hair, when he notices a tremor in her jawbone. There is drool on her lip, catching the light. The light lasers through the foliage, heating her hair, warming her cheek and falling across her throat. Sankey half rises and looks around him as though there may be a doctor lurking or an instruction pinned to a tree. But there is only him and a large tatty crow and the fallen Mary. What is this? Something in the day is shifted, something is realigned. He too is sliding with it. She is trembling now, a volcanic thing. He knows the cure for the faints: smelling salts to bring them round and tea for the shock. Good. Better that another female were present though, girls know the correct procedure when it comes to falls, shocks and ailments. Anthrax. The cattle had it, Cramer's herd. It was in their feed, the seed cake from Eygypt was contaminated. Surely girls didn't get anthrax? She suffered the fits from time to time, yes. The fits it could be. Sankey is afraid to touch her but he will force himself.

She makes a noise, a tiny leak out of her mouth. He can't tell if it was a sensible word or not. He crouches lower and places his face in front of hers so that she may see him through her unseeing eyes. 'Mary?' She stares blankly into the dim hollow of his devoted heart. He takes her hand and the light beams flare, igniting her. Surely she'll be right as rain in a moment. Girls do fall over, it is well known. He would like to help her, but cannot think of a way. On the other hand p'raps he ought to run. A person happening along may assume an incorrect assumption. He will get into trouble. Trouble that he does not deserve, in point of fact.

The light takes him by surprise as it refracts quite suddenly through the trees. It bounces into his face, making him start. Mary sits up in a single sudden animal movement. She is bright as gas. The light is pouring from her mouth and eyes, viscous and drifting, like nitrogen. It fills her up and spills brilliantly out. She is lit as though he had struck a match inside her. It electrifies the trees and blinds him with its whiteness. She is a human flare. What is this? Sankey clasps his hands to pray. O angel of God, preserve me this day from all sin and danger. But he knows of course. He realises he has suspected all along. Suspected but did not dare to hope. He kneels before Mary and bows his head.

'*Queen of Angels. Mother most pure. Virgin most merciful, have mercy on us.*'

> 'Never shone a light so fair,
> Never fell so sweet a song,
> As the chorus in the air,
> Chanted by the angel throng.
>
> Weary and sore distressed,
> Come, come, come unto me,
> Come, come, come unto me,
> Come unto me and rest.'

He has been a fool. It is all now quite beautifully clear.

Sankey has often wondered how the chosen few know they are called. Now he understands. The signs are unmistakable. A bright margin of light has appeared at the edges of his day, as though his life were catching alight. His blood is hurried up and his mouth is frothing with sacred talk. The burst of energy in his arms and legs makes him feel he could jump the houses, the hills, the earth itself. And the presence in his heart of a fiery truth, a *knowing*, quick and fizzing and waiting to be spoken, confirms his best suspicions.

Sankey runs to Uplands. He runs to the hill where the wind drags the giant trees to the ground. He falls to his knees and the wind roars into his throat and into the chambers of his faithful heart. The wind flings his prayers about and pulls the clouds apart. The light falling from the sky appears to Sankey to be as holy as the first light on the world. 'One there is who loves Thee,' he assures his God. And he lays himself down under a pink enflamed sky that is scratched with gold, weeping tired tears of joy.

CHAPTER 47

His face frightens her as it floats out from behind the big elm by Cockshoot Wood. She screams and dances into the air while Sankey clasps his hands in apology and bows his head.

'Mother most pure,' he murmurs.

'Shut your face,' she replies. 'Shut your cake-hole, Sank, d'you hear?'

'Yes.'

Sankey cannot bear to look at her, but longs to look, all the same. When he does he smiles, knowingly, fondly, and tears well in his eyes.

'Daft. Not daft, mad. Peeping Tom. Weeping Willie. Keep away or else.'

Sankey kneels before her, closes his eyes. He raises his palms to the sky.

'Keep away! Keep away!'

Sankey is surprised, hurt. Why does she persist in this way? She is ungrateful, truly. He does not deserve this, no indeed.

'Mary,' he says. 'He won't marry. Not you, not anyone. I think you ought to know.' There. She had it coming.

'Keep away, Charles Sankey. You're not the full shilling.'

'You are mistaken if you think he loves you.'

Mary cannot swallow the air squeezing up in her throat. It escapes behind her eyes and makes quick hot tears.

'What do you want? Clear off! Go on!' Her voice is an angry squeak.

'Don't be annoyed, Mary. I only want to talk to you.'

'Well, I do not want to listen.'

'It's only that I want you to be happy.'

'Well, I am not happy, so bugga you.'

'Mary.'

'Bugga you!'

Sankey watches her go. She runs like a little girl, he thinks, stumbling and crying. He wonders why she shuts him out when he only wants to help. Why does she do this? After all, it is he who understands her, he who can assist her, he who cherishes her; *he*. It is a poor show. It is he, after all, who is come to protect her, to guide her, to save her.

Mary runs. It is at first fear, then anger, and finally grief that drives her across the field and over the stile towards Grange Road. In the bag on her shoulder is the food she said she would deliver to Miss Ford for the Sunday school chapel. If it is spoiled she will have some explaining to do. She runs anyway. It is a small price to pay. A man who sees the Messiah's own mother when he looks at you, a man who waits for you in the woods, who begs and kneels and carries on and on. A man like this is worth fearing.

Sankey stands at the edge of the wood, waiting while he remembers why he has come. Nearby a bird speaks. Ah! it says. There is light the colour of rust filtering through the trees and a smell of dug earth. A cloud directly above Sankey's head slides back to reveal a soft ball of late sun. He waits. There is something between the forest and the sky and Sankey, a type of entanglement. He stands stiffly with his hands at his sides and his head fallen back, while the sky rolls out its secret messages for him to translate. It is a grave responsibility, this. It is not a lark or a lampoonery; it is not for Perfect or the others. It is for him, Charles. Poor young Charles, whose mother is with the angels. And what a good boy he is in truth. He shall be rewarded in heaven, yes he will. It is for he, Charles Sankey, an ordinary man to all intents and purposes, for whom an extraordinary task lies ahead. It is for him and him alone. Sankey is not ashamed to note that he has moved himself to tears.

He has a way of knocking. You know it's him. Walter waits until his mother has moved into the kitchen before he opens the door.

'The Virgin is here. Lord have mercy upon us.' Sankey says, matter-of-factly.

'Who is it?' Mrs Brown calls.

Sankey stands in a haze of dust. Mayflies bounce around his head.

'I am cleansed,' he says. 'She is come, Walter.'

Walter replies, 'You don't look well, Sank.' He realises, as he says it, that it is a dampening thing to say, a bucket of cold water over his friend's newly arrived Virgin. But Sankey continues brightly, unaffected.

'A vivid light brought her, Walt. White as the light of Heaven. You cannot look directly in actual fact. Like this it is.' And Sankey screws up his eyes, throws up his arms and twists away to demonstrate brightness. 'It will blind you, you see, if you look directly at it. You must look to one side, this way.'

Walter's mother has drifted up and bumped softly against her son's elbow. 'That man has got a parasite,' she comments. It is not the first time she has diagnosed infestation in Sankey, but he is always polite.

'Good afternoon, Mrs Brown.'

'You haven't the sense you were born with,' she replies, 'but it's too late now.' And she drifts away again, soundless as a water snake.

'Perhaps it were natural phenomena,' Walter tries, shifting to distract Sankey from his mother's words. 'A trick of weather perhaps.'

Sankey leans in to whisper, 'This was no trick, Walt. Not weather neither. This was the Queen of Angels.' Sankey grasps his friend's hand. He arranges his features as best he can for truth, for convincing. And Walter fancies as he looks into

Sankey's face that he can detect something tormented, ecstatic, not entirely natural, bordering on the unsound. It makes him think of the religious scenes, painted mainly by Italians, that hung in great galleries; the faces wrung with rapture.

'She is with Mary,' he says. He whispers, but still it leaves spit on his chin, a darkening in his eye. 'She is come unto Mary, Walt. You must believe that it is true.'

CHAPTER 48

He can see them, clear as day, through the trees. The one standing and the other kneeling with her dotty leaves and flowers and samesuch nonsense. On and on they talk, as if they are both of them women, thinks Sankey. He tries to follow their conversation. A lot of it is a muddle, he decides. If he talked this way he would expect nobody to reply, ever. What on earth is it all for? He sighs. What a waste of the Lord's time, and his time too. Walter pauses to glance over towards Sankey's hiding place in the ferns. Sankey hunches lower.

'What goes up comes down and what goes down stays down, is all I'm saying.' It is her speaking. Heaven knows what about.

'I'm afraid, Mary, there are perhaps things in science you do not understand.'

'I understand it all. You lump, you daft man. Try me.'

'It is you trying me, Mary. Ha ha ha.'

'That's a madman's laugh.'

'Only you would know it.'

'Come here and say it.'

'Daft.'

Walter moves. Sankey must adjust to keep him in sight.

'Come here.'

He has said it to her. This is precisely what happens. She is moving now. He has his arms around her, one arm; it is enough. It is how it starts. Shenanigans. That is what Dorrie Penn calls it when a man and a woman get up to things. She-nanigans. Because it is the female race who started it. Interesting how the Lord puts clues in words, in nature. It is His own remarkable mysterious way. Just yesterday Sankey had seen a clue in his fingernail, the letter J. Clear it was, unmistakable. Now he was waiting for J things to happen. He had his eyes and ears out and his wits about him. He wondered about it. Jerusalem. January. Jam. He would have to wait. He was waiting now. They are still talking but he cannot hear what they are saying. Speak up! It occurs to him that life is a long waiting game. Waiting for the kingdom, waiting for the gates to open. Waiting for Mary. Talk about gates; there was a pair of gates he saw in Regis years ago. Beautiful. You had to crane your neck to see the decorative finials at the top. He hoped Heaven's gates were like that, just like that, then it would be worth the wait. They are kissing. Oh, he has missed the part he should be noting. They have broken apart. Thank God. Uncomfortable crouched this way, his foot is numb. Pity any of this was necessary. They are doing it again. A tedious thing, kissing, if you are on the outside. Hurry up. Perhaps now, before it goes too far. Needs must. Not the easiest position to rise from, this, not with a sensationless foot to boot. Better to lean out to the left and swing up.

'Oh, who's there? Who is it?'

Keep down, keep hidden. He will assume it is an animal and resume. Better by far if you are a policeman in these circumstances and can say, 'What's going on here then? What do you think you two are up to?' The Lord's work is not all glory and hallelujahs, indeed it is not.

'Tut tut tut, Sank. Dearie me. Peeping Tom. Who'd have thought? Not I. Not on your nelly no no.'

'Is that you, Mary? I thought I was alone. Oh, and Walter too.'

'Sank! What the devil do you think you're doing?'

'He's not the full shilling, are you, Mr Sankey?'

'I must have slept. I thought it was an animal. Are you well?'

'Let's have an answer then.'

'He's got none, have you? Not on your nelly no-no.'

Sankey opens his Bible, a sudden stagy movement. A card marks the place. He clears his throat.

'Peep-peep peeping Tom, mind you keep your breeches on,' chants Mary.

Sankey considers them for a moment before lowering his Bible, abandoning his original plan, and rushing at Walter, swinging a left hook firmly into his face. Walter is aghast. When he looks up Sankey is coming again. There is no single punch this time, but a flurry of hits, slaps, a flailing of arms, a windmill delivery of blows; and Sankey, his face anguished, is finally able to unburden himself of the envy and frustration of so many months and years.

Walter is obliged to defend himself. He slaps his friend on the neck and ear. 'Ow!' complains Sankey.

Mary waits, hands on her hips, like any ringside referee. 'God sees you, Sank,' she warns. Sankey hesitates and turns to her as Walter swings his fist into his friend's nose and breaks it with a single cracking split.

Walter is standing on the railway station platform. He has his coat over his arm and his suitcase at his feet. He has bought some cigarettes and he is smoking one with great commitment. He feels as though he has at last recovered from a long, protracted illness and is returning with a clean bill of health to a happiness he once knew. He checks his ticket one more time and his fingers, he sees, are trembling. He looks up and down the platform. He blows smoke up at the clock. Though nobody knows it yet, Walter is leaving. He gave his notice at the Water Company. It was assumed there he was trying to escape conscription, which they say will come along, sure as eggs, but Walter has no thoughts of conscription or war or death or duty or anything like that. Walter is interested only in life and how he can obtain some. He is going to try his luck. That's what he says. 'I'm off to try my luck!' He makes it sound as jolly as a funfair.

He has decided he will write to Mary, far kinder that way. Poets always return. He will not be gone long, a few months perhaps. See the world, try his luck. When he returns he will write it all down, his rare experiences. She will be waiting and he will swing her off the ground. When he returns he will tell her that he loves her.

'If I die while you are on your holidays, I'm sure I don't know what will happen.' His mother's words. He never once suggested he was taking a holiday, much less used the word, but he did not argue her use of it now. Perhaps it was how she would comfort herself, with anger at his selfishness. He realises it is what she has decided to tell people. Her resentment over his departure from the Water Company gives way now to bitter tears.

'Everything will be all right, Ma,' he says and squeezes her shoulder. She feels, to him, tiny as a child, a bird in his arm. He, in contrast, has grown huge, inflated. He has to turn sideways to get himself and his suitcase through the door, so big has he become since making his decision. 'Everything will be all right, you'll see,' he says. These are the words that get spoken on the eve of disasters, great and small.

CHAPTER 49

Sankey has devised a plan. It involves Father Blagdon, but that cannot be helped. It is, Sankey knows, the right thing to do. He will speak with him this morning at the church rooms. He has shaved, cleaned his nails and washed behind his ears. It is a fine blue morning. Pasture and coppice hold still in preparation for the church bell, whose clang-te-clang tilts the sky and loosens the trees in the ground. Iron on iron like hammer on anvil, the sounds that tell you God is in His Heaven and men are at their work.

Sunlight squeezes songs from the hedgerow, livestock falls into a doze. The only eye-catching movement in the landscape is the top of Sankey's bowler travelling rapidly along the top of the hedgerow. His thoughts propel him along. Father Blagdon will weep when he realises the truth. He will embrace him. He will praise his fortitude and so on.

When Sankey arrives he is breathless and tearful with anticipation. In his agitation he knocks the prayer books from their pile on the table and they crash portentously to the floor. As he kneels to collect them Father Blagdon says with a sudden bounce in his voice, 'Well, Charles, well now. As I may have mentioned before, we have someone starting on Friday, Harold Rice, from the parish of Hazlemere, and so your assistance will no longer be required here for the time being. All right with you?'

Sankey tries to grasp the slippery prayer books. He looks up at Father Blagdon while he waits for him to admit he is only joking. But Father Blagdon admits nothing.

'Of course, yes, I expected that. Glad to be of some small usefulness meantime.'

Father Blagdon smiles, relieved. 'That's a good fellow. Whatever have you done to your nose?'

Sankey has a grip on the prayer books. He stands up and is surprised how light he feels, as if he weighed nothing at all.

'The Lord God is in my head, that is where He resides. The Lord God is in my heart, that is where He shall stay. I am on important business, the Lord's business. You must excuse me, I have no time to talk.'

Father Blagdon blinks patiently back. 'Yes, of course,' he replies. 'May the Lord always reside in your heart, Charles.'

At the door Sankey turns, blocking out the haze of sunlight. 'The Virgin is arrived in Gomms Wood. Her vessel is Mary Hatt. You are the first to know.'

And Father Blagdon, fearing all his suspicions about Charles are now, at last, about to be confirmed, says, 'Oh, thank you, Charles. Thank you very much indeed.' And when Charles Sankey is gone, he moves to lock the church-room door.

Sankey has bought Sid Perfect a half of ale. He has him cornered by the fireplace, away from the dartboard, in order to extract some advice. Sid is supping his half-jar quickly, however, and Sankey will find himself up at the bar again if he is not careful. He must get to the facts and be quick about it.

'Mary Hatt is visited by the Virgin, Sid. Don't argue, I have proof. It is a fact.'

Sid sups his beer. Though he raises it slowly, Sankey notes, the ale drains quickly away between his lips. His advice will equal the cost of a pint jar, whether Sankey likes it or not.

'What proof?'

'Many kinds. Numerous.'

'For example?'

'Light, Sid. For one. Not just any, not electrical, a brighter source than that.'

'What else?'

'Fainting on the feet. In an eyeblink she is gone, and the doctor says it is not caused by any ailment he can think of.'

'Has he examined her then?'

'No need. It's apparent.'

'And?'

'Her strangeness, Sid. She's not your usual type and moreover she's odd.'

'Dropped on her head, that's all. What's the game with your conk? Go on then, another quick one.'

Sankey digs into his pockets at the bar. He is anxious. Sid hasn't cottoned on at all. He is beginning to wonder why he is bothering with him. Perhaps the second half of ale will deliver an answer. On the other hand perhaps it is he alone who will see what is transparent. Perhaps nobody else will be blessed. Is it possible he alone will receive her light? He experiences a chill.

'Look, Sid, no mucking about. The Virgin more than likely has come to Mary. She is more than likely chosen – for why we do not know and who are we to argue? The Church must be informed.'

Sid takes a long draught of his drink.

'Right, well. Is that it?'

Sankey puts his pipe in the ashtray.

'Sid. Sid. Do you understand? The diocese must be involved. Interviews will be requested. Bishops will come, Cardinals, Archbishops!'

'Shut your fool mouth, Charlie. There is nothing coming except a war.' Sid's tone is surprisingly perfunctory. 'Nobody cares about this type of thing any more.' The smoke from Sankey's pipe curls in a rising noose. 'You've always been a bit of an idiot, Charlie. Shut up and join up, that's my advice.'

'I'm a passfist, Sid.'

'Shut up about that and all. Piece of advice? Shut up.'

Sankey stares through the smoke. He opens his

mouth to release his argument but none emerges. He searches his brain for the devastating remark that will crush Sid, annhilate him, force him to apologise. It must have been this way for the Apostles. It is not easy to find yourself unexpectedly at the centre of a miracle.

'He has gone, Mary, to another town. Near or far, hard to say. I do not know.' There was more he could have said, but did not. He forced himself to meet her eye, though it shivered him to do so, because even now he could see her light, her shine, the thing – divine or otherwise – that was hers alone. He pretended to see nothing.

Mary looked at his burst nose, bent like a spoon, crackling as it breathed.

'Sank.'

He regarded her steadily, as cheerfully as he could, so as not to startle her.

'D'you see light?'

Sankey crossed himself.

'I do.'

'Well then,' she continued evenly, 'you'd better kneel.'

She spoke it plain enough, though Sankey thought the words sounded lovely as the Psalms.

'You'd better, Sank.'

And so he did. And felt no shiver when he looked up at her this way to meet her eye directly.

'*Mary, Mother,*' he said. His tears surprised him, but he pressed on. '*All the day, close beside thee let me stay. Keep me pure from sinful stain, Till the night return again.*'

'There now,' Mary said gently, and smiled. 'There now.' And stroked her hand over his head.

31st March 1944, C.M.F.

My dear Mary,

Sorry for the long absence. I have been unable to write until now I'm afraid. How marvellous it was to receive two letters from you on the same day! Thank you for the catarrh pastilles, they were very good.

I wonder whether you've changed. I try to imagine your voice speaking the words you have written. Thank you for the pressed buttercups, and no, they did not make me sad at all, on the contrary. I have them safely in my pocket.

Well, lately I have had a few days' leave and I enjoyed my visit to the ruins of Pompeii – extraordinary. I feel not too bad just lately.

Jerry is fiendishly ingenious, you must be careful what you pick up. An explosion came the other day and a woman wailed. An Italian boy was staggering about with his arms torn off, a chest hole gaping, his face battered. He died in seconds while his mother wailed. I never pick anything up, not even a cigarette carton.

Ensa Rep Company did *Rope* the other night – quite a tonic! I wish I could get something for these chilblains. I have just soaked my boots in dubbin anyhow. The ground after rain is mud and more mud – one never knows what to expect in sunny Italy. The courage of these men and boys is a marvel to see, be it Yank, Pole, French or British. The men who lie beneath these crosses – very few enjoyed even the hopes of victory, and yet it is mostly their sacrifice that has made victory certain.

I have to close. I have spent so long looking at your picture these many months that when I close my eyes your lovely happy face is still there behind my eyelids. Are you my girl, Mary? Please tell me that you are. I'm sorry to ask but you say you feel 'not much' for Eric Hobbs. Does this mean you feel anything for me? I sometimes think my feelings for you appear to be stronger than yours for me. I am sorry to be gloomy. Everything becomes distorted through the hall of mirrors that is war.

Yours, Walter xx

P.S. Please don't mind when I say I love you.

Sean pushes the letter into his pocket. The line-marker has not moved. It lies on its side at the exact spot where it fell. A pool of congealed paint is gathered beneath it. Sean approaches cautiously. It could be a trick, or a trap. The line-marker makes no judgement; it will draw the line for a madman, murderer, loon or spaz. Sean is glad to see it again, he has missed drawing the line. There is still some paint left, he notices. *Peep-peep*. It still goes, good as new. He will draw the line, Sean decides, and lead the murderer in. He will find him, though the police did not. He has been clever with his blue moth-wing letters and stone-turning. He will catch him with his shining paint-line and he will be a hero then for ever and ever.

CHAPTER 50

Mary Hatt took her news to Gomms Wood. She hid within a crowd of shabby trees until the news felt less surprising, more paltry. She thought it through again. A waiter. A person who waits on tables. He had become a waiter, most likely due to her. Didn't she tell him of her ambition to become a Nippy in a Lyons Corner House? Yes, she did. So, he has copied her. Copycat. Sitting on the doormat. Walter Brown has stolen her dream and run away with it to London and turned it into his life, when he knows it is really *her* life.

He is a waiter at the Savoy Hotel, according to Evie Winter. 'Gossip,' Mavis Johns called it, but there is facts about it, Mary knows. Because even though Mrs Hilda Brown will not speak with Mary directly, she speaks to certain others, and the news filters through, and these are the filterings.

Mary allows herself to picture him hurrying gracefully around immaculate tables in a smart black jacket and elegant white apron. In certain magazines there are photographs of swank London places such as this. Whole menus are reproduced for the delectation of readers. She suspects there will be roasted meats served with golden potatoes, and fresh fish, steaming and fragrant with sprinklings of lemon, not to mention dainty cakes, fancies, fondants and glacé fruits. She tries to imagine the diners, particularly the women with their appreciative smiles and powdered chins and perky hats still damp from the rain. She supposes Walter would not light their cigarettes, their luncheon companion would do that. Though he might well snap open their napkins and drape them on to their laps. All that swank, wasted on Walter. He will not enjoy it. Instead he will write his dreadful poems, line after dreary line about how it all is now that he is a waiter at the Savoy Hotel in London. Bugga you and all who sail. She wonders what he gets in tips. And now Mary's tears arrive and though they choke and sting, she is glad of them. Perhaps she will marry Eric Hobbs. He is nineteen, two years younger than her, and he is unattractive and simple in the head but, on the good side, he has a job at the chair factory. If there is a war he will more than likely be considered too daft to join up, but you never know. And buggas can't be choosers, so.

Mary Hatt wipes her tears. Wally Walter Brown. Daft simpleton twerp poop-poet, bugga you. As a matter of fact, Mary thinks, that ought to do for his headstone.

There is more gossip. Filterings that have filtered through. The house is busy; nothing is quite the

434

same these days. The farm is filled with girls for a start, land girls they call them, and it is true they are landed on you without so much as a by-your-leave. The least bit of weather and they come chattering into the house.

The rain is still coming down outside after three days, so Mary Hatt squeezes underneath her bed for some peace and quiet and in order to think the latest news through. It is only a small filtering, but very definite. Confirmed, according to Evie Winter, by Mrs Brown herself. He is in Oxfordshire. He is at a training camp. He is to be with the Royal Artillery, Mrs Brown says. Royal! She says he will go abroad, certainly. She doesn't know where. Even he doesn't know where. Royal Artillery. Walter Brown. Daft daft daft. The army must have urgent need of a poop-poet. Perhaps he will come across her brother, Clem, in his tank. Poor Clem. Or Joseph, tall proud Joe, who says it is an honour to fight for his country and a greater one to die for it. Brave Joe, where will we find you? Mary closes her eyes.

The girls are laughing in the kitchen downstairs. A poor show, Mary reckons. She likes to frighten them with her behaviours, not necessarily fits. There have been no fits for a while. She put one on for them in the first week because she could see them looking, waiting. They must have been told. By Evie Winter more than likely. Royal Artillery. Royal! Wally Wally Wallflower, growing up so high.

19th April 1944, C.M.F.

Well now, my dear Mary,

I am sitting in a bivouac on a damp grassy hillside, looking at the water glinting in the churned-up fields in the valley. What else? I can see a fast-flowing river, brown with silt, a village of burned-out and bombed houses, the big Red Cross flag of a military hospital. Then there are more bivouacs and clothes hung to dry on the hedges, and a ceaseless stream of vehicles up and down along the road.

It may come as a surprise for you to hear from me this way. Daft, is likely the way you would view it, particularly when you have had a chance to take in my news and whereabouts. Daft is right, my dear girl, Mary. But in fairness there is much in the world that is gone daft these days.

I am with the Royal Sussex. We are up in the hills, about 2 or 3,000 feet, and everywhere is mist and rain. The mules do a remarkable job in these conditions and can carry more than you would imagine. How willing and biddable they are, not really stubborn at all!

Speaking of animals. Well now, did you know that almost every vehicle here has a dog or perhaps a cat, but more likely a chicken or two on board? Several now have sheep and lambs of course. Usually these creatures are acquired as we go through the deserted farms, together with the odd chair, table, alarm clock or cutlery items, though I personally have taken nothing that did not belong to me. The animals do lift our spirits and, excepting the grazers, would have starved.

So, Mary, I must tell you of our first spring snow. Two days ago it fell and on the higher hillsides it still lies, like writing on the wall, warning us of the contrariness here of weather and environment. Well, at the moment the weather is rather cold, with a touch of frost in the mornings. This morning, going down to the stream for a wash, the ice on the little pools crackled under our feet. Still, I am very lucky as, for a while, I was in charge of a house with a few chaps, waiting for the Coy to be relieved. We were well organised and the fire blazed high all day.

Well, Mary, do you have any details on Walter? I have it on fairly good authority that he is hereabouts. How I would dearly love to see him! I hope to manage it soon.

Interestingly, last night I woke up around 4 o'clock and about 30 yards away a nightingale was pouring out a beautiful song. It made me think of Walter, and of you. The moon was up and it really sounded lovely. True, there was a background of artillery, but that only made a setting of a deeper note.

Some sad news. Our signaller received a letter saying that his brother in the R.N.F. had just been killed. Our chap is only 19 and his brother just 18 months older. He seems so young and was rather badly cast down.

I have been praying at his side and he seems to find it comforting. I know you will pray for him too.

Well, Mary, I told him the story (well, I should tell it here to you too) of the day some weeks ago when we came to a village church that had been built some 300 years ago, 1621 to be exact. More than that we found the history of it from our friend the local priest (who is one year older than myself). Well, apparently in 1621 one of the village inhabitants swore that, wherever he saw snow on the 8th day of August, he would build a church in honour of the Blessed Virgin Mary. Possibly he thought he was on a good thing, for August being a very hot month it was hardly likely that there could possibly be snow. However, he must have been severely shaken when, on the morning of the 8th, snow an inch thick was *actually seen on the hill*. Yes! So, now there is a church, and the 8th of August is the fiesta day. The most beautiful true and lovely story I have ever heard. I thought you would like that story. I hope you do. I did.

Mary, how lovely it would be to see you and return home again! By the grace of God, I shall.

May God bless and protect you, Mary.

God bless you, dearest, Now and Always.

Yours,

Charles Sankey

A very small square of paper is pressed inside the larger one. Sean opens it and the tiny handwriting, curling like sewing, is revealed in neat rows.

Always remember: We shall never more suffer the lonely night when we sit together by the stream, nor hasten more to the demands of the clock. But only rest beneath a leafy canopy wherein shines the light of His eternal Love. We shall return to Him, each one of us, when it is our time. We shall go Home, Mary. We shall go Home.

Sean thinks he will draw the paint-line home and show this one to Ann. This one is different. He will go by the short cut.

CHAPTER 51

Sean sees him in the woods. The man is walking quickly, as though he has a train to catch. Sean watches. It is him, the one with the dead rabbit. It is the man in Mrs Roys' photograph. It is the man who writes the blue moth-wing letters. mista waltr. There are no trains here, however, as this is Gomms Wood. Sean thinks it is lucky that today of all days he is hidden behind this giant fern to witness these goings-on. The strange walkings and talkings of Mr Walter. Because, after all, the smoke-blurred detectives in their short raincoats are not here to slam any car doors or take photographs of leaves.

Mr Walter is snapping twigs and creepers as he goes. Things scrape his face but he does not put his hands out. It is unusual for a person to walk this urgently in dense woodland; ordinarily a person would pick their way, or run. Sean wonders whether there is any possibility at all that Mr Walter might be Martian. He wonders why he has not thought of it before. The man is already almost out of sight among the trees. Sean will have to move after him with jungle alertness. He must not let him out of his sight, he must not lose him now; he must not leave any stone unturned. Gomms Wood is one of the few places around where the weather cannot interfere. It simply can't get inside this wood. It tries; you see the sun straining itself through tattered leaves and poking through canopies, you see rainwater trickling and dripping. But the weather cannot invade and take over. Not like it does on the hills where there used to be fields and orchards and now there are nearly-houses – where once upon a time it would make or break a farmer and his workers and now it merely floods people's garages.

Sean has to run to keep up. He is used to running in these woods, except this time he is the hunter not the hunted. It is difficult because he is keeping his eye on the ball. The ball is Mr Walter. He moves almost as fast as a ball that someone throws at you along with the instruction, Catch!

Mr Walter is out of the wood and striding through the long lush meadow where insects balance on the tops of grass blades. Butterflies rise up in front of him and bounce out of his way. If he had a briefcase and a newspaper under his arm and he was on a railway platform and the whistle was blowing, he would not look at all out of place. Not like he does here, empty-handed, stone-faced, tearing through clouds of summer aphids.

He reaches the rushes and reeds where Ann usually sits and times Sean's weightless dives, where she once knitted indecipherable items in unwearable colours. Somewhere in those water grasses Sean's blue breathing tube still lies in the place it was flung.

Mr Walter has walked straight into the pond as though it were not there. He does not behave like a bather at all. He splashes in without pausing or considering or checking for fish or insects that may sting. He does not break his stride or turn his head or raise his arms. He walks until the water is up to his waist. And then up to his shoulders. And then he is just a head. Watch the ball. Why doesn't he swim? And then he is under. God.

Mr Walter is in the pond. Don't panic. It is just that Mr Walter is in the pond. Sean runs towards the water. He scatters mayflies and grasshoppers. He crashes into the reeds. He stands and looks in horror at the still brown surface, at the reflections of the trees, as they too peer curiously into the depths.

'Mr Walter!'

He is gone.

Bludyell. Sean runs around the edge of the pond. Rudyell. Mr Walter is in the pond without a breathing tube. Bludyell. This is the stone that will be unturned. Sean, you are a pie-faced spaz and I've always thought so. Rudyell. Mr Walter does not come up. Mr Walter is drowning. No one but Sean knows. He can run. Run! No one will ever know. Crine out loud. He wishes he had never even met Mr Walter. *You're a good lad. A fine lad you are*. He cannot run. He ran once before in

Gomms Wood and it brought the police in their smoky cars. He will not run. He will be brave. He will leave no stone unturned. Ann will blink when she hears.

Sean jumps. The water is colder than he remembers. He swims towards the centre where a leaf boat bobs. An astronaut must train for four years. He must prepare to go where it is silent and dark and cold and he will weigh less than a leaf when he gets there. Sean plunges down. He can hold his breath for almost a minute now. He opens his eyes and discovers he is no stranger to the brown murk this time. It has become his friend, and he stretches out his hands and he kicks himself down.

A mad woman lies at the bottom of the pond. It is said she was mad. It remains an unsolved mystery, another one. The villagers are used to living with mysteries; they are not afraid. But neither do they swim in the pond. Nobody has swum there since the drowning. The people on the estate do not know about this. Their coffee mornings and cheese-and-wine evenings are attended only by other estate residents. The village children whose family names are in the church-yard know not to swim there or play on the tip.

When a strong swimmer drowns everyone asks why. Why did Mad Mary drown? It was odd. Mary Hatt had swum in the woodland pool since she was a little girl. She swam like a fish.

A farmer knows; he knows nature makes the odd

miscalculation from time to time, and he accepts it. He witnesses her miscalculations every spring as his livestock give birth.

John Hatt waded up to his knees and he let his youngest daughter go. He watched while the infant Mary crawled forward beneath the surface of the water. Then he closed his eyes and prayed. He prayed to God for mercy, for forgiveness, for quick resolution in this most dreadful of tasks.

Mary Hatt suffered seizures from birth. John and Ida Hatt had watched their child contort and stiffen and struggle. They waited. Dr Summer paid a visit. One day, he said, she would simply asphyxiate, and that would be that. He did not know when. They spoke prayers to keep her, to protect her. Each time they thought she had gone, she returned. She would breathe herself pink again, pull herself back, though her heart swung too slow to hear. She died many small deaths in a day, and John Hatt thought it was kinder this way, to give her back quietly. In the water she would not struggle, she would not know. She would simply be returning to her element, to the buoyant memory of fluid. The water would neither frighten her nor carry her cries. It was, he thought, the kindest thing to do, natural, understood by God. The same God who, in His mercy, would forgive them, if not now then later.

John Hatt saw right away that she swam. He covered his face with his hands and asked for guidance. He cried. And then he walked away.

★ ★ ★

Mary Hatt was discovered by a cowman, watering his herd on their way to Wycombe. She was in the reeds, like Moses, laughing at dragonflies. Holding her breath was second nature to young Mary Hatt.

Mary's mother waited at the door with her news, and when John came in she slapped his face. He let her do it. He never knew whether it was because he had failed to drown Mary or because he had agreed to drown her in the first place. Mary Hatt swam like a fish, always had. Poor mad Mary. No one ever swam in the pond again.

CHAPTER 52

A Clarks sandal floats in the pond. It bobs to the side and waits there as though it would like to step out and walk away. The sun is high in the sky, but the big tree shadows the water, keeping it cool. A woodpecker taps into a tree, a sound like urgent knocking. As if to answer it, Sean comes up in the pond. He is slick like a seal. He gasps and coughs. The tree waits.

Sean walks home. He thinks he is always walking home this way, squelching. His progress is slower in only one sandal. The bare foot finds every stone, shard and thorn in Hughenden. 'Ow,' Sean says, and then again, like a peculiar wading bird. The sun follows him, burning the backs of his legs, pressing him on.

Once he is on tarmac he speeds up. She will not believe him of course, but he will tell her nonetheless. The truth will out. That's what people say. He hopes that is correct because the truth this time is more fantastic than any lie.

He sees her. She is at the top of a dirt mound with her hands on her hips. Yap yap yap, she is talking like that. When Sean's dad wants to indicate that, in his opinion, Sean's mother is talking too much, he makes little yap-yap motions with his hand, and says, 'Yap, yap, yap,' behind her back. Sean is always amazed as he has never noticed his mother talking more than the odd word or two.

Sean climbs the dirt mound. By the time he reaches the top he is bursting to tell it.

'P'sof, Spaz.'

'Guess what?'

'P'sof.'

'Mr Walter went in the pond bludyell I tried to stop him doing it God.'

'Yur a spaz and you don't know it.'

'Like some Martian I tell you what.'

On the hill the great orange crane stretches its neck left and right and raises its dinosaur head to the sky.

'Mr Walter went in the pond.' Perhaps, Sean considers, the smoky policemen will come again. Perhaps they will photograph the pond water. Maybe wade in up to their waists in their short raincoats. There was never a dull moment around here lately. Sean mentions this to Ann.

Gor stands at the sink, flicking his ash into the plughole, watching his youngest through the window. Sean appears to have been tarred and feathered or ducked or rolled in wet mud or something. Always the filthiest kid on the estate, Sean. How did he come to have such a funny kid? Who the bloody hell's he talking to? Other kids don't talk to themselves. Talking to himself all ruddy summer since she died, that girl. Not his fault. Nothing to be done about it. Police knew that. Ann Hooper. Nothing to be done now. Too late now. Poor kid's been buried almost three months. He'll have to snap out of it. Find another pal. Come on, son, come on. Chewing a ruddy brick. He's doing it again. Who in the bloody hell's he talking to? There's nobody there.

Ann Hooper's funeral had taken place on a warm spring day. She sailed past the estate in a gleaming black hearse. Wotcha, Spaz! She glided up the hill like an empress and the other cars followed. She sailed past the last tattered poster of her face: *Did you see anything? Did you hear anything? Were you in the vicinity on 4 May?* And the number to ring if you did. At the crossroads they waited for traffic but there were no other cars in Buckinghamshire. Sean heard the world go quiet. Just the scraping sound of insects and a burning sky. Ann had the roads to herself, like royalty. There was nothing else save for her big black wagon, the procession behind and a blank-eyed cuckoo in the wood.

The children from Cryers Hill Primary School were required to sit on the left-hand side of St Mary's Church on Cryers Hill Lane. Perhaps the Church of the Good Shepherd on the estate was considered too informal, with its concrete bell tower and smoky coffee mornings and come-as-you-are vicar. St Mary's on the other hand had a stained-glass window of St George and family tombs and was over four hundred years old. Here the local community could take comfort in a place that had witnessed the christenings, weddings and burials of their grandparents and great-grandparents. Here Ann Hooper could lie in peace and grow leaves in her hair. Here a village could bid a dignified farewell to its own lost child, its own unwitting angel snatched in the woods from under their noses.

A small group of girls shared a hanky to cry in, but mostly the children just swung their legs and stared.

The vicar read out things from the Bible. Sean didn't remember hearing anyone read from the Bible before. It was, Sean felt, not bad. Pleasant, Mrs Roys would have said. They sang hymns, 'Abide With Me', and 'Lead, Kindly Light'. Some of the adults knew the words and Sean watched their mouths making the rhymes. Ann would have been scornful, he thought, but he enjoyed it. When the service was over he wished they could do it again. Afterwards he heard the adults remarking on how small the coffin was, but Sean reckoned it was huge – enough room in it to roll over, to knit, to point out spazzery. He stared at it without blinking for old times' sake. But no one could stare without blinking longer than Ann.

Beside the altar lay a word made out of flowers. *Ann*, it said. Sean was glad he could read it. He read it again.

★   ★   ★

After the funeral he went to his room and closed the door. He sat on his bed and tried very many times to remember. He tried but he could not remember, not for the policeman, not for God, not for nothing. He remembered being in Gomms Wood and the sound of the leaves, as though they were moving by themselves. He remembered her saying, 'Don't be a twit, Sean Matthews. Why would I want a little spaz like you for a husband?' He hated her for that. For lots of things. He wandered off. He heard her calling him. He saw no one, nothing. No man, no murderer. But the leaves were moving, he remembered that. He kept wandering on. He heard her. 'Sean? *Seaner?*' He heard her scream. '*Seaner?*' She often screamed. He went home.

After that he forgot. He did a good job of forgetting. People arrived and asked what he remembered. But he could not remember and remember is what everyone wanted him to do. Try to remember, they said, try. But he could not. He forgot instead.

He saw her a few days later. She was sitting on a mound of dirt, arms folded. You see what you want to see.

'Spaz! Where'f you been?'

'To your funeral.'

'Ha bloody ha.'

Sean touched her hand. It was warm and as real as his own.

'Are you dead?'

'No, you spaz. Are you?'

He went indoors. His mum was in the kitchen listening to the plughole gurgle. Sean spoke to the back of her head.

'I've seen Ann. She's outside.' And his mum turned and stared at him.

'Don't be silly.'

'It's true. She's there. I swear.'

And then she looked towards the window. 'Where?' And he pointed her out on the dirt mound.

'There. She spoke to me.' And his mum turned and walked away. 'Mum?'

And his mum's words. 'There's nobody there, Sean.'

But there was. Now who was the spaz? She was as plain as the nose on your face. Anyone could see. Except no one could.

You're a pie-faced spaz. What are you?

That summer Sean and Ann went to the woods, to the tip, to the pond. Sean went all the way to the bottom with his breathing tube. Together they had looked at Ann's picture in the newspaper. *Local Tragedy*. They cut it out so that Sean could keep it in his pocket. Then they watched her photograph as it bloomed on the trunks of trees and lamp posts. Now she was everywhere and still no one could see her. I love you do you love me? Beneath her picture was the telephone number to call if you had information for the police. Sean and Ann called the number. 'Spaz,' murmured Ann. 'Spaz,' confirmed Sean. And replaced the receiver.

Ann Hooper was discovered by a local man walking his dog on 5 May 1969. No one could recall anything so dreadful happening in Cryers Hill before. They found her folded in bracken, sparkling with maggots, with leaves in her hair. Her skin was mauve. The policemen came to the woods with their measuring tapes and flash photography. They arrived sombre and determined in short dark coats. They crunched through the undergrowth and put their hands in the earth. They squatted and knelt, while above them the trees whispered shhh, shhh, and the shadows drew back.

Let bygones be bygones. Sean walks away, leaving her talking to herself on the dirt mound. Her hands are on her hips, her mouth is going yap yap yap. You see what you want to see.

He climbs upstairs to the bathroom. He has always liked this bathroom. It has waterproof flower-patterned wallpaper. No amount of splashing will wash those flowers off. If you stare, the flowers curl into faces. The modern world is remarkable. Nothing is what it seems. Except Ty. In the mirror Sean sees he could perhaps do with a quick wash. He looks again and this time he sees an astronaut. Tall, trained, fearless, ready for space. He is so tall in fact he can hardly fit his reflection inside the mirror. He has to bend to include his face. He smiles. Is this the smile of a man who turns steps into leaps? The smile of a space hero, a moonwalker? His suit is white and running with tubes and valves. On his left shoulder is his country's flag, and below that his name. Beneath his arm is his helmet with its dark visor, reflecting a smaller version of himself. You see what you want to see.

Sean and Ann are walking backwards up the hill for something to do. It looks simple, but it is not. The wind arrives from nowhere and lifts the red dust. The machines clatter and roar and the diggers raise their long yellow necks. There is a smell of dog-dirt and tar. Today they will go, same as every day, to the pond, the tip, the woods. Today Sean Matthews will learn to breathe without air, and jump without gravity. He will watch the lone ploughman without realising the horses are all gone, and listen to the birds he cannot name.

He calls this place home though it does not know him. It knows none of the flop-haired tykes on the estate, as smeared and dirty as their jungle ancestors, waiting for the day when, as adults, they will sit in commuter carriages nursing a bout of mild depression, as the empty farmland rushes by. The tykes who do not yet know their mortgages, their miserable marriages, their inability to recognise popular hymns. You could ask Sean to write the name of this place. You could ask.

When the nearly-houses are all complete Sean Matthews will look up at the night sky and wish he was there looking down. From space the earth is blue and white. Here among the diggers it is red and brown. And green. If you know where to walk it is still green. You will find it down narrow paths, over stiles and bursting up suddenly beside the tarmac roads: woodland and parkland and grazing acres, still shaded by the same beech and oak, now giant with age.

It is true that God moves in mysterious ways. The vicar says so. Everybody says so. Sean accepts it must be true. He thinks there is a song which points it out, perhaps by the Beatles. He cannot remember. There is an assortment of things he cannot remember. Assortment is a word by Mrs Roys. He remembers that. Mrs Roys says she ties a knot in her handkerchief if she wants to remember something. A bit loon that, like Debbie Sinclair lying naked in her garden all summer in the hope she will turn a darker colour, and Mr Dewitt walking about with a ticking box inserted in his heart because his heart forgets to beat. Forgets! The box electrocutes him and his heart remembers. He could have just tied a knot.

If Neil Armstrong had thought to write his name in the moon dust it would still be there today, beside his bootprints. He must have kicked himself. He could have done it easily, Sean thinks, with the flag stick. Anyone else would have, surely. There are names all over the estate, in the builders' sand, drying in cement: *Big Dave '69. Jef Burn luvs janet. Sod off brian.* Sean saw a man write his name on Blackpool beach. If it had been him, not Neil, then Sean knows he would have, yes he would most certainly have written his name on the moon. ʃhaurn. With smiley faces in the U.

April/May 1944, C.M.F.

My darling,
Your letter was sweet and has made me so happy. Winter is passing here. The women gather water in pitchers from a hillside spate and balance them on their heads. All the ploughs here are drawn by oxen and most people have an ass. The good earth of Italy is really good, soft and crumbly, and gives good and plentiful crops. Have I mentioned that before?

Did you know the Yanks have Spam and fruit and all sorts for their grub. Clearly we have been swindled. They are generous to a fault, however, and always share. Some of the lads hear from their wives that the wives have found someone else. Bill Palmer received one such letter. He cannot take it in.

2nd May '44

I am at this moment sitting on my camp bed at a rest camp writing this letter to you. It has been a change to be out of the line, and I feel much better for the break. We get up in the morning when we like!

You would imagine us all in our rooms 'til noon, and yet never in this billet has a man been in bed after 0800 hrs.

We saw a picture called *My Sister Eileen*, which was quite good, a laugh anyhow. I preferred another show called *Melody and Rhythm*, which had plenty of kick in it and some girls who were not afraid to show a little leg!

There are heaps of wild red poppies in the camp – and all kinds of wild flowers and trees in blossom, and there are walnut trees also. Just now clouds of dark blue butterflies appeared and then later on in the day hosts of lizards come out. If you are watching in the twilight you can see the quick-moving bats come out for the insects. So you see it is quite a paradise here! Rest camp, by the way, is another word (among our mob) for cemetery. But don't worry, I keep pinching myself, and I'm definitely not dead. Have to close as grub is up. How does it feel to be the most beautiful girl in the world?

Yours, Walter xx

CHAPTER 53

Mary Hatt would not have heard the news at all except for the fact that she wanted ribbon. Mrs Cleave at Scratch Corner had made a gift to her of some green ribbon when she'd heard about Mary receiving letters from Walter on active service. The airgraphs and letters looked smart tied up in this way and it had given Mary pleasure to see them in their little stack, each clasped to the next in a ladder of careful bows. But the unexpected arrival of Sankey's letter left Mary feeling inexplicably anxious, and she put this down to the absence of a differently coloured ribbon with which to fasten the new addition and the others that would surely follow. Mary was in no position to afford ribbon even if it had been off the ration, and Mrs Cleave's own precious ribbon collection had been tucked carefully away in tissue paper since her wedding day in 1926.

Mary's anxiety increased. She spent the morning with the land girls, outside and in, working, washing, clearing, airing the upstairs rooms while the sun was out. By two o'clock she was unable to think or sit or settle at all. She decided she would have to beg a small bit of ribbon from some-body or go mad with fidgetiness.

She had planned to collect some wild parsley in Gomms Wood for tea, but found herself walking too quickly and so by the time she arrived at Mrs Cleave's house, she was hot and breathless and unable to form a polite sentence or a neighbourly enquiry. Mrs Cleave was kind. She knew all the farming families hereabouts. She knew about Mary's lapses into strangeness. She made a pot of tea and produced a slim piece of red ribbon and Mary was finally able to say, 'Thank you very much, Mrs Cleave.'

Mrs Cleave didn't reply. A tiny clock on the mantelpiece sounded ting ting ting as though it were summoning elves. Mary drank her tea. She allowed the steam to prickle her nose and plaited the red ribbon tightly around her fingers until she felt suffi-ciently soothed to finish her drink without slurping.

'Walter has been killed, Mary.'

The words fell with the dust on to the sun-baked rug. They continued to fall, dropping out of order, until they began to form their own strange messages. Walter Been has killed Mary. Mary killed Walter Hasbeen. Mary Mary. Quite contrary. How does your garden grow?

'I know it's hard. Try to be brave. I'm very sorry, Mary, very sorry indeed.'

'With silver bells and cockle shells and pretty maids all in a row.'

'Yes. It's hard. I know, Mary. His mother received the news yesterday.'

I'm definitely not dead. How does it feel to be the most beautiful girl in the world?

'It was sniper fire, Hilda says.' Mrs Cleave's tears glittered. 'Very quick. They were on the move. They had just left a village and were moving northwards.'

Mrs Cleave stood to allow her tears to fall out from beneath her spectacles.

'I'll fetch you a handkerchief. I'll just go and fetch it.' And though Mary remained dry-eyed, Mrs Cleave rushed out to search for one. When she returned Mrs Cleave was startled to find Mary Hatt gone.

Here where we stood and kissed. Here where we chased. Here where you said my name. Here where we grew, me and you. Mary runs through Gomms Wood and the trees touch her as she goes. The breeze is mild and the trees tell her, Shush, shush, shush. They have seen it all before. Mary can smell blood in the woods, she is certain that is what it is. *Farm girls see more blood than soldiers.* Above her the clouds roll in the sky while beyond them the stars line up to burn their spoon, chair and bear pictures high in the black. Here (some say) is where your future is written, inside the gassy whirling patterns made by planets and stars. Here is all your bad luck, misfortune and ill gain, all spinning haphazardly in the dark. *You don't know nothing about blood and muck.* The trees cling and Mary runs. She runs until she hears her own heart bursting in her ears. As she reaches the farm track that leads to the lane she thinks she hears a cuckoo, and at precisely the same moment, Walter's voice. 'Cheerio, then,' he says. 'God bless. PS You're beautiful.'

Mary is not certain how she has slept. Perhaps she has not slept at all. She can feel the cool ground against her temple, grass on her neck. She has been listening to the cuckoo as it moved around the wood, but now there is no trace of it. She remembers a dream filled with shouts and a tall dark tree and a boy on a rock. But perhaps she was not asleep. Mary touches her cheek. It is puffy and hot. Her eyes are swollen and sore.

The pond, Mary sees, has become deeply green, bright-algaed at the edges and turning pewtery grey at the centre. Its soft surface is pinned here and there with sharp little insects. The biggest beech leans over until its towering reflection is returned with flattering watery magnification. A breeze moves quietly across the water; the reeds bow as it passes. Though she stands several feet away Mary can feel the pond's coolness on her hot skin. There is a smell, damp and sharp, the invisible business of disintegration and renewal.

Mary cannot remember the last time she and Walter came here. She can only remember him saying, 'Swim, swim, Mary Hatt, and I shall watch, like the king and the cat.' But she cannot remember how long ago this was. She remembers another time saying to him, 'Daft bugga, you,' because on that occasion, directly after she'd spoken it, he kissed her and she did not stop him.

The giant beech shivers and drops small pieces of itself into the water and waits while these leafy craft set sail. Through the smaller trees the evening sun sends flashes, spangles and bouncing discs of gold.

It is for you the nightingale sings her song. Mary has it still, neatly folded in her pocket, taken long ago from his coat. Poop words; she has kept them just the same. Now it is all that is left of Walter Brown.

Mary watches her foot as it enters the water, impossibly white against the algae, completely disappeared now as the weed regroups over it. She will swim; he liked to watch her swim. The water will hold her and her thoughts will simmer down. Bathing is a tonic for the sick, that's what they say. He said he could watch her swim all day. She can see him; well, he always stood in the same spot, arms folded, squinting against the sun, half smiling. He never sat down for fear of staining his trousers. She looks up at the clouds. If he is gone somewhere on high then perhaps he will see her. Yoohoo.

Her clothes fall on the grass and she doesn't stop to see the dragonfly land on her cardigan. The air is soft and cooling on her skin. She ties her hair with the red ribbon, a bit of luck as otherwise the wetness will ruin the collar of her best blouse. Happenstance. One of Walter's words. He liked to say it: 'Mere happenstance,' as though he were speaking German. She ties her happenstance ribbon. If any living thing other than the giant beech had been watching, they would have witnessed the red flash of that happenstance ribbon as it entered

461

the green pond, and immediately afterwards heard the splash of Mary's strong kick.

5th June 1944, C.M.F.

Darling Mary,

The corn is high, reaching my shoulders. It is being crushed under heavy armoured vehicles. It is possible to sniff rotting flesh. There are fields of vetch here just like the fields of clover in England. It is used as cattle fodder. Enormous fields of sunflowers too and the seeds are used for feeding poultry. Someone swore he saw an Italian milking a large dog – it must have been a goat. Four of our fellows were wounded yesterday.

You know, the fruit trees are lovely; pear, apple, peach, lemon, plum, apricot, and then of course the nuts and olives and vines – this country is blessed.

I had a dip in the Adriatic a few days ago, yes, me! The first sea-bathe for a year. I have no fear of water these days. Gee, kid, won't I be glad when this war is over. We seem never to have been out of the line for the duration and we are ready for a long rest. Funny, one lad said he'd be glad to get back to the front – it was too dangerous behind the lines, he said!

I have decided that when I come home I shall try to become a real writer, part-time for starters. I have so many plans. How about you? Will I be included in your plans, Mary? Don't keep me on tenterhooks!

We can have a happy life together, darling, I know that much. I promise you I shall write an excellent book one day, wait and see. We shall grow old together and be peaceful and content, and everything will be lovely and ordinary. I just want to come home and be with you.

I have some lava saved for you that I brought from Vesuvius. By the way, it has just started to rain here, turning the mud quite yellow. If I were to describe it (as a proper writer should) I would have to say it appears like saffroned porridge.

You say you are keeping these letters. What strange reading they will make for somebody one day, and somewhat dull I should say! Will you remember me to people? Frank and Joyce Wattings, I thought of them the other day, and the Deans and John Bain at the Royal and old George Osbourne and John, Ida and Isabel, and Mother of course. Tell them I'll be home soon. I think of Sankey often. I think of you always. You walk beside me, Mary. We are moving. I shall have to close.

In haste, I love you. You are the light in my life.

Yours, Walter xx

CHAPTER 54

Nowadays Sean has a desk with a lamp on it. His fingers touch the keys and the letters appear, one by one, and turn into words before his very eyes. True words these, for this is no liar alphabet.

Chapter Five. This is the first time he has written about where he grew up; the housing estate, the tip, the pond, the woods, Ann. wuns upon a tiem. He still has the yellowed newspaper story. *Local Tragedy.* And a photograph of her face before she died. Ann Hooper. First love lost love.

The published novels are on a shelf, smart in their book jackets. He is astonished when he sees his name along the spines. Inside, all the words are correctly spelled. Wur. Though spelling is not his strong point. In fact, he is an apauling speller. The characters who live inside his books, the nearly-people who walk and talk, stare at him from their respective pages. Wotcha, Spaz.

He can still picture people who are not there. He can still listen to them speak. They continue to live in his head, the people who are not real. They do not, however, stroll into his room and say, *Bludyell Sean crine out loud*. Not any more. They do not surprise him at the bus stop, or materialise in full battledress under the sycamore in his garden. He does not discover people out of photographs and letters smoking a pipe in his armchair.

He accepts the gone people are gone. There are no ghosts in Cryers Hill, he knows this. Only those who can't forget.

Sean is walking alone in Gomms Wood for the first time in twenty years. His father's funeral is tomorrow and Sean has returned to his childhood home. It is the same: the sun-lasered beech canopies, the birch and oak and tangles of bracken. He walks to the pond, where the bending tree continues to watch itself changing colour. He walks to the tip and discovers it is gone. He walks beside Cockshoot Wood where, once upon a time, there was a castle that was ruled by a ten-year-old queen, and up the estate hill to the Wilderness, but it is wilderness no more; it has been replaced by two identical box-faced houses. He walks and waits. But she is not here. *See ya, Spaz.*

There is no trace of her. There is nothing left. Perhaps his heart is mended. Perhaps he has forgiven himself. At the Royal Standard he raises a coloured drink to the memory of his father. *The male, as tribe leader, remains superior to the female, even in death.* And he puts the past to rest. Sean no longer conjures Ann Hooper or Walter Brown. Nobody now lives

465

in his mind's eye. He has let them go. Today his boyhood dreams are real. He is a cosmic traveller, a voyager in the bright universe. Small steps have become a giant leap. Wur.

Now is past – the happy *now*
  When we together roved
Beneath the wildwood's oak tree bough
  And nature said we loved.
    Winter's blast
The *now* since then has crept between,
  And left us both apart.
Winters that withered all the green
  Have froze the beating heart.
    Now is past.

'Now Is Past', John Clare

THE ITA EXPERIMENT

Between 1961 and the mid-1970s an educational experiment took place in the United Kingdom, sanctioned by the Conservative government of the day. Created during the 1950s by Conservative MP for Bath, Sir James Pitman (grandson of Sir Isaac Pitman), the Initial Teaching Alphabet would, it was hoped, revolutionise the process of teaching five-year-old children in Britain to read and write. The idea was to eradicate the inconsistencies found in the English language, making it less complicated for young children to master. The lack of a consistent code was deemed unnecessarily confusing: *through, though, bough, cough* were cited as examples. Consisting of forty-three symbols, each representing individual word sounds, Pitman's phonemic alphabet presented a logical code that disposed of the letters q and x, as well as capital letters, and enlisted characters from the Roman alphabet.

It was proposed that children would switch to traditional orthography (TO) at seven or eight years of age.

The experiment, begun in the Midlands, was

implemented nationwide at pre-selected schools. There was no formal training for teachers beyond the optional one-day course, held initially in some areas. Teachers were required to learn the system in practice. Parents were not consulted regarding the experiment. More schools joined the programme in 1962 and 1963. By 1966 140 of the 158 education authorities in the UK taught ITA in one or more of their schools. The experiment was controversial and the scheme was accused of being mishandled and poorly organised. The unfavourable conclusions of the Bullock Committee proved to be the beginning of the end for ITA in Britain, and subsequently it was gradually dropped by schools throughout the United Kingdom. Support for ITA in the form of associations still exists in Australia and the USA (where it is taught remedially by the ITA Foundation).

ACKNOWLEDGEMENTS

I would like to thank the Trustees of the Imperial War Museum for allowing access to the papers of L/Bdr J.R. Brown, Royal Regiment of Artillery (R.A.) and also Sgt. E.W. Cope, 2nd Bn. Rifle Brigade, Royal Sussex Regiment.

For information, research materials, documents, archives, photographs, childcare, memories and notes, I would like to thank Alison Gieler, Jeff Goodchild, Trevor Dean – for both his recollections and his account: *Widmer End: a village story* (Widmer End Residents Association) – Denise Knowles from the Bucks Family History Society, Stephanie Clarke (Dept of Documents, Imperial War Museum), Lizzie Richmond (Initial Teaching Alphabet archives, University of Bath), Jessica Bruce-Lockhart, Mrs Gillian Burn, Janice Bellamy, Rachel Johnson, Marylou Soto, Lorraine Hart, Robyn Becker, Mary Aldridge, Peter Aldridge, Jamie Lee, Dr Ruth Kennedy and Susan Campbell. My love and thanks to Mark, for his faith and encouragement. My thanks also to Clare Alexander and Dan Franklin.

Cryers Hill contains extracts from letters written

by L/Bdr J.R. Brown during his military service with the Mediterranean Expeditionary Force and the Central Mediterranean Forces between 1942 and 1944 and I would like gratefully to acknowledge this. An extract from a letter written by Sgt. E.W. Cope while serving with the Royal Sussex Regiment in central Italy also appears on page 318. The original letters are housed at the Department of Documents, Imperial War Museum, London SE1. In one such letter to his wife, L/Bdr J.R. Brown revealed both a desire to write of his experiences and also curiosity about who, if anyone, might one day read his words.

In acknowledgement, the following books proved helpful for reference:
The Way of a Countryman by Ian Niall (White Lion), *The Poacher's Handbook* by Ian Niall (White Lion), *Hallowed Acres* by Michael F. Twist (Farming Press), *The Countryside Remembered* by Sadie Ward (Select Editions), *Hughenden Valley* by John Veysey (Hughenden Valley Village Hall & Residents Committee), *Sacred Songs & Solos Compiled by Ira D. Sankey* (Morgan & Scott Ltd).

The author is grateful for permission to reprint lines from the following:
'Three Wheels on My Wagon': Words by Bob Hillard and Music by Burt Bacharach © Copyright 1961 by Better Half Music Co. and P&P Songs Ltd., New Hidden Valley Music Co. Copyright